Hinton Rowan Helper

Nojoque

A Question for a continent

Hinton Rowan Helper

Nojoque
A Question for a continent

ISBN/EAN: 9783337397616

Printed in Europe, USA, Canada, Australia, Japan

Cover: Foto ©Andreas Hilbeck / pixelio.de

More available books at **www.hansebooks.com**

A QUESTION FOR A CONTINENT.

BY

HINTON ROWAN HELPER,

OF NORTH CAROLINA,

AUTHOR OF "THE IMPENDING CRISIS OF THE SOUTH."

How natural has it been to assume that the motive of those who have protested against the extension of Slavery was an unnatural sympathy with the negro, instead of what it always has really been—concern for the welfare of the White Man.
SEWARD.

Deep-rooted prejudices entertained by the whites; ten thousand recollections by the blacks, of the injuries they have sustained; new provocations; the real distinctions which Nature has made, and many other circumstances, will divide us into parties, and produce convulsions, which will probably never end but in the extermination of the one or the other race.
JEFFERSON.

And thou, too, Ethiopia! against thee also will I unsheathe my sword.
ZEPHANIAH.

NEW YORK:

George W. Carleton & Co., Publishers.

LONDON: S. LOW, SON & CO.

MDCCCLXVII.

DEDICATION.

To

That most Enlightened and Progressive Portion of the People of the New World, who have the Far-reaching Foresight, and the Manly Patriotism, to Determine Irrevocably, by their Votes, in 1868—1872, Sooner or Later, that, after the Fourth of July, 1876, (or, at the very furthest, after the First of January, 1900,) No Slave nor Would-be Slave, No Negro nor Mulatto, No Chinaman nor unnative Indian, No Black nor Bi-colored Individual of whatever Name or Nationality, shall ever again find Domicile anywhere Within the Boundaries of the United States of America;—

To

All those Preëminently Sagacious and Good Men who are Deeply Impressed with the Conviction, that even the Firmest Founded and the Noblest Vindicated of all Republics, whether Ancient or Modern, and the Best System of Government ever yet Devised beneath the Sun, can never Fulfill its Promised Mission of Unexampled Greatness and Grandeur, until After it shall have been Brought under the Exclusive Occupancy and Control of the Heaven-descended and Incomparably Superior White Races of Mankind,

This Volume is Most Respectfully Dedicated,

By their Friend and Fellow-citizen,

THE AUTHOR.

PREFACE.

WERE I to state here, frankly and categorically, that the primary object of this work is to write the negro out of America, and that the secondary object is to write him, (and manifold millions of other black and bi-colored caitiffs, little better than himself,) out of exist-ence, God's simple truth would be told; wherefore, referring the reader to the body of the work itself for my incentives and reasons in the premises, I might now, not without propriety, desist from further prefatory remarks,—but yet I will say something more.

The highest temporal good of which the best men are capable, whether in regard to themselves individually or collectively, is, I believe, to be ultimately attained in America,—in America with more certainty, and with less delay, perhaps, than in any other country in the world. Nowhere else are men so profoundly actuated by pure and noble sentiments,—sentiments which, di-vested of all mawkish and irrational conceits, harmon-ize so exactly with the immutable requirements and conditions which, from the very beginning of time,

have been predetermined and decreed in the councils
of Heaven.

Yet there are many very despicable and worthless
men in America,—in all the Americas,—as, indeed, in
most other countries, who, so far from contributing in
any measure to the general progress and well-being of
society, who, so far from elevating any part of mankind to a higher standard of excellence, are always, to
a greater or less extent, repressing and neutralizing the
lofty efforts of those who are infinitely better than
themselves.

These sluggish and apathetic enemies of true progress, these unimpressible bafflers and repellers of good
intentions, have I frequently seen, in painfully loathsome and inauspicious numbers, on both sides of each
of the three great Americas,—North America, South
America, and Central America. I speak of negroes,
mulattoes, Indians, Chinese, and other obviously inferior races of mankind, whose colors are black or
brown,—but never white; and whose mental and moral characteristics are no less impure and revolting than
their swarthy complexions.

In nothing are any of these paltry creatures the sug-
gestors or promoters of the world's advancement. No
name peculiar to them has ever been coupled with any
generous or exalted purpose. Not one of them has
ever projected any notable or important work of general
utility. Not one of them has ever been, nor is it possible for any one of them ever to be, prominently instru-

mental in carrying out any liberal scheme of public improvement. Not in the least has any spirit of laudable enterprise ever manifested itself among them. Never, by word nor by deed, have they been the furtherers of any magnanimous or sublime undertaking.

Whether in reference to things past, things present, or things to come, (in reference to all things, indeed, except those which appertain immediately and especially to the stomach,) these coal-black and copper-colored caitiffs are, with rare exceptions, as absolutely thoughtless and improvident as the grasshoppers of autumn. Concerning them, however, there is one very consoling and cheerful consideration, and that is, that the appointed period of their tenancy upon the earth will soon be up; and then, like the short-lived ephemera of a summer afternoon, they shall all speedily pass away, and thenceforth and forever be known only, if known at all, in fossil form !

In the present economy of Nature, there are causes in constant operation, which, it is confidently hoped and believed, will ere long exterminate from the fair face of the earth, every one of the non-white drones and sluggards and vagabonds here referred to; and all persons who are not white, are, as an innate and inseparable condition of their existence, drones and sluggards and vagabonds of the worst possible sort. These steadfast and infallible efforts of Nature to rid herself of certain decrepit and effete races, which, like the toxodons, the glyptodons, the mastodons, and thousands of other extinct species of animals, have already fulfilled the comparatively unimportant ends for which they were created, will be candidly discussed in the following pages. Numerous other matters, which, if not exactly collateral or relevant, may nevertheless be regarded as not altogether foreign to the centre-subject here indicated, will also be treated with frank and earnest attention.

As for the author's paramount and ultimate object, as herein already referred to, that will be accomplished only when, from Spitzbergen to Cape Horn, and from the extreme East to the extreme West, the whole habitable globe shall be peopled exclusively by those naturally and superlatively superior races,—the pure White Races,—to whom we are indebted for all human achievements which may be fitly esteemed and described as at once wise and good, brilliant and powerful, splendid and imperishable.

H. R. H.

New York, *June* 3, 1867.

CONTENTS.*

---

* An alphabetical and copious index closes this volume ; and to this index the author would respectfully invite the reader's attention, even before perusing the body of the volume itself.

CHAPTER VI.

CHAPTER VII.

CHAPTER VIII.

CHAPTER IX.

CHAPTER X.

CHAPTER XI.

CHAPTER I.

THE NEGRO, ANTHROPOLOGICALLY CONSIDERED — AN INFERIOR FELLOW DONE FOR.

I have never read reasoning more absurd, sophistry more gross, in proof of the Athanasian creed, or Transubstantiation, than the subtle labors of Helvetius and Rousseau, to demonstrate the natural equality of mankind. The golden rule, do as you would be done by, is all the equality that can be supported or defended by reason, or reconciled to common sense.—JOHN ADAMS.

I do not mean to deny that there are varieties in the race of man, distinguished by their powers both of body and mind. I believe there are, as 1 see to be the case in the races of other animals.—THOMAS JEFFERSON.

I would not dwell with any particular emphasis upon the sentiment, which I nevertheless entertain, with respect to the great diversity in the races of men. I do not know how far in that respect I might not encroach.on those mysteries of Providence which, while I adore, I may not comprehend.—DANIEL WEBSTER.

WHAT matters it that my father and mother, and brothers and sisters, and myself, were all born and reared in the good old North State? What matters it that my father, who never saw, and scarcely ever heard of, a railroad, a steamer, or a telegraph, and who, without ever traveling more than twenty miles from home, owned land and slaves, and lived and died, on the eastern bank of Bear Creek, a small tributary of the South Yadkin, in the western part of North Carolina?

What matters it that my father's name (all except the surname) was Daniel? What matters it that my father, like certain other men,—of some of whom the reader has doubtless heard,—found a beautiful and bewitching blue-eyed damsel, fell in love with her, and got married? What matters it that my mother's maiden name (all except the surname) was Sarah? What matters it, indeed, that my father wooed, won and wedded Sarah Brown,—

an endeared and honored name, which, in these degenerate days of French folly would be but too apt to lose,
in some measure, at least, the Anglo-Saxon simplicity of
its consonants, and to glide into the vowel-terminating
appellation of Sallie Browne?

What matters it that, at intervals, respectively, of a
year, more or less, jolly-faced Dame Nature, the great
colonizer of the neighborhood, brought, and placed under the guardianship of my good parents, seven children,
five boys and two girls, all of whom, except the younger
daughter, were named by my father, and she by my
mother?   What matters it that my parents' children's
names (all except the surname) are thus recorded in a
ponderous old Family Bible,—an excellent compilation
of ancient writings, which, if a fact of this sort may be
here stated, my father's youngest, and homeliest, and most
mischievous son has twice read regularly through, from
Genesis to Revelation, inclusive, besides having perused
some of the finer poems thereof, especially those by Job,
David and Solomon, at least three dozen times?

HORACE HASTON, born January 27, 1819.
HENRIETTA MINERVA, born June 30, 1820.
HARDIE HOGAN, born March 21, 1822.
AMANDA MARIA, born November 22, 1823.
HANSON PINKNEY, born November 4, 1825.
HAMPTON LAFAYETTE, born October 8, 1827.
HINTON ROWAN, born December 27, 1829.

What matters it if, in these names, there is something
of an alliterative ampleness of the aspirate H?   May a
man not have pet letters as well as pet pigs, pet pups,
and pet parrots?   What matters it that my gentle and
revered mother pleased entirely her own fancy in the
nominal distinction of one of her own children?   Like
some other ladies whom I have known, she was determined to have her own way,—once at least; she just

would, and she would, and she did; and there was an end of it! And so, contrary to my father's suggestions, my second sister was not named Harriet, nor Hypatia, nor Helen.

What matters it that this alliterative characteristic of my father's mind was manifested even in the naming of his negroes,—Judy, Jinsy, Joe and Jack,—all of whom were as black as jet, and as ink-like in color as the juice of Japan? I dare say, also, that my father's horses, on the one hand, and his dogs on the other,—although I am not now quite certain how they were called,—might have recognized their names in words of such affinity of frame and pronunciation as Manser, Merley and Moxon; Bender, Bouncer and Bolton. In one case only can I conceive it possible that my father would have manifested a desire to depart from his usual preference for alliterative appellations. Had he been the owner of apes, monkeys or baboons, I have no doubt it would have been his pleasure to call them by such gimcrack cognomens as Vallandigham, Foote, Wise and Buchanan.

What matters it that my father died (somewhat suddenly, of a severe and unrelievable attack of the mumps) in the fall of 1830, when his youngest son, who had then been in the world but nine months, was still a close clinger to the breast,—a source of sweet solace and sustenance, which his elder brothers banteringly allege he did not desert until he was at least six years of age!

What matters it that any of these things were as they were, or are as they are? Little significance, indeed, have any of the intimations, or statement of facts, here advanced. In contrast with public interests and requirements, mere personal considerations are, or ought to be, of but very small moment. With heraldry, pedigrees and ancestry, I have, unlike John Chinaman, nothing to do. Ask a mandarin of Shanghai, of Canton or of Pekin, to lay before you the tree or diagram of his genealogy, and he will straightway prove to you, provided you will exercise full faith in what he says, that the venerated founder of his family was, tens of thousands of years before the days of Adam, a successful fish-monger, an expert knife-grinder, or a distinguished rag-picker, or something else equally honorable and aristocratic. We have no such ancient reckonings in the United States, and it is only by the aid of Pintoism and Munchausenism that they can count so far back in Europe.

As a plain American republican, possessed of a moderate share of common sense, and very much like the generality of my fellow-men, (my white fellow-men,) I was, and am, and shall be,—and that's sufficient. What, then, is the burden of my business in this book? Wait a moment, listen, and I will tell you.

I have come here both to ask and to answer certain questions, which are fraught with the greatest possible interest to the better part of the New World, and, in a somewhat modified degree, to every part and parcel of the habitable globe. It is quite unnecessary that the reader should be held in suspense on account of the questions and answers thus referred to—some of which are as follows:

Question. What is the best and only true remedy for the present and prospective troubles now brewing in the United States, between the White People and the Negroes?

Answer. An absolute and eternal separation of the two races.

Question. How could the separation here proposed be speedily and prudently effected?

Answer. By giving full and formal notice to the negroes—every one of them, including the mulattoes, the quadroons, the octoroons, and all the other non-whites, that, after the 4th of July, 1876, their presence would be no longer required nor tolerated north of the northern boundary of Mexico, and by assisting them, to a limited extent, to get somewhere (it would matter very little where) south of that south-moving boundary.

Question. Is there no other manner in which the negroes, who are fast becoming a consummate and unbearable nuisance, might be effectually and finally separated from that really estimable portion of the people of the United States—the white people—who, while they are eminently worthy, are also enlightened and progressive?

Answer. Yes. All impure-complexioned persons, of whatever nationality, whether black or brown, whether negroes, or Indians, or Chinese, or bi-colored hybrids, now resident in the United States, might (for the present at least) be colonized in a State or Territory by themselves, in Texas or in Arizona, for instance, and there, under suitable regulations, required to remain strictly within the limits assigned them.

Question. In any policy which we, the white people of the United States, may be induced to pursue toward the negroes, what should always be with us a controlling motive—what should unfailingly constitute one of the great and ultimate ends at which we should aim?

Answer. We should so far yield to the evident designs and purposes of Providence, as to be both willing and anxious to see the negroes, like the Indians and all other effete and dingy-hued races, gradually exterminated from the face of the whole earth.

Catechising thus, or in a somewhat similar vein, I might proceed much further; but, before either asking or answering any more questions, I deem it proper to bring forward abundant and irrefragable demonstrations of the fact, that the negro, as compared with the white man, is a very different creature, a grossly inferior being; and also that this difference of manhood, this despicable inferiority of the negro, is natural, conspicuous and permanent.

In the prosecution of this labor, I shall bring to my aid the investigations and discoveries of the most learned naturalists who have ever lived; and these, surely, are those whose voices, above all others, should be most attentively heard and heeded in the discussion of the specific subjects here mentioned. To begin, then, let us see, in the first place, what has been found to be true in reference to some of the most

PECULIAR AND DISTINGUISHING CHARACTERISTICS OF THE NEGRO.

Cuvier, in his "Animal Kingdom," page 50, says,

"The negro race is confined to the south of Mount Atlas; it is marked by a black complexion, crisped or woolly hair, compressed cranium, and a flat nose. The projection of the lower parts of the face, and the thick lips, evidently approximate it to the monkey tribe; and the hordes of which it consists have always remained in the most complete state of utter barbarism."

Again, in his "Theory of the Earth," page 341, Cuvier says,

"The negroes, the most degraded race among men, whose forms approach the nearest to those of the inferior animals, and whose intellect has not yet arrived at the institution of regular governments, or at anything having the least appearance of systematic knowledge, have preserved no sort of annals or of tradition."

Samuel George Morton, one of our own scientific and distinguished countrymen, who is, perhaps, (or was while he lived,) the very best authority extant upon the subjects of Anthropology and Ethnology, is quoted in Nott and Gliddon's "Types of Mankind," page 305, as håving said,

"After twenty years of observation and reflection, during which period I have always approached this subject with diffidence and caution; after investigating for myself the remarkable diversities of opinion to which it has given rise, and after weighing the difficulties that beset it on every side, I can find no satisfactory explanation of the diverse phenomena that characterize physical Man, excepting in the doctrine of an original plurality of races."

Again, in the course of a letter which he addressed to George Robbins Gliddon, in May, 1846, Dr. Morton said,

"I maintain, without reservation, the following among other opinions—that the human race has not sprung from one pair, but from a plurality of centres; that these were created *ab initio* in those parts of the world best adapted to their physical nature; that the epoch of creation was that undefined period of time spoken of in the first chapter of Genesis, wherein it is related that God formed man, 'male and female created he them;' that the deluge was a merely local phenomenon; that it affected but a small part of the then existing inhabitants of the earth; and, finally, that these views are consistent with the facts of the case, as well as with analogical evidence."

Again, in Nott and Gliddon's "Types of Mankind," page 307, Dr. Morton is quoted as having said,

"By the simultaneous creation of a plurality of original stocks, the population of the earth became, not an accidental result, but a matter of certainty. Many and distant regions which, in accordance with the doctrine of a single origin, would have remained for thousands of years unpeopled and unknown, received at once their allotted inhabitants; and these, instead of being left to struggle with the viscissitudes of chance, were, from the beginning, adapted to those varied circumstances of climate and locality which yet mark their respective positions upon the earth."

Hermann Burmeister, one of the most celebrated naturalists now living, in his work entitled "The Black Man," page 6, says,

"The first glance shows the negro to be of a peculiar race. The most striking marks of peculiarity are in the relative dimensions of the various parts of his body, the black color of his skin, and his curly head of wool. The great length of his arms is a peculiarity which strikes the experienced observer at once. The much shorter body and longer legs of the negro are also characteristics which serve to increase the difference between him and the European."

Again, in his work entitled "The Black Man," page 17, Burmeister says,

"The black man is more disposed to be submissive than the European. He feels and silently recognizes the superiority of the white man, and is conscious of his own inferiority in capacity and knowledge. From hence, perhaps, comes that cowardice of the negro which all observers have remarked. It is a well-known fact that the negro will yield with hardly any resistance, although numerically superior, to a white force, and thinks himself overcome even before a blow has been struck."

Again, in his work entitled "The Black Man," page 15, Burmeister says,

"The desire of amusing himself while at work, either by dancing or singing, or otherwise, is a marked feature of the negro. If he cannot have his amusement during his work, he must have it immediately after. The slave who has been at work in the field from sunrise to sunset, generally sings and dances for an hour or more afterward, in the company of his friends, around the fire in front of his hut, which he never fails to light, either for amusement, or for warmth when it happens to be cold. The observation of such groups was always a source of much amusement to me. The sunny, ape-like nature of the negro is then very evident. * * * It is quite interesting to observe a negro while walking alone, untroubled, on his way, perhaps carrying a load upon his head, as you most commonly meet him. Even then the negro is not in truth alone ; he has himself for a companion, with whom he talks or plays incessantly ; and the con-

versation is commonly very loud, and kept up without any regard to
the passers-by. In such moments, the negro, especially the slave, is
thoroughly in his element; he gives free course to his nature, and
enjoys himself with great delight although panting and gasping under his load, with the sweat pouring in torrents down his neck.
The subject of these monologues generally involves some incident or
event in the life, past or present, of the negro. * * * The words
of these negro monologues are always sung in the same monotonous
key, while the negro at the same time beats the load on his head with
a stick, or shakes an instrument he has—a tin box filled with shot. If
his burden be heavy, he runs on in a trotting gait, knocking incessantly with his stick, or shaking his tin instrument, and singing and
groaning in harmony. His groans are as rhythmical as his songs.
When his burden is light, the negro assumes a grave gait, and cries
aloud and very rapidly in a singing tone; he then stops a moment,
gesticulates with his hand, and shouts some compliment to some fel-
low-sufferer, which is answered in the same loud tone, and with similar gravity. As the head remains fixed, the movements of the negro
are accompanied by a free play of the features. The eye brightens,
the mouth is distorted as it gives utterance to these odd cries, and the
ape peeps out everywhere, as you look upon the old actor you have
before you.

Again, in his work entitled, "The Black Man," page
16, Burmeister says :

"The highest enjoyment of the negro generally consists in idle
lounging, and eating and drinking in quantity rather than in quality.
The negro female delights in ornaments of dress, such as ear-rings,
necklaces and finger-rings, and cares little for elegance or cleanliness.
* * * The negro is untidy in his dress, and will, at any time, prefer some worthless rag to a whole shirt or an entire pair of breeches.
The female is much more disposed to flaunt in finery than to wash
herself, or to keep herself free from vermin, or to have whole clothes,
or a supply of them. They have as little regard to economy as they
have to cleanliness. * * * They are fond of rich dress, a silk
handkerchief if they can get it, a pair of shining patent leather
shoes, or a fine beaver hat. They, however, take no care of these
objects; they do not wear them carefully, nor keep them for great
occasions, but they use them up at once. When they require a
change, and have not the means to purchase as good, they prefer
wearing their fine things to their last rag, rather than put on any-

thing less showy and costly. They recollect that they were once fine, and that thought consoles them."

Who is this Dr. Hermann Burmeister, this erudite and accurate observer, who speaks so knowingly and so interestingly about the negro? He is a German naturalist of world-wide repute ; and although he himself has never been in any part of the United States, yet an English translation of his graphic description of "The Black Man" appeared in New York as long ago as the year 1853, it having been published there, at that time, by William C. Bryant & Co., editors and proprietors of the New York *Evening Post;* and it was then that that excellent newspaper thus ably and enthusiastically criticised and sketched both the work and its author :

"This Treatise on 'The Black Man' presents the most complete study of the comparative anatomy and psychology of the negro which has ever been in print, so far as we know, and the only one, we believe, that has any pretensions to scientific accuracy. It has been prepared by Hermann Burmeister, one of the most distinguished of our living naturalists, and at present Professor of Zoology in the University of Halle, in Germany. He spent about fourteen months of the years 1850 and 1851 in Brazil, and has just submitted to the press the second volume of his work, entitled, "Geological Pictures of the Earth," one chapter of which embodies the result of his studies upon the Natural History of the African, and which is now, for the first time, presented in English to the American public.

" That the reader may know what value to attach to these observations, we may as well give a few particulars of their author's life and position in Germany.

" Burmeister was born in 1807, at Stralsund ; he published a 'Text-book of Natural History,' which was followed four years later by a larger manual of Natural History, which is a masterly work. Upon the death of Nitzsch, Burmeister was appointed, in 1837, 'Professor Extraordinary,' and, in 1842, Professor of Zoology in the University of Halle, where he now ranks as one of the most eminent and popular teachers in Germany. His greatest achievement as an author is his work on Entomology, in five volumes, the fullest treatise upon that subject in any language, and embracing the results of fifteen

years of devoted study to the subject. He is also the author of a
'History of Creation,' which has passed through five editions ; of a
work entitled, 'Geological Pictures of the Earth,' and a number of
essays and disquisitions upon subjects cognate to his profession,
which have appeared in various scientific journals.

"In 1848 he was chosen a member of the Berlin Parliament, where
he signalized himself by his eloquence and his industry. His health
compelled him to resign and go abroad. He arrived in Brazil in October, 1850, and spent fourteen months there, most of which time
was devoted to the study of the black race.—with what success the
reader will be able to judge. No one who gives these pages a faithful perusal will be long in discovering that nothing so elaborate or
satisfactory has ever been printed upon the subject ; and he will also
see precisely to what extent the white and the black races differ, and
how much further the former has progressed than the latter beyond
the apish type."

It was to this same Dr. Burmeister, who is now paying
his devotions to Nature in the Argentine Republic, that,
presuming somewhat upon a pleasant acquaintanceship,
I recently took the liberty to write as follows :

"When I tell you that we have twenty-eight millions of
white people in the United States, and only about four
millions of negroes, you could, if advised of all the facts
in the case, hardly fail to be surprised at the unduly
large percentage of black patients whom, during the four
years of my Consular residence in Buenos Ayres, I have
had occasion to send to the hospital for medical treatment. In this matter, your surprise would probably be
increased, were I to inform you that, of all the mariners
who come to this port on American vessels, only about
one in sixteen is of the black race, and that one is seldom
a mariner in the true sense of the word, but more generally a cook or a scullion, in which in-door situation he
is screened from the severer hardships of the weather.

"Yet I think that I am quite within the bounds of
truth when I say that nearly one-half of all the persons

who have come to me for assistance and relief, have been negroes. Of the large number of negroes who have thus applied to me for protection, most of them in an ill-clad and penniless condition, and with no wages due, many have needed, and have received, the attention of skillful physicians and surgeons. Once in the hospital, however, the negroes are, I have found, far less likely to come out alive and well than white patients.

"This much by way of preface. Now let me trouble you for a few items of information. You have, perhaps, already guessed one or two of the points upon which I wish to be enlightened. Why is it that the negroes are so rapidly falling a prey to every manner of fatal affliction? Is it not because Nature is becoming impatient to close her account with them? I ween so, and would be glad to have your opinion on the subject.

"A few years since, while temporarily residing in the city of New York, I frequently accepted the invitations of a youthful relative (I myself being somewhat younger then than I am now!) who was there studying medicine, to accompany him to the dissecting-rooms of the University Medical College, on Fourteenth Street, where, from first to last, I saw the corpses of a great many persons, of almost every age, color and nationality. Among these was no small number of negroes, to whom, as a rule, the peculiarities of extreme attenuation of the limbs, and general gauntness and imperfection of frame, attached in such manner as to excite my particular attention. At sundry times, while looking at them, I was impressed with the conviction,—a conviction which has since been greatly strengthened,—that, especially in communities of white people, there is an ever-obvious and uncheckable tendency on the part of the blacks, when put entirely upon their own resources, as they ought everywhere to be put, to decrease, to die, to disappear; in a word, to cease to retain a vital foothold upon the earth. So may it be!

In the views to which I have thus briefly given expression, am I right, or am I wrong? Not more firmly am I convinced of the bright and genial existence of the sun, than I am that the postulates here advanced are wholly founded in truth. Your reply, and the reasons upon which your own opinions on the subject are based, are awaited with great interest and respect.

To the foregoing communication, the nature-loving and learned Burmiester did me the honor to reply thus :

BUENOS AYRES, May 16, 1866.

HINTON R. HELPER, ESQ:

MY DEAR SIR—I have had the pleasure to receive your letter of yesterday, and have, with great interest, read your statement of the remarkable difference which has fallen under your observation in the number, respectively, of white and black men, who, in your official position, seem to have had claims upon you for relief. It is for me a new proof that, as I have already said in my description of "The Black Man," the negro race is inferior to the white race, particularly in the mental and spiritual forces; for it is a fact well known to every psychologist, that fullness of the spiritual forces, as in the case of the white man, has the happiest influences in promoting and preserving the good health of the body, and in predisposing the whole physical system to recovery, when once unwell.

These auspicious influences are steadily increasing in the white race, and will continue to do so with the grand progress of veritable civilization ; and, therefore, the higher and better grades of human society afford generally a stronger power of resistance to the attacks of all fatal disorders. The important truths here considered have always manifested themselves very conspicuously in times of long and terrible epidemics, and also during protracted and bloody wars and great battles.

We may not, therefore, be surprised to find that, in all cases of actual misfortune, and especially in cases of ill-health, the black race exhibits far less power of resistance than the white race. But not only, upon general considerations, is the higher civilization of the white race to be taken as a reason of its greater resistance to leveling causes. On this particular point, as already intimated, much may be admitted to be due to the very obvious superiority of the white man's mental and spiritual nature.

A man of inferior endowments is always superstitious and timid; and these are bad qualities which are notoriously common to the negro. Such a man has little faculty or inclination to create resources for himself, and is at all times too willing and too prone to rely upon others for assistance. If overtaken by sickness, and if left to himself, he at once resorts for remedies to one of a thousand or more species of witchcraft, or to some other monstrous system of absurdity, and, as a matter of course, soon falls a victim to his own folly. Indeed, once really sick, from whatever cause, he not unfrequently feels that, from that very moment, he is doomed to die—that his distressful aches and pains are past cure, and that his unsightly wounds and sores cannot be healed.

You know that, as a general rule, diseased or distempered animals cannot be cured. They should, if possible, always be kept in a state of good health ; for, except in rare instances, sickness proves fatal to them. Men are affected by a similar law, just in the proportion that they approximate to the condition of animals ; and the closest and most numerous approximations of this sort are furnished by the negro race.

Supposing that you would be satisfied with the mere expression of my opinion, I have given it to you in this way; but I am at your service to enter more elaborately into the discussion of the interesting subjects which seem to be now engaging your attention, should you consider it worth while to advance any new or additional hypothesis.

Your sincere friend,

HERMANN BURMEISTER.

Contemporary with **Dr. Burmeister,** and scarcely less distinguished as a Naturalist—a man who, regardless of pre-conceived errors on the part of the multitude, seeks to establish, before all the world, the eternal truth of things—is Prof. Agassiz, who, in Nott and Gliddon's "Types of Mankind," page 74, says,

"Accepting the definition with the qualifications just mentioned respecting hybridity, I am prepared to show that the differences existing between the races of men are of the same kind as the differences observed between the different families, genera, and species of monkeys or other animals; and that these different species of animals differ in the same degree one from the other as the races of men—nay, the differences between distinct races are often greater than those distinguishing species of animals one from the other. The Chimpanzee and Gorilla do not differ more one from the other than the Mandingo and the Guinea Negro; they together do not differ more from the Ourang-outang than the Malay or white man differs from the negro. In proof of this assertion, I need only refer the reader to the description of the anthropoid monkeys published by Prof. Owen and by Dr. J. Wyman, and to such descriptions of the races of men as notice more important peculiarities than the mere differences in the color of the skin. It is, however, but fair to exonerate these authors from the responsibility of any deduction I would draw from a renewed examination of the same facts, differing from theirs; for I maintain distinctly that the differences observed among the races of men are of the same kind and even greater than those upon which the anthropoid monkeys are considered as distinct species."

Again, Prof. Agassiz, (who, as he himself has pithily and notably declared, "has no time to waste in making money,") in Nott and Gliddon's "Types of Mankind," page 74, says,

"In the genus horse, we have two domesticated species, the common horse and the donkey; in the genus bull, one domesticated species, and the wild buffalo; the three species of bear mentioned are only found in the wild state. The ground upon which these animals are considered as distinct species is simply the fact that, since they have been known to man, they have always preserved the same characteristics. To make specific difference or identity depend upon genetic succession, is begging the principle and taking for granted what in reality is under discussion. It is true that animals of the same species are fertile among themselves, and that their fecundity is an easy test of this natural relation; but this character is not exclusive, since we know that the horse and the ass, the buffalo and our cattle, like many other animals, may be crossed; we are, therefore, not justified, in doubtful cases, in considering the fertility of two animals as decisive of their specific identity. Moreover, generation is not the only way in which certain animals may multiply, as there are entire classes in which the larger number of individuals do not originate from eggs. Any definition of species in which the question of generation is introduced is, therefore, objectionable."

Again, Prof. Agassiz, in Nott and Gliddon's "Types of Mankind," page 68, says,

"The earliest migrations recorded, in any form, show us man meeting man, wherever he moves upon the inhabitable surface of the globe, small islands excepted. * * * We have Semitic nations covering the north African and southwest Asiatic faunæ, while the south European peninsulas, including Asia Minor, are inhabited by Græco-Roman nations, and the cold, temperate zone, by Celto-Germanic nations; the eastern range of Europe being peopled by Schlaves. This coincidence may justify the inference of an independent origin for these different tribes, as soon as it can be admitted that the races of men were primitively created in nations; the more so, since all of them claim to have been autocthones of the countries they inhabit. This claim is so universal that it well deserves more attention."

Thomas Jefferson, who was, beyond all question, the most philosophic and far-seeing statesman who has yet left upon America the mark of his greatness, in his "Notes on Virginia," (see Jefferson's Works, Volume VIII., pages 380–383,) said,

"Deep-rooted prejudices entertained by the whites; ten thousand recollections, by the blacks, of the injuries they have sustained; new provocations; the real distinctions which nature has made; and many other circumstances, will divide us into parties, and produce convulsions, which will probably never end but in the extermination of the one or the other race. To these objections, which are political, may be added others, which are physical and moral. The first difference which strikes us is that of color. Whether the black of the negro resides in the reticular membrane between the skin and scarf-skin, or in the scarf-skin itself; whether it proceeds from the color of the blood, the color of the bile, or from that of some other secretion, the difference is fixed in nature, and is as real as if its seat and cause were better known to us. And is this difference of no importance? Is it not the foundation of a greater or less share of beauty in the two races? Are not the fine mixtures of red and white, the expression of every passion by greater or less suffusions of color in the one, preferable to that eternal monotony, which reigns in the countenances, that immovable veil of black which covers the emotions of the other race? Add to these, flowing hair, a more elegant symmetry of form, their own judgment in favor of the whites, declared by their preference of them, as uniformly as is the preference of the orang-outang for the black woman over those of his own species.

"The circumstance of superior beauty, is thought worthy of attention in the propagation of our horses, dogs, and other domestic animals; why not in that of man? Besides those of color, figure, and hair, there are other physical distinctions proving a difference of race. They have less hair on the face and body. They secrete less by the kidneys, and more by the glands of the skin, which gives them a very strong and disagreeable odor. This greater degree of transpiration, renders them more tolerant of heat, and less so of cold than the whites. Perhaps, too, a difference of structure in the pulmonary apparatus, which a late ingenious experimentalist has discovered to be the principal regulator of animal heat, may have disabled them from extricating, in the act of inspiration, so much of that fluid from the outer air, or obliged them in expiration to part with more of it. They seem to require less sleep. A black, after hard labor through the day, will be induced by the slightest amusements to sit up till midnight, or later, though knowing he must be out with the first dawn of the morning. * * * They are more ardent after their female; but love seems with them to be more an eager desire, than a tender, delicate mixture of sentiment and sensation. Their griefs are transient. Those numberless afflictions, which render it doubtful whether Heaven has given life to us in mercy or in wrath, are less felt, and sooner forgotten with them. In general, their existence appears to participate more of sensation than reflection. To this must be ascribed their disposition to sleep when abstracted from their diversions, and unemployed in labor. An animal whose body is at rest, and who does not reflect, must be disposed to sleep of course. Comparing them by their faculties of memory, reason, and imagination, it appears to me that in memory they are equal to the whites; in reason much inferior, as I think one could scarcely be found capable of tracing and comprehending the investigations of Euclid; and that in imagination they are dull, tasteless, and anomalous. It would be unfair to follow them to Africa for this investigation. We will consider them here, on the same stage with the whites, and where the facts are not apocryphal on which a judgment is to be formed. It will be right to make great allowances for the difference of condition, of education, of conversation and of the sphere in which they move. Many millions of them have been brought to, and born in America. Most of them, indeed, have been confined to tillage, to their own homes, and their own society; yet many have been so situated, that they might have availed themselves of the conversation of their masters; many have been brought up to the handicraft arts, and from that circumstance have always been associated with the whites. Some have been liberally educated, and all have lived in countries where the arts and sciences are cultivated to a considerable degree, and all have had before their eyes samples of the best works from abroad. The Indians, with no advantages of this kind, will often carve figures on their pipes not destitute of design and merit. They will crayon out an animal, a plant, or a country, so as to prove the existence of a germ in their minds which only wants cultivation. They astonish you with strokes of the most sublime oratory; such as prove their reason and sentiment strong, their imagination glowing and elevated. But never yet could I find that a black had uttered a thought above the level of plain narration; never saw even an elementary trait of painting or sculpture. * * * Misery is often the parent of the most affecting touches of poetry. Love is the peculiar œstrum of the poet. Their love is ardent, but it kindles the senses only, not the imagination. Religion, indeed, has produced a Phyllis Wheatley; but it could not produce a poet. The compositions published under her name are below the dignity of criticism. The heroes of the Dunciad are to her as Hercules to the author of that poem."

Again, in the first volume of his works, page 48, Jefferson, speaking of the negroes, said :

"Nothing is more certainly written in the book of fate than that these people are to be free ; *nor is it less certain that the two races, equally free, cannot live under the same government.*"

Of the sage of Monticello himself, it may not be amiss to note here, very briefly, what has been thought and said of him by those who have long enjoyed the reputation of being, or of having been, competent and impartial judges of men's merits. William Ellery Channing, the great moralist and theologian, in his work on "Emancipation," page 65, says :

"The South, with more of ardor and of bold and rapid genius, and the North, with more of wisdom and steady principle, furnish admirable materials for a State. * * * It is worthy of remark, that the most eminent men at the South have had a large infusion of the Northern character. Washington, in his calm dignity, his rigid order, his close attention to business, his reserve, almost approaching coldness, bore a striking affinity to the North ; and his sympathies led him to choose Northern men very often as confidential friends. Mr. Madison had much of the calm wisdom, the patient, studious research, the exactness and quiet manner of our part of the country, with little of the imagination and fervor of his own. Chief Justice Marshall had more than these two great men, of the genial, unreserved character of a warmer climate, but so blended with a spirit of moderation, and clear judgment, and serene wisdom, as to make him the delight and confidence of the whole land. There is one other distinguished name of the South, which I have not mentioned, Mr. Jefferson ; and the reason is, that his character seemed to belong to neither section of the country. He wanted the fiery, daring spirit of the South, and the calm energy of the North. He stood alone. He was a man of genius, given to bold and original speculations, and was, at the same time, a sagacious observer of men and events. He owed his vast influence, second only to Washington's, to his keen insight into the character of his countrymen, and into the spirit of his age."

Richard Hildreth, next to George Bancroft, the ablest historian of the United States, in his "Despotism in America," page 15, pays the following just tribute to Thomas Jefferson,—a tribute which is in perfect unity of sentiment with that paid above by Dr. Channing :

"Jefferson is revered, and justly, as the earliest, ablest, boldest, and most far-going of those who became the expounders and advocates of the democratical system in America. Most of the others, whether leaders or followers, seemed driven on by a blind instinct. They felt, but did not reason. Jefferson based his political opinions upon the general principles of human nature."

Sir Charles Lyell gives his valuable testimony, also, in proof of an original diversity of human races. Hear him. In his "Antiquity of Man," page 387, he says :

"As ethnologists have failed, as yet, to trace back the history of any one race to the area where it originated, some zoologists of eminence have declared their belief, that the different races, whether they be three, five, twenty, or a much greater number, (for on this point there is an endless diversity of opinion,) have all been primordial creations, having from the first been stamped with the characteristic features, mental and bodily, by which they are now distinguished, except where intermarriage has given rise to mixed or hybrid races. Were we to admit, say they, a unity of origin of such strongly-marked varieties as the negro and European, differing as they do in color and bodily constitution, each fitted for distinct climates, and exhibiting some marked peculiarities in their osteological, and even in some details of cranial and cerebral conformation, as well as in their average intellectual endowments,—if, in spite of the fact that all these attributes have been faithfully handed down unaltered for hundreds of generations, we are to believe that, in the course of time, they have all diverged from one common stock, how shall we resist the arguments of the transmutationist, who contends that all closely allied species of animals and plants have in like manner sprung from a common parentage, albeit that for the last three or four thousand years they may have been persistent in character? Where are we to stop, unless we make our stand at once on the independent creation of those distinct human races, the history of which is better known to us than that of any of the inferior animals?"

John Crawfurd, President of the Ethnological Society of London, in a communication addressed to the "Ethnological Magazine," Volume I., Part II., page 354, published in 1861, says :

"I propose in this paper to explain the views which I have myself been led to entertain respecting the Classification of Man, and may state at once that the conclusion I have come to is, that mankind consists of many originally created species, and that the hypothesis of unity of race is without foundation."

Again, John Crawfurd, in the "Ethnological Magazine," Volume I., Part II., pages 377–378, says :

"Although neither the skull nor any other single character is sufficient to distinguish the races of man,—nor, indeed, in the majority of cases, all possible characters combined,—still there are a few instances,—generally those of rude and isolated tribes,—in which the distinction of races seems clear enough. Among these may be reckoned the Australians, the negroes of New Guinea, those of New Ireland, those of Mallicollo, one of the Cyclades, those of Tauna, one of the New Hebrides, those of the Fejee Islands, those of the Andaman Islands, those of the Malayan Peninsula, those of the Philippines, and those of Madagascar, the Bhutias, the Tibetians, the Polynesians, the Kamschatdales, the Alutian Islanders, the Hottentots, and the Esquimaux. Here, then, instead of the five races of Cuvier and Blumenbach, or the seven of Prichard, we have no fewer than seventeen well defined ones, widely differing among themselves, and distinct from the rest of mankind. These rude races, however, embrace but a small portion of mankind, and we have large groups in which the race is sufficiently distinct, and the variations very trifling. These include the Chinese, the Japanese, the Hindoo-Chinese, the Hindus, the Malays, the native Americans, the Mauritanians or Berbers, and the Egyptians. These, although not so free from variety as the rude races above named, may still be considered as primordial species ; and, if so, the total will rise to five-and-twenty. Other large groups are more diversified, such as the European, the African negro, the Persian, the Syrian, and the Arab. Some of these contain within themselves races, probably as distinct at their creation, although closely allied, as Australians or Polynesians. In the European, for example, we have the Schlavonic, the German or Teutonic, the Celtic, the Greek, the Italian, and, very probably, the Spanish or Iberian. The African negro is still more split into races, such as the Caffres and the Zullas. These, however, are not all the races that might be enumerated, for north of the chain of the Himalaya, up to the Frozen Ocean, there are many tribes which, although agreeing in some respects with the Mongols, differ from them essentially in corporeal and mental endowments. In Western Asia we find races resembling Europeans, but palpably differing from them, such as Circassians, Georgians, and Armenians ; while to the North of Europe we have the Laplanders, and in Africa, the Nubians and the Abyssinians.

"Here, then, we have some forty races of man, which, to pack into the five pigeon-holes of Cuvier and Blumenbach, or the seven of Prichard, would produce confusion instead of order."

Again, John Crawfurd, in the "Ethnological Magazine," Volume I., Part II., page 363, says :

"As long as the race continues unmixed, no change of climate appears to make any essential change in it. Negroes from equatorial Africa have been settled in the temperate regions and high table lands of America for near three centuries without undergoing any appreciable physical change. A colony from the temperate parts of Persia has been settled for a thousand years in inter-tropical India, and, keeping themselves strictly unmixed, they still retain the physical form of Persians, and probably differ in no material respect from the contemporaries of Cyrus and Artaxerxes. The Spanish race has been settled within tropical America for three centuries and a half; but their pure descendants are, in complexion and personal form, in no essential point different from the Spaniards of old Spain. The Danes and Norwegians who have been settled in Greenland for more than two centuries, are still of the genuine Teutonic race; whereas, had there been any particular effect consequent on a change of climate, they would, by this time, have made some approach to the Esquimaux, who are the native inhabitants of the land."

.Dr. James Hunt, President of the Anthropological Society of London, in his work entitled, "The Negro's Place in Nature," page 52, says:

"No man who thoroughly investigates, with an unbiased mind, can doubt that the negro·belongs to a distinct type. The term species, in the present state of science, is not satisfactory; but we may safely say, that there is in the negro that assemblage of evidence which would, *ipso facto*, induce an unbiased observer to make the European and negro two distinct types of man."

Again, in the same work, "The Negro's Place in Nature," page 4, Dr. Hunt says:

"It is too generally taught, that the negro only differs from the European in the color of his skin, and in the peculiarity of his hair; but such opinions are not supported by facts. The skin and the hair are by no means the only characters which distinguish the negro from the European, even physically; and the difference is greater, mentally and morally, than the demonstrated physical difference."

Again, in the same work, "The Negro's Place in Nature," page 36, Dr. Hunt says:

"Some writers who advocate the specific difference of the Negro from the European, have very injudiciously admitted, that occasionally the negro is equal in intellect to the European; but this admission has materially weakened their argument in favor of a specific difference. If this is so, let me ask those who hold such an opinion, to give the name of one pure negro who has ever distinguished himself as a man of science, as an author, or a statesman, a warrior, a poet, an artist. Surely, if there is equality in the mental development of human races, some one instance can be quoted. From all the evidence we have examined, we see no reason to believe that the pure negro ever advances further in intellect than an intelligent European boy of fourteen years of age."

Again, in the same work, "The Negro's Place in Nature," page 10, Dr. Hunt says:

"There can be no doubt, that at puberty a great change takes place in relation to psychical development; and in the negro, there appears to be an arrested development of the mind, exactly harmonizing with the physical formation. Young negro children are nearly as intelligent as European children; but the older they grow the less intelligent they become. They exhibit, when young, an animal liveliness for play and tricks, far surpassing the European child."

John Pye Smith, (a very good Pye!) one of the ablest ecclesiastics known as English Dissenters, or Non-Conformists, in his work on "Geological Science," page 354, says:

"If we carry our concessions to the very last point—if the progress of investigation should indeed bring out such kinds and degrees of evidence, as shall rightfully turn the scale in favor of the hypothesis that there are several Races of Mankind, each having originated in a different pair of ancestors—what would be the consequence to our highest interests, as rational, accountable, and immortal beings? Would our faith, the fountain of motives for love and obedience to God, virtuous self-government, and universal justice and kindness—would this faith—'the substance of things hoped for, the evidence of things not seen'—sustain any detriment, after, by due meditation and prayer, we had surmounted the first shock? Let us survey the consequences.

2*

"If the two first inhabitants of Eden were the progenitors, not of all human beings, but only of the race whence sprung the Hebrew family, still it would remain the fact, that all were formed by immediate power of God; and all their circumstances, stated or implied in the Scriptures, would remain the same as to moral and practical purposes. * * * Some difficulties in the Scripture-history would be taken away—such as, the sons of Adam obtaining wives not their own sisters; Cain's acquiring instruments of husbandry, which must have been furnished by miracle immediately from God, upon the usual supposition; his apprehensions of summary punishment ('any man that findeth me will slay me ;') his fleeing into another region, of which Josephus so understands the text, as to affirm that Cain obtained confederates, and became a plunderer and robber, implying the existence of a population beyond his own family; and his building a ' city,' a considerable collection of habitations.

"The characteristic differences of the great divisions of mankind, physical and intellectual, would create no difficulty in our reasonings —for instance, the mental distinctions laid down by Dr. Morton : 'The Caucasian Race; distinguished for the facility with which it attains the highest intellectual endowments : The Mongolian; ingenious, imitative, and highly susceptible of cultivation : The Malay; active and ingenious, and possessing all the habits of a migratory, predaceous, and maritime people : The American; averse to cultivation, slow in acquiring knowledge, restless, revengeful, fond of war, and wholly destitute of maritime adventure : The Ethiopian; joyous, flexible and indolent, the many nations which compose this race presenting a singular diversity of intellectual character, of which the far extreme is the lowest grade of humanity.' The hypothesis also will diminish our surprise, but not our sorrow, that many fine nations of men have appeared incapable of being persuaded, by all the attempts of wisdom and humanity, as well as the stern demands of want; so that they prefer to perish by inches, rather than to cultivate the soil and adopt those habits of civilized life by which they might be preserved."

Charles Hamilton Smith, in his "Natural History of the Human Species," page 189, says :

"In the west African, we find the facial angle varying from 65 to 70 degrees ; the head being small and laterally compressed ; the dome of the skull arched and dense ; the forehead narrow, depressed, and the posterior parts more developed ; the nose broad and crushed, with the nostrils round ; the lower jaw protruding and angular, but more vertical in nonage ; the mouth wide, with very thick lips, and black to the commissure, which is red ; the teeth large and solid, and the incisors placed rather obliquely forward. The ears, which are roundish and rather small, standing somewhat high and detached, are said, like the scalp, to be occasionally movable ; the eyes always suffused with a bilious tint, and the irides very dark. The hair, in infants, rises from the skin in small mammillary tufts, disposed in irregular quincunx, and is in all parts of a crisp woolly texture, excepting the eyebrows and eyelashes. In men, it is scanty on the upper lip, generally confined to the point of the chin, without any at the sides of the face, excepting in late manhood. On the head, it forms a close hard frizzle of wool ; and the breast sometimes has a few tufts ; but the arms and legs are without any."

Again, in his "Natural History of the Human Species," page 192, Charles Hamilton Smith says :

"Negroes, of all human beings, are distinguished for fighting, by occasionally butting, with their heads foremost, like rams, at each other, the collision of their skulls giving a report that may be heard at some distance. Even women, in their brawls, have the same habit. The dense spherical structure of the head, likewise, enables several tribes to shave their crowns, and in this exposed state to remain, with the lower half of the body immersed in water, under a vertical sun."

Daniel Wilson, Professor of History and English Literature in the University College, Toronto, Canada, in his "Prehistoric Man," Volume II., page 334, says :

"From the very first, we perceive a strongly marked and clearly defined distinction between diverse branches of the human family ; and this, coupled with the apportionment of the several regions of the earth to distinct types of man, distinguished from each other not less definitely than are the varied faunæ of these regions, seems to express very clearly the subdivision of the genus Homo into diverse varieties, with a certain relation to their primary geographical distribution."

Again, in his "Prehistoric Man," Volume II., page 199, Prof. Wilson says :

·"The unsuccessful search after traces of an ante-Columbian intercourse with the New World, suffices to confirm the belief that, for unnumbered centuries throughout the ancient era, the Western Hemisphere was the exclusive heritage of nations native to the soil."

Henry Lichtenstein, who, in the early part of the present century, was one of the Professors of Natural History in the University of Berlin, and who was, moreover, for several years in the Dutch Service at the Cape of Good Hope, in his "Travels in Southern Africa," Volume II., page 224, says :

"I devoted a considerable time to observing these men very accurately ; and though, according to all that is related above, I must allow the validity of their claims to be classed among rational creatures, I cannot forbear saying that a Bosjesman, certainly in his mien, and all his gestures, has more resemblance to an ape than to a man. One of our present guests, who appeared about fifty years of age, whose forehead, nose, cheeks, and chin, were all smeared over with black grease, had the true physiognomy of the small blue ape of Caffraria.   What gives the more verity to such a comparison was the vivacity of his eyes, and the flexibility of his eye-brows, which he worked up and down with every change of countenance.   Even his nostrils and the corners of his mouth, nay, his very ears, moved involuntarily, expressing his hasty transitions from eager desire to watchful distrust.   There was not, on the contrary, a single feature in his countenance that evinced a consciousness of mental powers, or anything that denoted emotions of the mind of a milder species than what belong to man in his mere animal nature.   When a piece of meat was given him, and, half rising, he stretched out a distrustful arm to take it, he snatched it hastily, and stuck it immediately into the fire, peering around with his little keen eyes, as if fearing lest some one should take it away again.   All this was done with such looks and gestures, that any one must have been ready to swear that he had taken the example of them entirely from an ape.   He soon took the meat from the embers, wiped it hastily with his right hand upon his left arm, and tore out large half raw bits with his teeth, which I could see going entire down his meagre throat.   At length, when he came to the bones and entrails, as he could not manage this with his teeth, he had recourse to a knife, which was hanging round his neck.   With this he cut off the piece which he held in his teeth, close to the mouth, without touching his nose or eyes,—a feat of dexterity which a person with a Celtic countenance could not easily have performed. When the bone was picked clean, he stuck it again into the fire, and breaking it between two stones, sucked out the marrow ; this done, he immediately filled the emptied bone with tobacco. I offered him a clay pipe, which he declined ; and taking the thick bone a great way into his mouth, he drew in the smoke by long draughts, snapping his eyes like a person who, with more than usual pleasure, drinks a glass of costly wine."

Abraham Lincoln, during his first Presidential term, in the summer of 1862, while replying to a deputation of beggarly negroes who had waited on him in reference to a particular governmental scheme or plan of colonization, which was then a subject of much discussion throughout the country, used this highly significant and appropriate language :

"Why should not the people of your race be colonized? Why should they not leave this country? This is perhaps the first question for consideration. You and we are a different race. We have between us a broader difference than exists between almost any other two races. Whether it is right or wrong I need not discuss ; but this physical difference is a great disadvantage to us both, as I think your race suffers greatly, many of them by living with us, while ours suffer from your presence. In a word, we suffer on each side. If this is admitted, it shows a reason why we should be separated. You, here, are freemen, I suppose. Perhaps you have long been free, or all your lives. Your race are suffering, in my opinion, the greatest wrong inflicted on any people. But even when you cease to be slaves, you are yet far removed from being placed on an equality with the white race. You are still cut off from many of the advantages which are enjoyed by the other race. The aspiration of man is to enjoy equality with the best when free, but on this broad continent not a single man of your race is made the equal of ours. Go where you are treated the best, and the ban is still upon you. I do not propose to discuss this, but to present it as a fact with which we have to deal. I cannot alter it if I would. It is a fact about which we all think and feel alike. We look to our conditions owing to the existence of the races on this continent. I need not recount to you the effects upon white men growing out of the institution of slavery. I believe in its general evil effects upon the white race. See our present condition. The country is engaged in war. Our white men are cutting each other's throats, none knowing how far their frenzy may extend ; and then consider what we know to be the truth. But for your race among us, there could not be a war, although many men engaged on either side do not care for you one way or the other. Nevertheless, I repeat, without the institution of slavery, and the colored race as a basis, the war could not have had an existence. It is better for us both, therefore, to be separated. I know that there are free men among you who, even if they could better their condition, are not as much inclined to go out of the country as those who, being slaves, could obtain their freedom on this condition. I suppose one of the principal difficulties in the way of colonization is, that the free colored man cannot see that his comfort would be advanced by it. You may believe you can live in Washington, or elsewhere in the United States, the remainder of your lives, perhaps more comfortably than you could in any foreign country. Hence you may come to the conclusion that you have nothing to do with the idea of going to a foreign country. This (I speak in no unkind sense) is an extremely selfish view of the case. But you ought to do something to help those who are not so fortunate as yourselves. * * * For the sake of your race you should sacrifice something of your present comfort, for the purpose of being as grand in that respect as the white people. It is a cheering thought throughout life, that something can be done to ameliorate the condition of those who have been subject to the hard usages of the world. It is difficult to make a man miserable while he feels that he is worthy of himself, and claims kindred with the great God who made him ! In the American revolutionary war, sacrifices were made by men engaged in it, but they were cheered by the future. General Washington himself endured greater physical hardships than if he had remained a British subject ; yet he was a happy man, because he was engaged in benefiting his race, and in doing something for the children of his neighbors, having none of his own."

It was on these subjects of certain general and specific differences, which, even independently of color, are always clearly discernible between the whites, the blacks, and the browns, that I recently had occasion to write to the British Consul at Rosario, in the Argentine Republic, Thomas J. Hutchinson, Esq., as follows :

To-day I return to you, with many thanks, the works on Anthropology and Ethnology which you kindly sent me, some weeks since, through the hands of Consul Parish; also the second number of "The River Plate Magazine," containing your very curious and interesting paper on the Indians of the Gran Chaco.

Judging from what I know of Indians generally, (and I have seen many of them in each of the three great Americas, North, Central, and South,) I have reason to believe that you have succeeded with remarkable accuracy, considering the brevity of your personal observations and experiences among them, in depicting those of the Gran Chaco precisely as they are.

Your description of the Chacos brought vividly to my recollection groups of lingering offshoots of the Cherokees, the Mohawks, the Pequods, and the Diggers, whom I have seen in widely separated sections of the United States. Indeed, although I am deeply impressed with the conviction that there exists throughout the world a plurality of originally and specifically distinct creations of mankind, yet there is, I think, quite as much general resemblance between the Indians at large, of the United States and of the Argentine Republic, and also of most of the intervening countries, as there is between the negroes native of Africa and the negroes native of America. All the red men, on one hand, look much alike, and all the black men, on the other, exhibit, in every form, feature, and movement, unmistakable evidences of kinship; and all of both the red and the black, are, as I verily believe, equally and immutably barbarous, and good for nothing—mere human rubbish and *débris*, fit only to be detruded among the strata of fossiliferous remains, (as deposits for the speculative researches of the learned anthropological and ethnographical antiquaries who shall appear upon the stage of letters in the far future,) or to be aggregately and

unceremoniously hurled headlong into the vortex of oblivion.

Such, in brief, if I may be so frank as to say what I believe, is my opinion of the inferior races of men, and especially so of Cuffcy and of Cumjee, and of all their countrymen, companions and cousins of kindred complexion.

From the many strongly-marked differences in general,
which we have already found existing between the various races of mankind, we now come to that very important one called Color; or, in other words,

THE COMPLEXION.

It is with great reluctance that I quote at any time
from any anonymous publication, opposed as I am to
masks of every sort. Nevertheless, writers of such works as
the volume of Letters, by "Junius," on the one hand, and
of the "Vestiges of Creation," by some one whose name is
not given, even in pretence, on the other, although lacking in at least one essential characteristic of manliness,
may sometimes, with only a moderate degree of disapprobation, be tolerated. On the 136th page of this last-
named work, the author—whoever he is, or was—
says:

"Numerous as the varieties of the human race are, they have all
been found classifiable under five leading ones;—1st The Caucasian,
or Indo-European, which extends from India into Europe and northern Africa; 2nd The Mongolian, which occupies Northern and Eastern Asia; 3rd The Malayan, which extends from the Ultra-Gangetic
Peninsula into the numerous islands of the South Sea and the Pacific.
4th The Negro, chiefly confined to Africa; 5th The aboriginal American.
Each of these is distinguished by certain general features of so marked a kind as to give rise to a supposition that they have had distinct
or independent origins. Of these peculiarities, color is the most con-

spicuous; the Caucasians are generally white, the Mongolians yellow, the Negroes black, and the Americans red. The opposition of two of these in particular, white and black, is so striking, that of them, at least, it seems almost necessary to suppose separate origins."

John Crawfurd, in the course of an address published in the "Transactions of the London Ethnological Society," New Series, Volume II., page 257, says:

"Some writers, in their determination to trace all mankind to a single stock, insist that the very diversity of color is itself a sufficient proof of unity, seeing that there is no broad line of demarcation between them. This seems to me to be no better than insisting that there is no difference between white and black, because an infinite variety of shades lie between them. Surely there is as wide a difference between the color of an African Negro and an European,—between that of a Hindoo and a Chinese, and between that of an Australian and a Red American, as there is between the different species of the same genera of the lower animals, as for example, between the species of wolves, jackalls and foxes."

Again, in the "Transactions of the London Ethnological Society"—New Series, Volume II., page 251, John Crawfurd says:

"Color in the different races would seem to be a character imprinted upon them from the beginning. As far as our experience extends, neither time, climate, nor locality has produced any change. Egyptian paintings 4,000 years old, represent the complexions of ancient Egyptians and Ethiopians much the same as those of modern Copts and modern Nubians. Scripture itself represents the color of the last of these as unchangeable. A colony of Persians, well known to us under the name of Parsees, settled in India about a thousand years ago, and pertinaciously abstaining from intermixture with the black people among whom they settled, they are now of the same complexion with the present inhabitants of the country from which they migrated. The millions of African negroes that have, during three centuries, been transported to the New World and its islands, are of the same color as the present inhabitants of the parent country of their forefathers. The Spaniards and their descendants, who have for at least as long a time been settled in tropical America, are as fair as the people of Arragon and Andalusia, with the same variety of color in the hair and eye as their progenitors.   The pure Dutch-descended colonists of the Cape of Good Hope, after dwelling two centuries among black Caffres and yellow Hottentots, do not differ in color from the people of Holland."

Again, in "The London Ethnological Magazine," Volume I., Part II., page 365, John Crawfurd says:

"In color, the skin ranges from the pure clear white of the Scandinavian to the ebony black of the Congo negro.   Even within the same species there is always a wide range in the complexion.   The language which we employ in describing the color of different species—not to say that it is constantly varying even in the same species—is quite inadequate to convey a clear and distinct idea of the reality. We use the terms black, fair, yellow, red, brown, nut-brown, olive, cinnamon color, copper color, mahogany color, swarthy, sallow, coalblack, sooty-black.   These terms are, in fact, but approximations to the varieties in the tints of the human complexion, which are so great, and pass so insensibly from one shade to another, as to baffle description by words and even by painting.   Climate, I think it may safely be asserted, has no permanent influence in the production of color in the human complexion.   It has pleased the Creator—for reasons to us inscrutable—to plant certain fair races in the temperate regions of Europe, and there only, and certain black ones in the tropical and sub-tropical regions of Africa and Asia, to the exclusion of white ones, but it is certain that climate has nothing to do with the matter.   The Laplanders are much darker than the Norwegians, although much nearer to the Pole, or with less sun.   In the same latitude with fair Swedes we find olive-colored Kalmucks.   At the same distance from the equator we find fair Europeans, yellow Chinese, red Americans, and black Australians.   The Hindoos are black, Hindu-Chinese brown, and the Chinese yellow, in the very same parallels of latitude.   The Chinese do not vary in complexion over thirty degrees of latitude. The Hindoos of the Punjaub, thirty-five degrees distant from the equator, are as dark as those about Cape Cormorin, which is little more than eight degrees from it.   The Malays under the equator are far fairer than the Hindoos, who dwell under parallels corresponding with those of the south of Europe.   But, to give an extreme case, these Malays of the equator are nearly of the same complexion with the Esquimaux of the Arctic circle.   In the whole New World, there was no black man, and no white one."

And now to

THE HEAD.

Dr. William B. Carpenter, one of the most distinguished physiologists of modern times, in his "Principles of Human Physiology," page 827, says:

"Among the rudest tribes of men, hunters and savage inhabitants of forests, dependent for their supply of food on the accidental produce of the soil or on the chase,—among whom are the most degraded of the African nations, and the Australian savages—a form of head is prevalent which is most aptly distinguished by the term *Prognathous*, indicating a prolongation or forward-extension of the jaws. This character is most strongly marked in the negroes of the Gold Coast, whose skulls are usually so formed as to give the idea of lateral compression. The temporal muscles have a great extent, rising high on the parietal bones; the cheek-bones project forward, and not outward; the upper jaw is lengthened and projects forward, giving a similar projection to the alveolar ridge and to the teeth; and the lower jaw has somewhat of the same oblique projection, so that the upper and lower incisor teeth are set at an obtuse angle to each other, instead of being in nearly parallel planes, as in the European."

Dr. Hermann Burmeister, in his "Comparative Anatomy and Psychology of the African Negro," page 11, says:

"If we take a profile view of the European face, and sketch its outlines, we shall find that it can be divided by horizontal lines into four equal parts—the first inclosing the crown of the head; the second the forehead; the third the nose and ears; and the fourth the lips and chin. In the antique statues, the perfection of the beauty of which is justly admired, these four parts are exactly equal; in living individuals slight deviations occur, but in proportion as the formation of the face is more handsome and perfect, these sections approach a mathematical equality. The vertical length of the head to the cheeks is measured by three of these equal parts. The larger the face and smaller the head, the more unhandsome they become; it is especially in this deviation from the normal measurement that the human features become coarse and ugly."

"In a comparison of the negro head with this ideal, we get the surprising result that the rule with the former is not the equality of the four parts, but a regular increase in length from above downward. The measurement, made by the help of drawings, showed a very considerable difference in the four sections, and an increase of that difference with the age. This latter peculiarity is more significant than the mere inequality between the four parts of the head."

Again, Dr. Burmeister, in his "Comparative Anatomy and Psychology of the African Negro," page 11, says :

"The narrow, flat crown ; the low, slanting forehead; the projection of the upper edges of the orbit of the eye; the short, flat, and, at the lower part, broad nose; the prominent, but slightly turned-up lips, which are more thick than curved; the broad, retreating chin, and the peculiarly small eyes, in which so little of the white eye-ball can be seen; the very small, thick ears, which stand off from the head; the short, crisp, woolly hair, and the black color of the skin— are the most marked peculiarities of the negro type. The southern races, which inhabit Loanda and Benguela, have a longer nose, with its bridge more elevated and its wings contracted; they have, however, the full lips, while their hair is somewhat thicker."

And now to

THE HAIR.

Burmeister, in his work entitled "The Black Man," page 12, says:

"The hair of the negro, when minutely examined, presents many peculiarities. It is unquestionably the most constant characteristic of the negro conformation. Its peculiarities never undergo any change. I have always found it equally black, glistening, curly and thick. It is much stronger than that of the European, especially than the light brown hair of the German. The curls of the negro hair are very small; each hair describes a series of circles which have a diameter of not more than three to four lines, and each hair is seldom more than three to four inches in length. * * * The oval form of the section of a negro's hair is an interesting fact. It is not circular like ours, but elliptical; it appears, therefore, unequally thick when viewed on different sides. This peculiarity may give it its disposition to curl."

Mayne Reid, in his "Odd People," page 17, says :

"The features of the Bushman, as well as the Hottentot, bear a strong similarity to those of the Chinese ; and the Bushman's eye is essentially of the Mongolian type. His hair, however, is entirely of another character. Instead of being long, straight, and lank, it is short, crisp, and curly—in reality, wool. Its scantiness is a characteristic ; and, in this respect, the Bushman differs from the woolly-haired tribes both of Africa and Australasia."

Sir John Barrow, in his "Travels into the Interior of Southern Africa," Volume I., page 107, says:

"The hair of the Hottentot is of a very singular nature ; it does not cover the whole surface of the scalp, but grows in small tufts at certain distances from each other, and, when kept short, has the appearance and feel of a hard shoe-brush, with this difference, that it is curled and twisted into small round lumps about the size of a marrowfat pea. When suffered to grow, it hangs on the neck in twisted tassels, not unlike some kinds of fringe."

And now to

THE SKIN.

Dr. John Mitchell, in a paper which he read before the Royal Society of London, in 1744, entitled "Colors of People," said:

"The skins of negroes are of a thicker substance, and denser texture than those of white people, and transmit no color through them. For the truth of the first part of this proposition, we need only appeal to our senses, and examine the skins of negroes when separated from the body ; when not only the cutis, but even the epidermis, will appear to be much thicker and tougher than in white people. But because the substance and texture, especially of the epidermis, is not a little altered in anatomical preparations, and that in such a measure as to alter the texture, perhaps, on which the color depends, by boiling, soaking and peeling, let us examine the skins of negroes on their body ; where they will appear, from the following considerations, to have all the properties assigned. 1st. In bleeding, or otherwise cutting their skins, they feel more tough and thick than in white people. 2d. When the epidermis is separated by cantharides, or fire, it is much tougher and thicker, and more difficult to raise in black than in white people. 3d. Negroes are never subject to sun-burn, or to have their skins blistered by any such degree of heat, as the whites are. 4th. Though their skins, in some particular subjects, should not be so very thick in substance, yet in winter, when they are dry, and not covered with that greasy sweat which transudes through them in summer, their skins feel more coarse, hard, and rigid ; 5th. Their exemption from some cutaneous diseases, as the prickly heat, or essera, which no adult negroes are ever troubled with, but which those of fine and thin skins are most subject to, show the thickness or callosity of their skins, which are not easily affected from slight causes. 6th. And not only the thickness, but also the opacity of their skins, will appear, from their never looking red in blushing, nor when under ardent fevers with internal inflammations, nor in the measles, nor small-pox ; where, though the blood must be forcibly impelled into the subcutaneous vessels, yet it does not appear through the epidermis. The like may be said of their veins ; which, though large and shallow, yet do not appear blue, till the skin is cut."

And now to

THE SKULL.

Sir Charles Lyell, in his late work entitled the " Antiquity of Man," page 90, says:

"The average negro skull differs from that of the European in having a more receding forehead, more prominent superciliary ridges, and more largely-developed prominences and furrows for the attachment of muscles ; the face, also, and its lines, are larger proportionally. The brain is somewhat less voluminous on the average in the lower races of mankind, its convolutions rather less complicated, and those of the two hemispheres more symmetrical, in all which points an approach is made to the Simian type."

Dr. Robert Knox, in the " Anthropological Review," No. II., page 268, says:

"A conformation of the osteological head distinct from all other races characterizes the Australian and Tasmanian, the Esquimaux, Bosjesman, the Kaffir, the Negro, the pure Mongul, the Carib, the Peruvian. All these races have *race* characters more or less marked, and not to be observed in other races. That these races may be converted by education into white men is, I fear, an entire delusion."

Dr. Samuel George Morton, as quoted in Nott and Gliddon's "Types of Mankind," page 321, says:

"I shall conclude these remarks on this part of the inquiry, by observing, that no mean has been taken of the Caucasian races collectively, because of the very great preponderance of Hindoo, Egyptian, and Fellah skulls, over those of the Germanic, Pelasgic, and Celtic families. Nor could any just collective comparison be instituted between the Caucasian and Negro groups in such a table as we have presented, unless the small-brained people of the latter division were proportionate in number to the Hindoos, Egyptians, and Fellahs of the other group. Such a comparison, were it practicable, would probably reduce the Caucasian average to about eighty-seven cubic inches, and the Negro to seventy-eight at most—perhaps even to seventy-five; and thus confirmatively establish the difference of at least nine cubic inches between the mean of the two races."

And now to

THE BRAIN.

Charles Hamilton Smith, in his "Natural History of the Human Species," page 126, says:

"The higher order of animals, according to the investigations of M. de Serres, passes successively through the state of inferior animals, as it were, *in transitu*, adopting the characteristics that are permanently imprinted on those below them in the scale of organization. Thus, the brain of Man excels that of any other animal, in complexity of organization, and fullness of development. But this is only attained by gradual steps. At the earliest period that it is cognizable to the senses, it appears a simple fold of nervous matter, with difficulty distinguishable into three parts, and having a little tail-like prolongation, which indicates the spinal marrow. In this state it perfectly resembles the brain of an adult fish—thus assuming, *in transitu*, the form that is permanent in fish. Shortly after, the structure becomes more complex, the parts more distinct, the spinal marrow better marked. It is now the brain of a reptile. The change continues by a singular motion. The *corpora quadrigemina*, which had hitherto appeared on the upper surface, now pass toward the lower; the former is their permanent situation in fishes and reptiles, the latter in birds and mammalia. This is another step in the scale. The complication increases; cavities or ventricles are formed, which do not exist in either fishes, reptiles, or birds. Curiously organized parts, such as the *corpora striata*, are added. It is now the brain of mammalia. Its last and final change is wanted, that which shall render it the brain of Man, in the structure of its full and human development. But although in this progressive augmentation of organized parts, the full complement of the human brain is thus attained, the Caucasian form of Man has still other transitions to undergo, before the complete *chef d'œuvre* of nature is perfected. Thus the human brain successively assumes the form of the Negro's, the Malay's, the American's, and the Mongolian's, before it attains the Caucasian's."

Again, in his "Natural History of the Human Species," page 159, Charles Hamilton Smith, says :

"The volume of brain in relation to the intellectual faculties, is clearly proved by Dr. Morton's researches, who, having filled for this purpose the cerebral chamber of skulls, belonging to numerous specimens of the Caucasian, Mongolian, Malay, American, and Ethiopian stock, with seeds of white pepper, found the first the most capacious, and the Ethiopian the smallest—though there may be some doubt whether the negro crania that served for his experiment were not, in part at least, derived from slaves of the Southern States of North America, who, being descended from mixed African tribes, and much more educated, have larger heads than new negroes from the coast."

Professor Tiedemann, of Heidelberg, quoted in Nott and Gliddon's "Types of Mankind," page 299, says :

"The weight of the brain in an adult European, varies between three pounds two ounces, and four pounds six ounces, Troy. The brain of men who have distinguished themselves by their great talents, are often very large. The brain of the celebrated Cuvier weighed four pounds, eleven ounces, four drachms, thirty grains, Troy; and that of the distinguished surgeon Dupuytren weighed four pounds ten ounces, Troy. The brain of men endowed with but feeble intellectual powers, is, on the contrary, often very small, particularly in congenital idiotismus. The female brain is lighter than that of the male. It varies between two pounds eight ounces, and three pounds eleven ounces. I never found a female brain that weighed four pounds. The female brain weighs, on an average, from four to eight ounces less than that of the male ; and this difference is already perceptible in a new-born child."

Burmeister, in his essay on "The Black man," page 10, says :

"The brain is the most important organ for the establishment of the dignity of man ; and its comparative condition is, therefore, a very important consideration in forming an idea of the differences and the relations between the various human races. Soemmering has thoroughly investigated the characteristics of the negro brain. Tiedemann, the anatomist, has followed in the same direction. The result of their inquiries coincides with the previous conclusions. The brain of the negro is relatively smaller than that of the European, especially in the front part, which is called the larger brain. In the brain of man, as in all the higher animals, there are certain convolutions, which are subject to variety in number and size. In the negro, their number is smaller and their size larger, which appears to me a fact of great importance."

Dr. James Hunt, in his work entitled, "The Negro's Place in Nature," page 17, says :

"With regard to the chemical constituents of the brain of the negro, little that is positive is yct known. It has been found, however, that the grey substance of the brain of a negro is of a darker color than that of the European ; that the whole brain has a smoky tint, and that the *pia mater* contains brown spots, which are never found in the brain of a European."

Dr. Josiah Clark Nott, in Nott and Gliddon's "Types of Mankind," page 189, says :

"Much as the success of the infant colony at Liberia is to be desired by every true philanthropist, it is with regret that, while wishing well to the negroes, we cannot divest our minds of melancholy forebodings. Dr. Morton, quoted in another chapter, has proven that the negro races possess about nine cubic inches less of brain than

3

the Teuton ; and, unless there were really some facts in history, something beyond bare hypothesis, to teach us how these deficient inches could be artificially added, it would seem that the negroes in Africa must remain substantially in that same benighted state, wherein Nature has placed them, and in which they have stood, according to Egyptian monuments, for at least five thousand years."

And now to

THE EYES AND EARS.

In his Pope-surpassing essay on "The Black Man," page 12, Burmeister says :

"The white of the eye has, in all negroes, a yellowish tinge. The lips are always brown, never red-colored ; they hardly differ in color from the skin in the neighborhood ; toward the interior edges, however, they become lighter, and assume the dark-red fresh-color of the inside of the mouth. The teeth are very strong, and are of a · glistening whiteness. The tongue is of a large size, and remarkable in thickness. The ear is surprisingly small. * * * The small ear of the negro cannot, however, be called handsome ; its substance is too thick for its size. The whole ear gives the impression of an organ that is stunted in its growth, and its upper part stands off to a great distance from the head."

And now to

THE CHIN.

Ripley and Dana, in their "New American Cyclopedia," Volume V., page 561, say that,

"No animal but man has a chin, and even this begins to decrease in the negro races; in all below him the anterior arch of the lower jaw is convex vertically and retreating at its lower margin."

And now to

THE NECK.

In his work entitled "The Black Man," page 10, Burmeister says:

"The thickness of the nape appears more striking in consequence of the shortness of the negro neck. * * * This shortness of neck is as much an approximation to the type of the ape as are the small skull and large face of the negro, for all the monkey tribe are short-necked. The short neck of the African gives him the necessary strength for carrying burdens upon his head, and explains his readiness to do so, while the European is less able and willing, in consequence of his neck being both longer and weaker."

And now to

THE BREASTS.

John Ogilby, in his "History of Africa," page 451, says:

"The women of the Gold Cost are slender-bodied, and cheerful of disposition, but have such great breasts that they can fling them over their shoulders, and give their children suck that hang at their backs."

John Duncan, in his "Travels in Western Africa," Volume I., page 88, says:

"In Accrah, the women's breasts are generally much larger and looser than those of an European, and frequently hang down as low as the waist."

Henry Lichtenstein, in his "Travels in Southern Africa," Volume I., page 117, says:

"The loose, long hanging breasts, and disproportionate thickness of the hinder parts, make a Bosjesman woman, in the eyes of an European, a real object of horror."

And now to

THE ARMS AND LEGS.

Burmeister, in his matchless essay on "The Black Man," page 9, says:

"From the long arm of the negro there results an ugliness that always adheres to him. It gives to his attitude and movements a certain stiff awkwardness, like as his flatness of foot does to his dragging gait. The negro seems to be instinctively aware of his ugly arms, and generally strives to conceal their awkward length. A black servant never stands in the presence of his master, nor a negro soldier in the presence of his officer, with his arms hanging down. If he is not engaged in carrying anything, or is at repose, he is sure to have his arms folded. This attitude, which would be esteemed with us insolent, and which a servant only assumes when at his ease by himself, is universally taken by every negro slave, male as well as female, whenever they stand behind their master or guests, to serve them at table. It strikes the European eye very oddly to behold, not a single negro, but a whole range of them, standing behind a table with their arms folded. I at first supposed it to be a mark of insolence, or secret ill-humor, which seemed to express itself in the ugly black face; but after a while I was fully persuaded that it was nothing but the instinctive desire on the part of the negro to conceal from the observer as much as possible his long black arms, which, if allowed to hang down, would expose all their ugliness to the fullest extent."

Again, in his essay on "The Black Man," page 9, Burmeister says :

"I need not enlarge upon the long hands, slender fingers and flat feet of the African. Any one who has ever visited a menagerie cannot fail to have observed the long hand, slender fingers, long nails, the flat foot, the deficient calf and compressed, sharp thigh of the ape, which so much resemble, in every respect, the peculiarities of the negro."

Again, in his essay on "The Black Man," page 9, Burmeister says :

"We have traced the peculiar form of the negro in the formation of his arm and foot, and arrived at the result, that both have a relatively greater length than the arm and foot of the European. We have found that the increase of length is not so marked in the upper portions of the extremities,—the arm and thigh,—as in the lower—the fore-arm and leg, as well as the hand and foot. To the greater length there are added the peculiarities of a greater thinness, an inferior muscular development, particularly in the thigh and calf, and an absence of the arch of the foot. It will be seen that all the divergencies of the negro from the European are so many approximations towards the type of the ape."

Again, in his essay on "The Black Man," page 6, Burmeister says :

"The arm of the female negro is relatively longer than that of the European ; and her leg also surpasses that of the latter in length, and assumes, to a certain degree, the male type. I found the arm, from the shoulder to the elbow, relatively shorter, and the hand relatively longer, in the negress than in the European female."

Again, in his essay on "The Black Man," page 6, Burmeister says :

"The thigh of a full-sized European female generally measures 17 inches ; the leg, from the knee to the ankle, 15 inches at the most. The negress I measured gave 17 inches for the thigh, and 15¾ for the leg.* From which it will be observed that the leg of the negro female is a little longer than that of the white. In spite of this, the negress appears short-legged, in consequence of her exceedingly flat foot. In the European, with a regularly formed foot, the ankle rises from 2¼ to 2½ inches above the ground, while in the negress it does not reach higher than from 1¼ to 1½ inches.

Again, in his essay on "The Black Man," page 8, Burmeister says :

"From the foot upwards the ugliness of the negro type does not diminish, but rather increases. A thin leg without a calf presents an undoubtedly ugly aspect. Such a one is possessed by the negro, and especially by the negro female. When you behold the leg from before, its narrowness and deficiency in muscle are especially observable. The calf is hardly apparent, and cannot, as in the European, be clearly distinguished from the muscles beneath ; it has the appearance of being compressed laterally. The part of the leg below the

---

* When Burmeister shall have more of this sort of work to do, it is definitely understood and arranged that he is to have, as a fellow-helper in the labor, an American friend, who has made special application for the privilege of assisting in the delicate service thus anticipated,—provided that none of the subjects for admeasurement shall, at any time, be either black or brown, but always white !

calf, as far as the ankle, is also very thin. The whole leg appears wooden, deficient in muscle, and rudely shaped. There is none of the peculiar swelling contour of the European leg beneath the skin, and the skin itself appears tightly stretched upon a uniform plane. This is the more remarkable and ugly in the tallest and finest specimens of the negro race. My servant, who was very short, but well built, had a finer calf than usual. The kitchen-maid of the house in which I lived displayed before me every day, when she was washing in the court-yard or in the house, with her clothes hoisted, a pair of very ugly, thin legs. I was reminded, in spite of myself, of an ape, when I beheld her black legs uncovered to the knees, with their deficient roundness, their flat sides, and their meagerness of muscles. It is the same with the negro thigh, which is equally deficient in that fleshy fullness which belongs to the well-formed European. On a careful examination, you will find the thigh flattened laterally, thus approaching, in its conformation, the peculiarity which distinguishes the lower animals from man."

> Here bachelors all, of every age,
> May quickly skip one little page ;
> And if they clamor for the reason,
> Let them know—to ask is treason! *

And now to

THE NYMPHÆ.

Sir John Barrow, in his "Travels in the Interior of Southern Africa," Volume I., page 235, says :

"The well-known story of the Hottentot women possessing an unusual appendage to those parts that are seldom exposed to view, which belongs not to the sex in general, ridiculous as it may appear, is perfectly true with regard to the Bosjesmans. The horde we met with possessed it in every subject, whether young or old, and without the least offence to modesty, there was no difficulty in satisfying our curiosity on this point. It appeared on examination to be an elongation, or more correctly speaking, a protrusion, of the nymphæ, or

---

* As this is the author's first attempt at rhyming, he hopes to be pardoned, not meaning to offend again !

interior labia, which were more or less extended, according to the age or habit of the person. That there is in this race of human beings a predisposition to this anomalous formation of the parts, was obvious from its evident appearance in infants, and from its length being in general proportioned to the age of the female. The longest that was measured somewhat exceeded five inches, and this was in a subject of middle age. Many were said to have them much longer. These protruded nymphæ, collapsed and pendent, leave the spectator in doubt as to what sex they belong. Their color is that of livid blue, inclining to a reddish tint, not unlike the excrescence on the beak of a turkey, which indeed may serve to convey a tolerably good idea of the whole appearance, both as to color, shape and size."

And now to

THE PELVIS.

Dr. William B. Carpenter, in his "Principles of Human Physiology," page 831, says :

"Next to the characters derived from the form of the head, those which are founded upon the form of the pelvis seem entitled to rank. These have been particularly examined by Professors Vrolik and Weber. The former was led by his examinations of this part of the skeleton to consider that the pelvis of the negress, and still more that of the female Hottentot, approximates to that of the Simial in its general configuration, especially in its length and narrowness, the iliac bones having a more vertical position, so that the anterior spines approach one another much more closely than they do in the European ; and the Sacrum also being longer and narrower. On the other hand, Professor Weber concludes, from a more comprehensive survey, that no particular figure is a permanent characteristic of any one race. He groups the principal varieties which he has met with, according to the form of the upper opening, into oval, round, four-sided, and wedge-shaped. The first of these is most frequent in the European races ; the second among the American races ; the third, most common among the Mongolian nations, corresponds remarkably with their form of head ; whilst the last chiefly occurs among the nations of Africa, and is in like manner conformable with the oblong compressed form usually presented by their cranium."

Burmeister, in his remarkable essay on "The Black Man," page 10, says:

"Although the smaller dimensions of the negro pelvis depend essentially upon the smaller negro head, which is much smaller in the African than in the European, they also indicate another approximation to the apes, all of which have pelvises relatively smaller to other parts of their bodies, than men. The small musculuar development of the thigh and leg, to which I have already alluded, corresponds with the small pelvis or basin ; for where the muscles are slightly developed, smaller points of attachment are sufficient. The pelvis, which is the chief point of attachment for the muscles of the hip and thigh, is not required to be so large in the negro, whose muscles are small.

"The plane of the sacrum—the bone at the lowest end of the spine—should extend further down and be more steep, whenever the pelvis or basin is smaller, in order to afford a stronger support to the intestines, which press in a downward direction. The pendulous belly of the African, which has been observed by all travelers, even when covered, is a consequence and illustration of the conformation. I have observed it as very striking in small, naked negro children. It is another well-marked analogy with the ape. The disgusting-looking protruded belly of the orang-outang can be observed in all the delineations of that ugly animal, and is a feature of the negro, which is an essential cause of his ugliness, and that peculiar corporal appearance which I cannot help terming beastlike."

Sir John Barrow, in his "Travels into the Interior of Southern Africa," Volume I., page 234, says,

"The Bosjesmans, indeed, are amongst the ugliest of all human beings. The flat nose, high cheek-bones, prominent chin, and concave visage, partake much of the apish character, which their keen eye, always in motion, tends not to diminish. The upper lid of this organ, as in that of the Chinese, is rounded into the lower on the side next the nose, and forms not an angle, as is the case in the eye of an European, but a circular sweep, so that the point of union between the upper and lower eyelid is not ascertainable. Their bellies are uncommonly protuberant, and their backs hollow. * * * As a means of increasing their speed in the chase, or when pursued by an enemy, the men had adopted a custom, which was sufficiently remarkable, of pushing the testicles to the upper part of the root of the penis, where they seemed to remain as firmly fixed, and as conveniently placed, as if nature had stationed them there."

And now to

THE POSTERIORS.

In his "Travels into the Interior of Southern Africa," Volume I., page 237, Sir John Barrow says:

"The great curvature of the spine inwards, and the remarkably extended posteriors, are characteristic of the whole Hottentot race; but in some of the small Bosjesmans they are carried to such an extravagant degree as to excite laughter. If the letter S be considered as one expression of the line of beauty to which degrees of approximation are admissible, some of the women of this nation are entitled to the first rank in point of form. A section of the body, from the breast to the knee, forms really the shape of the above letter. The projection of the posterior part, in one subject, measured five inches and a half from the line touching the spine. This protuberance consisted entirely of fat, and, when the woman walked, it exhibited the most ridiculous appearance imaginable, every step being accompanied with a quivering and tremulous motion, as if two masses of jelly had been attached behind her."

Dixon Denham, in his "Narrative of Travels and Discoveries in Northern and Central Africa," Volume II., page 89, says:

"The women of this part of Africa are certainly singularly gifted with the Hottentot protuberance. * * * So much depends on the magnitude of those attractions for which their southern sisters are so celebrated, that I have known a man about to make a purchase of one out of three, regardless of the charms of feature, turn their faces from him, and looking at them behind, in the vicinity of the hips, make choice of her whose person most projected beyond that of her companions."

And now to

THE FEET.

Burmeister, in his learned essay on "The Black Man," page 7, says:

"The negro foot impresses the beholder very disagreeably; its ex-

3*

ceeding flatness, its low heel, projecting backwards, the prominent yet flat contour of the sides, the thick bolster of fat in the inner hollow of the foot, and the spread-out toes, serve to make it excessively ugly. * * * Here we observe at once a distinct characteristic of the lower animals. The smaller size of the second toe, in proportion to the first, is a marked peculiarity of the white man, and the short great toe of the negro a decided approximation to the type of the ape. This resemblance to the ape is further strengthened by the wide separation between the first and second toes of the negro foot. This is a peculiarity which strikes only the experienced eye. It is, however, the excessively flat foot which impresses every one so disagreeably. * * * You observe that that part of the negro foot presses most directly on the ground, which in the European is the most elevated, and which is so admirably adapted in the latter, for a graceful lightness of gait. The high heels of our boots are adapted to this natural conformation of the white foot, and serve to increase the lightness of step, and the natural beauty of the feet of the European. The purpose of the heels is to add to the beauty of the foot, and it may accordingly be traced far back in the history of boot and shoe-making. The negro is totally deficient in this peculiar beauty of the arch of the foot. A popular American song characterizes, very aptly, the want of the hollow in the foot of the negro, thus :

> "De hollow ob his foot
> Make a hole in de groun !"

And now to

THE BLOOD.

David Livingstone, in his "Missionary Travels and Researches in South Africa," page 548, says,

"The thermometer, placed upon a deal box in the sun, rose to 138°. It stood at 108° in the shade by day, and 96° at sunset. If my experiments were correct, the blood of a European is of a higher temperature than that of an African. The bulb, held under my tongue, stood at 100° ; under that of the natives, at 98°."

Mungo Park, in his "First Journal of an Expedition to the Niger," page 41, says,

"I found his majesty sitting upon a bullock's hide, warming himself before a large fire; for the Africans are sensible of the smallest variation in the temperature of the air, and frequently complain of cold when a European is oppressed with heat.

Dr. James Hunt, in his work entitled "The Negro's Place in Nature," page viii., quoting from a communication adressed to him by one of his friends, says:

"The blood of the negro, as compared with the blood of the white man, is vastly dissimilar. The red corpuscles are greatly in excess, and the colorless have an extraordinary tendency to run together; the molecular movement within the disks differs in every respect, and when tried with a solution of potash, the protrusions from the cell-walls take every intermediate form, reverting with great rapidity to the normal condition. It is an attested fact, that if there is a drop of negro blood in the system of a white person, it will show itself upon the scalp. The greater the proximity, the darker the hue, the larger the space; there may not be the slightest taint perceptible in any other part of the body, but this spot can never be wiped out—no intervening time can ever efface it."

And now to

THE BONES.

Sir Charles Lyell, in his "Antiquity of Man," page, 19, says:

"Eminent anatomists have shown, that in the average proportion of some of the bones, the negro differs from the European, and that in most of these characters he makes a slightly nearer approach to the anthropoid quadrumana."

Dr. William B. Carpenter, in his "Principles of Human Physiology," page 831, says:

"In nearly all the less civilized races of man, the limbs are more crooked and badly-formed than the average of those of Europeans; and this is particularly the case with the negro, the bones of whose legs bow outwards, and whose feet are remarkably flat. It has been generally believed, that the length of the fore-arm of the negro is so much greater than in the European, as to constitute a real character of approximation to the apes."

Charles Hamilton Smith, in his "Natural History of the Human Species," page 191, says:

"Some tribes in Dongola and Sennaar have one lumbar vertebra more than the Caucasian, and the stomach corrugated."

Dr. James Hunt, in his work entitled "The Negro's Place in Nature," page 5, says:

"The average height of the negro is less than the European, and although there are occasionally exceptions, the skeleton of the negro is generally heavier, and the bones larger and thicker in proportion to the muscles, than those of the European. The bones are also whiter, from the greater abundance of calcareous salts. The thorax is generally laterally compressed, and, in thin individuals, presents a cylindrical form, and is generally smaller in proportion to the extremities. The extremities of the negro differ from other races more by proportion than by form: the arm generally reaches below the middle of the femur. The leg is on the whole longer, but is made to look short on account of the ankle being only between $1\frac{1}{3}$ inches to $1\frac{1}{2}$ inches above the ground; this character is often seen in mulattoes."

Again, in his work entitled "The Negro's Place in Nature," page viii., Dr. James Hunt, quoting from a communication addressed to him by one of his friends, says:

"The skeleton of the negro can never be placed upright. There is always a slight angle in the legs, a greater in the thigh-bones, and still more in the body, until, in some instances, it curves backwards. All the bones of the legs are flattened, and wider than in the European; and the arm-bones have always a tendency to fall forward, while the head stoops from the shoulders, and not from the neck, as in other nations."

Time and space here press me to say, that it will now be convenient to notice, demonstratively, but one of the many other specific physical differences which are everywhere signally apparent between the whites and the blacks, and which, like the battle spoken of by Job, in his rampant description of a war horse, may always be scented afar off—and that is,

THE NEGRO'S VILE AND VOMIT-PROVOKING STENCH.

Charles Hamilton Smith, in his "Natural History of the Human Species," page 191, says :

"Beneath the epidermis of the negro, the mucous membrane, loaded with a coloring matter in the bile, causes the melanic appearance of the skin, which varies, however, from deep sallow to intense sepia black—darkest in health ; and that color always distinctly affects the external glands. It is likewise the source of an overpowering offensive odor, spreading through the atmosphere, when many are congregated in the hot sun."

Richard F. Burton, in his book of travels, entitled "The Lake Regions of Central Africa," page 89, says :

"The sebaceous odor of the skin, among all these races, is overpowering, and is emitted with the greatest effect during and after excitement, whether of mind or body."

Dr. Burmeister, in his masterly essay on the slavish "Black Man," page 12, says :

"In the examination of the negro body, I cannot venture to pass without notice a disagreeable property which it possesses, and which always produces disgust on the part of the European, in his intercourse with colored people. I allude to the disagreeable smell emitted by their perspiration. All individuals do not possess it in an equal degree, and it can be diminished, but never completely destroyed, by cleanliness. The more the negro perspires, the more apparent the odor becomes."

What are the facts established by the numerous and eclectic testimonies here adduced? Most conclusive have been the proofs, that the negro, as already stated, is a grossly inferior man, of separate and distinct origin ; and that, from the hair of his head to the extremities of his hands and feet, every part of him, however large, or however small, whether internal or external, whether physical or mental, or moral, loses in comparison with the white, much in the same ratio or proportion as darkness loses in comparison with light, or as evil loses in comparison with good.

In absolute dissimilarity of nature, and in point of superiority, the Caucasian differs quite as much from the African, as does the Horse from the Ass ; the Sheep from the Goat ; the Dog from the Wolf ; the Tiger from the Cat ; the Rat from the Mouse ; the Whale from the Porpoise ; the Halibut from the Herring ; the Lobster from the Craw-fish ; the Eagle from the Hawk ; the Owl from the Screech-owl ; the Macaw from the Parrot ; the Martin from the Swallow ; the Swan from the Goose ; the Duck from the Gull ; the Butterfly from the Moth ; the Bee from the Bug ; the Alligator from the Lizard ; the Turtle from the Tortoise ; the Anaconda from the Copperhead ; or the Eel from the Earthworm.

Now come I to a subject of somewhat novel importance, a subject which has occupied my attention for a great while, and one for the discussion of which, it is believed, the present is a suitable time. I allude to the presence of so many negroes in our cities and towns—places where not one of them should ever be permitted to reside at all ; and if I shall succeed, as I hope and believe I shall, in presenting such a combination of facts and arguments as will demonstrate the propriety of removing them all into the country (if far and forever beyond the limits of the United States, so much the better.) I shall regard it as evidence complete, that these lines have been judiciously penned.

In this life, it not unfrequently happens that we find things out of their proper place. If careless servants—and none are so careless as negroes—leave the parlor encumbered with uncouth utensils, with greasy vessels, or with rusty implements, our sense of the fitness of things is at once shocked, and we immediately give orders for the removal of the unseemly articles. People, too, are very often found beyond the pale of their proper sphere. For instance: the population of every city is composed of a greater or less number of illiterate poor persons; but those who are best acquainted with the world and its ways, know very well, that cities, even in the very best parts of the earth, are notedly unpropitious places for poverty and ignorance.

It may, I think, be safely assumed that, as a general rule, no person ought to be admitted as a resident of any city, unless he can readily command one of two things, namely, Capital or Talent. Of these two indispensable requisites, the negro can command neither the one nor the other; he should, therefore, never be allowed to live in any situation, or under any circumstances, within the corporate limits of any city or town.

With few exceptions, all sane white persons have sufficient tact to render themselves useful in some manner or other, to gain an honorable livelihood, and to add something to the general stock of human achievements. If their minds can accomplish nothing in the domains of science, their hands may be rewarded in the fields of art. If they cannot invent labor-saving machines, they can make duplicates of such as have already been invented. If they cannot enrich and embellish their country by building factories, stores, warehouses, hotels, and banks, they can always fill situations in such establishments, with profit to themselves, and with advantage to others. The negro can do none of these things. On the contrary, he is, indeed, a very inferior, dull, stupid, good-for-nothing sort of man. Past experience proves positively that he is not, and never has been, susceptible of a high standard of improvement. His capacities have been fully and frequently tested, and have always been found sadly deficient.

To the neglect of a large and meritorious class of our own race, we have made numerous experiments in favor of the worthless negro. We have earnestly endeavored, time and again, to infuse into the brain of the benighted black a ray of intellectual light, to teach him trades and professions, and to prepare him for the discharge of higher duties than the common drudgeries of every-day life. Thus far, however, all our efforts in his behalf have proved abortive; and so will they continue to prove, so long as he remains what he always has been, and still is —a negro. Further attempts, on our part, to elevate him to a rank equal to that held by the white man, would certainly betray in us an extraordinary and unpardonable degree of folly and obtuseness. Just as impossible is it for us to divest the negro of his foul and betattered garb of inferiority, and to raise him to a position of equality among men of European descent, as it is for us to transform the Baboon into a Gorilla; the Lynx into a Lion; the Gemsbok into a Reindeer; the Opossum into a Kangaroo; or the Ground-squirrel into a Rabbit.

Variety, indeed, seems to have been a paramount condition of the creation; and we may honestly and reasonably doubt whether any two things, animate or inanimate, have ever yet been found, or ever will be found, exactly alike. Whether we look into the animal, the vegetable, or the mineral kingdom, we observe, emblazoned before us, in every 'direction, the greatest diversity in size, in shape, and in color. There are numerous species of quadrupeds, birds, insects, fishes, and reptiles; and why, why, forsooth, should there not also be different and distinct races of men? Has there been fixed—and if so, how? why? where? when? and by whom?—has there been fixed a limitation to the power of the Almighty?

In augmentation of his own good pleasure, God called into existence the Mastodon and the Mole; the Condor and the Cuckoo; the Cricket and the Cockchafer; the Shad and the Sardine; the Boa Constrictor and the Coluber—but were all of these, or were any two of them, created equal? Examine the Oak and the Ash; the Apple and the Quince; the Melon and the Gourd; the Beet and the Turnip; the Wheat and the Rye—were all of these, or were any two of them, created equal? Look at the Diamond and the Topaz; the Gold and the Silver; the Granite and the Limestone; the Soil and the Clay—were all of these, or were any two of them created equal? Look up also at the vast and variegated vault, the brilliantly bejeweled foundation of heaven, that adorns the night; see Jupiter and Pallas; Saturn and Ceres; Uranus and Vesta; Sirius and Phecda, Arcturus, and Mirfak; Rigel and Kocab—were all of these, or were any two of them, created equal? No, no; by no means. "One star differeth from another star in glory;" and every man in the world differs from every other man, in stature, in weight, in color, in physiognomy, in strength of body, or in power of mind.

Negroes are, in truth, so far inferior to white people, that, for many reasons consequent on that inferiority, the two races should never inhabit the same community, city, nor state. The good which accrues to the black from the privileges of social contact with the white, is more than counterpoised by the evils which invariably overtake the latter when brought into any manner of regular fellowship with the former.

Whatever determination may be come to with regard to a final settlement or disposition of the negroes—whether it be decided to colonize them in Africa, in Mexico, in Central America, in South America, or in one or more of the West India Islands, or elsewhere beyond our present limits; or whether they be permitted to remain (a while longer) in the United States—it is to be sincerely hoped that there may be no important division of opinion as to the expediency of soon removing them all from the cities and towns. A city is not, by any means, a suitable place for them. They are positively unfit for the performance of in-door duties. Sunshine is both congenial and essential to their natures; and they ought not to be employed or retained in situations that could be so much more advantageously filled by white people. One good white person will, as a general rule, do from two to five times as much as a negro, and will, in addition, always do it with a great deal more care, cleanliness and thoroughness. A negro or a negress in or about a white man's house, no matter where, or in what capacity, is a thing monstrously improper and indecent.

By removing all the negroes into the country, our agricultural districts would receive a large addition of laborers, and, consequently, the quantity of our staple products, cotton, corn, wheat, sugar, rice, and tobacco, would be greatly increased. Crowds of enterprising white people would flock to our cities and towns, fill the vacancies occasioned by the egress of the negroes, and give a fresh and powerful impetus to commerce and manufactures. The tides of both domestic and foreign immigration, which have been moving westward for so long a period, would also soon begin to flow southward, and everywhere, throughout the whole length and breadth

of our land, new avenues to various branches of profitable industry would be opened.

Let it not be forgotten, however, that this proposition
does not contemplate any permanent settlement of the
negroes, even in the agricultural districts of our country.
Only a temporary accommodation of the case is here held
in view. Perhaps the best thing that we could do just
now, would be to take immediate and complete possession
of Mexico, (we shall acquire the whole of North America,
from Behring's Strait to the Isthmus of Darien, by and
by,) and at once push the negroes—every one of them—
south of the Rio Grande. On no part—to say the least
—on no part of the territory of the United States, as at
present organized, should any but the pure white races
ever find permanent domicile.

Now comes the last, not the least, reason why I advocate the removal of the negroes from the cities and towns.
I believe that the Yellow Fever (which is only another
name for the African Fever) and other epidemic diseases
—those terrible scourges which have so signally retarded
the growth of Southern seaports—have, to a very great
degree, been induced by the peculiarly obnoxious filth
engendered by the black population. Who has ever
heard of the yellow fever prevailing to an alarming extent in any city or state inhabited almost exclusively by
white people? How fearfully, how frequently, does it
rage in such despicable, negro-cursed communities as
Norfolk, Charleston, Savannah, Mobile and New Orleans!

Only from the base-colored races is it, as a rule, that
we are overwhelmed and prostrated by wide-spread con-
tagions and epidemics. Even the cattle-plague, the mur-
rain among sheep, and other fatal distempers to which
our domestic animals are subject, have almost invariably
had their origin in the countries which are inhabited by

the blacks and the browns, who are themselves but the rickety-framed and leprous remnants of those unworthy races of men who have been irrevocably doomed to destruction.

This is a subject which deserves far greater attention and treatment than can be bestowed upon it at the present time. Merely by way of suggestion, it must suffice to say, on this occasion, that when the pure Caucasian races shall have become the exclusive occupants of all those vast territories, both east and west (with a wide range both north and south) of the Bosphorus—territories comprised within the boundaries of at least two great continents—and when the last individual of the negro race shall have been fossilized, then, but not till then, may we look for complete exemption from Asiatic Cholera on the one hand, and from African Fever—in other words, Yellow Fever—on the other.

It is, indeed, fully and firmly believed that the only way to get rid of yellow fever is to get rid of the negroes; and the best way to get rid of the negroes is now the particular question which, of all other questions, should most earnestly engage the undivided attention of the American people.

Strikingly apparent is it that the negro is a fellow of many natural defects and deformities. The wretched race to which he belongs exhibits, among its several members, more cases of *lusus naturæ* than any other. Seldom, indeed, is he to be seen except as a preordained embodiment of uncouth grotesqueness, malformation, or ailments. Not only is he cursed with a black complexion, an apish aspect, and a woolly head; he is also rendered odious by an intolerable stench, a thick skull, and a booby brain. An accurate description of him calls into requisition a larger number of uncomplimentary terms than are necessary to be used in describing any other creature out of tophet; and it is truly astonishing how many of the terms so peculiarly appropriate to him are compound words of obloquy and detraction.

The night-born ogre stands before us; we observe his low, receding forehead; his broad, depressed nose; his stammering, stuttering speech; and his general actions, evidencing monkey-like littleness and imbecility of mind. By close attention and examination, we may also discover in the sable individual before us, if, indeed, he be not an exception to the generality of his race, numerous other prominent defects and deficiencies. Admit that he be not warp-jawed, maffle-tongued, nor tongue-tied, is he not skue-sighted, blear-eyed, or blobber-lipped? If he be not wry-necked, wen-marked, nor shoulder-shotten, is he not stiff-jointed, hump-backed, or hollow-bellied? If he be not slab-sided, knock-kneed, nor bow-legged, is he not (to say the least) spindle-shanked, cock-heeled, or flat-footed? If he be not maimed, halt, nor blind, is he not feverish with inflammations, festerings, or fungosities? If he be not afflicted with itch, blains nor blisters, does he not squirm under the pains of boils, burns, or bruises? If he be not the child of contusions, sprains, nor dislocations, is he not the man of scalds, sores, or scabs? If he be not an endurer of the aches of pneumonia, pleurisy, nor rheumatism, does he not feel the fatal exacerbations of rankling wounds, tumors, or ulcers? If he be no complainer over the cramps of coughs, colics, nor constipation, doth he not decline and droop under the discomforts of dizziness, dropsy, or diarrhœa? If he be no sufferer from hemorrhoids, erysipelas, nor exfoliation, is he not a victim of goitre, intumescence, or paralysis? If he experience no inconvenience from gum-rash, cholera-morbus, nor moon-madness, doth he not wince under the pangs of the hip-gout, the tape-worm, or the mulli-grubs? If he be free from idiocy, insanity, or syncope, is he not subject to fits, spasms, or convulsions? Aye, in almost every possible respect, he is a person of ill-proportion, blemish and disfigurement; and no truer is it that the Turk (in Europe) is the sick man of the East, than that the negro (in America) is the sick man of tho West. Neither the one nor the other will ever recover. The malady of each is absolutely incurable. Both are doomed to take upon themselves—and that very soon—the cold and inanimate condition of complete fossilization.

Shabbiness and drollery of dress, and awkwardness of gait, are also notable characteristics of the negro. Faultless garments, and well-shaped hats and shoes, arc things that are never found upon his person. Once or twice a year he buys (or begs) a suit of second-hand clothing; but seldom does he wear any article of apparel more than two or three weeks before the outer edges of the same become ragged; then unsightly holes and shreds and patches follow in quick succession—and the slovenly and slipshod tatterdemalion is as contented and mirthful as a merrymaking monkey.

As for the negro's repulsive complexion, his curse-incurring color, his hideous blackness—than which there can be no greater contrast in comparison with the white man, nor one more adverse to the negro—that is a subject which will be treated more elaborately in the next succeeding chapter. Nor is the blackness of the negro the only black thing that will be examined within the scope and compass of these pages.

Blackness, whether it attaches to things animate or inanimate, is, in most cases, the brand (in other words, the indication and the evidence) of a vile and infamous quality; and of this important but 'somewhat infant fact, a thorough exposition shall be made. Afterward, having emerged from the filthy and pestiferous fogs of Blackness, the reader shall have revealed to him, in unmistakable prominence, the enrapturing beauties and glories of Whiteness—beauties and glories which shall fill his heart fuller of delight than was the heart of Moses of old, when, from Mount Nebo, one of the peaks of Pisgah, he was graciously permitted to behold the promised land.

Among other black monstrosities which shall be herein arraigned for castigation, is a high-handed assemblage of conspirators against public rights, public morals, public safety, public interests, and public decency, now (or but recently) organized in the good city of Washington—a sectional and seditious assemblage, which shall be everywhere stigmatized and detested, in all future time, as the Black Congress. Without an open and complete renouncement of all past errors, conjoined with a full and solemn promise of better behavior hereafter, few members of the Black Congress, whether Senators or Representatives, should ever again be elevated to any office, whether national or municipal, or of any other grade or nature whatever, within the gift of the American people. The whys and the wherefores of this just and necessary stricture on the Black Congress, together with numerous other weighty and relevant considerations, shall be brought forward and adequately explained in due time.

It must be by the election to office of better men than those who compose the majority of the Black Congress, that the Black Congress itself, and other black abominations, shall be constrained, sooner or later—the sooner the better—to terminate their pernicious existence. Who are some of the better men here referred to—men of real might and merit, whom, to the exclusion of others less able and less worthy, we should place and retain in the very highest positions of honor and trust? These are some of them—some of the best;—not Black Republicans of low and groveling instincts, but White Republicans of godlike aspirations and purposes :

CHARLES FRANCIS ADAMS, of Massachusetts.
WILLIAM H. SEWARD, of New York.
REVERDY JOHNSON, of Maryland.
JOSEPH HOLT, of Kentucky.
GEORGE BANCROFT, of New York.
HUGH McCULLOCH, of Indiana.
EDWARD BATES, of Missouri.
MONTGOMERY BLAIR, of Maryland.
WILLIAM PITT FESSENDEN, of Maine.
DAVID DUDLEY FIELD, of New York.
BARTHOLOMEW F. MOORE, of North Carolina.
CASSIUS M. CLAY, of Kentucky.
JOHN A. BINGHAM, of Ohio.
HENRY J. RAYMOND, of New York.
JOSHUA HILL, of Georgia.
JOHN POOL, of North Carolina.
JAMES R. DOOLITTLE, of Wisconsin.
OLIVER H. BROWNING, of Illinois.
JOHN MINOR BOTTS, of Virginia.
THOMAS E. BRAMLETTE, of Kentucky.
EDWIN M. STANTON, of Pennsylvania.
EDWIN D. MORGAN, of New York.
JAMES GUTHRIE, of Kentucky.
WILLIAM AIKEN, of South Carolina.
EDGAR COWAN, of Pennsylvania.
JAMES E. ENGLISH, of Connecticut.
JOHN B. HENDERSON, of Missouri.
FRANCIS H. PEIRPONT, of Virginia.

Edwards Pierrepont, of New York.
James Dixon, of Connecticut.
Emerson Etheridge, of Tennessee.
Alfred Dockery, of North Carolina.
Alexander W. Randall, of Wisconsin.
Daniel S. Norton, of Minnesota.*

Is it remarked that this list is not lengthened nor en-

---

* It may not be amiss for me to state here, that not one of the gentlemen mentioned in the foregoing list—a list embracing some of the wisest and worthiest statesmen now living in the world—is aware of the liberty which I have thus taken; nor does any one of them possess any knowledge whatever of any desire or purpose on my part to publish this book; nor yet will any one of them know aught about it until after it shall have come complete from the hands of the publisher. Had they not been among the very ablest and best men of America, the complimentary attention and prominence which have here been accorded to their names, would have been withheld. At the same time, I may also declare, that with the exception of the quotations which, as such, are clearly and unmistakably designated, I alone am responsible for every sentiment and expression herein contained. It is my pleasure to make this declaration, because, feeling an interest in the exact identification of American writers, I am unwilling that the authorship of any work written by myself, however esteemed on the one hand, or however disesteemed on the other, should ever be attributed to any one else. It is, no doubt, well remembered how generally, some years ago, the authorship of my "Impending Crisis of the South," was alternately and absurdly accredited to James Gordon Bennett, Horace Greeley, John Sherman, Dr. Jones, Abraham Lincoln, and others! These silly reports were in keeping with the floods of lamentable follies, of almost every kind, which prevailed so widely and so banefully during the weak and wicked Presidency of one James Buchanan.　　　　　　　　　　　　　　　H. R. H.

4

larged by the presentation of any name or names distinguished in the annals of war?—and why? Purposely has the writer refrained from the mention of such names, because he is firmly fixed in the belief that the spirit and the genius of genuine republican government (the most rational and befitting form of government for the peace and prosperity of all truly enlightened and magnanimous peoples) require that the military authorities should always, and everywhere, be held subordinate to the civil. God knows how greatly the author's heart glows with gratitude to Grant, Sherman, Thomas, Canby, and others, for their heroic achievements in suppressing the Slaveholders' Rebellion ; but, in doing that, they, like millions of other loyal and patriotic citizens, only did their duty to their country; and their services have already been appropriately acknowledged and rewarded.

If, then, we are to depart so far from the true principles of republican government as to have military Presidents and military Governors,—which, in his kind and watchful care over our country, may the great God forbid!—the grave responsibility of emblazoning their names in such connections shall, under no consideration whatever, rest with the writer hereof.

But for the fact of their being Generals, there are, perhaps, few men in all the United States more worthy of the Presidency than John A. Dix, of New York, George H. Thomas, of Virginia, and Nathaniel P. Banks, of Massachusetts. So, too, it was only while he was a Colonel that, in regard to the Chief Magistracy, there could be no serious objection to the valiant John Charles Fremont. Now, however, that he has become a General,—and the place for the General is the tented field (or that better and more beautiful field of glory, the corn-field!) —let us no longer think nor speak of him, nor of any other General, for the high and peace-promoting office of President.

Besides, it is currently rumored that one of the military celebrities,—not the last one just mentioned,—whose name has been occasionally spoken of in connection with the White House, is a Roman Catholic; and if this be true, a fact so entirely at variance with the real character of an American Republican, a fact so palpably inconsistent with the vigorous and lofty aims of a New World gentleman, a fact so obviously unaccordant with the dignified qualities and bearing of high-principled manhood, will certainly not fail to frustrate the disingenuous and jesuitical influences which may be used for his unworthy promotion. Let Catholicism take itself back to the very darkest of the Dark Ages, to the primordial and musty periods of the Hindoos, whence it came; or to the monarchic and other despotic powers of our own time, where, as a diminisher and enslaver of the minds of the masses, it is always sure to find a most hearty welcome. In republics, however, it has, and can have, no legitimate business, if, indeed, it can have legitimate business anywhere; and not a whit more, not a moment sooner, should it be tolerated on the one hand, than Mormonism or Mohammedanism should be tolerated on the other.

In the future, therefore, as in the past, let us, for the most part, keep the United States of America under the direction of our ablest and best civilians; and with Peace and Justice for our guides, (and with the negroes, Indians, and all the other inferior and effete races well fossilized in the background,) we shall not be long in unfolding to the world the unsurpassable greatness and grandeur and glory of a vast and indissoluble commonwealth.

What more shall be said of that morbid-minded faction of inveterate grumblers and growlers in our country, that fanatical cabal of white men, whose inexplicable preference for the negro is at once unnatural, wrong, absurd and ridiculous? Very justly have these monsters been stigmatized as Black Republicans. Let that stigma rest upon them forever. It is an appropriate designation of black-hearted criminals, whose black crime is black treason to a superior race! Let us stoutly protest, however, against the wholesale and atrocious misapplication of this term to those who, in no manner, deserve it. All the sound and alert patriots who voted for Fremont in 1866, and all the ardent lovers of their country who supported Lincoln for the Presidency in 1860, and again in 1864, were, without discrimination, most villainously berated and denounced as Black Republicans.

In truth, however, a very large majority of all those who, at different times, cast their suffrages for the two gentlemen just named, so far from having been Black Republicans, were, in the highest and best sense of a better term, White Republicans. Still, that the country has been, for a great while past, and is even yet, grievously infested with Black Republicans, of the very rankest and meanest sort, cannot be denied. Just now, especially, there is a most foul and flagrant fullness of Black Republicans in the Black Congress. No Black Congress would there ever have been, in fact, but for the Black Republicans who compose it, and from whom alone it has derived its black and base existence. Yet there remains to the good people of the United States this cheering consolation, that the usurpatory and tyrannical legislative assemblage now (or but recently) in session at the city of Washington, which, for the most part, has been so appropriately denominated the Black Congress, is not entirely black, nor altogether usurpatory and tyrannical.

A few excellent men,—White Republicans, of great ability and worth,—some of whose names may be found in the foregoing list, are also in that assemblage ; and to these, and to those who will faithfully and unswervingly coöperative with them, must we look for the final and complete salvation of America.

Black Republicans, banded together cheek by jole in a Black Congress, are the shameless advocates and enactors of Negro Bureau Bills, Negro Suffrage Bills, and numerous other bills of most abominable blackness and infamy. They are also the unblushing and despotic framers of military establishments in times of peace. The very least that can be truthfully said of them is, that they are a frenzied faction of rough-shod overriders of the Constitution. White Republicans, on the other hand, are the hearty supporters of such measures as have for their object the rightful recognition of nature's laws ; and for this reason they are always careful to keep themselves placed in a position of uncompromising opposition to the base efforts of the Black Republicans, whose detestable and atrocious policy, if successfully carried out, would have a tendency to degrade the heaven-born and high-souled Caucasian down to the low level of the African. If, therefore, we are to be additionally disgraced in the United States by the continued existence, intrigues and wrangling of a Black Republican party, we should at once thoroughly organize (for the irretrievable discomfiture and prostration of these and all other negrophilists) a White Republican party. During many years past, much have we heard of Red Republicans in Paris, and also of Black Republicans in Boston. More things and better things than it was possible for us ever to hear of either or both of these, are we soon to hear of White Republicans in and throughout every State and Territory of the American Union.

Why is Massachusetts a greater State than South Carolina?   Because, while Massachusetts is inhabited chiefly by industrious and enterprising white people, South Carolina is burdened by a large and lazy commonalty of mean-spirited and good-for-nothing blacks.   Why is New York a greater State than Virginia?   Because, while New York is white with Anglo-Saxons and Anglo-Americans, Virginia is black with Congo negroes and Guinea niggers.   Why is Pennsylvania a greater State than North Carolina?   Because, while Pennsylvania is blessed with a population of heaven-descended and heaven-destined Caucasians, North Carolina is cursed with a tenantry of hell-hatched and hell-doomed Ethiopians.   How may Kentucky become as great a State as Ohio?   By waiting until Nature shall have shown all the Kentucky Quashees and Dinahs the way into the Mammoth Cave, or into some other vast subterranean cavity, or into the whirlpools of the Mississippi, or into the labyrinthian wilderness of some foreign country, and then by being very particular not to show any of them the way out again, and by filling their places with a race of mankind, —a white race,—fit to live longer upon the earth.

Great States are made up only of white men, white women and white children ; and nations generally are powerful and important only in proportion to their freedom from admixture with swarth-complexioned bipeds. Would we of the South, in emulation of the bright and noble examples set us by our White Republican brothers of the North, foster the development of great commonwealths, great cities, and great enterprises?   To white emigrants, then, from every part of the known world, but more especially from the eastern and northern sections of our own country, must we open wide our entrance-gates and front-doors, and give to the new comers warm and sincere salutations and welcome. In the first place, however, it behooves us to open at once, for the speedy and pell-mell exit of all the negroes, Indians, and bi-colored hybrids, every back-door in our land; and to assist them to retire, totally and forever, to some appropriate nook or corner, where,—if, indeed, there be such a nook or corner in any part of the universe,—their presence may not be generally and justly considered a most consummate and unmitigated nuisance.

Less than ten thousand miles from the place where these lines are penned, a lady and gentleman were recently wedded. Prior to their marriage, certain rules and regulations, by which they were to be more or less governed in all the future of their earthly existence, were well defined, understood, and agreed upon. Among these matters of mutual agreement was one that, under no circumstances whatever, was any negro, Indian, nor bi-colored hybrid, whether bond or free, old or young, male or female, ever to find either service or welcome within any house or other building, or upon any foot of land, or on or about any ship or other vessel or thing whatsoever, whether at sea or elsewhere, over which it might be their prerogative to exercise control. These rules and regulations, as adopted by the couple in question, have been, and will always continue to be, rigidly observed.

As a matter of high and sacred duty to their own supremely blessed race, not as an act of harsh dealing toward those upon whom Nature has been pleased to fasten the curse of foul and fatal blackness, every white man and every white woman in the world, whether married or unmarried, ought at once to subscribe to rules and regulations similar to those above mentioned, and to be always and undeviatingly governed by them. Under such an efficacious and salutary White Republican policy as is thus faintly foreshadowed, we may soon look for the ignominious *finale* of Black Republican folly. Faithful adherence to the same policy will also soon rid us of the negroes themselves, and likewise of all the other base-colored, base-blooded and base-minded species of mankind, whose pernicious presence, in any place inhabited by white people, is a thousand times worse than a threefold pestilence.

Particular portions of the subsoils of America are known to possess special affinities for *coal*-black materials; and other portions for *copper*-colored substances. These respective subterranean localities are also remarkable for possessing certain attrahent and fossilizing properties, which, with a power far greater than that of the loadstone, manifest a nature-implanted destiny to attract and overclod all jet-black and killow-colored bipeds. Fossilization then—speedy and complete fossilization— is alike the doom of the negro, the Indian, and the bi-colored hybrid. If, in his great mercy and kindness, God wills it, let every one of these reprobate creatures be fossilized to-morrow—in which case, the delectable dawn of the millennium will be less than two days distant!

CHAPTER II.

BLACK ; A THING OF UGLINESS, DISEASE, AND DEATH.

> Black is the badge of hell, the hue of
> Dungeons, and the scowl of night.—SHAKSPEARE.

If the world were intended for a house of mourning, every flower would be painted black; every bird would be a crow or a buzzard; the ocean would be one vast ink pot; a black veil would be drawn over the face of heaven, and an everlasting string of crape hung around the borders of creation.—*Eclectic Magazine. July*, 1863.

Of the negro race, it may fairly be said, that it is the one most likely to have had an independent origin: seeing that it is a type so peculiar in an inveterate black color, and so mean in development.—*Vestiges of Creation, page* 145.

To men of acute and well-balanced perceptive faculties, no fact in nature can be more obvious than that Black is a thing of universal ill-omen and detestation. Everywhere, also, is it plainly observable, that the displeasing and repulsive characteristics of blackness are affixed to faulty and effete things in general, and to the negroes in particular. These black persons and things (all of them, without any manner of exception) have been irrevocably foredoomed to utter destruction. Why is this? For the same reason that anything is as it is—simply because God himself, in his infinite wisdom and power and justice, has so decreed it.

Black, indeed, is a most hatable thing ; and it is quite as natural and right, for white people at least, to hate black, as it is for the angels in heaven to abhor hideous Satan, or for bachelors on the earth to love pretty maids.

He who is the Creator and the Ruler, the Upholder and the Disposer, of the heavens and the earth and the seas, and of all the things that therein are—of every thing in the universe, both great and small—will be exact in requiring of us perfect fulfillment of all the conditions of our being. In no manner, in no degree, may we, with impunity, shirk the obligations, whether altogether as we would wish them or otherwise, which he hath imposed upon us. What he hath made for us to love, that we must love ; and what he hath made for us to hate, that we must hate.

If, in a spirit of rebellion against the laws of nature, we love the negroes and other black things, we shall thereby only gain the low distinction of gratifying the devil ; but if, on the other hand, assuming attitudes of antagonism toward the imps of Africa, toward the prince of darkness, and toward all the other monstrous representatives of blackness and abomination, "we hate them with perfect hatred," as they deserve to be hated, and as we are required and expected to hate them, we shall thereby render highly acceptable and pleasing service to the Deity ; and, continuing to please him, will secure for ourselves unlimited and everlasting felicity in heaven.

During the myriads of ages which have élapsed since the first appearance of animal life, certain genera and species of creatures peculiar to each grand cycle, have, without intermission of time, and independently of their own election, been endowed with both the means and the irresistible inclination to exterminate others. So steadily and extensively has this natural process of extermination affected sentient (or once sentient) beings, that there is much reason for believing that the earth and the ocean contain, to-day, the fossils of at least as many families and varieties of formerly numerous but now entirely extinct organisms, as are known to exist in full vigor at the present period.

From the application of this fossilizing law of nature, only the more favored branches of the white races of mankind can, thus far, truthfully claim to have enjoyed exemption—and even the more meritorious and tenacious of these, after the lapse of eighty-nine millions of years, more or less, may, and probably will, be superseded by other white races, as far superior to those of the present, as those of the present are superior to the Orang-outangs and the Hottentots.

We may not, in this particular place, speak of the numerous aboriginal tribes of Palestine, and other countries of the Old World, who, according to oft-quoted and well-recéived authority, have been totally "cut off from the face of the earth;" but we may here, with unquestioned propriety, invite attention to the cheering fact, that, under the operations of the great law of nature just mentioned—a law of which we white people have, in so great a measure, been made the executors—no less than one hundred millions of American Indians have already found, at the depth of five or six feet beneath the soil, their appropriate and final resting-place. Just so many of these worthless creatures as still survive—whether they survive in North America, in Central America, in South America, or in the islands adjacent—are now (having already arrived at the very doors of the house of death) rapidly learning, like all the Indians in other parts of, the world, how specifically this law was framed for them. Under the operations of the same law, fourteen millions of negroes on this side of the Atlantic, and fifty-five millions on the other side, will soon be taught that the time allotted for their tenancy above ground is now fast expiring, and that they, too, must all speedily depart for

> "The undiscovered country, from whose bourne
> No traveller returns."

Strange it is, however, passing strange, that in the

face of all the manifest and irrefragable evidences of nature's abhorrence of . Black, there are men, in the United States, white men, men reputed to be possessed of highly cultivated minds, men occupying exalted positions of honor and trust—such men, for instance, as those who compose the majority of the Black Congress—who, nevertheless, persist in the nocent and notorious nonsense of attempting to ignore and conceal the noisome nigritude of the negroes. "No antipathy to color," say they, "no hatred nor exclusion of the negroes because of their blackness." Indeed! Ah! Umph! So! Then let us at once do away with all our antipathy to snakes! Let us cease to hate fiends! and, from the firesides of our families, let there be no further exclusion of courtesans!

Nor is it men only, who, with the unreasoning tongues of parrots, are, ever and anon, clamorously and preposterously prating about the aversion to color, and who, at the same time, are most wrongfully striving to palliate the baneful blackness of the negro. Women also, or rather a species of sexless creatures in petticoats—human hermaphrodites in female garb—have, in like manner, begun to betray equal folly, by holding public meetings for the purpose of propping up and sustaining the nature-blasted representatives of Black. How infinitely better would it be for these brazen-faced and babyless personators of women, if they were but women in reality —first maidens, then mothers and matrons, and surrounded by a goodly number of adolescent candidates male and female—for welcoming, with loud and jubilant honors, the advent of the twentieth century!

What more ridiculous and absurd spectacle can be presented than women as the conveners of political gatherings! women on the platform! women at the polls!—

as if, forsooth, the proper place for women was not at home, ready there, at all times, to hold in check the excesses of their mischievous boys and giggling girls (every one of whom ought, now and then, to be well spanked!), and to bestow, as occasion may require, certain minuter attentions upon their mewling infants!

It is, however, more especially the white masculine apologists of Black, from whom we beg leave to differ on this occasion. White women, or rather the white hermaphrodites who personate women, like all the Indians, negroes, mulattoes, and other swarthy numskulls, are utterly unfit to be allowed to participate, in any manner, in the more important political affairs of our country—in such affairs, for instance, as voting, legislating, representing, and governing. Certain it is, also, that the willingness to incur the public notoriety, scandal and disgrace, which would inevitably result from such amazonian interference in the business of the State as is here contemplated, has its home only in the breasts of those (if, indeed, they have breasts at all) who are destitute of all the finer and purer qualities of true ladyship.

Now for a word of wholesome condemnation against certain white men, who, because of their unnatural affinity and affiliation with things of base blackness, have become an opprobrium to their kind. What is the character of these men? Truth requires the admission that many of them are honest, sincere, and well-intentioned, and that some of them, in reference to matters and things generally, have acquired much solid and correct information. Many of them are estimable and kindly-hearted in all their personal relations. Many of them are good sons, good husbands, good fathers, good neighbors. Yet, in their thoughts of the negro, (a paltry wretch, totally unworthy of a millionth part of the

thoughts which white people have already bestowed upon
him,) they have been so unfortunate as to be brought
under the control of a most morbid and mischievous
sentimentality.   Perfectly rational on almost every other
subject, on this they have become quite insane; and
hence it is, that many of their teachings are, it is conscientiously believed, no less inimical to the welfare of the
country at large, than were the teachings of Jeff. Davis
and other pro-slavery traitors, just prior to the great
Rebellion.

What must we do with these wrong-headed and unnatural white lovers of the negro,—these wayward and
dissentious authors and accessories of the Black Congress?   We must cease to vote for them.   We must no
longer encourage them in their unmeritorious aspirations
for political preferment.   We must withdraw them entirely from the high offices which they are so grossly
dishonoring.   Soundly rebuking them for their folly, we
must remand them to private life, and there leave them
unnoticed, free to rave and rant at their pleasure, but
with no power to harm the State.

Yet, in justice to these crotchety and misguided men
of our own race, these fanatical and mischief-making
champions of Black, these deluded and undignified asso-
ciates of the negro, it is very proper that, even in their
retirement, we should continue to demonstrate to them,
that our dislike of the African is not, as they erroneously
allege, a mere blind and bitter "prejudice against color,"
but that it is a natural and ineradicable aversion, a right
and necessary antipathy, implanted in us by the Almighty
Himself, who can do nothing wrong.

With as little impunity might we, who are fortunately
possessed of a moderate share of common sense unbiased and unabused, persistently refuse to eat when hun-

gry, decline to drink when thirsty, or scorn to repose when sleepy, as strive to repress our inborn and nature-nurtured repugnance to the negro. To give free play to this rèpugnance is as much a matter of duty with us as it is to yield to any other innate and ever-healthful requirement,—a duty, indeed, which God has made absolutely obligatory on us ; and if we fail to obey His precepts in this regard, or in any other regard whatever, He will assuredly visit us with the severest possible condemnation.

If, now, we would learn to entertain a just, and salutary abomination of Black, let us at once acquaint ourselves with its specific and distinguishing qualities, its nature and its functions ; and in order to do this, it may be well for us (being beforehand provided with return tickets) to descend, for a few moments, to its home and its author—

HELL AND THE DEVIL.

If we may believe those who have seriously written on the subject, among them the Italian monk Pinamonti, (whose statements, however, are unworthy of belief,) the outer walls of hell are composed of an impenetrably adamantine or other stony substance of the unvarying and sorely distressing color of ebony ; and are, besides, "more than four thousand miles thick!" Within the dismal space thus impregnably walled up, there is, it is said, always perceptible one vast and never-ceasing storm of utter and tormenting darkness, where the confined smoke of burning brimstone has, from the very beginning of time, been so black and dense as to completely and forever hide from view, not only the ferocious fiends and serpents and other hideous monsters therein, but also even the fire itself, so that no ray of light, no object in contrast with the horrible and overwhelming blackness, can ever afford to the eye of any one of the victims thereof a single moment's relief.

Let, therefore, all the hare-brained and wrong-doing champions of Black, (including the Black Congress,) and the whole gang of their sable and heaven-debarred *protégés*, beware !—for like will seek and attract its like, and the Prince of Darkness will have his own.

John Ford, the eminent English dramatist, has bequeathed to his fellow-men the following appalling picture of the infernal regions :

> "There is a place, in a black and hollow vault,
> Where day is never seen ; there shines no sun,
> But flaming horror of consuming fires ;
> A lightless sulphur, choked with smoky fogs
> Of an infected darkness ; in this place
> Dwell many thousand thousand sundry sorts
> Of never-dying deaths ; there damned souls
> Roar without pity ; there are gluttons fed
> With toads and adders ; there is burning oil
> Poured down the drunkard's throat ; the usurer
> Is forced to sup with draughts of molten gold ;
> There is the murderer forever stabb'd,
> Yet can he never die ; there lies the wanton
> On racks of burning steel, while in his soul
> He feels the torment of his raging lust ;
> There stand those wretched things,
> Who have dream'd out whole years in lawless sheets
> And secret incests, cursing one another."

Of the same sinner-punishing place, John Milton speaks thus :

> "A dungeon horrible on all sides round,
> As one great furnace flamed ; yet from those flames
> No light ; but rather darkness visible,
> Served only to discover sights of woe,
> Regions of sorrow, doleful shades, where peace

> And rest can never dwell ; hope never comes
> That comes to all ; but tortures without end.
> Such place eternal justice had prepared
> For those rebellious ; here their prison ordained
> In utter darkness, and their portion set
> As far removed from God and light of heaven,
> As from the centre thrice to the utmost pole."

Prescott, in his " History of the Conquest of Mexico," Volume I., page 33, says :

"The Mexicans imagined three separate states of existence in the future life. The wicked, comprehending the greater part of mankind, were to expiate their sins in a place of everlasting darkness. Another class, with no other merit than that of having died of certain diseases, capriciously selected, were to enjoy a negative existence of indolent contentment. The highest place was reserved, as in most warlike nations, for the heroes who fell in battle, or in sacrifice. They passed at once into the presence of the Sun, whom they accompanied with songs and choral dances, in his bright progress through the heavens ; and after some years, their spirits went to animate the clouds and singing birds of beautiful plumage, and to revel amidst the rich blossoms and odors of the gardens of paradise."

In one of his Sonnets, (CXLVII.,) Shakspeare complains that,

> " I have sworn thee fair, and thought thee bright,
> Who art as black as hell, as dark as night."

As if directly addressing the debased white aiders and abettors of the abandoned blacks, (as if addressing the Black Congress, for instance,) Fawcett very pertinently exclaims—

> " Your way is dark and leads to hell ;
> Why will you persevere ?
> Can you in endless torments dwell,
> Shut up in black despair ?"

An old Hebrew author (1 Samuel ii., 9) warns the blacks and their white accomplices in deviltry, that,

"The wicked shall be silent in darkness."

Another writer has foretold that all the black and would-be-black reprobates shall be

" Consigned to a fiery place of punishment in perpetual night."

Again, in reference to the God-forsaken creatures of whom we are now speaking, Heaven's immutable decree has gone forth, that,

"Nameless in dark oblivion they must dwell."

One of the authors of the Catholic Bible (Tobias IV., ii.) tells us that,

"Alms deliver from all sin, and from death, and will not suffer the soul to go into darkness."

From our very earliest childhood, as is well and generally known, we are accustomed to hear both the "The Black Man" and "The Prince of Darkness" used as common designations for the devil.

Draper, in his "Intellectual Development of Europe," page 29, says :

"In the interior of the solid earth, or perhaps on the other side of its plane—under world as it was well termed—is the realm of Pluto, the region of Night. From the midst of his dominion, that divinity, crowned with a diadem of ebony, and seated on a throne framed out of massive darkness, looks into the infinite abyss beyond, invisible himself to mortal eyes, but made known by the nocturnal thunder which is his weapon."

Worcester, next to Webster the greatest American lexicographer, in his " Chart of Mythology," tells us that,

"Pluto, the god of the infernal regions, of death and funerals, is represented sitting on an ebony throne."

Again, in his "Chart of Mythology," Worcester tells us—and this is worthy of the attention of those foolish persons who, on certain sad occasions, and for long periods, clothe themselves in the disgusting habiliments of mourning—that,

"The Furies are represented of grim and frightful aspect, with serpents entwined about their heads instead of hair; their garments black and bloody; attended by Terror, Paleness, and Death, with Care, Sorrow, Disease, and Famine, in their train."

Under the incitement of virtuous indignation, one of our patriotic poets has recently castigated, in a most thorough manner, the treason and rebellion of

'Jeff. Davis, our blackest foe, of devilish origin."

Although it has already been suggested, yet here it may be more definitely premised, that Blackness and Darkness, as representing the. opposites of White and Light, are but one and the same thing. On the right hand, White and Light are emanations from Heaven; on the left hand, Blackness and Darkness are emanations from hell. Further on, in the next succeeding chapter, we shall have occasion to revert to this subject again. Here let it suffice that we expose, in part, the horrible aspects and infamous characteristics of Black, as it is generally seen, like a shapeless and gigantic monster, prowling about the earth under the guise of

NIGHT—DARKNESS.

In the ninth book of his "Odyssey," Homer, as translated by Pope, speaks of

"The black palace of eternal night,
The dolesome realms of darkness and of death."

Shakspeare, in his poem entitled "The Rape of Lucrece," says,

"Solemn night, with slow sad gait descended
To ugly hell; when lo, the blushing morrow
Sends light to all fair eyes that light will borrow."

Again, Shakspeare speaks of

> "The dreadful deeds of dark midnight."

Again, in his "Titus Andronicus," Act V., Scene I.,
Shakspeare tells us that,

> "'Twill vex thy soul to hear what I shall speak;
> For I must talk of murders, rapes, and massacres,
> Acts of black night, abominable deeds,
> Complots of mischief, treason; villainies
> Ruthful to hear, yet piteously performed."

Again, in his "Julius Cæsar," Act II., Scene I., Shakspeare inquiringly, and indignantly exclaims:

> "O conspiracy!
> Sham'st thou to show thy dangerous brow by night,
> When evils are most free?　O, then, by day,
> Where wilt thou find a cavern dark enough
> To mask thy monstrous visage?"

Again, in his poem entitled "The Rape of Lucrece,"
Shakspeare exclaims;

> "O night, thou furnace of foul-reeking smoke,
> Let not the jealous day behold that face
> Which, underneath thy black all-hiding cloak,
> Immodestly lies martyred with disgrace!
> Keep still possession of thy gloomy place,
> That all the faults that in thy reign are made,
> May likewise be sepulchred in thy shade!"

Again, the bard of Avon exclaims:

> "The dragon wing of night o'erspreads the earth;
> O hateful, vaporous and foggy night."

Milton also tells us that,

> "When night
> Darkens the streets, then wander forth the sons
> Of Belial, flown with insolence and wine."

In his First Night, Edward Young, the author of "Night Thoughts," is heard giving utterance to these solemn words:

> "Night, sable goddess! from her ebon throne,
> In rayless majesty now stretches forth
> Her leaden sceptre o'er a slumbering world.
> Silence how dead! and darkness how profound!
> Nor eye nor listening ear an object finds;
> Creation sleeps.   'Tis as the general pulse
> Of life stood still, and Nature made a pause;
> An awful pause! prophetic of her end."

Judging from the concurring accounts given by a host of truth-telling travelers, there is to be heard at all times, day and night, throughout the entire length and breadth of negroland,

"Horrid, hideous sounds of woe, sadder than owl-songs on the midnight blast."

According to the Douay version of the Bible, it appears that, of all the plagues of Egypt, absolute darkness was the only one that proved sufficiently appalling to produce among the Thoth-worshiping and Jew-enslaving countrymen of the obdurate Pharaoh a profound and universal thrill of horror.

Edward Thomson, of Ohio, an eloquent minister of the Methodist Episcopal Church, in a sermon which he preached some years ago, on "The Missionary Enterprise," said, with fullness of truth,

"Turn to Africa, and along its northern borders and throughout its interior, you have Mahommedanism, while, with the exception of a few missionary stations on the coast, all else is one black cloud of pagan darkness."

It would now seem to be proper that we should here

institute a somewhat more minute inquiry into the nature, qualities and significance of

BLACKNESS IN GENERAL.

On this subject, the "London Encyclopædia," Volumo IV., page 177, has favored us with the following brief but pointed remarks :

"Black is literally applied to the color of the night ; to darkness ; and figuratively, to what obscures, pollutes or soils a character or reputation ; to whatever is gloomy, dismal, fearful, and terrific ; to that which is concealed ; to nefarious, wicked, foul, atrocious and disgusting criminality. It therefore describes natural objects, mental apprehensions, and moral delinquencies. Over them all it throws the pall of night, the gloomy horrors of the outer darkness."

From the "Encyclopædia Britannica," Volume IV., page 740, we learn that,

"Black from a remote antiquity has been regarded as the symbol of mourning and calamity. It is sometimes imposed as a mark of humiliating distinction ; the most familiar instance of which is the obligation laid upon the Jews in Turkey of wearing black turbans.'

The "Encyclopædia Metropolitana," Volume XV., page 606, says :

"Black is applied to that which has the dismalness, the gloominess the forbiddingness of darkness; to that which is dark, dismal, gloomy, forbidding, fearful, dreadful."

Edmund Burke, in his admirable work on "The Sublime and Beautiful," page 179, says :

"Perhaps it may appear, on inquiry, that blackness and darkness are, in some degree, painful by their natural operation, independent of any associations whatsoever. I must observe that the ideas of darkness and blackness are much the same ; and they differ only in this that blackness is a more confined idea. Mr. Cheselden has given us a very curious story of a boy who had been born blind, and continued so until he was thirteen or fourteen years old; he was then couched for a cataract, by which operation he received his sight. Among many remarkable particulars that attended his first perceptions and judgments on visual objects, Cheselden tells us, that the first time the boy saw a black object, it gave him great uneasiness; and that some time after, upon accidentally seeing a negro woman, he was struck with great horror at the sight.

It has been said, on good authority, that the mere sight of anything black, invariably excites in the Chameleon a most feverish and fearful horror, and that, though possessing the extraordinary power of changing its own color into a great variety of rare and beautiful tints, it has never been known to assume, even for one moment, a single shade of the hatable and hideous hue of the negro.

From the latest edition of the unabridged "American Dictionary of the English Language," by Noah Webster, (a man who has displayed more genius in the definition of words than any other lexicographer that has ever lived,) the following extracts tell their own story. As will be observed, the brood of evils thus fathered by Black and its corrupt compounds, is, alas! hardly less numerous or less fatal, than was the brood of evils which, many centuries ago, to the great and irreparable misfortune of mankind, escaped from Pandora's box:

"Black.—Mournful; calamitous; horrible; wicked.'

"Blackness.—The quality of being black * * * atrociousness or enormity in wickedness."

"Black-vomit.—A copious vomiting of dark-colored matter * * * one of the most fatal symptoms of yellow fever."

"Black-death.—The black plague of the fourteenth century.

"Blackleg.—A notorious gambler and cheat."

"Blackguard.—A person of low character, accustomed to use scurrilous language, or to treat others with foul abuse."

"Black-book.—A book kept at a university for the purpose of
registering crimes or misdemeanors."

"Black-flag.—The flag of a pirate."

"Black-mail.—A certain rate of money, corn, cattle, or other thing,
anciently paid in the north of England and south of Scotland,
to certain men, who were allied to robbers, to be by them
protected from pillage. * * * Extortion of money from a person by threats of accusation or exposure, or opposition in the
public prints."

David A. Wells, in his "Things not Generally Known,"
page 74, says:

"To be in the Black Books, implies out of favor; a phrase said to
be borrowed from the black-book of the English monasteries, which
was a detail of the scandalous enormities practiced in religious
houses."

Kirkland, in his "Commercial Anecdotes," Volume II.,
page 420, speaking of the "English Stock Brokers' Blackboard, says:

"The origin of the blackboard—that moral pillory of the English
stock exchange—dates back to 1787. There were, said a journal of
that day, no less than twenty-five 'lame ducks,' who waddled out
of the alley. Their deficiencies were estimated at one million and a
quarter of dollars; and it was upon this occasion that the plan in
question was first proposed; and, at a very full meeting, if was resolved that those who did not either pay their deficiencies or name
their principals, should be publicly exposed on a blackboard, to be
provided for such occasion. Thus the above deficiencies—larger than
had been previously known—alarmed the gentlemen devoted to stock
dealing, and produced that system which is yet regarded with wholesome awe."

The poets, true to their divine mission, invariably use
the word Black in an ill sense. Take, for instance, and
for the sake of brevity, the following disconnected expressions from Shakespeare:

"Black envy."

"Black scandal."

"Black villainy."

"Black defiance."

"Black strife."

"Black tidings."

"Black vengeance."

"Black funerals."

"Black and portentous."

"Night's black agents."

"The black brow of night."

"Acts of black night, abominable deeds."

"As black as incest."

"Bitter, black, and tragical."

"That black word death."

" Let the devil wear black."

"The devil damn thee black."

"Dimmed with death's black veil.'

"It was a black soul burning."

" As gross as black from white."

"As black as if besmeared in hell."

" This dread and black complexion smeared."

"A black day will it be to somebody."

"Richard yet lives, hell's black intelligencer."

"The coal-black clouds that shadow heaven's light."

"Look, how the black slave smiles."

"Sable arms, black as his purpose."

"Will have his soul black like his face."

Milton supposes a case when,

> " At our heels all hell should rise
>   With blackest insurrection."

Young, in his " Night Thoughts," speaks of

> "The black waste of murdered time."

Lamb deeply laments that there are still in the world persons who, like the negroes and their depraved white

5

confederates and defenders, are so reprobate as to be the willing recipients of

> "Sin's black wages."

The following proverbs and sententious sayings, extracted from the writings of various distinguished authors, are worthy of attention in this connection :

"Two blacks make no white."

"Black will take no other hue."

"Necessity is coal-black."

"The black fear of death that saddens all."

"Crows are never the whiter for washing themselves."

"The raven chides blackness.

"The raven said to the rook, stand away, black coat!"

Black birds generally—not all that are called black without being so—but such as are entirely and unrelievedly black, from the beak of the bill to the end of the tail, have always, in every age and country, been regarded as

> "The hateful messengers of heavy things,
> Of death and dolor telling;"

And many of these, and more especially those which feed on putrid flesh, such, for instance, as the carrion-crow and the buzzard, are, as may also be justly said of the negro,

> "Like a collier's sack, bad without, but worse within."

There be black birds, however, that is to say, there are birds which are called black, which are so only in part, and which are, therefore, the victims of a most mischievous and monstrous misnomer. It was of such birds as these (redwinged, or otherwise saved from the curse of entire blackness; good in themselves, and good to eat) that, as the nursery song will have it, the king's pie was made.

Conjoined with other words, the word black is also wrongly used in reference to many other things. An instance of this is found in the compound word blackcattle—a term which is thus defined by Noah Webster:

"Black-cattle.—Cattle of the bovine genus reared for slaughter, in distinction from dairy-cattle. The term has no reference to their color."

So, too, of tea, and bread, and grapes, as Black Tea, Black Bread, Black Grapes, and many other misnamed things, which are merely brown, or blue, or purple. Any leaf or drop of tea, any particle of bread, any atom of grape, or any quantity, however minute, of any other thing whatever, if absolutely black, is absolutely dead, poisonous, or unpalatable ; and, therefore, absolutely unfit and dangerous to be introduced into the stomach of any undoomed living creature.

Another striking proof of the very loathsome and accursed character of Black, is, that it thoroughly abhors its own self, and carries in itself the seeds of self-destruction. This fact is fully illustrated in the African's detestation of his own color, and in

THE NEGRO'S PREDILECTION FOR WHITE.

The writer hereof has frequently heard his father's negroes (in North Carolina, near the banks of the South Yadkin) when disagreeing among themselves, tauntingly call each other "nigger," "black rascal," "crow-colored scoundrel," and numerous other epithets of similar sable softness. He also recollects very distinctly, that, on one occasion, when, in his boyhood, he himself called Jack a nigger, Jack, who was also youthful, became quite indignant, and said that, as his mother Judy had told him, there was no nigger except the devil, "for mammy say," said he, "for mammy say de debble am black for all de time, and can nebber be wash white; and for dat reezun de debble am a nigger; but we slabes is black only in dis prezzen worle; in de nex worle, we is gwine to be white fokes too!   You see den dat we's not niggers."

Whether his ebony-crowned highness accepted the appellation thus bestowed upon him, is not known.   Yet a strong impression was produced, and still lingers with the writer, that the word nigger was a very appropriate word, as descriptive of both of the black fellows here mentioned, and that, while Old Nick was and is undoubtedly a most hideous Big Nigger, young Jack was, with equal certainty, a very ugly Little Nigger.

Livingstone, during his "Travels and Researches in South Africa," (page 26) held, on a certain occasion, a dialogue with a native Rain-doctor—in other words, a black fool—who, notwithstanding, thus intelligently and truthfully replied to his distinguished white interlocutor:

"God made black men first, and did not love us as he did the white men.   He made you beautiful, and gave you clothing, and guns, and gunpowder, and horses, and wagons, and many other things about which we know nothing.   But toward us he had no heart."

Again, on the 204th page of his "Travels and Researches in South Africa," Livingstone says :

"The whole of the colored tribes consider that beauty and fairness are associated, and women long for children of light color so much, that they sometimes chew the bark of a certain tree in hopes of producing that effect.   To my eye the dark color is much more agreeable than the tawny hue of the half-caste, which that of the Makololo ladies closely resembles.   The women generally escape the fever, but they are less fruitful than formerly ; and to their complaint of being undervalued on account of the disproportion of the sexes, they now add their regrets at the want of children, of whom they are all excessively fond."

Again, in his "Travels and Researches in South Africa," page 445, Livingstone says,

"The people under Bango are divided into a number of classes. There are his councilors, as the highest, who are generally head men of several villages, and the carriers the lowest free men. One class above the last obtains the privilege of wearing shoes from the chief by paying for it; another, the soldiers or militia, pay for the privilege of serving, the advantage being that they are not afterward liable to be made carriers. They are also divided into gentlemen and and little gentlemen, and, though quite black, speak of themselves as white men, and of others, who may not wear shoes, as 'blacks,' The men of all these classes trust to their wives for food, and spend most of their time in drinking the palm-toddy."

Again, Livingstone, in his "Travels and Researches in South Africa," page 517, says:

"Katema, the ruler of the village, asked if I could not make a dress for him like the one I wore, so that he might appear as a white man when any stranger visited him."

Wilson, in his "Western Africa: Its History, Condition, and Prospects," page 343, says:

"The negro feels that, in energy of character, in scope of understanding, in the exercise of mechanical skill, and in the practice of all the useful arts of life, he is hopelessly distanced by the white man."

Again, in his "Western Africa," page 192, Wilson, (without stopping to remark on this new infamy of the Catholic church) says:

"Many years since, according to Barbot, the King of Benin engaged to bring his entire kingdom over to the Roman Catholic faith, if the priests would provide him with a white wife. An embassy was immediately dispatched to the neighboring island of St. Thomas, where there was a considerable white population, and a strong appeal was made to the Christian feeling of the sisterhood, one of whom had the courage to look the matter in the face, and actually accepted

the hand of his sable majesty.   She ought to have been canonized,[*]
but it is not known that the deed of self-sacrifice ever received any
special notice from the Father of the Church."

Again, in his "Western Africa," page 191, Wilson
says :

"From the time that white men first visited their shores and
spread before them the products of civilized arts, it became a ruling
passion with the African to court their favor, and secure for himself
as large a share of these coveted treasures as he possibly could.
Rivalries grew out of this passion, and no pains or means were
spared in endeavors to supplant each other in the white man's
esteem."

Again, in his "Western Africa," page 311, Wilson
says :

"Albinos may be found in almost every community in Southern
Guinea.   Everywhere they are regarded as somewhat sacred, and
their persons are considered inviolable.   On no condition whatever
would a man strike one of them.   Generally they are very mild ;
and I have never heard of their taking advantage of their acknowledged inviolability.   In features they are not unlike the rest of their
race, but their complexion is very nearly a pure white, their hair of
the ordinary texture, but of a cream color, and their eyes are gray
and always in motion."

Mungo Park, in his first "Journal of an Expedition
into the Interior of Africa," page 259, says :

"Observing the improved state of our manufactures, and our manifest superiority in the arts of civilized life, Harfa, the intelligent
negro merchant, would sometimes appear pensive, and exclaim, with

---

* There are others who believe that this shameless woman
and her Catholic seducers from common decency, should all
have been banished forever from the presence of respectable
society, and left, during the whole term of their natural lives,
to grope their way in sorrow and solitude, through the dismal
Wilderness of Sin.

an involuntary sigh, '*Fato fing inta feng*'—black men are good for nothing."

Clapperton, in his "Narrative of Travels and Discoveries in Central Africa," Volume IV., page 199, says:

"The whole court, which was large, was filled, crowded, crammed with people, except a space in front, where we sat, into which his highness led Mr. Houston and myself, one in each hand; and there we performed an African dance, to the great delight of the surrounding multitude. The *tout ensemble* would doubtless have formed an excellent subject for a caricaturist, and we regretted the absence of Captain Pearce, to sketch off the old black caboceer, sailing majestically around in his damask robe, with a train-bearer behind him, and every now and then turning up his old, withered face, first to myself, then to Mr. Houston; then whisking round on one foot, then marching slowly, with solemn gait; twining our hands in his—proud that a white man should dance with him."

Again, in his "Narrative of Travels and Discoveries in Central Africa," Volume IV., page 222, Clapperton says:

"Zuma, a rich widow of Wava, the owner of a thousand slaves, told me that her husband had been dead these ten years; that she had only one son, and he was darker than herself; that she loved white men, and would go to Boussa with me."

Burton, in his "Lake Regions of Central Africa," page 216, says:

"The women are well disposed toward strangers of fair complexion, apparently with the permission of their husbands."

Hutchinson, another African traveler, in an article published in the London *Ethnological Magazine*, Volume I., Part II., page 333, issued in 1861, says:

"At the mouths of several of the Palm Oil Rivers, in former times (even of those of Brass and New Kalabar at the present) there existed the custom to sacrifice an Albino female child to the sharks, which were considered the Ju-ju of these rivers. No case has ever been recorded of any such victim objecting to her fate; for they are indoctrinated with the belief, that in the world of spirits to which they are going, it is their destiny to be married to a white man."

Again, in his "Impressions of Western Africa," page 112, Hutchinson says:

"A curious superstition is connected with Parrot Island, and is observed with religious punctuality by the natives of Old Kalabar, on the occasion of need arising for its performance. Whenever a scarcity of European trading ships exists, or is apprehended, the Duketown authorities are accustomed to take an Albino child of their own race, and offer it up as a sacrifice, at Parrot Island, to the God of the white man."

Baldwin, in his "Hunting in South Africa," page 266, says:

"The Kaffirs believe that white men can do anything."

Waitz, in his "Anthropology of Primitive Peoples," Volume I., page 304, says:

"Among the Mandingoes, in the region of Sierra Leone, white is the symbol of peace. Among the Ashantees and other negro people, white is the color of joy ; and they paint themselves white on their birth-days. Priests, ambassadors, and warriors are dressed in white among the Tebus."

What then, as thus far seen, what is Black ? Just what, when rightly examined, it appears to be—a thing of Deterioration, Uncomeliness, and Repugnance ; a thing indicative of Gloom, Sadness, and Sorrow ; a thing concomitant to Cruelty, Corruption, and Crime ; a thing appallingly significant of Disaster, Disease and Death ; a thing justly exciting Aversion, Antipathy, and Disgust ; a thing fit to be Despised, Hated, and Abhorred ; a thing proper to be Discarded, Shunned, and forever Excluded.

Many additional evidences of the negroes' intense dislike and abomination of Black, and of their inborn fondness for White, might be here cited, and would be cited, were it not that the space alloted for this chapter is already filled. In the next succeeding chapter, many of the subjects herein barely mentioned, shall receive further attention. And as we proceed, if we be truly diligent and faithful in our inquiries and investigations, we shall doubt-less find, in reference to the swarthiness of the negroes, as was found by Sir Thomas Browne, in his researches touching the blackness of their skin, "no less of darkness in the cause than in the effect itself." Thus, in full accord with the will of Heaven, may we learn to strengthen our natural and healthful aversion to all the basely black and bi-colored underworld of humanity; thus also, preparing, in our humble way, for the dawn of that glorious period promised in the future, may we co-operate more immedi-ately and efficiently with Providence in those wise and wonderful fossilizing processes which are now rapidly re-moving from the fair face of the earth all ugly and useless organisms.

Meanwhile, however, it behooves us to keep it prominent-ly before the public, that it is not alone the horrible and hurtful blackness of the negroes, which impels us to de-test them. Blackness is only one of the many vile qualities of their nature. We must consider attentively all their mean and loathsome characteristics; and from the sum total of these, we shall, if clear and unbiased in our judgments, quickly perceive that, like hyenas, jackals, wolves, skunks, rats, snakes, scorpions, spiders, centipedes, locusts, chinch-es, fleas, lice, and other noxious creatures, the negroes are not upon the earth to be loved and preserved, but, under the unobstructed and salutary operations of the laws of nature, to be permited to decay and die, and then to disappear, at once and forever, down, down, deep down, in the vortex of oblivion!

CHAPTER III.

WHITE: A THING OF LIFE, HEALTH, AND BEAUTY.

White, as it is the color of day, is expressive to us of the cheerfulness or
gayety which the return of day brings. Black, as the color of darkness, is expressive of gloom and melancholy. The color of the heavens, in serene weather,
is blue; blue, therefore, is expressive to us of somewhat the same pleasing and
temperate character. Green is the color of the earth in spring; it is consequently
expressive to us of those delightful images which we associate with that season.—
ALISON.

White is applied metaphorically to denote what is pure, unspotted, unstained,
unblemished, innocent, harmless.—ENCYCLOPŒDIA METROPOLITANA.

White men alone possess the intellectual and moral energy which creates that
development of free government, industry, science, literature, and the arts, which
we call civilization. Black men, can neither originate, maintain, nor comprehend
civilization.—SIDNEY GEORGE FISHER.

THE act of proving that White is a positive good, will,
at the same time, constitute proof, in addition to the
proof already adduced, that Black is a positive evil—
the one thing being the veritable extreme or antithesis
of the other.

From the very dawn of the earliest antiquity to the
present moment, among the people of every clime and
country, White, as a color, or as the negation of color,
has been recognized as the symbol of Innocence, Purity,
and Peace. Nay, not only has it been so among all mundane nations, tongues, and tribes, but, judging from the
highest authorities we have upon the subject, so likewise
has it ever been—even more intensely so, indeed—with
the celestial beings above us.

White is Light, and Light is White; the meaning of
the one term, as here used, may be unequivocally accepted as the signification of the other. Heaven, and all
the vast expanse of space exposed to the view of man,
are but soul-refreshing emanations from the source of su-

preme and perfect whiteness. God, himself, the mighty Father of All, in whose all-gracious and all-glorious presence, no particle of blackness is ever tolerated, and upon whose benignant head no hairs but white were ever seen, is the Eternal Centre and Substance of Light.

Not only, however, is it by God, angels, and men, that White has always been held in the highest possible favor and esteem. There is strong presumptive evidence that the heroes and demi-gods of the prehistoric age, as well as those of a later period, were equally inclined to regard White as a thing of divine origin—as a thing of the most auspicious and sacred associations. In the reign of Ægeus, king of Athens, who, as ancient history informs us, lived contemporaneously with Solomon, king of Israel, Theseus, one of the very greatest of the great Grecian heroes, and son to Ægeus, conditionally volunteered to be one of seven Athenians who were destined by treaty with cruel Minos, king of Crete, either to be thrown alive to the man-eating monster Minotaur, or to be blind-folded and cast into the Cretan Labyrinth, there to wander among its inextricable mazes, hopelessly lost, forlorn, hungry, and thirsty, to the end of time. The condition on which Theseus volunteered to become one of the seven victims, was, that he and all his comrades should be exempt from the terrible fate assigned them, provided he himself, alone and without weapons, should succeed in taking the life of the ferocious Minotaur. On the departure of the seven Grecians from Athens for Crete, to fulfill the engagement so heroically entered into by Theseus, or to answer with their persons the provisions of the treaty, the sorrowing Athenians, in tears, and never expecting to see their half-doomed countrymen again, embarked them, as peerless Plutarch tells us, in a "ship with a black sail, as carrying them to certain ruin. But when Theseus encouraged his father by

his confidence of success against the Minotaur, Ægeus
gave another sail, a white one, to the pilot, ordering him,
if he brought Theseus back, to hoist the white; but if
not, to sail with the black one, in token of his misfortune." It is gratifying to be able to inform the unmyth-
ological reader that Theseus slew the fell monster, and,
with his compatriots, all under white sail, returned to
Athens, where he received a welcome similar to the one
which but recently awaited the great Ulysses of modern
times, on his victorious return from Richmond, after having there vanquished a certain slaveholding monster from
the mounds of Mississippi.

Let us see, for a moment, how white is spoken of in
connection with

THE GREATER AND THE LESSER DIVINITIES.

Dunlap, in his "Spirit-History of Man," page 191,
quotes from the principal hymn of the ancient Egyptians
to their Supreme deity, these words:

"Thou art the God swift-coming from the Sun, the greatly-glorious,
the lion-shaped, the very white forever!"

From Botta's "Universal Literature," page 366, we
learn that,

"The antithesis of a good and evil principle is met with among
most of the Sclavonic tribes ; and even at the present time, in some
of their dialects, everything good and beautiful is to them synonymous with the purity of the white color ; they call the good spirit the
white God, and the evil spirit the black God."

Again, from Botta's "Universal Literature," page 41,
we learn that,

"Availing himself of the doctrines of the Chaldeans and of the
Hebrews, Zoroaster, endowed by nature with extraordinary powers,
sustained by popular enthusiasm, and aided by the favor of powerful
princes, extended his reform throughout Persia, and founded a new religion on the ancient worship. According to this religion, the two

great principles of the world were represented by Ormuzd and Ahriman, both born from eternity, and both contending for the dominion of the world. Ormuzd, the principle of good, is represented by light, and Ahriman, the principle of evil, by darkness. Light, then, being the body or symbol of Ormuzd, is worshiped in the sun and stars, in fire, and wherever it is found. Men are either the servants of Ormuzd, through virtue and wisdom, or the slaves of Ahriman, through folly and vice. Zoroaster explained the history of the world as the long contest of these two principles, which was to close with the conquest of Ormuzd over Ahriman."

Prescott, in his "History of the Conquest of Mexico," Volume II., page 333, says:

"None of the Mexican deities suggested such astonishing analogies with Scripture, as Quetzalcoatl, with whom the reader has already been made acquainted. He was the White Man, wearing a long beard, who came from the East; and who, after presiding over the golden age of Anahuac, disappeared as mysteriously as he had come, on the great Atlantic Ocean.

Of the most distinguished Moral Philosopher who has ever lived upon the earth, one of his disciples (Mark ix., 2–4) has said:

"After six days, Jesus taketh with him Peter, and James, and John, and leadeth them up into an high mountain, apart by themselves; and he was transfigured before them. And his raiment became shining, exceeding white as snow; so that no fuller on earth can white them."

One of the compilers of the New Testament (Matthew xxviii., 3) describing an angel reported to have just descended from Heaven, says:

"His countenance was like lightning, and his raiment white as snow."

John, of Patmos, seems to have had few or no visions, except through white clouds. Hear him—first in Revelation i., 12–15:

"I turned to see the voice that spake with me. And being turned,

I saw seven golden candlesticks; and in the midst of the seven candlesticks one like unto the Son of Man, clothed with a garment down to the foot, and girt about the paps with a golden girdle. His head and his hairs were white like wool, as white as snow; and his eyes were as a flame of fire; and his feet like unto fine brass, as if they burned in a furnace; and his voice as the sound of many waters."

Again—Revelation ii., 17 :

"He that hath an ear, let him hear what the spirit saith unto the churches: To him that overcometh will I give to eat of the hidden manna, and will give him a white stone, and in the stone a new name written, which no man knoweth saving he that receiveth it."

Again—Revelation iii., 1, 4, 5 :

"And unto the angel of the Church in Sardis write * * * Thou hast a few names even in Sardis which have not defiled their garments; and they shall walk with me in white; for they are worthy. He that overcometh, the same shall be clothed in white raiment; and I will not blot his name out of the book of life, but I will confess his name before my Father, and before his angels."

Again—Revelation iii., 17, 19 :

"Because thou sayest, I am rich, and increased with goods, and have need of nothing; and knowest not that thou art wretched, and miserable, and poor, and blind, and naked; I counsel thee to buy of me gold tried in the fire, that thou mayest be rich; and white rayment, that thou mayest be clothed, and that the shame of thy nakedness do not appear."

Again—Revelation iv., 2–5 :

"A throne was set in heaven, and one sat on the throne. And he that sat was to look upon like a jasper and a sardine stone; and there was a rainbow round about the throne, in sight like unto an emerald. And round about the throne were four and twenty seats; and upon the seats I saw four and twenty elders sitting, clothed in white raiment; and they had on their heads crowns of gold."

Again—Revelation vi., 9–11 :

"When he had opened the fifth seal, I saw under the altar the souls of them that were slain for the word of God, and for the testimony which they held; and they cried with a loud voice, saying: How long, O Lord, holy and true, dost thou not judge and avenge our blood on them that dwell on the earth. And white robes were given unto every one of them."

Again—Revelation vii., 9, 13:

"A great multitude which no man could number, of all nations, and kindreds, and people, and tongues, stood before the throne, and before the Lamb, clothed with white robes, and palms in their hands; and cried with a loud voice, saying, Salvation to our God which sitteth upon the throne, and unto the Lamb. * * * One of the elders answered, saying unto me, What are these which are arrayed in white robes? and whence came they? And I said unto him, Sir, thou knowest. And he said to me, These are they which came out of great tribulation, and have washed their robes, and made them white in the blood of the Lamb. Therefore are they before the throne of God, and serve him day and night in his temple; and he that sitteth on the throne shall dwell among them."

Again—Revelation xiv., 14:

"I looked, and behold a white cloud, and upon the cloud one sat like unto the Son of man, having on his head a golden crown, and in his hand a sharp sickle."

Again—Revelation xix., 7–9:

"Let us be glad and rejoice, and give honor to him; for the marriage of the Lamb is come, and his wife hath made herself ready. And to her was granted that she should be arrayed in fine linen, clean and white."

The readers of that curious collection of books called "The Apocryphal New Testament," will find that the Seers, or reputed Seers, whose foretellings are emblazoned therein, were also quite familiar with the merits of White. The following extract, from the fourth chapter of the "Visions of Hermas," will suffice as an instance:

"The beast had upon its head four colors, first black, then a red and bloody color, then a golden, and then a white."

"After that I had passed by it, and was gone forward about thirty feet, behold there met me a certain virgin well adorned, as if she had been just come out of her bride-chamber, all in white, having on white shoes, and a veil down her face, and covered with shining hair."

"Now I knew by my former visions that it was the Church, and thereupon grew the more cheerful. She saluted me, saying, Hail O man! I returned the salutation, saying, Lady, Hail! * * * Then I asked her concerning the four colors which the beast had upon its head. But she answered me, saying, Again thou art curious, in that thou askest concerning these things. And I said unto her, Lady show me what they are."

"Hear, said she; the black which thou sawest, denotes the world in which you dwell. The fiery and bloody color signifies that this age must be destroyed by fire and blood."

"The golden part are ye, who have escaped out of it. For as gold is tried by the fire, and is made profitable, so are ye also in like manner tried who dwell among the men of this world."

"They, therefore, that shall endure to the end, and be proved by them, shall be purged. And as gold, by this trial is cleansed, and loses its dross, so shall ye also cast away all sorrow and trouble; and be made pure for the building of the tower."

"But the white color denotes the time of the world which is to come, in which the elect of God shall dwell; because the elect of God shall be pure and without spot unto life eternal."

The pious and poetical writers of "psalms and hymns and spiritual songs," in their glowing descriptions of Heaven, and of the happy hosts thereof, have always seemed to be more and more under the influence of the divine *afflatus*, just in proportion as they manifested a disposition to deal liberally in the elegant tropes and metaphors of White. Thus significantly inquires Charles Wesley :

  "Who are these arrayed in white,
   Brighter than the noonday sun?
   Foremost of the sons of light
   Nearest the eternal throne?"

Again, he prays :

> "Cast my sins behind thy back
> And wash me white as snow."

Again, he says of God :

> "Descending on His great white throne,
> He claims the kingdoms for His own."

Another poet speaks of

> "The pearly gates of Heaven."

Daniel, the prophet, (chapter xii, verse 10,) vouchsafes to us the consoling assurance that,

> "Many shall be purified and made white."

Whether any reference is here had to the African is not stated. It may be gravely doubted, however, whether any process of albification will ever suffice to change the hateful hue of the negro from the accursed color of the crow.

Zeus, the great Grecian father of gods and men, is thus spoken of, under his Latin name, in Dwight's Mythology, page 122 :

"As Jupiter was the prince of light, the white color was sacred to him. The animals sacrificed to him were white; his chariot was believed to be drawn by four white horses; his priests wore white caps, and the consuls were attired in white, when they offered sacrifices."

Hera, the Olympian queen of heaven, is thus referred to, under her Latin name, in "Dwight's Mythology," page 139 :

"During the worship of Juno, there were always two processions to the temple of the goddess without the city; the first was of the men in armor, and the second of the women, when her priestess, mounted on a splendid chariot, rode in triumph to the temple of the goddess to offer a hecatomb of white heifers. The goddess was here particularly venerated in the person of her high priestess; a veneration with which the touching history of Cleobis and Biton is connected. On one occasion, when the white heifers which were to have drawn their mother were not at hand, they, with filial devotion, yoked themselves to her chariot, and drew it to the temple, forty-five stadia from the gates of Argos, lest she should be deprived of the honor of the day."

Of a very celebrated Roman goddess, we have this account in "Dwight's Mythology," page 283:

"The Goddess of Liberty was commonly represented in the figure of a woman in white robes, holding a rod in one hand, and a cap in the other. The cap, according to Valerius Maximus, and other ancient writers, was a badge of liberty used on all occasions. It, as well as the rod or wand, referred to the custom of the Romans giving slaves their freedom. In the performance of that ceremony, the rod was held by the magistrate, and the cap by the slave, even for some period previous. Sometimes a cat is found placed at the feet of the deity, this animal being very fond of liberty, and impatient when confined."

Another Roman goddess, whose precepts every one would do well to follow, is thus spoken of, in "Dwight's Mythology," page 290:

"Virtue, daughter of Truth, is represented clothed in white, as an emblem of purity; sometimes holding a sceptre, at others crowned with laurel. In some instances, she is represented with wings, and placed upon a block of marble to intimate her immovable firmness."

It has already been remarked that White. finds one of its broadest and best definitions in

LIGHT.

In the first Epistle of John (chapter i., verses 5–7) may be found this expressive passage:

"This then is the message which we have heard of him, and declare unto you, that God is light, and in him is no darkness at all. If we say that we have fellowship with him, and walk in darkness, we lie, and do not the truth ; but if we walk in the light, as he is in the light, we have fellowship one with another."

The Koran, according to Sale's translation, page 292, informs us that,

"God is the light of heaven and earth ; the similitude of his light is as a niche in a wall, wherein a lamp is placed, and the lamp inclosed in a case of glass ; the glass appears as it were a shining star. It is lighted with the oil of a blessed tree, · an olive neither of the east, nor of the west ; it wanteth little but that the oil thereof would give light, although no fire touched it.   This is light added unto light; and God will direct unto his light whom he pleaseth."

Confucius, the great Chinese philosopher and moralist, taught that,

"The principle of good is entirely absorbed in light ; the principle of evil entirely buried in darkness."

Mythological writers are ever delighted to speak of

"Jupiter, the god of heaven and light."

And also of

"Apollo, the pure and shining god of light."

Lord Bacon has assured us that

"God's first creature was light."

Dryden truly tells us that

"At the cheerful light
The groaning ghosts and birds obscene take flight."

In "The Rape of Lucrece," Shakspeare tells us that

"Light and lust are deadly enemies."

Poor Milton, after he became blind, lamented his misfortunes in these touching words :

"Light, the prime work of God, to me's extinct,
And all her various objects of delight
Annulled, which might in part my grief have eased."

Another poet well assures us that

"A virtuous soul is pure and unmixed light."

Adam Clarke, in one of his Commentaries (Volume IV., page 924) says :

"Light implies every essential excellence ; especially wisdom, holiness, and happiness. Darkness implies all inperfection ; and principally ignorance, sinfulness, and misery. Light is the purest, the most subtle, the most useful, and the most diffusive of all God's creatures ; it is, therefore, a very proper emblem of the purity, perfection, and goodness of the Divine nature. God is to human souls what the light is to the world ; without the latter, all would be dismal and uncomfortable ; and terror and death would universally prevail."

Fullom, in his "Marvels of Science," page 175, says :

"The color of light in direct emanation is white, but in its elements, it embraces seven different tints—namely, red, orange, yellow, green, blue, indigo, and violet. The particular hue is regulated, as already mentioned, by the ratio of ethereal vibration ; blue requiring more numerous undulations than red, while a graduating number of waves produce the various intervening tints. White light, compounded of the whole, may be resolved by absorption and refraction into the seven component parts. Three colors—red, yellow, and blue—are called primary ; the remaining four result from the combination of these, and are designated secondary."

Chevreul, in his excellent work on "Color," page 3, says :

"A ray of solar light is composed of an indeterminate number of differently-colored rays ; and since, on the one hand, it is impossible to distinguish each particular one, and as, on the other, they do not all differ equally from one another, they have been divided into groups, to which are applied the terms red rays, orange rays, yellow rays, green rays, blue rays, indigo rays, and violet rays ; but it must not be supposed that all the rays comprised in the same group, red for instance, are identical in color ; on the contrary, they are generally considered as differing, more or less, among themselves, although we recognize the impression they separately produce as comprised in that which we ascribe to red."

Burke, in his work "On the Sublime and Beautiful," page 178, says:

"In utter darkness, it is impossible to know in what degree of safety we stand; we are ignorant of the objects that surround us; we may every moment strike against some dangerous obstruction; we may fall down a precipice the first step we take; and, if an enemy approach, we know not in what quarter to defend ourselves; in such a case, strength is no sure protection; wisdom can only act by guess; the boldest are staggered; and he who would pray for nothing else toward his defence, is forced to pray for light."

Draper, in his "Intellectual Development of Europe," page 605, says:

"The investigation of the nature and properties of light rivals in interest and value that of electricity. What is this agent, light, which clothes the earth with verdure, making animal life possible, extending man's intellectual sphere, bringing to his knowledge the forms and colors of things, and giving him information of the existence of countless myriads of worlds? What is this light which, in the midst of so many realities, presents him with so many delusive fictions, which rests the colored bow against the cloud—the bow once said, when men transferred their own motives and actions to the Divinity, to be the weapon of God."

Again, in his "Intellectual Development of Europe," page 608, Draper says:

"To the chemical agency of light, much attention has in recent times been devoted. Already, in photography, it has furnished us an art which, though yet in its infancy, presents exquisite representations of scenery, past events, and the countenances of our friends. In an almost magical way it evokes invisible impressions, and gives duration to fleeting shadows. Moreover, these chemical influences of light give birth to the whole vegetable world, with all its varied charms of color, form, and property, and, as we have seen in the last chapter, on them animal life itself depends."

From Tytler's "Elements of General History," page 282, we learn that,

"The Egyptians had a solemn festival called the *Feast of the Lights;* the Chinese have the *Feast of the Lanterns.*"

To which the learned historian might very properly have added, that the Greeks of Argos had the *Feast of the Flambeaux.*

Dr. John Moore, a celebrated Scottish physician and traveler, writing in relation to the effect of light on body and mind, says :

"A tadpole confined in darkness would never become a frog ; and an infant being deprived of Heaven's free light will only grow into a shapeless idiot, instead of a beautiful and reasonable being. Hence, in the deep, dark gorges and ravines of the Swiss Valais, where the direct sunshine never reaches, the hideous prevalence of idiocy startles the traveler. It is a strange, melancholy idiocy. Many citizens are incapable of any articulate speech ; some are deaf, some are blind, some labor under all these privations, and all are misshapen, in almost every part of the body. I believe there is in all places a marked difference in the healthiness of houses according to their aspect with regard to the sun ; and those are decidedly the healthiest, other things being equal, in which all the rooms are, during some parts of the day, fully exposed to the direct light. Epidemics attack inhabitants on the shady side of the street, and totally exempt those on the other side ; and even in epidemics such as ague the morbid influence is often thus partial in its labors."

That very learned biblical commentator, Adam Clarke, from whose high and accurate estimate of Light, we have already quoted, says, in his first volume, page 31 :

"Light is one of the most astonishing productions of the creative skill and power of God. It is the grand medium by which all his other works are discovered, examined, and understood, so far as they can be known."

In his infinite goodness and mercy to man, God has permitted no nebula, no constellation, no ball of black, to be suspended in the firmament. All above us is blue, or white, and light, and bright, and beautiful. One moment's change of the sun, or of any one of the stars, from its luminous qualities into the dismal and death-boding color of the negro, would so corrupt and disarrange the universe, that it could be saved from falling into irremediable chaos, only by the most instantaneous interposition of the Deity.

If we but place ourselves in the open air, and turn our eyes upward, casting them hither and thither, in every possible direction, we shall at once perceive how immutably determined an all-wise Providence is, and ever has been, to hold everything of positive blackness aloof from the regions of

THE SKY AND THE BRIGHT SHINING ORBS.

In happy allusion to the manifold beauties and sublimities of the celestial spaces, Dryden tells us that,

> "There fields of light and liquid ether flow,
> Purged from the ponderous dregs of earth below."

Lord Byron was enraptured with

> "The blue wilderness of interminable air."

Mrs. Hemans was happy in her contemplations of

> "The blue, deep, glorious heavens."

Addison, in the 565th number of the "Spectator," says :

"I was yesterday, about sunset, walking in the open fields, until the night insensibly fell upon me. I at first amused myself with all the richness and variety of colors which appeared in the western part of heaven; in proportion as they faded away and went out, several stars and planets appeared, one after another, until the whole firmament was in a glow. The blueness of the ether was exceedingly heightened and enlivened by the season of the year, and by the rays of all those luminaries that passed through it. The galaxy appeared in its most beautiful white. To complete the scene, the full moon rose at length in that clouded majesty which Milton takes notice of, and opened to the eye a new picture, which was more finely shaded and disposed among softer lights, than that which the sun had before discovered to us."

"As I was surveying the moon walking in her brightness, and taking her progress among the constellations, a thought rose in me which, I believe, very often perplexes and disturbs men of serious and contemplative natures. David himself fell into it in that reflection, 'When I consider the heavens, the work of thy fingers, the moon and the stars, which thou hast ordained: what is man that thou art mindful of him? and the son of man, that thou regardest him?' In the same manner, when I considered that infinite host of stars, or, to speak more philosophically, of suns which were then shining upon me, with those innumerable sets of planets or worlds which were moving round their respective suns; when I still enlarged the idea, and supposed another heaven of suns and worlds rising still above this which we discovered, and these still enlightened by a superior firmament of luminaries, which are planted at so great a distance, that they may appear to the inhabitants of the former as the stars do to us: in short, while I pursued this thought, I could not but reflect on that little, insignificant figure which I myself bore amidst the immensity of God's works."

Ruskin, in his admirable work on "Architecture and Painting," page 23, says:

"You see the broad blue sky every day over your heads; but you do not for that reason determine blue to be less or more beautiful than you did at first; you are unaccustomed to see stones as blue as the sapphire, but you do not for that reason think the sapphire less beautiful than other stones. The blue color is everlastingly appointed by the Deity to be a source of delight; and whether seen perpetually over your head, or crystallized once in a thousand years into a single and incomparable stone, your acknowledgment of its beauty is equally natural, simple, and instantaneous."

Maury, in his "Physical Geography of the Sea," page 127—although he was so unpatriotic as to become a rebel—uses this graphic and beautiful language:

"In the summer of the southern hemisphere the sea breeze is more powerfully developed at Valparaiso than at any other place to which my services afloat have led me. Here regularly in the afternoon, at this season, the sea breeze blows furiously; pebbles are torn up from the walks and whirled about the streets; people seek shelter, the Almendral is descrted, business interrupted, and all communication from the shipping to the shore is cut off. Suddenly the winds and the sea, as if they had again heard the voice of rebuke, are hushed, and there is a great calm. The lull that follows is delightful. The sky is without a cloud; the atmosphere is transparency itself; the Andes seem to draw near; the climate, always mild and soft, becomes now doubly sweet by the contrast. The evening invites abroad, and the population sally forth—the ladies in ball costume, for now there is not wind enough to disarrange the lightest curl. In the southern summer this change takes place day after day with the utmost regularity, and yet the calm always seems to surprise, and to come before one has time to realize that the furious seawind could so soon be hushed. Presently the stars begin to peep out, timidly at first, as if to see whether the elements here below had ceased their strife, and if the scene on earth be such as they, from bright spheres aloft, may shed their sweet influences upon. Sirius, or that blazing world Argus, may be the first watcher to send down a feeble ray; then follow another and another, all smiling meekly; but presently, in the short twilight of the latitude, the bright leaders of the starry host blaze forth in all their glory, and the sky is decked and spangled with superb brilliants. In the twinkling of an eye, and faster than the admiring gazer can tell, the stars seem to leap out from their hiding-places. By invisible hands, and in quick succession, the constellations are hung out; but first of all, and with dazzling glory, in the azure depths of space appears the Great Southern Cross. That shining symbol lends a holy grandeur to the scene, making it still more impressive. Alone in the night-watch, after the sea breeze has sunk to rest, I have stood on the deck under those beautiful skies, gazing, admiring, rapt. I have seen there, above the horizon at once, and shining with a splendor unknown to these latitudes, every star of the first magnitude—save only six—that is contained in the catalogue of 100 principal fixed stars of astronomers. There lies the city on the sea shore, wrapped in sleep. The sky looks solid, like a vault of steel set with diamonds. The stillness below is in harmony with the silence above; and one almost fears to speak, lest the harsh sound of the human voice, reverberating through those vaulted ʻchambers of the south,ʼ should wake up an echo, and drown the music that fills the soul. On looking aloft, the first emotion gives birth to a homeward thought; bright and lovely as they are, those, to northern sons, are not the stars nor the skies of fatherland."

6

Hadfield, in his work on Brazil, page 135, says:

"The sunsets in Bahia are sometimes very fine, and I have noticed that when the twilight is hastening on, a brighter glow will appear, with very vivid and distinct bands of blue and pink, alternately shaded off into each other, and radiating from the spot when the sun has gone down. The difference in the apparent sunset is about half an hour between winter and summer. Bright as the sky is by day, it is brighter far by night, when the spangled heavens are spread out like a curtain. The air is so pure that the stars seem to shine with an increasing brightness. The Southern Cross is a beautiful object; and so different are the heavens from the northern hemisphere, that nothing seems to produce the effect of the long distance from home so much as the difference of the starry constellations. The Milky Way seems to have received fresh refulgence; and all is magnificence."

Says the "New American Cyclopædia," Volume V., page 367:

"Little is known of the causes that produce the brilliant and varied colors often assumed by the sky, particularly at sunset. They are unquestionably, however, connected with the aqueous vapor contained in the atmosphere; and the reddish hue, the most common of all, is probably owing to the greater facility with which these rays are transmitted through the watery vesicles. Reflected from the surface of distant hills, they even give to these a delicate roseate hue."

Milner, in his "Gallery of Nature," page 176, says:

"The contrasted color of the multiple stars, the rich and varied hues with which they shine, is one of their most striking peculiarities. The stars visible to the naked eye, differ in the tints which they display. This, though very apparent, is not so clearly remarked in our own country by the unaided vision, owing to the general haziness of the atmosphere, as in other parts of the globe. But if we were encamped at night upon the plains of Syria, or on those of High Asia, the greatest projection upon the surface of our planet, where the firmament is displayed with greater clearness through the rarity of the circumambient air, the diverse coloring of the stellar light would at once be observed. Sirius, whose advance to the field of view, on directing a telescope to it, has been likened to the dawn of the morning, is so refulgent, that for a time it has been found impossible to endure it, is brilliantly white. There have been some extraordinary changes in the history of this splendid object ; for Sirius, now white, was known to the ancients as a red star, and is so characterized by Ptolemy and Seneca. This is not a solitary phenomenon, but one upon which it is quite useless to speculate. Within the last half century, Leonis and Delphini have very perceptibly changed color. Lyra, Spica, Virginis, Bellatrix, Altair, and Vega are white stars. Procyon and Capella are orange. Aldebaran, Antares, Arcturus, Pollux, and Betelguese are red."

Humboldt, the greatest of modern *Savans*, in his "Cosmos," Volume III., pages 207–209, says:

"The frequent occurrence of contrasted colors constitutes an extremely remarkable peculiarity of multiple stars. Struve, in his great work published in 1837, gave the following results with regard to the colors presented by six hundred of the brighter double stars. In 375 of these, the color of both principal stars and companion was the same and equally intense. In 101, a mere difference of intensity could be discovered. The stars with perfectly different colors were 120 in number, or one-fifth of the whole ; and in the remaining four-fifths the principal and companion stars were uniform in color. In nearly one-half of these six hundred, the principal star and its companion were white. Among those of different colors, combinations of yellow with blue, and of orange with green, are of frequent occurrence."

"Arago was the first to call attention to the fact that the diversity of color in the binary systems principally, or at least in very many cases, has reference to the complementary colors — the subjective colors, which, when united, form white. It is a well-known optical phenomenon, that a faint white light appears green, when a strong red light is brought near it, and that a white light becomes blue, when the stronger surrounding light is yellowish. Arago, however, with his usual caution, has reminded us of the fact, that even though the green or blue tint of the companion star is sometimes the result of contrast, still, on the whole, it is impossible to deny the actual existence of green or blue stars. There are instances in which a brilliant white star is accompanied by a small blue star ; others where, in a double star, both the principal and its companion are blue. In order to determine whether the contrast of colors is merely subjective, he proposes (when the distance allows) to cover the principal star in the telescope by a thread or diaphragm. Commonly it

is only the smaller star that is blue ; this, however, is not the case in
the double star 23 Orionis, where the principal star is bluish, and the
companion pure white.   If, in the multiple stars, the differently
colored suns are frequently surrounded by planets invisible to us,
the latter, being differently illuminated, must have their white, blue,
red and green days !"

"As the periodical variability of the stars is, as we have already
pointed out, by no means necessarily connected with their red or
reddish color, so also coloring in general, or a contrasting difference
of the tones of color between the principal star and its companion, is
far from being peculiar to the multiple stars.   Circumstances which
we find to be frequent are not, on that account, necessary conditions
of the phenomena, whether relating to a periodical change of light
or to the revolution in partial systems round a common centre of
gravity.   A careful examination of the bright double stars (and color
can be determined even in those of the ninth magnitude) teaches
that, besides white, all the colors of the solar spectrum are to be
found in the double stars, but that the principal star, whenever it is
not white, approximates, in general, to the red extreme, (that of the
least refrangible rays,) but the companion to the violet extreme (the
limit of the most refrangible rays.)   The reddish stars are twice as
frequent as the blue and bluish ; the white are about two and a half
times as numerous as the red and reddish.

Again, in the third volume of his "Cosmos," page 130,
Humboldt says :

"A difference of color in the proper light of the fixed stars, as well
as in the reflected light of the planets, was recognized at a very early
period ; but our knowledge of this remarkable phenomenon has been
greatly extended by the aid of telescopic vision, more especially
since attention has been so particularly directed to the double
stars.   We do not here allude to the change of color which, as already
observed, accompanies scintillation even in the whitest star, and
still less to the transient and generally red color exhibited by stellar
light near the horizon, (a phenemenon owing to the character of the
atmospheric medium through which we see it,) but to the white or
colored stellar light radiated from each cosmical body, in consequence of its peculiar luminous process, and the different constitution
of its surface.   The Greek astronomers were acquainted with the red
stars only, while modern science has discovered, by the aid of the
telescope, in the radiant fields of the starry heaven, almost all the

gradations of the prismatic spectrum between the extremes of re-frangibility of the red and the violet ray."

It may also be worth while to invite the reader's attention to some of the non-black but high-colored

PHENOMENA OF THE NEARER ETHEREAL REGIONS

W. Mullinger Higgins, Fellow of the Royal Geological Society, and Lecturer on Natural Philosophy at Guy's Hospital in London, in his work on the "Physical Condition of the Earth," page 177, says:

"There is as much beauty of coloring in aerial as in terrestrial scenery. It is scarcely possible to trace the successions of color in clouds, whether in the light and resplendent hues of the evening cloud, or in the deep and sombre tints of the threatening nimbus. These varied appearances are produced by the absorption, refraction, and reflection of light. * * * The edges of clouds are, generally, much more luminous than their centres, which may be traced to the thinning of the body of vapor at its edges, so that we may determine the density of a cloud by its color. This same cause, absorption, may influence the color of clouds by the abstraction of a portion or the entire of one or more constituent rays. Atmospheric vapor may be variously constituted, and its effects on light may be different, according to its character and mode of combination ; thus, one cloud may absorb the blue, and another the red rays, or such proportions of each may be successively taken away as shall produce a rapid and evanescent series of resplendent colors. * * * The position of clouds in relation to the sun has no small influence in occasioning those rapid changes of form and color for which they are remarkable. It is scarcely possible to imagine that the clouds, which at sunset may be absolutely drenched in golden hues, have before floated over the hemisphere as colorless and flaccid masses ; yet we cannot watch a mass of vapor over the face of the heavenly vault, without observing the infinite variety of colors and shades which it assumes, as fickle, and frequently not less vivid, than the hues of the celestial bow."

Again, in his "Physical Condition of the Earth," page 179, Mr. Mullinger Higgins says :

"The rainbow is always seen in that part of the sky opposite to the sun.   There are, however, two bows, of which the interior is the stronger, being formed by one reflection, the exterior by two. Supernumerary bows have been occasionally seen. The primary or inner bow, which is commonly seen alone, consists of arches of color in the following order, commencing with the innermost: violet, indigo, blue, green, yellow, orange, and red. These, as we have already stated, are the primitive colors, and we may be led to a suspicion of the cause of the rainbow by the fact that they have the same proportion in the bow as in the prismatic spectrum."

Humboldt, in his " Cosmos," Volume V., page 149, says :

"In the higher latitudes, the prevailing color of the polar light is usually white, while it presents a milky hue when the aurora is of faint intensity. When the colors brighten, they assume a yellow tinge ; the middle of the broad ray becomes golden yellow, while both the edges are marked by separate bands of red and green. When the radiation extends in narrow bands, the red is seen above the green. When the aurora moves sideways, from left to right, or from right to left, the red appears invariably in the direction toward which the ray is advancing, and the green remains behind it. It is only in very rare cases that either one of the complementary colors, green or red, has been seen alone. Blue is never seen, while dark red, such as is presented by the reflection of a great fire, is so rarely observed in the north that Siljestrom noticed it only on one occasion. The luminous intensity of the aurora never, even in Finmark, quite equals that of the full moon."

Byron, in his " Childe Harold's Pilgrimage," Canto II, Stanza XLVIII., exclaims :

"Where'er we gaze, around, above, below,
What rainbow tints, what magic charms are found !
Rock, river, forest, mountain, all abound,
And bluest skies that harmonize the whole."

Light and White, White and Light, and all the Primary Colors, are pure and everlasting emanations from Deity, and have, for their fields of gorgeous display, their own native heavens and the earth, and all the measureless ex-

panse of intervening space.   Black is an alien and pernicious shade upon our planet—a most base and baneful
dye from hell—limited as to the period of its existence
among us—and has for its principal companions and representatives, its originator the devil, the negro, and the
night-raven.

White, in addition to its own supremacy of purity and
perfection, when alone and unmixed, is, in a greater
or less degree, blended with every other bright and beautiful color.   We may, therefore, at this stage of our imperfect inquiries into the unbounded and imperishable
merits of white, pay some little attention to the

CLEAR AND GAY COLORS IN GENERAL.

Henry Home (Lord Kames) in his "Elements of Criticism," page 161, says:

"Nature in no particular seems more profuse of ornament, than
in the beautiful coloring of her works.   The flowers of plants, the
furs of beasts, and the feathers of birds, vie with each other in the
beauty of their colors, which in lustre as well as in harmony are beyond the power of imitation.   Of all natural appearances, the coloring of the human face is the most exquisite; it is the strongest instance of the ineffable art of nature, in adapting and proportioning
its colors to the magnitude, figure, and position, of the parts.   In a
word, color seems to live in nature only, and to languish under the
finest touches of art."

W. Mullinger Higgins, in his "Physical Condition of
the Earth," page 177, says:

"If the infinite variety of color which we observe in nature did
not exist, then all the forms, however beautiful, which decorate the
earth, would lose their charm, and the eye would ever rest upon a
dull, monotonous scene, incapable of exciting a single feeling of interest."

Eugene Chevreul, the learned and distinguished superintendent of the celebrated Dyeing Establishment of the

Gobelins, in Paris, in his elaborate work on "Color," page 322, says:

"Whether we contemplate the works of nature or of art, the varied colors under which we view them is one of the finest spectacles man is permitted to enjoy. This explains how the desire of reproducing the colored images of objects we admire, or which under any name interest us, has produced the art of painting ; how the imitation of the works of the painter, by means of threads or small prisms, has given birth to the arts of weaving tapestry and carpets, and to mosaics ; how the necessity for multiplying certain designs economically has led to printing of all kinds, and to coloring. Finally, this explains how man has been led to paint the walls and wood-work of his buildings, as well as to dye the stuffs for his clothing, and for the interior decoration of his dwellings."

Chevreul, again, in his work on "Color," page 360, says:

"Whenever man seeks distraction from without, whether the pleasures of meditation are unknown to him, or thought fatigues him for a time, he feels the necessity of seeing a variety of objects. In the first case, he goes in quest of excitement, in order to escape from ennui ; in the second he is desirous of diverting his thoughts, at least for a time, into another channel. In both cases man flies monotony ; a variety of external objects is what he desires. Finally, the artist, the enlightened amateur, and less cultivated minds, all seek variety in works of art and nature. It is to satisfy this want that various colors in objects please more than a single color, at least when these objects occupy a certain space, that our monuments have many accessory parts which are only ornaments ; that in furniture we use many things which, without being useful, strictly speaking, please by their elegance of form, their colors, their brilliancy."

Timothy Dwight favors us with these just and apposite reflections:

"Were all the interesting diversities of color and form to disappear, how unsightly, dull, and wearisome would be the aspect of the world. * * * The ever-varying brilliancy and grandeur of the landscape, and the magnificence of the sky, sun, moon, and stars, enter more extensively into the enjoyment of mankind, than, perhaps, we ever think, or can possibly apprehend, without frequent and extensive investigation. This beauty and splendor of the objects around us, it is ever to be remembered, are not necessary to their existence, nor to what we commonly intend by their usefulness. It is, therefore, to be regarded as a source of pleasure gratuitously superinduced upon the general nature of the objects themselves, and in this light as a testimony of the Divine goodness peculiarly affecting."

The "Encyclopædia Britannica," Volume IV., page 551, says:

"All bright and clear colors are naturally typical of cheerfulness and purity of mind, and are hailed as emblems of moral qualities, to which no one can be indifferent. * * * Darkness, and all that approaches it, is naturally associated with ideas of melancholy, of helplessness, and danger; and the gloomy hues that remind us of it, or seem to draw upon it, must share in the same association."

Sir Isaac Newton, in a paper entitled "Theory of Light and Colors," which was read before the Royal Society of London, in 1672, and which may be found in the "Treasury of Natural and Experimental Philosophy," page 34, says:

"There are two sorts of colors; the one original and simple, the other compounded of these. The original or primary colors are red, yellow, green, blue, and a violet-purple, together with orange, indigo, and an indefinite variety of intermediate gradations. But the most surprising and wonderful composition is that of whiteness. There is no one sort of rays which alone can exhibit this. It is ever compounded, and to its composition are requisite all the aforesaid primary colors, mixed in a due proportion. I have often with admiration beheld, that all the colors of the prism being made to converge, and thereby to be again mixed as they were in the light before it was incident upon the prism, reproduced light, entirely and perfectly white, and not at all sensibly differing from a direct light of the sun, unless when the glasses I used were not sufficiently clear; for then they would a little incline it to their own color."

The "New American Cyclopædia," Volume V., page 494, says:

"When white or solar light is transmitted through triangular

6*

prisms of glass, or other media .differing in dispersive power from the air, the beam or ray of white is analyzed, being separated into the seven primary colors, red, orange, ycllow, green, blue, indigo, and violet. The prism turns all these colors out of the straight line pursued by the white light, the violct most, the red least, so that instead of a round white spot, it throws upon a screen an elongated or oval figure, containing in succession the several colors already named. The most bent or refracted color, violet, may be called the highest color, the red the lowest ; the whole figure is the solar spectrum. The primary colors have never been further decomposed by any process to which they have been submitted ; hence they are considered as elementary or simple. Recombined by a second inverted prism or a lens, they again form white light. The colors are those of the rainbow, but reversed in order, owing to a difference in the mode of viewing. The proof that these are the elements of white light was first furnished by the experiments of Sir Isaac Newton, in 1672. It must be added, however, that, between any two of the simple colors . of the spectrum, there is a gradual interchange of hue, so that, in fact, the different colored rays existing in and obtainable from the white ray are not seven only, but indefinite in number."

The "Enclyclopædia Britannica," volume VIII., page 153, says :

"A yellow color generally indicates a bitter taste ; as in gentian, aloe, celandine, and turmeric. Red indicates an acid or sour taste ; as in cranberries, currants, raspberries, mulberries, cherries, and the service. Green indicates a crude alkaline taste ; as in leaves and unripe fruits. White promises a sweet, luscious taste ; as in white currants, plums, and apples. Black indicates a harsh, nauseous, disagreeable taste ; as in the berries of deadly night-shade, myrtle-leaved sumach, herb Christopher, and others, many of which are not only unpleasant to the taste, but pernicious and deadly in their effects.

The "London Encyclopædia," Volume VI., page 196, says :

"Colors in the Latin and Greek churches, are used to distinguish several mysteries and feasts celebrated therein. Five colors only are regularly admitted, namely : white, green, red, violet, and black. The white is for the mysteries of Christ, the feast of the Virgin, those of the angels, saints and confessors ; the red is for the solemnities of the holy sacrament, and for the feasts of the apostles and martyrs ; the green is for the time between pentecost and advent, and from epiphany to septnagessima ; the violet in advent, and Christmas, in vigils, rogations, and in votive masses in time of war ; lastly the black is for the dead, and the ceremonies thereto belonging.

Chevreul, in his treatise on " Color, " page 161, says:

" The stained glass of Gothic churches, by intercepting the white light which gives too vivid and unsuitable a glare for meditation, have always the most beautiful effect. If we seek the cause, we shall find it not only in the contrast of their colors so favorably opposed, but also in the contrast of their transparency with the opacity of the walls which surround them and of the lead which binds them together. The impression produced on the eye, in virtue of this twofold cause, is the more vivid the more frequently and the longer they are viewed each time. The windows of a Gothic church are generally either circular, or pointed at the tops in *ogive*, with vertical sides. The stained glass of the first usually represent great rose-windows, where yellow, blue, violet, orange, red, and green, appear jewels of the most precious stones. The windows of the second almost always represent, amid a border or a ground analogous to the rose-windows, a figure of a saint in perfect harmony with those which stand in relief about the portals of the edifice; and these latter figures, to be appreciated at their true value, must be judged as parts of a whole, and not as a Greek statue, which is intended to be seen isolated on all sides."

Again, in his treatise on " Color," page 192, Chevreul says:

"The coloring of Geographical Charts, as is well known, gives many advantages in presenting readily to the eyes their different component parts, whether continent, empire, kingdom, or republic, state or country. Until lately, the coloring of maps has always depended upon the caprice of the colorer; yet it appears to me there are some rules which it would not be useless to observe. The colors should be as pale as possible, especially those which are naturally sombre, as blue and violet, so that the reading of the names may always be easy; but preference must be given to the luminous colors, red, orange, yellow, and light green, and to employing only their bright tones."

Alison, in his "Principles of Taste," page 185, says:

"Rose-color is a more beautiful color than that of mahogany; yet if any man were to paint his doors and windows with rose-color, he would certainly not add to their beauty. The color of a polished steel grate is agreeable, but is not, in itself, very beautiful. Suppose it to be painted green, or violet, or crimson, all of which are much more beautiful colors, and the beauty of it will be altogether destroyed. The colors of cedar, of mahogany, of satin-wood, are not nearly so beautiful as many other colors that may be mentioned. There is no color, however, with which such woods can be painted that would be so beautiful as the colors of the woods themselves; because they are very valuable, and the colors are, in some measure, significant to us of this value."

From a note to the "Gospel of the Infancy of Jesus Christ"—one of the books of "The Apocryphal New Testament," page 23—we learn that,

"There are several stories believed of Christ, proceeding from the Gospel of the Infancy, as that which Professor Sike relates out of La Brosse's Persic Lexicon, that Christ practiced the trade of a dyer, and his working a miracle with the colors; from whence the Persian dyers honor him as their patron, and a dye-house is called the shop of Christ."

Dr. Charles Pickering, in his "Races of Man," page 151, says:

"A change had taken place in the national taste in regard to colors; yellow, the favorite with the Malayan race, giving place, among the Feejeans, to vermilion-red. White seemed in some measure a rival; for the lace-like tapa covering the hair of the men in the semblance of a turban, together with the belt or sash completing their dress, were invariably white. By a coincidence showing actual accordance with the complexion, red and white were subsequently found to be the favorite colors with the equally dark Telingans of Hindoostan; and were used almost exclusively in the dress of those seen at Singapore."

Again, in his "Races of Man," page 46, Dr. Pickering says:

"Yellow is the favorite color throughout the countries inhabited by the Malay race; and it appears to be really the one most becoming to the deep brown complexion."

Haydn, in his "Dictionary of Dates," page 98, says:

"Blue was the favorite color of the Scotch Covenanters in the 16th century.   Blue and orange or yellow, became the Whig colors, after the revolution in 1688; and were adopted on the cover of the Whig periodical, the *Edinburgh Review*, first published in 1802.   The Prussian Blue dye was discovered by Diesbach, at Berlin, in 1710."

Munsell, in his "Every Day Book of History and Chronology," page 470, says:

"Pope Innocent IV., about the middle of the 13th century, invested the cardinals, for the first time, with a red hat, as a mark of dignity."

Robert Boyle, the "able and sedulous Investigator of Nature by Experiment," asks this quaint but philosophical question:

"What principle manages the white and yolk of an egg into such variety of textures, as is requisite to fashion a chick?"

Goldsmith, in his "History of the Earth and Animated Nature," Volume I., page 247, says :

"Of all the colors by which mankind is diversified, it is easy to perceive that ours is not only the most beautiful to the eye, but also the most advantageous.   The fair complexion seems, if I may so express it, as a transparent covering to the soul ; all the variations of the passions, every expression of joy or sorrow, flows to the cheek, and, without language, marks the mind.   In the slightest change of health also, the color of the European face is the most exact index, and often teaches us to prevent those disorders that we do not as yet perceive."

In his treatise on "Color," page 69, Chevreul says :

"The splendor of the White is so dominant, that, whatever be the difference of light or of brilliancy observable between the different colors associated, there will always be harmony of contrast, as must follow from what has already been stated of the influence of White in elevating the tone and augmenting the intensity of the color which is next to it."

Again, Chevreul, in his treatise on "Color," pages 19, 20, 251, says :

"White heightens the tone of the colors with which it is placed in contact. * * * The lowering of the tone of a color in contact with black is always perceptible. * * * White always exalts all colors by raising their tone."

The "Encyclopædia Metropolitana," Volume XXV., page 1243, says :

"White things are most conspicuous."

Except the negroes, who are uninstructable and unimprovable dunces by destiny, there are, it may be reasonably inferred, but few creatures in "the human form divine" who are not more or less familiar with

"The glowing colors of poetry."

Shakspeare's works are almost universally known—the more known the better for the world—to be replete with chaste and sublime expressions, such, for instance, as those of which the following are but mere fragments :

"Angel whiteness."
"Purity and whiteness."
"Pure congealed whiteness."
"White and spotless hue."
"Immaculate white and red."
"Good white head."
"Pure white robes."

Whittier, in his "Nature's Worship," and in his other poems, speaks of

"The white wings of prayer."
"The white soul."
"In the white robes of angels clad."

Bryant, true patriot and poet as he is, has ever been solicitous to foster in his countrymen a just and lively admiration of

"Freedom's white hands."

Ripley and Dana, in their "New American Cyclopædia," Volume VI., page 107, have incidentally made us acquainted with a very special and becoming use of gold letters on white satin. In their biographical sketch of Derzhavin, the great lyrical poet of Russia—one of the most heaven-inspired poets of any country—they say :

"Many of his poems abound in beautiful moral sentiments and expressions, especially his Ode to God, which was not only translated into several European languages, but also into Chinese and Japanese. It is said to have been hung up in the palace of the emperor of China, printed in gold letters on white satin, and, according to Golownin's account, it was placed in the same manner in the temple of Jeddo."

Yet it is not only in the upper heavens, nor in the lower heavens ; not only in the higher regions of ether, nor in the less elevated realms of the atmosphere ; not only in the rarefied altitudes of mid-air, nor in the zephyr-cooled eminences of cloud-space ; not only about the towering summits of the mountains, nor in the vicinity of the tall steeples and the house-tops ; not only along the far-out-stretched horizon, and upon the ever-tangible levels of our own heads and hands—that there is always a profuse display of varied and beautiful colors. Around us, above us, beneath us—everywhere, indeed, out of the dominions of absolute darkness and death—all Nature is continually bedecked in light-colored and comely attire. Incontrovertible evidences of this fact, so pleasingly apparent elsewhere, are also pleasingly apparent in both—

LAND AND WATER.

Sir Charles Lyell, in his "Manual of Elementary Geology," page 240, says :

"The area over which the white chalk preserves a nearly homogeneous aspect is so vast, that the earlier geologists despaired of discovering any analogous deposits of recent date. Pure chalk of nearly uniform aspect and composition, is met with in a northwest and southeast direction, from the north of Ireland to the Crimea, a distance of 1,140 geographical miles, and, in an opposite direction, it extends from the south of Sweden to the south of Bordeaux, a distance of about 840 geographical miles. In Southern Russia, according to Sir R. Murchison, it is sometimes 600 feet thick, and retains the same mineral character as in France and England, with the same fossils."

It is said that the Roman conquerors, under Julius Cæsar, called England *Albion*, from the chalky cliffs and soil of its southern shore ; and that the Phœnicians and other traders from the Orient called it the *White Island.*

Thomas Witlam Atkinson, in the course of his graphic and very interesting description of his seven years' travels through "Oriental and Western Siberia," pages 368, 369, after speaking at considerable length of the beautifully colored porphyries, agates, beryls, amethysts, and other rocks and precious stones which he saw there, says :

"Along the borders of the lakes of the Altai, we found the plants and flowers growing with a tropical luxuriance, which imparted to the scene quite an enchanting aspect. Indeed, it was savage nature adorned with some of her most lovely ornaments. The deep red on the granite, the gray, purple and orange on the slate, with the bright yellow of the birches on the distant rocks, overtopped as they were by deep, purple mountains, rendered this a study of inestimable value. Had Ruskin been with us in the painted solitude of the Altai, he must have acknowledged that Dame Nature was a colorist more Turneresque than Turner himself. * * * The rocks are of every variety of color—some bright-red, others purple, yellow, and green.

I saw several beautiful specimens of marble, one a white with purple spots; another, white with bluish-purple veins; also masses of a deep plum-colored jasper."

John Campbell, an English missionary to the negroes, in the early part of the present century, in his "Travels in South Africa," page 362, says :

"Some of us walked after breakfast to examine the Asbestos Mountains, where we found plenty of that rare mineral, between the strata of the rocks. That which becomes by a little beating soft as cotton, is of the color of Prussian blue. When ascending a mountain alone, I found some of the color of gold; but it was not soft, or of a cotton texture, like the blue; some I found white, and brown, and green. Had this part of Africa been known to the ancients, in the days of imperial Rome, many a mercantile pilgrimage would have been made to the Asbestos Mountains in Griqua land. Were the ladies' gowns, in England, woven of this substance, many lives would annually be saved that are now lost by their dresses catching fire; for cloth made from it stands the fire, and the ancients burned their dead in such cloth to retain their real ashes."

Marble white, granite gray, and sandstone brown, have always, in all parts of the world, been selected as the material for the most imposing and enduring edifices, whether public or private; and also for pillars, arches, abutments, monuments and tombs. Carrara Marble, Parian Marble, and Alabaster, fashioned into vases and other useful ornaments, many of which are most pleasingly white and transparent, are now rapidly finding their way into the houses of the opulent in every part of the habitable globe.

Very beautiful, also, are the Gneiss Ashlers of Carolina, the Feldspar of Labrador, the Fluor-spar of England, the orange-colored Crystals of Sicily, and many other rocks and stones all over the world.

Almost the only black things emboweled in the earth are things which, like Coal and Jet, have become black, after having undergone the fatal change from life to death. Between these things and the negro, however, there is this trifling difference, that while they are black in death, he is black in life. They, in their original woody or fibrous state, seem always to have been, like the negro, good for nothing ; they were barren ; they cumbered the ground ; and, by command of the Almighty, they were cut down and hid from the fair face of Nature. This obvious fact in the vegeto-geological world clearly indicates what is to be the nigh-drawing doom of the African. The only possible advantage, or even semblance of advantage, which the respectable and permanent races of mankind may ever reasonably expect to accrue to them from the circumstance of the negro's ever having had an existence, will make its appearance, if at all, long ages after he and every one of his worthless kith and kin shall have been detruded and fossilized among the earth's deep-dipping strata.

Not one of the precious metals—not a single one of the elementary substances — is black. Indeed, but for the beautiful colors of gold and silver and precious stones, there would be far less charm or inducement for man to struggle so hard to obtain them. In every case, to a greater or less extent, it is their very color which give them value. The colors of Gold, Silver, Copper, Iron, Lead, Nickel, Zinc, Mercury, Bismuth, Cobalt, and other useful metals, are too well known to require description ; Cadmium, Aluminum, Magnesium, Antimony, and others, are white ; Potassium, Sodium, Calcium, Manganese, Tellurium, Rhodium, and others, are grayish white ; while Platinum, Palladium, and others, are bluish white.

Edgar A. Poe, in the second volume of his miscellaneous works, page 299, tells us that,

"The Italians have little sentiment beyond marble and colors."

Allen, in one of his Moral Sonnets, thus alludes to the beautiful colors of certain well-known gems:

> "I've struck the milk-white quartz with gentle blow,
> And split with hammer, fragments from the rock,
> When lo, unquarried by the shivering shock,
> The precious emerald's crystal beauties glow!
> Thus from the mine of thought, obscure and low,
> Does force of argument the gem unlock,
> Whose charms the beams of star-born diamond mock;
> That gem is truth—the truth which angels know!"

Maury, in his "Physical Geography of the Sea," page 19, tells us, not of the pearls, nor of the corals, nor of the conches, nor of any of the other solid and shining treasures of the ocean; nor yet of the brilliant phosphorescent phenomena of the blue and briny deep; but, with his terse powers of description, he does tell us of the color of the Gulf Stream; thus:

> "There is a river in the ocean: in the severest droughts it never fails, and in the mightiest floods it never overflows; its banks and its bottom are of cold water, while its current is of warm; the Gulf of Mexico is its fountain, and its mouth is in the Arctic Seas. It is the Gulf Stream. There is in the world no other such majestic flow of waters. Its current is more rapid than the Mississippi or the Amazon, and its volume more than a thousand times greater. Its waters, as far out from the Gulf as the Carolina coasts, are of an indigo blue. They are so distinctly marked, that their line of junction with the common sea-water may be traced by the eye. Often one half of the vessel may be perceived floating in Gulf Stream water, while the other half is in the common water of the sea—so sharp is the line, and such the want of affinity between these waters, and such, too, the reluctance, so to speak, on the part of those of the Gulf Stream to mingle with the littoral waters of the sea."

Could we but lift the mighty volume of waters from the bed of the ocean, the ample display of dolphins, bonitoes, wrasses, sticklebacks, shells, corals, and other beautifully colored marine objects, which we should there behold (including the mermaids, if any, all divested of their liquid drapery) would doubtless cause us to join enthusiastically in the exclamation of Somerville,

> "What bright enamel, and what various dyes !
> What lively tints delight our wondering eyes !"

Now hasten we to pay our *devoirs* to the

BELLES AND BRIDES OF BEAUTY.

Fairness of complexion is one of the very first requisites of beauty and loveliness in women. No negro woman ever was, or will be, blessed with a fair complexion; *ergo*, no negro woman ever could, or can be, either beautiful or lovely. How elegantly and bewitchingly ladies are generally set off by their own inherent conditions of whiteness, and by a judicious display of white paraphernalia, may be inferred from the advice to them by their old but gallant friend Ovid, who, in the third book of his "Art of Love," says :

> "I need not warn you of two pow'rful smells,
> Which sometimes health or kindly heat expels ;
> Nor from your tender legs to pluck with care
> The casual growth of all unseemly hair.
> Tho' not to nymphs of Caucasus I sing,
> Nor such who taste remote the Mysian spring,
> Yet let me warn you that thro' no neglect
> You let your teeth disclose the least defect.
> You know the use of white to make you fair,
> And how with red lost color to repair ;
> Imperfect eyebrows you by art can mend,
> And skin, when wanting, o'er a scar extend ;
> Nor need the fair one be asham'd who tries
> By art to add new lustre to her eyes.
> *　　*　　*　　*　　*
> Whose fingers are too fat, and nails too coarse,
> Should always shun much gesture in discourse ;
> And you whose breath is touch'd, this caution take,
> Nor fasting, nor too near another, speak.

Let not the nymph with laughter much abound,
Whose teeth are black, uneven, or unsound.
You'd hardly think how much on this depends,
And how a laugh or spoils a face or mends.
Gape not too wide, lest you disclose your gums,
And lose the dimple which the cheek becomes.
Nor let your sides too long concussions shake,
Lest you the softness of the sex forsake :
In some, distortions quite the face disguise ;
Another laughs, that you would think she cries.
In one, too hoarse a voice we hear betray'd ;
Another's is as harsh as if she bray'd.

*　　*　　*　　*　　*

If snowy white your neck, you still should wear
That, and the shoulder of the left arm bare ;
Such sights ne'er fail to fire my am'rous heart,
And make me pant to kiss the naked part !"

Chaucer, in his " Court of Love," says :

"She made no answer, and I soon retir'd,
  To press not daring, tho' by love inspir'd ;
  But still her image dwelt within my breast,
  Too excellent to be in verse express'd.
  Her head is round, and flaxen is her hair ;
  Her eyebrows darker, but her forehead fair ;
  Straight is her nose ; her eyes like emeralds bright ;
  Her well-made cheeks are lovely red and white ;
  Short is her mouth, her lips are made to kiss,
  Rosy and full, and prodigal of bliss ;
  Her teeth like ivory are, well-sized and even,
  And to her breath ethereal sweets are given ;
  Her hands are snowy white, and small her waist,
  And what is yet untold is sure the best."

Sir Walter Scott, in his "Ivanhoe," page 61, says :

"Of Rowena's beauty you shall soon be judge ; and if the purity
of her complexion, and the majestic, yet soft expression of a mild
blue eye, do not chase from your memory the black-dressed girls of
Palestine, ay, or the houris of old Mahomet's paradise, I am an in-
fidel, and no true son of the church."

Oliver Goldsmith, in the second number of "The Bee,"
says:

"I remember, a few days ago, to have walked behind a damsel
tossed out in all the gayety of fifteen; her dress was loose, un-
studied, and seemed the result of conscious beauty. I called up all
my poetry on this occasion, and fancied twenty Cupids prepared for
execution in every folding of her white négligée."

The readers of Cervantes will remember the glowing
description given by the facetious Sancho Panza, to his
renowned master Don Quixote, of the beautiful lady Dul-
cinea, of Toboso, and her pretty maids, who were all
"one blaze of flaming gold, all strings of pearl, all
diamonds, rubies, cloth of tissue above ten hands deep;
their tresses loose about their shoulders, like so many
sunbeams playing with the wind," and who, in the plain
of La Mancha, were severally mounted on palfreys "white
as the driven snow."
Says Ovid, in his "Art of love,"

"White's the expressive image of the fair."

Solomon, whose remarkably high and extensive appre-
ciation of the sex, seems never to have been surpassed,
sang thus :

"My beloved is white and ruddy,
The chiefest among ten thousand."

Edward Young, the author of "Night Thoughts," in
his tragedy entitled "The Revenge," Act I., Scene II.,
says :

"Those eyes that tell us what the sun is made of;
Those lips whose touch is to be bought with life;
Those hills of driven snow, which seen are felt;
All these possest are naught, but as they are
The proof, the substance of an inward passion,
And the rich plunder of a taken heart."

Shakspeare, in his poem entitled "The Rape of Lucrece," says :

> "With more than admiration he admired
> Her azure veins, her alabaster skin,
> Her coral lips, her snow-white dimpled chin.

Madame de Chatelain, in her "Bridal Etiquette," says :

"What interests the bride even more than her outfit, is the choice of the dress she is to wear on her wedding day. This, like all the rest, must depend upon her fortune and position in life ; still, whatever be the material, it should be white. Although not quite sharing in the superstitious notion of a lady we once met with, who attributed her want of happiness in the marriage state to the fatal fault of having put a black mantilla over her bridal attire, still we confess we do not like to see a young lady, especially, go to the altar in any but a white dress. If a widow likes to wear a colored silk, let her do so by all means—there is almost a modest propriety on her part in declining to play the bride a second time in her life— and if those of limited means prefer, like the Vicar of Wakefield's wife, to choose their dress for its solidity rather than its beauty, we can but respect their economical motives ; but where no such reasons exist, we cannot fancy any young maiden dressed otherwise than in white.

The "New American Cyclopædia," Volume I., page 683, says :

"Among the Romans the wedding day was fixed, at least in early times, by consulting the auspices, and the bride was attired in bright yellow shoes, and a veil of the same color, and in a long white robe, adorned with a purple fringe and with ribbons, and bound about the waist with a girdle or zone, to be unloosed by the bridegroom."

The foregoing extracts (with the one now added from Shakspeare) are, it is believed, quite sufficient to establish the fact that there has always been, and still is, but one appropriate color for the dress of brides,

> "Whose white investments figure innocence."

Here it may not be amiss to offer some suggestions as to certain important advantages of health and pleasure, which, it is believed, would be likely to result to mankind at large, by a universal adoption of white and other light colors, in

ARTICLES OF DRESS AND OTHER FABRICS.

He who is reputed to have been the wisest man that ever lived, not even excepting Solon nor Socrates—Solomon king of Israel—has, in Ecclesiastes ix., 8, bequeathed to posterity this very just and wholesome injunction :

"Let thy garments be always white."

The following extract from Percival's "Library of Useful Information," page 467, is, on the part of white people all over the habitable globe, worthy to be perused and pondered with the most earnest and undivided attention :

"Dr. Stark, an English physician, has instituted a series of experiments, the result of which proves, that varieties of color greatly modify the capability of substances for imbibing and giving out odors. Dr. Stark's attention was drawn to this subject by observing that a black dress, which he happened to wear while performing dissections at the anatomical rooms, contracted a most intolerable smell from the dead bodies ; whereas, the light olive colored garments, which he had usually worn, were almost entirely free from the like inconvenience. His first experiment was made by inclosing equal quantities of black and white wool, with a small piece of camphor ; the black wool was found to have become much the more odorous of the two. The result was the same, when wool of each color was shut up in a drawer with assafœtida. He afterward inclosed black, blue, red, green, yellow, and white wool, with assafœtida and with camphor ; the black imbibed the strongest odor ; then the blue, then the red, and next the green ; the yellow wool was but very faintly scented, and the white scarcely at all. The wool of sheep attracted a stronger odor than cotton wool ; and all animal substances become scented in a greater degree than those of a vegetable nature, and appear to have a particular attraction for fetid odors."

"These facts suggest many important hints, as to the regulations which it may be proper to adopt, in cases of contagious disease, and during the prevalence of epidemics. It is usual to purify infected places by raising a high temperature within them, and by the use of chlorine, fumigation with sulphur, washing with quick-lime, and freely ventilating them. Dr. Stark is of opinion, that, in many cases, mere white-washing may be more efficacous than these, or any other measures. When the cholera visited Scotland, most of the narrow lanes, alleys and staircases of Edinburgh were white-washed; and to this is attributed the mildness of the disease, in that metropolis. The deleterious emanations, meeting with no dark surfaces to absorb them, were swept away by the currents of air. The walls of hospitals, prisons, and of all apartments where a number of occupants are congregated together, should be white-washed ; the bedsteads, chairs, tables, and other furniture, should be white, and likewise the garments of the attendants. The black suits, almost invariably worn by physicians, unquestionably render them more liable to communicate disease in going their daily rounds among the sick and well. Instead of black broadcloth, (which, besides its color, attracts bad smells the more powerfully, as being an animal substance,) the dress of the medical profession ought to be white cotton— a garb little suited, it must be owned, to the gravity of an M. D."

"Most persons have heard of the Black Assize, as it was called, where the Judges, while holding at a court of Oxford, together with a great number of people, were suddenly taken sick and died. This occurred in July, 1577 ; and Lord Bacon observes, that similar instances of sickness and mortality happened two or three times, within his memory. There was another instance in 1750, at the Old Bailey in London, where four Judges, several Counselors, an under Sheriff, with Jurymen and others, to the number of above forty, lost their lives by a sudden attack of some mysterious disorder. In all these cases, the mortality was attributed to a putrid effluvium, which either came from the neighboring jail, or was exhaled from the persons of the prisoners, when brought into court. This doubtless was its true origin ; and Dr. Stark conceives that the infectious odor was attracted to the judges, counselors, sheriffs, and other official persons, by the black garments which they wore in the discharge of their duties."

7

Abraham Rees, in the course of an article on BLACK, in the fourth volume of "Rees's Cyclopædia," says :

"The inflammability of black bodies, and their disposition to acquire heat beyond those of other colors, are easily evinced.' Some persons appeal to the experiment of a white and black glove worn in the same sun ; and the consequence in such case, is a very sensibly greater degree of heat in the one than in the other. Others allege the phenomena of burning glasses, by which black bodies are always found to kindle soonest ; thus a burning glass, too weak to have any visible effect at all upon white paper, will readily kindle the same paper rubbed over with ink. Mr. Boyle gives other proofs still more obvious ; he took a large tile, and having whited over one-half of its superficies, and blacked the other, exposed it to the sun ; where, having let it lie a convenient time, he found that, whilst the whited part remained still cool, the black part was grown very hot. For further satisfaction, the same author has sometimes left on the surface of the tile a part retaining its native red, and, exposing all to the sun, has found the latter to have contracted a heat in comparison of the white part, but inferior to that of the black. So also on his exposing two pieces of silk, one white the other black, in the same window to the sun, he often found the latter considerably heated, when the former has remained cool. It is observable, likewise, that rooms hung with black are not only darker, but warmer than others. * * * To all which may be added, that a virtuoso of unsuspected credit assured Mr. Boyle, that, in a hot climate, he had, by carefully blackening the shells of eggs, and exposing them to the sun, seen them thereby well roasted in a short time. * * * Dr. Watson, the present bishop of Londoff, covered the bulb of a thermometer with a black coating of Indian ink, in consequence of which the mercury rose ten degrees."

Again, the learned encyclopædist, in the fourth volume of "Rees's Cyclopaedia," says :

"Black is something that imbibes the greatest part of the light that falls on it, and reflects little or none. In matters of dress, black is the distinguishing habit of mourners. Clothes dyed of this color wear out faster than those of any other, because their substance is more penetrated and corroded by the vitriol necessary to strike their dye, than other bodies are by the galls and alum which suffice for them. Black clothes heat more, and dry sooner in the sun, than white clothes. Black is, therefore, a bad color for clothes in hot climates."

Boyle, one of the most eminent philosophers of the seventeenth century, says :

"Cloths imbued with black cannot afterward be dyed into lighter colors."

Kirkland, in his "Commercial Anecdotes," Volume II., page 425, speaking of the "Bankruptcy of a Dealer in 'Women's Blacks,' says :

"Women's blacks is the term for the common black worsted stockings formerly an article of very extensive consumption ; they are now little made, because little worn. One of the greatest wholesale dealers in these 'women's blacks,' in an English manufacturing town, was celebrated for the largeness of his stock ; his means enabled him to purchase all that were offered to him for sale, and it was his favorite article. He was an old-fashioned man, and while the servant maids were leaving them off, he was unconscious of the change, because he could not believe it ; he insisted that it was impossible that household work could be done in 'white cottons,' staking his judgment as a business man on this assertion. Offers of quantities were made to him at reduced prices, which he bought ; his immense capital thus became locked up in his favorite 'women's blacks ; whenever their price in the market lowered, he could not make his mind up to put his stock low enough to invite purchasers ; his warehouses were filled with them. When, however, he at last determined to sell, the demand had wholly ceased ; he could effect no sales ; and becoming bankrupt, he literally died of a broken heart."

It is to be hoped that the fate of this gruff and ungallant dealer in "Women's Blacks," may serve as a warning to every other "lord of creation," who would so far forget his duty to the sex as to be willing to have their pretty ankles hid within the unsightly and deleterious network of black stockings. The under-clothing, even with fewer exceptions than the outer, should be of pure white, both for men and for women ; and he who would wear black shirts or black drawers ; or she who would

voluntarily put upon herself black petticoats or black
chemisettes, ought to be regarded as a ghoul or a hob-
goblin, utterly unfit for association with any of God's
earth-inhabiting creatures, except negroes and monkeys.

Speaking of stockings, how is it (if the question may
be here asked by way of parenthesis)—how is it, that
the fond mother of to-day, no mattter on what street
or avenue we may find her promenading, is so persistently ambitious to make a liberal display of her little
daughter's comparatively stockingless legs? Is it not,
partly at least, for the purpose of leading the gentlemen
to infer—a very natural and consoling inference, to be
sure—that, at a riper and more interesting period of life,
she (the sweet one!) will probably still be possessed of
those precious appendages?

Fany Fern, who ought to know, and probably does
know, the truth of the things whereof she speaks, says :

"Show but a strip of white stocking above your boot, or a bit of
embroidered skirt or a Balmoral, and you may lead a man anywhere
by the nose!"

Ovid, (as quoted by Haydn, in his "Dictionary of
Dates," page 222,) tells us that,

"The women of Cos, whose country was famous for the silk-worm,
wore a manufacture of cotton and silk of so beautiful and delicate a
texture, that their garments, which were always white, were so clear
and thin that their bodies could be seen through them."

Which being so, and if the fabric and costume here described are still in fashion on the island, the writer hereof
knows a gentlemen (a particular friend of the ladies) who
would be delighted to live in Cos ; but the reader must
not be too curious or inquisitive as to the identity of the
gentleman to whom allusion is here made, as his name
cannot be communicated, except verbally, and even then
only in the strictest confidence!

Of the quaint and foppish style of dress, which characterized English noblemen in the days of good Queen Bess, when, as it would seem, the white and other light colors enjoyed their rightful preference and pre-eminence, we may form a tolerably correct idea from the following brief sketch of the first and most distinguished settler of North Carolina, of whom Secretary Vincent, of the Royal Institution of Great Britain, says :

"Sir Walter Raleigh wore a white satin-pinked vest, close-sleeved to the wrist, and over the body a brown doublet, finely flowered, and embroidered with pearls. In the feather of his hat, a large ruby-and-pearl-drop at the bottom of the sprig, in place of a button. His breeches, with his stockings and ribbon garters, fringed at the end, all white ; and buff shoes, which on great court days were so gorgeously covered with precious stones as to have exceeded the value of £6,600 ; and he had a suit of armor of solid silver, with sword and belt blazing with diamonds, rubies, and pearls."

Chevreul, in his work on "Color," page 240, says :

"Let us suppose a uniform of Red and Green, like that of many regiments of cavalry ; by the law of contrast, the two colors being complementary, mutually strengthen each other ; the Green renders the Red redder, and the Red renders the Green greener. I suppose the augmentation of color resulting from contrast to be one tenth for each of the cloths, the color of which, seen separately, is represented by unity ; by means of the juxtaposition, each color becomes, then, equal to $1+.1$. I suppose also that a dress made simply of green or of red cloth, after having been worn a year, has lost one-tenth of its color ; it is evident that a uniform composed of green and of red cloth, after being worn for the same length of time, will not appear to the eye formed of two cloths which will have lost each one-tenth of their original color, since the Green gives Red to the Red, and the Red gives Green to the Green ; and if we do not admit that the strengthening is precisely equal to one-tenth of the original color, nevertheless observation proves, that the real fraction which expresses it, is not far from that ; so that if, on the supposition I have made, we cannot say that at the year's end a piece of a bi-colored uniform exhibits cloths which have exactly the same color as that of each new cloth seen separately, yet we are obliged to admit that the difference is small. I forgot to say that the two colors are taken at the same tone."

"This reasoning applies to bi-colored uniforms of which the colors, as Orange and Blue, Violet and Greenish-yellow, Indigo and Orange-yellow, are complementary to each other; only we must take into account the difference of tone, more or less great, that may exist between them when they are not taken at the same tone, as I have supposed in the preceding example."

Again, in his work on "Color," page 239, Chevreul says :

"A uniform composed of cloths of different colors may be worn much longer and appear better to the eye, although nearly worn out, than a suit of a single color, even when this latter is of a piece of cloth identical with one of those composing the first. The law of contrast gives the reason of this fact perfectly."

Count Rumford, (Benjamin Thompson,) in his "Inquiry Concerning the Nature of Heat"—a paper read before the Royal Society of London, in 1804, says :

"Upon careful examination, it will be found that those substances which supply us with the warmest coverings, as furs, feathers, and silks, are not only smooth, but highly polished ; it will also be found, other circumstances being equal, that those substances are the warmest which are the finest or which are composed of the greatest number of fine polished, detached threads or fibres. The fine, white, shining fur of a Russian hare is much warmer than coarse hair : and fine silk, as spun from the silk-worm, is warmer than the same silk twisted together into coarse threads. * * * The warmth of clothing depends much on the polish of the surface of which it is made ; hence, in choosing winter garments, those dyes are to be avoided which tend most to destroy that polish ; and as a white surface reflects more light than an equal surface equally polished of any other color, there is reason to believe, that white garments are warmer than any other in cold weather. They are universally considered as the coolest that can be worn in very hot weather, and, especially, when a person is exposed to the direct rays of the sun ; and if they are well calculated to reflect calorific rays in Summer, they must be equally well calculated to reflect those frigorific rays by which we are cooled and annoyed in Winter."

In a late work of advice to the sterner sex, in matters of dress, it is rightfully insisted upon that,

"Clean linen, white as snow, is indispensable, if you wish to support the character of a gentleman."

According to Botta's "Universal Literature," page 133,

"The Roman characters upon the stage, whether in comedy or in tragedy, were known by a conventional custom ; old men wore robes of white ; young men were attired in gay clothes ; rich men in purple ; soldiers in scarlet ; and poor men and slaves in dark and scanty dresses."

The "New American Cyclopædia," Volume V., page 750, says :

"The national and peculiar garment of the Romans was the toga. It was a full semicircular robe of white woolen, thrown freely about the body, flowing into many folds, and worn in different styles by every age and rank, that for priests and magistrates being bordered or striped with purple."

Again, the "New American Cyclopædia," Volume I., page 174, says :

"The dress of the Moors consists of a shirt with wide sleeves, and of very wide trousers of white linen, over which they wear the caftan, usually of a very bright color, with short sleeves buttoned at the wrist and fastened around the waist with a colored sash ; over this they wear a cloak of colored cotton or silk after the manner of the Roman toga. Sometimes a garment of blue cloth with a cowl is added, or a light undervest, usually of a white cassimere ; the covering for the head consists of a white cap ; such as have made a pilgrimage to Mecca add a turban of white muslin ; the feet are covered with yellow leather shoes or half boots."

Stocqueler, in his "History of India," page 87, says :

"There are a number of natives resident at Serampore. Some of their houses having rather a castellated appearance, and being more secluded from view than those of the Europeans, may be seen half-shadowed by trees, and half abutting into the river, adding considerably to the beauty and variety of the landscape. They also assemble in huge parties in the streets and thoroughfares, all clad in the purest white muslin."

Again, in his "History of India," page 128, Stocqueler says :

"In India, every scheme that human ingenuity can devise to mitigate the discomfort of heat is resorted to. The pumkah is continually kept swinging over the head of the European; * * * matting of fragrant grass is placed at doors and windows, and continually watered; and every possible attention is paid by the prudent to clothing and to diet. From November to March, woolen clothes may be worn with advantage. During the rest of the year, everybody is clad in white cotton.

Under date of May 22, 1862, the New York *Journal of Commerce* says :

"The object of this article is not to write a disquisition upon dress, but to call attention to the recent discoveries of the French chemists in the production of rare and brilliant dyes. More progress has been made in this department within the last two or three years than for the previous quarter of a century.

"The most wonderful of these discoveries has been in the adaptation of Aniline colors to the various processes of printing and dyeing silk, woolen, and cotton fabrics. Aniline is found in coal tar, and it is from this that the beautiful hues have been obtained which have now become so fashionable. Fuchsine is the red dye obtained from Aniline, and includes the shade known as Magenta, first patented two years ago by Messrs. Renard & Franc. Slight modifications of the fuchsine give an endless variety of brilliant reds and pinks, which can be used both in dyeing and printing.

"The violet imperial, or reddish violet, is a magnificent purple, of a far finer hue than the celebrated orchil purple of Marnas, made from lichens, and may be graduated from the deepest royalty to a delicate tint suited to the coolest summer drapery.

"The Bleu de Lyon is the most exquisite, perhaps, of the new colors, since it has a slight tinge of red, which makes it easily distinguishable from green in an artificial light, and it therefore retains its brilliancy in the evening. It can be graduated from the mazarine to the palest azure, and contrasts well with the different shades of yellow and orange.

"The Aniline colors were at first used upon calico with no mordant, being simply mixed with starch and printed upon the cloth. Of course the first slight washing, or even a small shower was sufficient to remove them. They are now fixed by a suitable chemical process, and are said to resist both light and soap without fading. The most brilliant silks and worsteds are dyed with them; the delaine (cotton and wool) printers of this country have adopted them; and they are making their way among the calico printers.

"Before closing, we may notice a very ingenious process, now in use, for dyeing silks white. Singular as it may appear to the uninitiated, this is successfully done to a very considerable extent. It is well known, even to mere tyros in science, that a mixture of the three primitive colors (red, blue and yellow) in the exact proportions of the spectrum, will produce the effect of a full ray of light, that is, white if reflected, and black if absorbed. This is now practically demonstrated in the dyeing room. The silk itself furnishes the yellow, for that is its primitive hue; it is therefore boiled, dipped in a light solution of Ammonia, then in a tank of water tinged with French purple, and then in another to which is added successive portions of carmine of indigo. The purple gives the red, and the carmine of indigo the blue, while the result is a clear lustrous white."

The Rev. Dr. Clarke, in the third volume of his Commentaries, page 276, speaking of an angel, a heavenly messenger, who is reported to have made his appearance upon the earth nearly two thousand years ago, in "raiment white as snow," says, with far more candor and fitness of expression than we are accustomed to hear from the black-coats generally :

"He was clothed in garments emblematical of the glad tidings which he came to announce. It would have been inconsistent with the message he brought, had the angel appeared in black robes, such as those preposterously wear, who call themselves his successors in the ministry of a once suffering, but now risen and highly exalted Saviour. But the world is as full of nonsense as of sin; and who can correct and bring it to reason and piety?"

Only one right and sensible thing did the Southern rebels do during the late civil war; the Northern rebels (that is to say, the Copperheads) failed to do even that much; for, from the beginning to the end, all that they did was both wrong and foolish. It was in the almost universal use of a beautiful gray-colored cloth, and in that alone, that the rebels of the South have succeeded in saving themselves from the charge of total purblindness and folly. Good cloth of the elegant color here referred to, cannot be too generally worn by our people, whether in the North, in the South, in the East, or in the West; and if the whole country would at once adopt it, and tenaciously adhere to it, or if not that, some other light-colored material—forthwith and forever discarding all garments of black and sombre hue—the improved health and longevity of Americans, in the years now coming on apace, might, perhaps, in great measure compensate for the dreadful sufferings and mortality which were occasioned by the conflict! Thus, in a greater or less degree, might we be the happy and honored instruments of bringing good out of evil. And why should this not be so? What is the point or advantage of capturing an enemy's colors, unless we make use of them?

Before leaving the subject of Dress, the reader—especially the lady-reader, who has an unfortunate weakness for expensive and dazzling outfits—may do well, with an eye more to economy than to color, to heed the following very opportune complaint from the poet Cowper:

> "We sacrifice to dress till household joys
> And comforts cease. Dress drains our cellars dry,
> And keeps our larder bare; puts out our fires,
> And introduces hunger, frost and woe,
> Where peace and hospitality might reign."

Judging from the large number of immense bleach-fields and factories which are to be found in France, Germany, Great Britain, and the United States, it would seem that there is, on the part of the more civilized and progressive nation, an instinctive and growing demand for white clothing, and for white and other light-colored fabrics generally. Think of bed-clothes—sheets, counterpanes, pillow-cases, quilts and blankets; in these, what color is so befitting and pleasing as white?—in these what color would be so improper and repulsive as black? So, too, with canvas, muslin, linen, dimity, lace, and numerous other qualities of goods, which are used for a thousand and one purposes, and in all of which, as a rule, whiteness of color, or non-blackness of color, is an indispensable condition.

Who, indeed, on this side of the infernal regions, would ever think of having a black carpet, a black-window curtain, a black table-cloth, a black napkin, or a black handkerchief? Where is the shipmaster, not wishing or expecting to be ship-wrecked, who would ever think of going to sea with black sails? The large number of white caps now worn by our military and naval officers, and the many white hats upon the heads of our civilians, show that men of sane and thoughtful minds, whether on land or on water, are at last beginning to feel the necessity of protecting their brains against such concentrated rays of the sun as have too long been accustomed to find their way for mischief through the black artificial coverings of the scalp.

It is an important and very interesting fact, now coming into notice, that the Quakers generally, are afflicted with but little sickness, except just before they die, after having attained a good old age. Of course, however, this fact is, in the main, owing to their remarkably and most commendably regular and temperate habits; yet who knows how much of their exemption from disease may not, at the same time, be justly attributed to their total rejection of all dark-colored clothes—most of them wisely shunning a black garment with as much loathing and disgust as they would shun the devil! With what positive and lasting advantage to our health might we not all try, in regular succession, a few full suits of drab? Yet it is truly lamentable that the great mass of the Quakers, who, wherever we find them, are possessed of so much good sound sense and simplicity of manners, while learning to entertain a wholesome detestation of the foul and ill-boding blackness of almost every inanimate object, have, nevertheless, strangely failed to acquire a just abhorrence of the more abominable blackness of the negro.

From sundry inferior rivals, who would deride him, much have we heard, from time time, about Horace Greeley's "old white coat;" but little or nothing have we heard about Horace Greeley's fevers, pleurisies, or rheumatisms—if, indeed, he ever suffered from any of these diseases. Verily it is the man with the white coat, who may, with good reason, pity the man with the black coat; and not the man with the black coat, who may with propriety laugh or jeer at the man with the white coat. He who, unlike Horace Greeley, is so unfortunate as not to be the owner of an old white coat, nor of a new white coat, nor of a white coat of any sort, had better do himself the justice to repair to the tailor's immediately, and buy one.

As for those foolish persons who patronize the mourning stores—every whit as foolish as those who patronize the groggeries—they ought to be heavily fined, or otherwise visited with severe penalties, for the wrongs which, by dressing in deleterious and disgusting black, they inflict, not only on themselves, but also on the several communities in which they reside. And as for the proprietors themselves, the demoralized and gloom-spreading proprietors, of the death-presaging and death-rememorative establishments called mourning-stores, they ought at once to be persuaded and encouraged to an early abandonment of their black business ; but in the event that these gentle methods did not prove to them a sufficient warning, then they should all be unceremoniously put under such urgent disabilities as would cause an immediate and lasting suspension of their traffic in devil-dyed fabrics. Too long already has the world been saddened and disgraced by the existence in it of such plague-engendering nuisances as mourning-stores, whiskey-shops, negro-huts, and negro-rookeries. All these, including the festeringly filthy and effete negroes themselves, should be forthwith and forever effaced from every part of the earth. Much the same also should it be with the black-gowned, bigoted and besotted Catholic priests—a set of very ignorant and scurvy fellows, who, as the loud and incessant proclaimers of great evils to come, and as the inveterate enemies of all free institutions, are woeful hinderers of the healthful progress of all true religion on the one hand, and of all genuine republicanism on the other.

In order to be fully convinced of the fact that nature never intended that man should be habited in black garments, it is but necessary for us to examine the colors of the raw materials which are generally used, or which are usable, for purposes of clothing—not a single one of which carries with it even an approximation to blackness. If we look out upon the fields or plantations of cotton, when it is fairly ripe and ready to be picked, our view is met by myriads of beautifully-expanded and nature-bleached bolls of blazing whiteness. Flax and hemp are both of a grayish white or yellowish white color ; and all the fibrous barks and grasses used in the manufacture of articles of apparel, are also, if free from the application of artificial dyes, white or light colored. If we gaze upon the flocks of sheep, grazing or browsing like the cattle upon a thousand hills, we shall find them all, with very rare exceptions, covered with wool of most warmful and wholesome whiteness. The color of the cocoon—always of a light golden tinge—affords ample proof that the silk-worm (to the miniature but effective spinning processes of which the ladies are so largely indebted for their finery) laudably disdains to emit into the world a single fibre of black.

In flags also, in the ensigns of nations, we may often behold most beautiful combinations of color—almost always with more or less white, but very seldom, indeed, with even a particle of black. Pirates and land-savages are, it is believed, the only carriers of black banners.

The American flag is, thank God! so everlastingly complete, so inimitably gorgeous, in its juxtapositions and conjunctions of the Red, White, and Blue, that there is no room on it, and never can be room, for the smallest possible speck of black.

In session at Philadelphia, on the 14th of June, 1777, the Continental Congress of America, evincing on the part of its members a notably nice discrimination of colors, resolved,

"That the flag of the thirteen United States be thirteen stripes, alternately red and white; and that the Union be thirteen stars, white on a blue field, representing a new constellation."

James Rodman Drake, in his poem on "The American Flag," uses this patriotic and appropriate language:

"When Freedom from her mountain height,
Unfurled her standard to the air,
She tore the azure robe of night,
And set the stars of glory there;
She mingled with its gorgeous dyes
The milky baldric of the skies,
And striped its pure celestial white
With streakings of the morning light.

Flag of the free hearts' hope and home,
By angel hands to valor given;
The stars have lit the welkin dome,
And all thy hues were born in heaven,
Forever float that standard sheet!
Where breathes the foe but falls before us,
With Freedom's soil beneath our feet,
And Freedom's banner streaming o'er us?

Francis Scott Key, in his beautiful and immortal "Star-spangled Banner," which, although written in 1814, is so applicable to the present times, that any one, not knowing better, might be easily led into the error of supposing that it was first published in 1861–'65, says:

"On the shore dimly seen through the mists of the deep,
    Where the foe's haughty host in dread silence reposes,
What is that which the breeze, o'er the towering steep,
    As it fitfully blows, half conceals, half discloses?
Now it catches the gleam of the morning's first beam—
In full glory reflected, now shines on the stream;
    'Tis the Star-Spangled Banner; O! long may it wave
    O'er the land of the free, and the home of the brave.

" And where is the band who so vauntingly swore
    That the havoc of war and the battle's confusion
A home and a country should leave us no more?
    Their blood has wash'd out their foul footsteps' pollution.
No refuge could save the hireling and slave
From the terror of flight or the gloom of the grave;
    And the Star-spangled Banner in triumph doth wave
    O'er the land of the free, and the home of the brave.

"O! thus be it ever, when freemen shall stand
    Between their loved homes and the war's desolation;
Blest with victory and peace, may our Heaven-rescued land
    Praise the Power that hath made and preserved us a nation.
Then conquer we must, for our cause it is just;
And this be our motto—"In God is our trust!"—
    And the Star-spangled Banner in triumph shall wave
    O'er the land of the free and the home of the brave."

Munsell, in his "Every Day Book of History and Chronology," page 293, informs us that, in 1789,

"Lafayette added to his cockade the white of the royal arms, declaring, at the same time, that the tri-color should go round the world."

History is very explicit as to the colors which were respectively chosen, as marks of distinction, by the Houses of York and Lancaster, during England's thirty years' Wars of the Roses. Fortunate, indeed, was it for the country at large, that there lived in it, in 1486, a certain loving couple, Henry VII. and the Princess Elizabeth,

"Whose marriage conjoined the white rose and the red."

Between belligerents, as is well known, the hoisting of a white flag (except in cases of the basest and blackest treachery on the part of those who upraise the signal) always indicates pure and peaceful purposes. In his "Pericles, Prince of Tyre," Act I., Scene IV., Shakspeare says:

"By the semblance
Of their white flags displayed, they bring us peace,
And come to us as favorers, not as foes."

Come we now to consider briefly, the various shades of color common to the

HAIR AND EYES.

Some persons have a preference for black hair; some for brown; some for flaxen; some for gray; some for golden: some for silvery; some for light; some for white—and a few for red. Almost every being or personage, real or imaginary, who has ever been the recipient of divine honors, and most of our preëminently distinguished fellow-men, especially those of past ages, who are widely known for their great knowledge and good actions, are generally represented with hair, either of perfect whiteness, or of a golden tinge. Of this latter type was Jesus Christ, whose hair, if we may believe the painters and the poets, was very fine, and always wore the appearance of having been most elegantly but unaffectedly glossed with a rich-colored solution of amber.

One of the newspaper correspondents who was connected with Grant's army in Virginia, and who had ample opportunities for observation there and elsewhere, writes thus:

"In the army, and among returned soldiers, I have noted one fact, in particular, somewhat at variance with the usual theories. It is that light-haired men, of the nervous, sanguine type, stand campaigning better than the dark-haired men, of bilious temperament. Look through a raw regiment, on its way to the field, and you will find fully one-half its members to be of the black-haired, dark-skinned, large-boned bilious type. See that same regiment on its return for muster-out, and you will find that the black-haired element has melted away, leaving at least two-thirds, perhaps three-fourths, of the regiment to be represented by red, brown, and flaxen hair."

Smiles, in his "Self-Help," page 100, says:

"Addison amassed as much as three folios of manuscript materials before he began his 'Spectator.' Newton wrote his 'Chronology' fifteen times over before he was satisfied with it; and Gibbon wrote out his 'Memoir' nine times. Hale studied for many years at the rate of sixteen hours a day, and when wearied with the study of the law, he would recreate himself with philosophy and the study of the mathematics. Hume wrote thirteen hours a day while preparing his 'History of England.' Montesquieu, speaking of one part of his writings, said to a friend, 'You will read it in a few hours; but I assure you it cost me so much labor that it has whitened my hair.'"

Smollett, in one of his best novels, "The Expedition of Humphrey Clinker," Volume I., page 123, complains that,

"Since Grenville was turned out, there has been no minister in this nation, worth the meal that whitened his periwig.—They are so ignorant, they scarce know a crab from a cauliflower; and then they are such dunces, there's no making them comprehend the plainest proposition."

Byron, in his "Siege of Corinth," Stanza XXV., says:

"There stood an old man—his hairs were white,
But his veteran arm was full of might:
So gallantly bore he the brunt of the fray,
The dead before him on that day,
In a semicircle lay;
Still he combated unwounded,
Though retreating, unsurrounded,
Many a scar of former fight
Lurked beneath his corslet bright,
But every wound his body bore,
Each and all had been ta'en before;
Though aged, he was so iron of limb,
Few of our youth could cope with him;
And the foes, whom he singly kept at bay,
Outnumber'd his thin hairs of silver gray."

Shakspeare, in his poem entitled "The Rape of Lucrece," describing some of the more distinguished of the Grecian heroes in their besiegement of Troy, says:

"In Ajax and Ulysses, O what art
Of physiognomy might one behold!
The face of either ciphered either's heart;
Their face their manners most expressly told;
In Ajax' eyes blunt rage and rigor roll'd
But the mild glance that sly Ulysses lent,
Show'd deep regard and smiling government.

"There pleading might you see grave Nestor stand,
As 't were encouraging the Greeks to fight;
Making such sober action with his hand,
That it beguil'd attention, charm'd the sight:
In speech, it seemed, his beard, all silver white,
Wagg'd up and down, and from his lips did fly
Thin winding breath, which purl'd up to the sky."

Again, in his "Antony and Cleopatra," Act III., Scene IX., Shakspeare makes Antony, whose hair seems to have been gray, say:

> "My very hairs do mutiny, for the white
> Reprove the brown for rashness."

Again, the Bard of Avon would have us pay all due respect to

> "The silvery livery of advised age."

Moses, in the nineteenth chapter of Leviticus, verse 32, says:

> "Thou shalt rise up before the hoary head, and honor the face of the old man, and fear thy God."

Ovid speaks of Cupid's locks, as

> "Those graceful curls which wantouly did flow,
> The whiter rivals of the falling snow."

Says a late number of *The Town Talk:*

> "Middle-aged men are apt to be sensitive with the incipient turning gray of the beard, but they are often mistaken as to its effect. Black hair, which turns earliest, is not only picturesquely embellished by a sprinkling of gray, but exceedingly intellectualized and made sympathetically expressive. * * * A white beard is so exceedingly distinguished that every man whose hair prematurely turns should be glad to wear it, while for an old man's face it is so softening a veil, so winning an embellishment, that it is wonderful how such an advantage could ever be thrown away. That old age should be always long bearded, to be properly veiled and venerable, is the feeling, we are sure, of every lover of nature, as well as of every cultivated and deferential heart."

One of the London magazines, *Temple Bar*, has but recently remarked that,

> "The beard is now so very generally worn *au naturel* with us, as it has been for a longer time by the continental nations and the

Americans, that the "movement" appears to have settled down into a regular custom. * * * The fashion has become so far accepted that beards of every shape and color are to be seen, from the golden and silky growth of the young Hercules, to the stiff iron-gray of the middle-aged man, and the flowing white of the comfortable old gentleman."

It is well known that many distinguished ladies have had golden hair. Of these were Beatrice Cenci; Laura (of Petrarch-memory;) Elizabeth Woodville; Queen Catherine Parr; and Queen Elizabeth. Others, who either lived anterior to the age of authentic history, or were mere creations of the imagination, were, according to the accounts of the poets, also adorned with auburn locks. Of these were Eve, Aphrodite, Lucrece, Portia, and the Bride of Lammermoor—also both the wife and the daughter of Pericles.

Sir Walter Scott, in his song called "The Crusader's Return," asks—

"Seest thou her locks, whose sunny glow
Half shows, half shades, her neck of snow?"

Of the color of the eyes, the Portuguese have a ditty from which the following is an extract:

"Black eyes and brown
You may every day see;
But blue like my lover's
The gods made for me."

Addressing his sweetheart at "the Hub of the Universe," Oliver Wendell Holmes, in the words of a true poet, says,

"I look upon the fair blue skies,
And naught but empty air I see;
But when I turn me to thine eyes,
It seemeth unto me
Ten thousand angels spread their wings
Within those little azure rings."

Byron, in his little poem addressed "To Woman," exclaims,

> "How throbs the pulse when first we view
> The eye that rolls in glossy blue."

According to Botta, there lived, in the sixteenth century, a French poet, who made the extraordinary declaration, that the eyes of his mistress were "as large as his grief, and as black as his fate."

A mere cursory view will suffice to show us how universally conspicuous and pleasing are the offices of White and its attendant colors, and how circumscribed and detestable are the functions of Black, among

BIRDS AND INSECTS.

Classical mythology informs us that the amorous and mighty Jupiter took the form of a white swan, when, by Leda, he became the father of Castor and Pollux, and subsequently of Helen, the most beautiful woman in the world.

Duncan, in his "Western Africa," Volume II., page 233, says:

"I asked permission to shoot some cranes in the cranery we passed yesterday, but the caboceer would only allow me to shoot the gray ones. The white cranes, he said, were the fetich-men (or gods) to the gray ones."

Buffon, in his "Natural History," page 204, says:

"In some cold countries a variety of the blackbird is found of a pure white color."

An old proverb will have it, that

"A black hen will lay a white egg."

A newspaper correspondent, writing from Marysville, California, some time since, related a truly interesting

and touching incident, which occurred there during the
active operations of the United States Sanitary Commission in 1864, and which he unassumingly described in
these words:

"A poor little boy brought a white chicken to the fair, which was
all he had to offer, saying it might make some broth for a poor sick
soldier. He had decked his little offering with ribbons of 'red, white
and blue;' but as he had no money to pay the admittance fee, when
he came to the door he was rejected. As he went down the street,
some gentleman seeing his distress listened to his story, gave him a
ticket and sent him in. The simplicity of the donor and the beauty
of the offering attracted attention, and the chicken was put up at auc-
tion and sold to the highest bidder for $460 in gold, for the benefit of
the Sanitary Commission."

Query: Had the pretty white pullet, which was thus
auctioned for $460, been black and ugly, like a negro,
could she have been disposed of, at either public or private sale, for more than two shillings—and would the
boy have been admitted, or the soldier benefited?

It was at the baptism of Jesus Christ, in the river Jordan, near Gilgal, south of Galilee, not far from Jericho,
and less than three days' journey from Jerusalem, that
many are represented as having

> "Beheld upon his sacred head
> A snow-white dove alight."

From an advertisement of Van Amburgh's Menagerie,
published in the New York *Herald*, February 6, 1864, it
would appear that he, there and then, had on exhibition

"A pair of white peacocks, recently imported from Germany—as
white as the driven snow, and the first of their kind ever before seen
in any country. Their tails form a magnificent plume, which they
elevate at pleasure over their bodies. Not one spot or a single dark
shade tarnishes their dazzling whiteness."

Addison, in the 265th number of the "Spectator," pertinently remarks, that,

"Among birds nature has lavished all her ornaments upon the

male, who very often appears in a most beautiful head-dress; whether it be a crest, a comb, a tuft of feathers, or a natural little plume, erected like a kind of pinnacle on the very top of the head. As Nature on the contrary has poured out her charms in the greatest abundance upon the female part of our species, so they are very assiduous in bestowing upon themselves the finest garnitures of art. The peacock, in all his pride, does not display half the colors, that appear in the garments of a fashionable lady, when she is dressed either for a ball or a birthday."

Goldsmith, in his "History of the Earth and Animated Nature," Volume III., page 91, says:

"The Greeks were so much struck with the beauty of the peacock, when first brought among them, that every person paid a fixed price for seeing it; and several people came to Athens, from Lacedæmon and Thessaly, purely to satisfy their curiosity."

John Crawfurd, in an article "On the Relation of Animals to Civilization," published in a work entitled "Transactions of the London Ethnological Society: New Series," Volume II., page 451, says:

"The peacock is incomparably the most gorgeous of the whole feathered creation."

Buffon, in his "Natural History" page 241, says,

"It is proverbial in Italy, that the peacock has the plumage of an angel."

Young, the author of "Night Thoughts," in his poem entitled "A Paraphrase of the Book of Job," exclaims:

"How rich the peacock! what bright glories run
From plume to plume, and vary in the sun!
He proudly spreads them to the golden ray,
Gives all his colors, and adorns the day;
With conscious state the spacious round displays,
And slowly moves amid the waving blaze."

Goldsmith, in his "History of the Earth and Animated Nature," Volume III., page 156, says:

"Having given some history of the manners of the most remarka-

ble birds of which accounts can be obtained, I might now go to a very
extensive tribe, remarkable for the splendor and the variety of their
plumage; but the description of the colors of a beautiful bird, has
nothing in it that can inform or entertain; it rather excites a longing,
which it is impossible for words to satisfy. Naturalists, indeed, have
endeavored to satisfy this desire, by colored prints; but, beside that
these at best give only a faint resemblance of Nature, and are a very
indifferent kind of painting, the bird itself has a thousand beauties,
that the most exquisite artist is incapable of imitating. They, for instance, who imagine they have a complete idea of the beauty of the
little tribe of Manikin birds, from the pictures we have of them, will
find themselves deceived, when they compare their draughts with Nature. The shining greens, the changeable purples, and the glossy
reds, are beyond the reach of the pencil; and very far beyond the colored print, which is but a poor substitute for painting. I have therefore
declined entering into a minute description of foreign birds of the
sparrow kind; as sounds would never convey an adequate idea of colors."

At the same time that a rightful sneer is meted out to
Black, a handsome compliment is paid to White, in
Æsop's Fable of the Fox and the Crow—as follows:

"A Crow having taken a piece of cheese out of a cottage window,
flew up into a high tree with it, in order to eat it. Which a Fox observing, came and sat underneath, and began to compliment the
Crow, upon the subject of her beauty. I protest, says he, I never observed it before, but your feathers are of a more delicate white than
any I ever saw in my life. Ah! what a fine shape and graceful turn
of body is there. And I make no question but you have a tolerable
voice. If it is but as fine as your complexion, I do not know a bird
that can pretend to stand in competition with you. The Crow, tickled
with this very civil language, nestled and wriggled about, and hardly
knew where she was; but thinking the Fox a little dubious as to the
particular of her voice, and having a mind to set him right in that
matter, began to sing, and in the same instant, let the cheese drop
out of her mouth. This being what the Fox wanted, he chopped it
up in a moment, and trotted away, laughing to himself at the easy
credulity of the Crow."

In his Third Night, Young complains of

"The black raven hovering o'er my peace,
    Not less a bird of omen than of prey."

Bare reference to the beautiful colors displayed by Butterflies, Lightning-bugs, Lady-cows, Cochineals, and other little bright-winged creatures, will be amply sufficient to show that Black is universally and deservedly held at unexpressibly odious discount in the world of insects.

Stocqueler, in his " History of India," page 85, says,

"Many of the trees of India actually seem encircled by a halo, in consequence of the multitudes of fire-flies which glance in and out, emitting a greenish golden light, like that which would proceed from a lamp formed of emeralds. Though the greater number of these luminous insects disport themselves round the trees, many flash like meteors along the air, crossing the path, whether on shore or on the water, and rendering night more beautiful, even in the presence of the stars, which come out so thickly and so brightly in this glittering hemisphere, that, excepting during the cloudy season of the rains, the nights are never dark."

How the Glow-worms and the Fire-flies relieved a certain night of its oppressive darkness, is thus described by the poet Southey:

> " Sorrowing we beheld
> The night come on; but soon did night display
> More wonders than it veiled; innumerable tribes
> From the wood-cover swarm'd, and darkness made
> Their beauties visible: one while they streamed
> A bright blue radiance upon flowers that closed
> Their gorgeous colors from the eye of day;
> Now, motionless and dark, eluded search,
> Self-shrouded; and anon, starring the sky,
> Rose like a shower of fire."

Black is also exceptional, and White and its attendant colors general, among

ANIMALS AND FISHES.

White Bulls, White Sheep, and White Goats—and none of any other color—were always tendered and accepted as sacred offerings to Jupiter, the supreme deity of the

ancients.   Strange to say, white Elephants, even in the
present day, are held sacred in Siam.   In Africa, many
white creatures, animate and inanimate, are, at this
very moment, objects of profound adoration.

Of the White Elephant, Haydn, in his "Dictionary of
Dates," page 731, says:

"Xacca was the mythological founder of idolatry in the Indies and
other eastern countries.   The history of his life reports, that when
his mother was enceinte with him, she dreamt that she brought forth a
white elephant, which is the reason the kings of Siam, Tonquin, and
China, have so great a value for them.   The Brahmins affirm that
Xacca has gone through a metempsychosis 80,000 times, and that
his soul has passed into so many different kinds of beasts, whereof
the last was a white elephant.   They add that, after all these changes,
he was received into the company of the gods."

Gordon, in a sarcastic article on the causes of war, in
his "Cato's Letters," Volume II., Number 48, says:

"White elephants are rare in nature, and so greatly valued in the
Indies, that the king of Pegu, hearing that the king of Siam had got
two, sent an embassy in form, to desire one of them of his royal
brother at any price; but being refused, he thought his honor concerned to wage war for so great an affront.   So he entered Siam
with a vast army, and with the loss of five hundred thousand of his
own men, and the destruction of as many of the Siamese, he made
himself master of the elephant, and thus retrieved his honor !"

Sir John Bowring, who, in 1856, was sent by the British government, on a special mission to the king of Siam,
has recently published, in the *Fortnightly Review*, the
following elephantine items:

"Elephants, especially white elephants, are all-important person-
ages in Siam.   In the multitudinous incarnations of Buddha, it is
believed that the white elephant is one of his necessary domiciles,
and the possession of a white elephant is the possession of the presence and the patronage of the Deity.   I was escorted by one of the
great ministers of state to the domicile of the white elephant in
Bangkok, whose death not many years ago filled the court and na-

tion with mourning. He had been discovered in the forests of the interior ; a large reward was paid to the fortunate discoverer, and the first king left his capital to meet with becoming ostentatious welcome and reverence the newly-acquired treasure. In Siamese history there are many chapters giving an account of invasions and repulses in wars waged solely for the acquisition of some white elephant in the possession of a neighboring sovereign. There are instances where two existed in the same capital, and when negotiations failed for the acquisition of one by friendly surrender, the territory of the doubly-blessed monarch was violated and the superfluous elephant demanded *vi et armis*. The court of Siam had been for some time unhonored by the presence and the patronage of a white elephant. Elephants there were not wholly dark brown or pale black, with pendent ears of a lighter color and spots on the skin, which showed some affinity to a purer and diviner race. These were adorned with rich jewels, attended by special servitors, and accompanied by music when they left their stalls ; but they became as nothing when the elephant of higher aristocracy, or rather of celestial genealogy appeared. The king, on the announcement of his capture, wrote to me in terms of high satisfaction at his good fortune. When he escorted his prize to his capital, I was conducted to the palace of the honored dignitary ; to say the truth, his color was not white, but coppery, like that of a red Indian. His stable was painted like a Parisian drawing-room ; there was an elevated platform, on whose adjacent walls handsome warlike ornaments were hung, and nobles of high rank were in attendance, who took care he should be supplied with delicious food, principally the sugarcane. When the white elephant went to bathe, caparisoned in splendid decorations, he was preceded by musicians, escorted by courtiers, and was received by the people with prostration and reverence. On my departure from Bangkok, after the signature of the treaties, when the royal letters were delivered engraved on golden slabs for the great Queen of England and placed in a gold box locked with a gold key, though many handsome presents accompanied the royal missives, one offering was placed in my hands with the assurance that it was by far the most precious of the gifts to be conveyed—and the invaluable offering was a bunch of hairs from the white elephant's tail, tied together with a golden thread."

In many parts of the East, it is considered an honor, and a peculiar privilege of the aristocracy, to be able to ride on white animals, of whatever sort, whether Elephants, Horses, Asses, or Mules; and these, when entirely white, are ridden in preference to riding in the finest vehicles.

In all ages of the world, mankind, especially the more martial races of mankind, seem to have evinced a sort of universal partiality for White Horses. We have all heard of Alexander's famous white charger Bucephalus, which, proudly and nobly bore the conqueror of the world, through all his brilliant campaigns, from Greece to India.

Nor, if we may place implicit faith in the statements of certain writers and traditionists of the far past, is it allowed to the earth alone to boast of the possession of white horses. In his "Revelation xix., 11–14, John, of Patmos, says·:

"I saw heaven opened, and behold a white horse ; and he that sat upon him was called Faithful and True, and in righteousness he doth judge and make war. * * * And the armies which were in heaven followed him upon white horses, clothed in fine linen, white and clean."

The readers of classical mythology will recollect that

"Aurora, the goddess of the morning, is represented riding in a gold-colored chariot, drawn by white horses."

Herodotus, of Halicarnassus, one of the first and most veracious of the Grecian historians—though, as just indicated, not a native of Greece—in his "Clio," section 189, tells us that,

"When Cyrus, in his march against Babylon, arrived at the river Gyndes, whose fountains are in the Matiaman mountains, and which flows through the land of the Dardanians, and falls into another river, the Tigris ; which latter, flowing by the city of Opis, discharges itself into the Red Sea :—now, when Cyrus was endeavoring to cross this river Gyndes, which can be passed only in boats, one of the sacred white horses, through wantonness, plunged into tho stream, and attempted to swim over ; but the stream having carried him away and drowned him, Cyrus was much enraged with the river for this affront, and threatened to make his stream so weak, that henceforth women should easily cross it without wetting their knees. After this menace, deferring his expedition against Babylon, ho divided his army into two parts ; and having so divided it, he marked out by lines one hundred and eighty channels, on each side of the river, diverging every way ; then having distributed his army, he commanded them to dig. His design was indeed executed by the great numbers he employed ; but they spent the whole summer in the work."

In his "History and Chronology," page 277, Munsell says :

"At the battle of Regillum, in the year 496 before Christ, it is said that the twin knights Castor and Pollux, appeared upon white horses and assisted the Romans. In memory of this event an annual cavalcade was instituted at Rome, during which the knights, robed in purple, and crowned with olive wreaths, rode in solemn procession from the temple of Honor to the Capitol, where the censor, seated on his curule chair, passed judgment on their character."

Again, in his "History and Chronology," page 272, Munsell, says :

"On the 26th of July, in the year 46 before Christ, Julius Cæsar, arrived at Rome from Utica, celebrated the fourfold triumph in a quadriga of white horses, for the victories over the Gauls, over Ptolemy in Egypt, over Pharnace in Pontus, and over Juba in Africa; entertained the people with naumachian and pentachlic or circensian games during 40 days ; rewarded and feasted them at 22,000 tables ; was declared consul the fourth time, and dictator for ten years ; and, to place him on the summit of human glory, his statue was erected in the Capitol, opposite to that of Jupiter, with the globe at his feet."

Prescott, in his "History of the Reign of Ferdinand and Isabella," Volume I., page 272, recounting the more prominent and important features of the war in Granada, says :

"The young King Abdallah, who had been conspicuous during
that day in the hottest of the fight, mounted on a milk-white charger
richly caparisoned, saw fifty of his royal guard fall around him."

The readers of Froissart's quaint Chronicles.(page
466) will readily recall to mind the gay scene, where the
Duke of Brittany, in the 14th century, presented the
Count d'Estampes with "a handsome white palfrey, sad-
dled and equipped as if for a king."

One of Lafayette's biographers says of him,

"He usually rode a white charger, and shone the very imperson-
ation of chivalry."

Modern writers, in dealing with facts, have had frequent occasions to denounce the sanctimonious arro-
gance and tyranny of those rakish and ridiculous rascals
in Rome, called Popes and Cardinals—the promoters of
villainous priestcraft and superstition—all of whom, like
all the negroes and the Mormons of our own country,
ought to be (forcibly if necessary) placed, for all time to
come, a thousand miles, at least, beyond the pale of respectable society.   It is said that the detestably pre-
sumptious Pope Adrian IV., compelled Frederick I.,
Emperor of Germany, in the latter half of the 12th century, to prostrate himself before him, kiss his feet, hold
his stirrup, and lead the white palfrey on which he rode!
The compulsory power, in this case, was the monstrous
and absurd threat, on the part of the Catholic Church,
to absolve the subjects of Frederick from their allegiance
to him ; to excommunicate him in this world ; and to
consign him to eternal darkness and damnation in the
next!—a silly but successful effort at intimidation, which
it is profoundly humiliating to know an Emperor of
Germany had the weakness to heed.   Any person, of
whatever calling, however high his station, or however

humble, who would regard any such threat, or any threat at all from the Romish Church, otherwise than with unmitigated contempt and derision, is pitiably destitute of the primary and most essential requisites of manhood.

It was on the plains of Bosworth, on the 21st of August, 1485, that Richard III.—the night preceding his death in battle—ordered Catesby, as Shakspeare informs us, to

> "Saddle white Surrey for the field to-morrow."

Burns has told us, as only Burns could tell us, an amusing story of Tam O'Shanter, who,

> "Well mounted on his gray mare, Meg,
> A better never lifted leg——"

The Flemings have a proverb which alleges that

> "The gray mare is the better horse."

It is generally understood that the utterer of this proverb means to say, that the wife is more of a man than her husband, or that she wears the breeches—in which latter case, the poor fellow's to be pitied!—but, if we may credit Macaulay, it had its origin in the fact that, formerly, preference was usually given to the gray mares of Flanders over the finest coach horses of England.

Herodotus, the "Father of History," who lived nearly five hundred years before Christ, in his "Euterpe," section 38, speaking of the religion and of the gods of the Egyptians, says:

"The male kine the Egyptians deem sacred to Epaphus, and to that end prove them in the following manner. If the examiner finds one black hair upon him, he adjudges him to be unclean; and one of the priests appointed for this purpose makes this examination, both when the animal is standing up and lying down."

Valdez, in his "Six Years of a Traveler's Life in Western Africa," Volume II., page 331, says :

"On the occasion of the appointment of a chief to the supreme command, a bullock is sacrificed by the Samba Golambole, as also a white sheep, and a white or fawn-colored pigeon, together with various other victims. But the principal sacrifice is that of one slave from each of the nations under the dominion of the paramount chief, the heads of whom are carried in triumph and exhibited to the populace, accompanied by drums and other instruments. The bodies are added to those of the other animals, and all cooked together, and distributed as a savory dish to the chief and the other nobles."

Baldwin, in his "Hunting in South Africa," page 187, says :

"Desiring to secure the good will of the king, we sent him many presents. * * * At last all our doubts were set at rest by a present of a snow-white heifer which was meant to show that his heart was white toward us, and that we had nothing to fear.

Shakspeare, in his "Titus Andronicus," Act V., Scene I., assures us that,

> "Where the bull and cow are both milk-white,
> They never do beget a coal-black calf."

Seldom, indeed, does more than one black sheep show itself in a flock of fifty white ones ; it is, therefore, a very easy task to answer the question—frequently asked by the propounders of conundrums—

"What is the reason that white sheep eat more than black ones?"

Darwin, in his "Origin of Species," page 81, says :

"I can see no reason to doubt that natural selection might be most effective in giving the proper color to each kind of grouse, and in keeping that color, when once acquired, true and constant. Nor ought we to think that the occasional destruction of an animal of any particular color would produce little effect ; we should remember how essential it is, in a flock of white sheep, to destroy every lamb with the faintest trace of black."

Benjamin Thompson (Count Rumford) in his "Inquiry Concerning the Nature of Heat"—a paper read before the Royal Society of London, in 1804, says :

"The fur of several delicate animals becomes white in winter in cold countries ; and that of bears, which inhabit the polar regions, is white in all seasons. These last are exposed alternately in the open air to the most intense cold, and to the continual action of the sun's rays during several months. If it should be true that heat and cold are excited in the manner already described, and that white is the color most favorable to the reflection of calorific and frigorific rays, it must be acknowledged that these animals have been exceedingly fortunate in obtaining clothing so well adapted to their local circumstances."

The "New American Cyclopædia," Volume V., page 568, says :

"The scales of certain fishes are ornamented with the most beautiful and varied colors, presenting all the metallic reflections."

Reference has already been made to the very pleasing colors displayed by the Wrasse, the Stickleback, and the Bonito.   Other fishes are equally beautiful.   Of the Dolphin, Fullom, in his "Marvels of Science," page 288, says:

"I must not omit to mention the variations of color in the dolphin, which, despite the declarations of travelers, many naturalists still consider fabulous.   That this finny chameleon, however, does actually change his hue, and, in his dying hour, glow with a hundred beautiful tints, ought not to be disputed, and I must add my testimony, that the statement is strictly true."

Campbell, in his "Travels in South Africa," page 503, writing while on his homeward-bound voyage to England, says :

"On the 18th we were much amused by several beautiful dolphins, following and playing about the ship.   They appeared in the water of a verdigris green, and sometimes of a beautiful brown color. After several unsuccessful throws of the harpoon, the captain at length stuck it into one, and brought it on deck, to the no small

8*

gratification of such of us as had not seen one before. We all pronounced it a complete beauty, not inferior to any creature on land, not even excepting the golden pheasant, or the bird of paradise. The back was dark green, mixed with large blue spots, in the middle of which was a red spot, like a drop of blood—the green as it descended gradually became lighter, till lost in the color of the finest gold—this yellow became paler, till lost in white, which was the color of the belly. The fins were equally ornamented. The shape of the finest symmetry. It was about three feet and a half long. When boiled, it was nearly as white under the skin as snow, and had a delicate taste."

Hugh Miller, a truly remarkable and renowned reader of rocks, in his "Old Red Sandstone," page 252, says :

"Color is a mighty matter to the ichthyologist. The fins and shining scales, the rainbow-dyes of beauty of the watery tribes, are connected often with more than mere external character. It is a curious and interesting fact, that the hues of splendor in which they are bedecked, are, in some instances, as intimately associated with their instincts—with their feelings, if I may so speak—as the blush which suffuses the human countenance is associated with the sense of shame, or its tint of ashy paleness or of sallow with emotions of rage or feelings of a panic terror. Pain and triumph have each their index of color among the mute inhabitants of our seas and rivers. Poets themselves have bewailed the utter inadequacy of words to describe the varying tints and shades of beauty with which the agonies of death dye the scales of the dolphin, and how every various pang calls up a various suffusion of splendor. Even the common stickleback of our ponds and ditches can put on its colors to picture its emotions. There is, it seems, a mighty amount of ambition, and a vast deal of fighting, sheerly for conquest's sake, among the myriads of this pigmy little fish which inhabit our smaller streams ; and no sooner does an individual succeed in expelling his weaker companions from some eighteen inches or two feet of territory, than straightway the exultation of conquest converts the faded and freckled olive of his back and sides into a glow of crimson and bright green. Nature, it would seem, furnishes him with a regal robe for the occasion."

Of Jelly Fishes, the younger Agassiz, in the "Atlantic Monthly" for December, 1865, wrote thus :

"The Jelly-Fishes, so sparkling and brilliant in the sunshine, have a still lovelier light of their own at night; they give out a greenish golden light, as brilliant as that of the brightest glow-worm, and on a calm summer night, at the spawning season, when they come to the surface in swarms, if you do but dip your hand into the water, it breaks into sparkling drops beneath your touch. There are no more beautiful phosphorescent animals in the sea than the Medusæ. It would seem that the expression, 'rills of molten metal,' could hardly apply to anything so impalpable as a Jelly-Fish, but, although so delicate in structure, their gelatinous disks give them a weight and substance; and at night, when their transparency is not perceived, and their whole mass is aglow with phosphorescent light, they truly have an appearance of solidity which is most striking when they are lifted out of the water and flow down the sides of the net. * * * A thousand lesser creatures add their tiny lamps to the illumination of the ocean: for this so-called phosphorescence of the sea is by no means due to the Jelly-Fishes alone, but is also produced by many other animals, differing in the color as well as the intensity of their light; and it is a curious fact that they seem to take possession of the field by turns. You may row or sail over the same course which a few nights since glowed with a greenish-golden light wherever the surface of the water was disturbed, and though equally brilliant, the phosphorescence has now a pure white light."

Nature's strong and loving predilection for White, and for its attendant colors, and her immutable and wholesome abhorrence of Black, are also universally evinced in

FLOWERS AND BLOSSOMS.

No such abnormal production as a black flower, or a black blossom, has, it is believed, ever been known. Flowers of a great variety of indescribably beautiful hues and tints—but many more of pure white than of any other color—do, indeed, constitute some of the most delightful and fascinating adornments of the earth.

Chevreul, in his work on "Color," page 262, says:

"Among the pleasures afforded us by the cultivation of choice plants, there are few so intense as the sight of a collection of flowers, varied in color, form, and size, and in their position on the stems that support them. If the perfume they exhale has been extolled by the poets as equal to their colors, it must be admitted that they never create, through the medium of sight, disagreeable sensations analogous to those which some nervous organizations experience from their exhalations through the sense of smell. Color, then, is doubtless, of all their qualities, that which is most prized."

Again, in his work on "Color," page 264, Chevreul says :

"White flowers are the only ones that possess the advantage of heightening the tone of flowers which have only a light tint of any color whatever. They are also the only ones that possess the advantage of separating all flowers whose colors mutually injure each other."

Leigh Hunt, in his "Chorus of the Flowers," says :

"See (and scorn all duller
Taste) how heaven loves color ;
How great Nature, clearly, joys in red and green—
What sweet thoughts she thinks
Of violets and pinks,
And a thousand flushing hues, made solely to be seen ;
See her whitest lilies
Chill the silver showers,
And what a red mouth is her rose, the woman of her flowers."

Milton describes an occasion, when

"Crocus and hyacinth, with rich inlay
Broidered the ground, more colored than with stone
Of costliest gem."

It is stated in Adams's "Language of Flowers," page 156, that,

"In the South of England, a chaplet of white roses is borne before the corpse of a maiden by a young girl, nearest in age and resemblance to the deceased, and afterwards hung up over her accustomed seat at church. They are emblematical, says Washington Irving, of purity, and the crown of glory which she has received in heaven."

Lucy Hooper, in her "Lady's Book of Flowers and Poetry," page 206, says:

"In the by-gone days of chivalry, when a lady wished to intimate to her lover that she was undecided whether she would accept his offer or not,.she decorated her head with a frontlet of white daisies, which was understood to say, 'I will think of it.'"

Again, from Hooper's "Lady's Book of Flowers and Poetry," page 160, we learn that,

"Orange flowers are made the emblem of chastity, from the purity of their white petals."

Again, on page 184, Miss Hooper, in her "Lady's Book of Flowers and Poetry," says:

"The white pink, so richly gifted with odor, is emblematic of those persons who benefit society by their talents."

Keightley, in his "Mythology of Ancient Greece and Italy," page 49, says:

"Of flowers, Juno was most partial to the dittany, the poppy, and the lily. It is said that the lily was once yellow, but that the infant Hercules being put to the breast of the goddess as she slept, on waking she thrust the babe indignantly from her with such precipitation that a part of her milk was spilt. What fell on the heaven produced the Galaxy or Milky Way; the portion which reached the earth, tinged the lilies white."

Leigh Hunt, in his "Chorus of the Flowers," says:

> "We are lilies fair,
> The flowers of virgin light;
> Nature held us forth and said,
> 'Lo! my thoughts of white.'"

Camoens, Portugal's greatest poet, kindly reminds us that,

> "Bending beneath the tears of pearly dawn,
> The snow-white lily glitters o'er the lawn;
> Lo! from the bough reclines the damask rose,
> And o'er the lily's milk-white bosom glows;
> Fresh in the dew, far o'er the painted dales,
> Each fragrant herb her sweetest scent exhales."

Lucy Hooper, in her "Lady's Book of Flowers and Poetry," page 93, says :

"We usually associate the idea of extreme whiteness with the Lily; so that it is as common to express a pure white by comparison with this flower, as with snow."

Again, in her "Lady's Book of Flowers and Poetry," page 124, Miss Hooper says :

"The Cactus grandi-floris is one of our most splendid hot-house plants, and is a native of Jamaica and some other of the West India Islands. Its stem is creeping, and thickly set with spines. The flower is white and very large, sometimes nearly a foot in diameter. Its petals are of a pure and dazzling white; and a vast number of recurved stamens, surrounding the style in the centre, add to its beauty."

Of the broad-leaved and magnificent Lincoln Lily, of South America, called by our English cousins, and by some of the other Europeans, the Victoria Regia, Guyot, in his "Earth and Man," page 210, says :

"On the bosom of the peaceful waters of tropical America swims the Victoria Regia, the elegant rival of the Rafflesia, that odorous and gigantic water lily, whose white and rosy corolla, fifteen inches in diameter, rises with dazzling brilliancy from the midst of a train of immense leaves, softly spread upon the waves, a single one covering a space of six feet in width."

According to Noah Webster's description of the Lincoln Lily—although he (or one of his lexicographical successors) describes it under another and less appropriate name:

"Its large, spreading leaves are from three to five feet in diameter, and have a rim from three to five inches high ; and its immense rose-white flowers, when fully expanded, sometimes attain a diameter of twenty-three inches."

It is a very significant fact, also, and one well worthy to be attentively considered in this connection, that

Black is an extremely distasteful and dangerous thing—a thing which the great and good God of Nature has been particularly careful to exclude from every wholesome article of

FOOD AND DRINK.

Bread—that of which man eats most, or that which is used as a substitute for bread, whether of wheat or of corn, as with us ; of rice, as with the Chinese ; of millet, as with the people of the East Indies ; or of mandioca, as with many of the nations of tropical America and Africa, is always, if pure, and if properly made, either white or golden—never black.

Upon this subject, we may here adduce the following very pertinent extract from the writings of Moses, who, in the sixteenth chapter of Exodus, says :

"When the dew that lay was gone up, behold, upon the face of the wilderness there lay a small round thing, as small as the hoar frost on the ground. And when the children of Israel saw it, they said one to another, It is manna ; for they knew not what it was. And Moses said unto them, This is the bread which the Lord hath given you to eat. * * * And the house of Israel called the name thereof Manna ; and it was like coriander seed, white, and the taste of it was like wafers made with honey."

Another ancient Jewish writer, Artabanus, who, as we learn from a very curious compilation entitled " Old and Rare Fragments," page 275, says :

" When the Egyptians came up with the Jews, and followed after them, the fire flashed on them from before, and the sea inundated their path, so that all the Egyptians perished, either by the fire, or by the return of the waters. But the Jews escaped the danger, and passed thirty years in the desert, where God rained upon them a kind of grain, like that called Panic, whose color was like snow. Moses was ruddy, with white hair, and of dignified deportment, and, when he did these things, he was in the eighty-ninth year of his age."

It may have been, and doubtless was, well enough for the manna to be of the color and general appearance of "hoar frost on the ground"—although, in that form and guise, it may, at first, have impressed the hungry Israelites who had already begun to long and murmur for the flesh-pots of Egypt, with the idea of a rather cold breakfast—yet it by no means follows that, therefore, bread made of the meal or flour of corn, wheat, rye, oats, or barley, should be altogether as white as snow.

Everything has, by nature, its own appropriate and peculiar color. Reasonably may we infer that, with a single exception, all the colors, hues, dyes, shades and tints, are, in themselves, absolutely good and proper. Upon Black alone, among colors, has the Deity placed the seal of his eternal disapprobation. It would seem, then, that we should not only be willing to retain, but also careful to preserve, the distinguishing chromatic signals with which the Almighty has been pleased to perfect his favorite and countless creations—all the chromatic signals, indeed, except Black, with which latter, however, the Lord of Hosts never has been, and never will be, pleased to perfect anything—Black being, by his own supreme and irreversible decree, the badge of all imperfection, ugliness, disease, and death.

In an anonymous pamphlet, recently published, entitled "How to Detect Adulterations in our Daily Food and Drink," page 11, it is very opportunely and truthfully stated that,

"Bread made of good flour, fermented in the usual way, with no admixture of either salt or alum, is not only the sweetest bread that can be eaten, but the only kind which should be eaten ; and were the public to demand such, and refuse to purchase the falsely white bread, there would be much less need for the physician, and a lower rate of mortality. The best bread is not the whitest ; nor is excessive fineness of the flour desirable, either for purposes of nutriment or digestibility."

Bread tinged with the pale golden color natural to many of the smaller cereals, is certainly more palatable, and far more healthful, than that made of the costlier qualities of extra-white and extra-superfine flour. It may be safely assumed, therefore, that the almost universal inquiries and demands for snow-white flour, and for snow-white bread, are positively ridiculous and unwholesome.

The object of these pages is not so much to prove that all the good things are white, as to establish the fact —however fatally such fact may affect the negro—that, with very rare exceptions, no good thing is black.

Hardly may we suppose that there is, in all the universe, one intelligent creature who would not retain intact the refulgent splendor of the heavens; the radiance of the sun; the blueness of the sky; the azure of the ocean; the grayness of the earth; the verdure of the foliage; the greenness of the grass; the delightfully variegated colors of the flowers; the rosiness of the apple; the pink of the peach; the scarlet of the nectarine; the crimson of the cherry; the carnation of the currant; the purple of the grape; the yellowness of the orange; the redness of the beet—and, with the sole exception of Black, every other hue and tint inherent in the respective things of nature.

In most of the fruits, however, as, indeed, in most of the cereals, pod-produce, garden-vegetables, tubers, nuts, and other eatables, whiteness, or a near approach to whiteness, is always conspicuous and predominant. Nor does any healthy animal, bird, or fish, or other creature, yield black flesh, black eggs, black oil, black fat, black albumen, black gelatine, black cartilage, black gristle, black tendons, black ligaments, black arteries, black veins, black milk, black blood, black bones, nor black teeth.

Well known is it, also, that clarification, leading to, a

greater or less degree of whiteness, is a universal and invariable result of every well-conducted refining process whether such process be with grain, with sugar, with salt, with wines, with liquors, with resins, with syrups, with medicines, with meats, with metals, or with any other substance whatever, whether liquid or solid.   As a rule, things which by nature are not white, become white just in proportion as they are purified by being separated from gross or feculent matters ; but those things which are naturally white, while undergoing processes of still greater refinement, merely change from one grade or degree of whiteness to another — in many cases, from only the bare tinge of superiority to the full-color of perfection.

From the things eaten and drunk, to the things off of which and out of which we eat and drink, there is so short a distance, that we may here very properly pay some little attention to the colors of both crockery and glass-ware. Has any one ever seen, or has any one any desire to see, a black dish, a black plate, a black cup, a black saucer, a black pitcher, a black tureen, a black bowl, a black goblet, or a black wine-glass? No; the more usual and appropriate color of all these things is white; and if we would enjoy our dinner, and be fully benefited by it, there must be no black thing upon the table; and more especially is it necessary and desirable, when we sit down to partake of the substantially good things of this life, that there be no black person in the dining room—no swarthy guest, nor negro waiter. Pure porcelain, Delft-ware, China-ware and stone ware—all of glittering and spotless whiteness—are, among other things, quite indispensable to every well furnished side-board.   Even the casters, the salt-cellars, the knives, the forks, and the spoons, must be burnished brightly, so that they, too, may both be and appear as white as possible.

In many other important particulars do men constantly

exhibit their instinctive and salutary preference for White. We may look at the houses in our own country—in the United States, in Great Britain, in Germany, in Russia, in France, in Italy, in Spain, in Portugal; we may examine those in Asia, in Africa, in South America—in all parts of the world, indeed, where houses have ever been built; but nowhere may we find a black house—a house of which either the exterior or the interior, as finished by the owner, by the architect, or by the painter, has been subjected to the polluting and pestilential process of nigrification. On the contrary, in many large cities, as, for instance, in Lisbon, in Calcutta, in Tunis, and in Buenos Ayres, almost every house is white, both within and without.

Even the bare thought of a black residence awakens within us feelings of dread and horror akin to those which proved so fatal to the many poor fellows who, in 1756, were diabolically forced into the " Black Hole " of Calcutta.

As having a direct bearing on the very interesting and important subject of white houses and white apartments it may be well to introduce, in this connection, the following extract from a letter recently written by a correspondent of the London *Builder*, who, in speaking of the " Effects of Colors upon Health," says:

" From several years' observation in rooms of various sizes, used as manufacturing rooms, and occupied by females for twelve hours per day, I found that the workers who occupied those rooms which had large windows with large panes of glass in the four sides of the room, so that the sun's rays penetrated through the room during the whole day, were much more healthy than the workers who occupied rooms lighted from one side only, or rooms lighted through very small panes of glass. I observed another very singular fact, namely, that the workers who occupied one room were very cheerful and healthy, while the occupiers of another similar room, who were employed on the same kind of work, were all inclined to melancholy, and complained of pains in the forehead and eyes, and were often ill and unable to work. Upon examining the rooms in question, I found they were both equally well ventilated and lighted; I could not discover anything about the drainage of the premises that could affect the one room any more than the other; but I observed that the room occupied by the healthy workers was wholly whitewashed, and the room occupied by the melancholy workers was colored with yellow ochre.

I had the yellow ochre all washed off, and the walls and ceilings whitewashed. The workers ever after felt more cheerful and healthy. After making this discovery, I extended my observation to a number of smaller rooms and garrets, and found, without exception, that the occupiers of the white rooms were much more healthy than the occupiers of the yellow or buff colored rooms; and I succeeded in inducing occupiers of the yellow rooms to change the color for whitewash. I always found a corresponding improvement in the health and spirits of the occupiers. From these observations I would respectfully drop a hint to the authorities of schools, asylums, and hospitals, to eschew yellow, buff, or anything approaching to yellow, as the grand color of the interior of their buildings. "

Various writers of high repute, some at one time, and some at another, have used certain terms as the symbols or types of White and Black, respectively; and, from the terms thus used, the following selection is offered as fairly representing this laconic but very suggestive method of defining the two extremely opposite principles or things now under consideration:

WHITE.	BLACK.	WHITE.	BLACK.
God	Devil	Wealth	Want
Heaven	Hell	Abundance	Beggary
Day	Night	Affluence	Pauperism
Light	Darkness	Honor	Ignominy
Good	Evil	Glory	Shame
Virtue	Vice	Liberty	Slavery
Right	Wrong	Freedom	Subjection
Wisdom	Folly	Independence	Vassalage
Knowledge	Ignorance	Sovereignty	Subordination
Prudence	Improvidence	Friendship	Enmity
Energy	Inertness	Kindness	Cruelty
Progress	Retrogression	Humanity	Brutality
Improvement	Deterioration	Fortitude	Fear

White.	Black.	White.	Black.
Safety	Danger	Harmony	Discord
Success	Failure	Peace	War
Riches	Poverty	Courage	Cowardice
Victory	Defeat	Mirth	Melancholy
Candor	Duplicity	Gayety	Gloom
Truth	Error	Gladness	Grief
Veracity	Falsehood	Delight	Horror
Modesty	Obscenity	Rapture	Wretchedness
Chastity	Licentiousness	Happiness	Misery
Innocence	Guilt	Love	Hatred
Fragrance	Fetor	Hope	Despair
Cleanliness	Filthiness	Weal	Woe
Neatness	Nastiness	Felicity	Agony
Sobriety	Drunkenness	Bliss	Torment

Considered, then, in the incalculable amplitude and multiplicity of the meanings which belong to it, what is White? Precisely what, in the preceding pages, it has been represented to be—a thing of Life, Health, and Beauty; a thing of Hope, Mirth, and Merit; a thing of Improvement, Progress, and Permanence; a thing of Goodness, Glory, and Grandeur; a thing of Harmony Sublimity, and Perfection; a thing of Amiability, Peace, and Heaven-born Excellence; a thing of Sympathy, Attraction, and Delight; a thing of Innocence, Virtue, and Purity; a thing of most wholesome Enchantments, Benefits, and Blessings: a thing worthy to be eternally Loved, Courted, Kissed, Caressed, Embraced, Cherished, Protected, Increased, Multiplied and Replenished.

Numerous other instances might be cited to show that, while Black is one of the worst of bad things, and is under the bitter and blasting ban of Nature, White is one of the best of good things, and is under the especial and all-powerful protection of Heaven. But, for this chapter, already much lengthened beyond the limits assigned it, we must now find a conclusion.

Henceforth, who, in the councils of our nation, shall be so idiotic or so impudent, so deceitful or so audacious, so demagogical or so degenerate, so shameless or so reprobate, as to demand that America shall become the theatre of a forcibly and gigantical organized system of amalgamation between good and evil, and that the pernicious blackness of the African shall, by acts of Congress, be placed upon an equality with the salutary whiteness of the Caucasian?—as if, forsooth, a thing so impossible in nature could be feasible in legislation! If our National and State legislatures are still haunted by the presence of ghouls and ogres who persist in howling out demands so odious and preposterous as these, those ghouls and ogres must at once give way to men of common sense, to men of clear heads and practicable ideas, who, recognizing the fact that the whole universe is but an aggregation of ever-obvious and immutable distinctions, will not waste time, nor render themselves ridiculous, by attempting to annul or modify the irrevocable decrees of fate.

Scarcely possible is it, within the compass of a single language, to find words of sufficient number and force to reprehend with adequate severity that particular class of demagogues who are here but too feebly, too imperfectly denounced. In the midst of their career of criminal folly, let the execrable two-thirds majority of the Black Congress, who have so shamelessly and so wickedly proposed to strike from all our State Constitutions, and from the Constitution of the United States, the blest and sacred word White, pause for a few moments, and listen to the manly and significant protests of their insulted and aroused constituents.

This day, indeed, may the stentorian voices of the greater and better portion of the American people, pointing toward Hartford and New Haven, and directly addressing the Black Congress, be heard pithily exclaiming,

in effect—Remember the result of the late election in
Connecticut! Observe how gloriously the White Republicans and the Loyal Democrats, acting together in a
spirit of most laudable and patriotic harmony, have
saved the State from irreparable disgrace. Near at hand
is the time for this opportune and wholesome lesson of
Connecticut to be carried into every other State of the
American Union! Since the old Republican party has
been debased into a black and vile-smelling negro party,
it, as a party, has forfeited all just claims upon us for support; now it may take care of itself; from this time forward,
we are firmly resolved not to have anything whatever to
do with it, nor for it; only, as a solemn duty which we
owe to the commonwealth and to ourselves, we are determined to use every legitimate means in our power to di-
•vide it, to defeat it, and to destroy it! Untrue to its
mission, false to the faith of its founders and its followers,
the old Republican party may henceforth look for the precarious life and maintenance which yet await it, to the
negroes and to such other Black Republicans as may unfortunately encumber and curse with their presence our
common country! Assembling together the better elements of the old Republican party, in affiliation with the
Loyal Democrats, (and sloughing off, and pushing out, all
Black Republicans, Copperheads, and Secessionists) it is
our purpose to form a White Republican party, one of
the functions of which shall be the early bringing, and
the perpetual keeping, of the whole continent of North
America under one good republican government—precisely such a good republican government as is provided
for in the Constitution of the United States—to be pre-
sided over and controlled, from first to last, and all the
time, exclusively by men who inherit the natural greatness
and glory of unsullied descent from the pure white races!
What! strike from an American Constitution the hea-

ven-born and immaculate word White! No, no, never,
never; this beautiful and salutary monosyllable (one of
the best terms recorded in the annals of time, one of the
most elegant and sublime vocables of the English language) must be preserved in full vigor and force as the
palladium of an elevated and progressive American manhood. Rather than that the sorry-witted and recreant
members of the Black Congress should busy themselves
in the base attempt to strike from the archives of their
country the pure and precious word White, infinitely
better would it be if, at once, they would but take service
in striking from themselves their own duncical and degraded heads!

Countless ages ago, God was pleased to create the Tox-
odon, the Mylodon, the Glyptodon, and numerous other
gigantic quadrupeds, not a single representative of which
can now anywhere be found, save only in fossil form.
Previously, or subsequently, or at the same time, he also
created a certain species of black bipeds, of the genus
homo, to whom he allotted, as the proper period of their
aggregate existence upon the earth, a fixed number of centuries, the last of which is now rapidly approaching (if,
indeed, it be not the one now actually drawing to a close)
and with the last day of which will inevitably pass away,
forever, the last servile and slothful scion of the House of
Ebony—a most slavish and shabby scion, fitted finally,
and from the first, like all of his fugitive and forgotten
forefathers, only for fossilization!

CHAPTER IV.

THE SERVILE BASENESS AND BEGGARY OF THE BLACKS.

There has never been the slightest danger of an insurrection of the slaves. The real victim of slavery is the white man. Whatever little good there is in the system, the black man has had ; while most of the evil has fallen to the white man's share.—*Parton's Gen. Butler in New Orleans, page 99.*

> What can ennoble sots, or slaves, or cowards?
> Alas! not all the blood of all the Howards.—POPE.

> Who so base as be a slave?
> The coward slave! we pass him by.—BURNS.

WHEN the negro, in Africa, in the year 1620, fastening anew upon both himself and his posterity the condition of perpetual bondage, allowed himself, as a guarantee of his passive and prodigious dastardy, to be brought in chains all the way across the Atlantic—it was then that, for the first time, was reached the uttermost depth of human degradation. That the negro had, and has, always been a slave in his own country or elsewhere, according to the habitat or journeyings of his master, is well known; but it was only when, as the cringing tool of the meaner sort of white men, he came to America, that his obsequiousness and pusillanimity began to assume monstrous proportions.

Of all the miscreants and outcasts who have brought irreparable disgrace upon mankind, the slave is at once the most despicable and the most infamous. To be a slave of the white man, yet, if possible to be a slave exempt from the necessity of labor, has always been the ruling ambition of the negro—not less so now than it was four thousand years ago, and not less so then than it is now. Does the reader demand proofs of these astoundingly disgusting facts? Proofs of one part of the statement are already too notorious to require repetition ; proofs of the other part are here adduced.

Under date of July 3, 1858, the *Frontier* (Texas) *News* said :

"While in attendance on the District Court, in Tarrant County, one day of the previous week, we witnessed the ceremonies on the occasion of a free negro, named Jerry, voluntarily going into slavery. He came into court cheerfully, and there stated, in answer to questions propounded by the court, that he knew the consequence of the act—that he had selected as his master W. M. Robinson, without any compulsion or persuasion, but of his own free will and accord. Two gentlemen came in and stated under oath that they had signed his petition at his request, and that the gentleman he had selected as his master, was a good citizen and an honorable man. Jerry is a fine looking negro, some forty years of age, and appears to be smart."

The following legal notice was duly advertised in Rogersville, Tennessee, at the time indicated in the advertisement itself.

"PETITION FOR VOLUNTARY ENSLAVEMENT.—*In Chancery at Rogersville, Tennessee.*—BEN, A MAN OF COLOR, AND WILLIAM MILLER, ESQ.— Notice is hereby given that Ben, a man of color, has this day filed his Petition in our said Court, asking to become the slave of the said Miller, under an act of the General Assembly of said State, passed the 8th of March, 1858.

R. C. FAIN,
Clerk and Master in Chancery."

"*May 29th*, 1858."

In a paragraph headed "*Departure of Emancipated Negroes—Don't Want to Leave*," the Lynchburgh (Virginia) *Republican*, only a little while before the outbreak of the great rebellion, said :

"On Sunday last, a crowd of not less than one thousand negroes assembled on the basin to take leave of the negroes belonging to the estate of the late Mr. Francis B. Shackleford, of Amherst County, who, in accordance with the will of the deceased, were about to depart, by way of the canal, for a free State. The whole number set free was forty-four, men, women, and children, but only thirty-seven left, the balance preferring to remain in servitude in Old Virginia, rather than enjoy their freedom elsewhere. Some of those who did leave were thrown on the boat by main force, so much opposed were they to leaving, and many expressed their determination of returning to Virginia as soon as an opportunity offered."

During the proceedings of the Legislature of Virginia, in the early part of 1856,

"Mr. Seddon presented the petition of Critty, a free negro, emancipated by the will of Elizabeth Woodson, late of Powhatan. Critty is tired of freedom, and wants to become a slave again."

"Mr. Renold presented the petition of Frank Harman for his voluntary enslavement."

"Mr. White presented the petition of Jesse Spencer, a free negro, to be allowed to enslave himself."

The Richmond *Enquirer*, of June, 1855, informed us that,

"About three years ago, Miss Anne W. Taliaferro, of King William County, Virginia, emancipated 40 negroes, giving each $150. They were placed in a Quaker settlement in Ohio, by E. W. Scott, executor of the estate. A few weeks since, Mr. Scott had occasion to visit them on business, and found them in a wretched condition, almost starving. One of the children had been stolen, and several had died for want of attention and the necessaries of life. They begged Mr. Scott to allow them to return with him to Virginia and go into slavery."

In 1858, the Louisville *Courier*, in an article headed "Returning to Slavery," said

"By the will of the late David Glass, of this city, his negroes who desired to go to Liberia were ordered to be set free upon arriving at the age of 18 years. In accordance with the provisions of this will, two of the negro men were manumitted by the County Court, and delivered to Mr. Cowan, the agent of the Kentucky Colonization Society. Mr. C. started with them a few days ago. When they reached Lexington, they expressed a wish to see one of their young mistresses who resided there. Mr. Cowan readily acceded to this request, but they did not return. Mr. C. went after them, when they positively refused to go to Liberia. They have returned to this city, and the executor of Mr. Glass's estate has taken charge of them. They will fall back on the heirs and probably be sold."

The New Orleans *Picayune* of February, 1859, said:

"In the Mississippi Legislature, on the 1st inst., Mr. Suratt, from the Committee on Propositions and Grievances, to whom was referred the petition of William Webster, a free negro, to be permitted to become the slave of Dr. Athnald Ball, of Charleston, Tallahatchie County, Mississippi, reported the same back to the House with a bill recommending that the same become a law. Received and agreed to. Bill passed."

According to the Nashville *Banner*, of March, 1859,

"William Bass, a free person of color, residing in the District of Marlborough, has petitioned the General Assembly of South Carolina, praying to become a slave."

The Memphis *Bulletin*, of September, 1858, said:

"About thirteen months ago, a bright mulatto girl belonging to Mrs. J. P. Pryor, ran off from Memphis and went to Cincinnati, where she remained for over a year. About two days ago she voluntarily returned to this city and delivered herself up to Mr. J. W. Wilkinson, a friend of the family, requesting him to write to Mr. R. H. Parkham, who lives near La Grange, and is the father of Mrs. Prior, and who reared the girl, to come down to Memphis and receive her again into slavery, as she preferred slavery to Cincinnati freedom. The girl is named Emily, and is well known in this city. She says she had a hard time in Cincinnati—that she was sick a good deal and found a great difference in having a master and mistress to take care of her when sick, and having to take care of herself. She says she ran away from Memphis, and had to run away from Cincinnati to get back. The foregoing facts may be relied on as authentic. By reference to our Chancery advertisements, there will be found another instance of voluntarily seeking to return to slavery, in the case of a girl named Hannah, with the facts of which we are not acquainted."

In a paragraph headed "Preferred Slavery to Freedom," the Galveston (Texas) *News*, of January 5, 1861, said :

"On Tuesday last, a negro woman named Margaret arrived here from Connecticut, accompanying Miss Ellen Lee (granddaughter of Col. James Morgan) as her slave. This woman Margaret was given by Col. Morgan to his granddaughter, and accompanied her to Connecticut in 1849, when Miss Lee was a child, and she was then given her freedom. During this period of fourteen years, she has lived in various parts of the free States, enjoying her freedom the same as others of her color. Learning that her former mistress was about to return to reside in Texas, she went back to her and asked the privilege of accompanying her and of resuming her former condition as a slave. She was told by Col. Morgan that she could live here in no other condition than as a slave, and that she would at any time be liable to be sold. She, however, persisted in returning, as she said she preferred to be a slave in the South, rather than have her freedom in the North."

The New York *Evening Post*, of April 30, 1860, under the heading "A NEGRO FATHER DESIRES TO SELL HIS CHILDREN INTO SERFDOM—A DESPERATE RENCONTRE THE CONSEQUENCE," said :

"A difficulty occurred on Saturday evening last in that part of Cincinnati known as Bucktown, which arose from the following circumstances : A negro named Frank Buckner called at the house of Mary Emerson, a negress, and demanded the custody of his two children, alleging that since the death of their mother they had been of no particular value to him, and he was determined to sell them into slavery and realize a handsome thing out of them. This very unnatural and hard-hearted desire on the part of the father, so roused the feelings of the woman Emerson, that she seized a skillet and commenced such a vigorous onslaught upon Buckner that he fled incontinently from the premises. About half an hour subsequently he ventured to return, this time, however, provided with a huge bowie-knife, the brandishing of which he supposed would intimidate the Amazonian Mary from any further use of the culinary utensil ; but, instead of quieting her, it only added the more to her aggravation, and calling upon a second female who occupied an adjoining apartment, the twain sat upon Buckner and came nigh using him up, when he managed to gain the mastery by felling them both to the floor with his knife ; and but for the timely arrival of the police, he would have killed them outright.   As it was, each of the women, as well as Buckner himself, were badly hurt, he from the effects of the skillet, and they from the knife.   They were all locked up in the station-house to await an examination."

Governor Hammond, of South Carolina, who, like all the other slaveholders of the Southern States, ought to have had more common decency than to wish to be the centre (or anything else) of the exceedingly foul and noxious surroundings of negroes and negro slavery, says:

"Sometimes it happens that a negro prefers to give up his family rather than separate from his master.   I have known such instances."

Here follows something unique and exquisite.   In 1859, the Rev. Daniel Worth, of North Carolina, a truly estimable old gentleman, who was born and reared in Guilford County, began to preach against slavery, and to circulate anti-slavery literature—especially a work entitled "The Impending Crisis of the South."   He was arrested, imprisoned, fined $3,000, and then banished from the State, with the judicial warning that the penalty of his second offence, if committed, would be death!   His trial and conviction took place in Greensborough, about ninety miles west of Raleigh.   What occurred immediately after the court had sentenced the good old man, may be learned by reading the following extract from the Greensborough correspondence of the New York *Herald*, under date of January 4, 1860 :

"After Worth was convicted, the slaves of this place gave a grand banquet in honor of the event, to which the Court and Bar and many of our prominent citizens were invited.   It was truly a magnificent affair, and the table would have done credit to a Fifth Avenue palace. To show you the feeling of the negroes, a slave belonging to Colonel E. P. Jones, a large tobacco manufacturer of this place, remarked that he could read his Bible as well as Worth, and he prayed to the Lord to let all the Abolitionists be hung, because if it were not for them the master would not be half as strict with the slave; and that he loved the Lord the best and his master next, and hated an Abolitionist worst and the devil next."

If Heaven spares the life of the author of the book above mentioned, he hopes to be able to induce the State of North Carolina (his own dear native land) to repair, in a measure at least, the wrong it did to Daniel Worth; that is to say, he means to ask that the whole amount of the fine, with six per cent. interest added, be refunded to the heirs of the brave and venerable Worth—who, having undergone many barbarous persecutions at the hands of slavery, has but recently quitted the scenes of earth. In the sincere hope and confidence of being able to render at least a modicum of good service to a much larger number of his countrymen, the same author also means to solicit North Carolina and Massachusetts, Louisiana and New York, Georgia and Pennsylvania, Alabama and Ohio, Virginia and Minnesota, Florida and Illinois, Texas and Maine, Tennessee and Oregon, Maryland and California, and, indeed, every other State of the United States—or rather, he means to solicit the people of America at large—to sweep away from themselves, quickly, thoroughly, and forever, every trace and vestige of the negro race.

In perfect keeping with the last foregoing extract, is the following item, headed "An Abolitionist Betrayed by Slaves," from the Raleigh (North Carolina) *Register*, of November 12, 1859:

"We learn from a friend that a man who says his name is John D. Williams has been arrested and confined in Hillsborough jail, on a charge of tampering with slaves. He is about 25 years of age, and is traveling as a book-agent. *He was twice betrayed by slaves to whom he communicated his Abolition sentiments.* He was still in jail on the 3d. We would not be surprised to hear that he has been lynched, He no doubt will be, if he should not leave as soon as he is turned out of jail."

So much—without the unnecessary multiplication of instances—so much for the grovelling servility of the negroes before the war. How did they act during the progress of actual hostilities? As a mass, with scarcely an exception, what were they, indeed, but

"A set of simpletons and superstitious sneaks?"

It is true that many negroes were enrolled or ranged on the side of the Union ; but not one of them assumed the character of a soldier from any patriotic impulse or admonition—not one of them was either a true lover of Liberty, or a genuine hater of Slavery. On the contrary, they all sought the camp from venal motives, and from an absurd and cowardly disposition to be placed beyond any further necessity to labor. The exceeding baseness of their natural predilections and proclivities, and the unparalleled infamy of their real purposes and proceedings, are revoltingly apparent in the following extracts.

Soon after the rebel assault on Fort Sumter, in April, 1861, the Richmond *Enquirer*, under the heading of "The Blue Cockade Worn by Negroes," said :

"We learn from the *Southerner*, a paper published at Bolivar, Tenn., that the negroes of A. S. Coleman, Esq., of that place, created quite a sensation in that town a few days ago, by appearing in the streets with blue cockades on their hats. It learns from Mr. Coleman that they requested the privilege of wearing them, as they said, to show their contempt for the Abolitionists, and their love for their native South."

Early in the month of May, 1861, the Mobile *Advertiser*, in an announcement of the names of certain "Subscribers to the Southern Loan," published the following telegram :

"DEMOPOLIS, April 26, 1861.

"Two negroes of Marengo have taken $900 of the Confederate Loan. Peter, the property of Mrs. Ann Tarbert, and a blacksmith at Spring Hill, took $400 ; and the foreman of A. Hatch, Esq., on his plantation at Arcola, took $500. Some of our most wealthy planters have not taken a dollar, and others that are able to take thousands, have only subscribed $50 to $100. Shame on the patriotism of our wealthy men, that the negroes should be more patriotic than they."

About the same time, the Montgomery (Alabama) *Mail*, in a paragraph ironically entitled "Lo! The Poor Slave," said :

"William, a slave belonging to our townsman, Dr. W. H. Rives, has invested one hundred and fifty dollars in the Confederate States Loan Bonds."

Just after the farce of Secession had been enacted in Louisiana, the New Orleans *Picayune*, speaking of "The Poor African and the Confederate Loan," said :

"Albert, a slave, the property of General S. G. Hadaway, accosted Mr. Knox, President of the Central Bank, and Chairman of the Board of Loan Commissioners, this morning, on the steps of the Central Bank, when the following conversation ensued :

"'Good morning, Mr. Knox; I am told you have some Southern Confederacy bonds for sale.'

"'Yes, Albert, *the loan is not all taken*, although it is being rapidly subscribed for.'

"'Well, Mr. Knox, I want to take some. I have got three hundred dollars which I have saved out of my earnings in odd times, and I want to put it in these bonds, if you will let me.'

"'You cannot do so without your master's consent,' replied Mr. Knox, 'but if he is willing, there will be no difficulty about it.'

"Albert went out, found his master, obtained his consent, and the books of the loan subscription show three hundred dollars of coupon bonds subscribed for and paid 'by Samuel G. Hadaway, trustee for his slave Albert,' and with the money of Albert.

"Alfred, the slave of Colonel W. Crawford Bibb, being told of Albert's subscription, drew out one hundred dollars which he had on deposit, and subscribed for coupon bonds for that amount."

The following item appeared in the Charleston *Mercury* of May 28, 1861 :

"The free colored men of Charleston have contributed $450 to

9*

sustain the cause of the South. The zealous and unfailing alacrity with which this class of our population have always devoted their labor and their means to promote the safety of the State, is alike honorable to themselves and gratifying to the community."

A correspondent of the New York *Herald*, writing from Montgomery, Alabama, under date of February 14, 1861, said :

"I am informed that the Governor of this State has received a letter from a 'head man' on a plantation, who says he has been drilling sixty of his master's men, on moonlight nights and Sundays, and with his master's permission is now ready to go to Fort Morgan and do all he can for his master against 'the damned buckram abolitionists,' who have done so much to cut off Sam's privileges."

The Philadelphia *Enquirer*, under date of July 24, 1861, speaking of the battle of Bull Run, said :

"Upward of 12,000 negroes were employed to work on the intrenchments of Manassas, and about the same number were employed to work on the intrenchments at Richmond.

"Our informant is the owner of a large number of slaves, and was required to furnish a certain number of them to work for the Rebels every day.

"There are two regiments of well-drilled negroes at Richmond."

The Richmond *Examiner*, in the summer of 1861, in an article in reference to "The Free Colored Men of Virginia," said :

"A list of thirty-five worthy free negroes of this city, who have offered their services in the work of defence, or in any other capacity required, has been sent in to the Captain of the Woodis Riflemen. We noticed colored men in uniform. They came as musicians with the Georgia troops."

In harmony with the foregoing account from the *Examiner*, the Richmond *Enquirer*, about the same time, in an article entitled "Negroes Volunteering," said :

"Free negroes in Amelia County have offered themselves to the Government for any service. In our neighboring city of Petersburgh, two hundred free negroes offered for any work that might be assigned to them, either to fight under white officers, dig ditches, or anything that could show their desire to serve Old Virginia. In the same city, a negro hackman came to his master, and insisted, with tears in his eyes, that he should accept all his savings, $100, to help equip the volunteers. The free negroes of Chesterfield have made a similar proposition. Such is the spirit, among bond and free, through the whole of the State."

Shamelessly boasting of the negroes' scandalous and criminal devotion to slavery, the New Orleans *Crescent*, soon after the general outbreak of hostilities, in an article entitled " Slaves with the Confederate Army," said :

"Tom, the slave of our citizen James H. Phelps, took a fancy to go soldiering, and his master willingly gratified him, and Tom was engaged by Captain Kountz, of the De Soto Rifles, to attend him through the war. There are hundreds of other slaves like Tom gone to kill the Yankees. Tom's highest ambition appears to be to kill a Yankee."

Under the heading "Black Troops in the Rebel Army," the Hartford (Connecticut) *Times* published a letter, dated at Pittsborough, Chatham County, North Carolina, May 10, 1861, from which the following is an extract :

"Every free negro in this county, so far as I can learn, has enlisted to fight the Abolitionists, and there are enough to make a regiment. All the slaves who can obtain consent have also enlisted."

An instance of the remarkable solicitude and faithfulness with which the negroes befriended the Union soldiers during the war, is furnished in the following item, which appeared in the Richmond *Enquirer*, of January 28, 1865 :

"A corporal and four men, escaped Yankee prisoners from Florence, South Carolina, were captured near Elizabethtown, Bladen County, North Carolina, last week, endeavoring to cross the Cape Fear, making their way to Newbern. They were detected by a negro, who gave information of their whereabouts, and were delivered to the military authorities at Wilmington on Friday."

Of the faint-heartedness and poltroonery of the negroes, an officer of one of the Michigan regiments wrote to the *National* (Washington) *Intelligencer*, on the 13th of August, 1862, as follows :

"I witnessed their drill exercise a short time before leaving Port Royal, and it was truly amusing. During the exercises, they practised them in the manual of arms and loading and firing blank cartridge ; and when the command 'fire' was given, nearly one half of the line squatted and dropped down, frightened at the noise of the guns in their own hands. I also conversed with several of them. They told me they never expected it of the Yankees to make them fight ; that they could not fight ; 'me drap right down gone dead, I get so skeered !'"

But for the intolerably disgraceful and disgusting scenes which would be certain to await us, we might follow the chicken-hearted negroes from the drill-ground, to the battle-field, where, (as at the abortive attempt to undermine and blow up Petersburgh, in Virginia, on the 30th of July, 1864, when "the black troops broke and fled, a demoralized mob, to the rear, their white officers, who strove in vain to rally them, being nearly all cut off,") we should find them, on all occasions, enfeebled with fear, quivering with fright, skulking with trepidation, and otherwise behaving with the most shameless and unpardonable cowardice.

He who says that the negro ever was, is, or can be, a brave man, gives expression to as great an absurdity as would be uttered by the asserter that soot is as white and pure as snow, or that coal is of the color and consistence of cream. It is in the very nature of the negro to be an arrant coward; and to expect him at any time, or under any circumstances whatever, to evince even a passable degree of valor or courage, is to regard as possible that which, in the wise dispensations of Providence, is absolutely impossible.

No form nor power of speech is adequate to a sufficient reprobation of such unnatural and infamous crimes, on the part of the blacks, as are brought to our notice in many of the foregoing extracts. It has been enough to dumfound us to see—and yet, even in this nineteenth century, we have seen—negroes going before courts of record, and there, with the most cringing baseness, begging to be permitted to enslave forever, both themselves and their posterity!

Others, to whom Freedom had been generously proffered, have we seen voluntarily remaining in slavery!

We have seen others who were literally forced to accept Liberty as a thing of value!

Others have we seen denying the ownership of themselves in the Free States, and, of their own accord, by change of residence, becoming the property of negro-drivers in the Slave States!

We have seen others who were willing and even anxious to sell their own free-born children into a condition of absolute and perpetual bondage!

Others, from whom the shackles of slavery have been kindly removed, have we seen piteously imploring permission to return to their ex-masters!

We have seen others who, completely besmeared and saturated with the slime of slavery, have manifested for their masters and mistresses far more regard than they ever entertained for their own families!

Others have we seen obsequiously eager to subscribe to the vast fund which was proposed for prosecuting with success the slaveholders' rebellion!

We have seen others "praying to the Lord to let all the Abolitionists be hung," and declaring "that they loved the Lord the best and their masters next, and hated the Abolitionists worst and the devil next!"

Others have we seen exercising their indescribably vile

and vulgar tongues with the fulsome assurances that they would do everything they could for their masters against the "damned buckram Abolitionists!"

We have seen others who took pleasure in willfully betraying poor white Union prisoners, who had temporarily escaped confinement, and averring that their (the negroes') "highest ambition was to kill Yankees!"

Yet these are the fellows—tell it not in Gath!—these are the fellows who, upon terms of perfect equality, are at once to be socially and politically adopted into the great family of the American poeple! These are the fellows—publish it not in the streets of Ashkelon!—these are the fellows who, without any manner of distinction or qualification, are henceforth to be recognized and greeted as worthy citizens of the United States! These are the fellows upon whom it is said we should at once confer the elective franchise! These are the fellows in whose behalf we are audaciously asked to establish and support Freedmen's Bureaus and Negro Asylums *ad infinitum*. These are the fellows (so entirely and glaringly deserving of outlawry) in whose behalf the factious demagogues of the Black Congress have but recently been concocting and consummating all manner of mean measures!

Let the Black Congress, the American Congress now (or but recently) in session at Washington, the Congress which finds so much time to legislate for negroes, and so little time, or no time at all, to legislate for white men, the Rump Congress, the Congress which believes in taxation without representation, the Congress which devises and frames military establishments in times of peace, the Congress which, through a blind and malignant policy, would make a Poland or an Ireland of one section of our Republic, rather than have it equally free and prosperous in every part, and greater in its totality than Russia and England and all Europe combined—let this unworthy, half-witted and vindictive Congress beware! Ay, remembering the late lofty and luminous lesson of Connecticut—in, beholding which it is easy to read an avenging handwriting upon the wall—let the Black Congress both blush and beware! Its unpatriotic and degenerate members are, thank God, rapidly losing their prestige and power. The days which they are now so shamefully misspending in unmerited and mawkish praise of the negroes, are quickly passing away. Their wanton disregard of the rights and interests of the whites, and their deep concern in the despicable affairs of the disserviceable and deathdoomed blacks, are, after all, but temporary mischiefs and misfortunes to the commonwealth. After the expiration of the present term, respectively, of their official service, two-thirds or more of them must be remanded to the pursuits of private life. Neither at home nor abroad shall they ever again have the opportunity either to betray or to misrepresent the good people of America. Most perversely and dissolutely have they cast their lot with the demons of darkness; with the demons of darkness let them at once, voluntarily or otherwise, slink into the doleful shades of dishonor!

America, and all the other continents and islands, for white men! Erebus for the negroes! Limbo for the mulattoes! Pandemonium for the Indians! Hades for the Chinese! and Tophet for all the other swarthy and copper-colored ghouls!

There can be little doubt that our late civil war would have ended much sooner, with far less loss of valuable lives and treasure, and with infinitely greater honor and glory to America, had our Government, from the very first outbreak of hostilities, done full justice to itself by treating both the negroes and their masters for exactly what they were—direful enemies of the Republic ; and by vigorously operating with ample and irresistible bat-

teries of blunderbusses against the one, and with an
equal number of formidable and effective howitzers
against the other; only with this difference, that the
blunderbusses should have been kept blazing away at the
blacks, until there had not been left, in any State of the
Union, one vital drop of negro blood!

It may not be questioned that an abundance of salt-
petre, rightly applied to the woolly-heads, would have
proved a most excellent means of unloosing the Gordian
knot of American politics. By such applications, or by
other applications no less efficient, all the negroes, not
only of the United States, but also of the whole world,
are destined, erelong, to suffer the mortiferous penalties
of their atrociously servile and criminal misdoings—their
utterly effete and useless existence. They have been
weighed in ten thousand balances; and, in every balance,
without exception, they have been found wanting. Their
doom has been legibly written in the Book of Fate. The
keynote of their sentence has been clearly sounded in the
word Fossilization!

Of the habitual and shameless Beggary of the Blacks,
language again fails to furnish terms of adequate condemnation. If there is a law or condition of our nature
impelling us to an unmitigated abhorrence of being
sprinkled with the malodorous juices of skunks and pole-
cats; if we would be filled with unrelieved disgust at the
sight of venomous toads and reptiles; if we would retreat with spasmodic horror from the hideousness of
fiends and devils; then must we also profoundly and intensely loathe the common penury and pauperism, the
usual destitution and mendicancy, of all the black and
bi-colored families of men—mean and misfashioned men,
who ought everywhere and on all occasions,

"To be despised and avoided in the street."

Only it is to be most earnestly and unyieldingly regretted that they are ever permitted to appear in the street at all. Erelong, this foul indecency must be disallowed. As an equitable and proper measure preliminary to their final exit from America, all the negroes ought to be immediately assigned to such unsettled and unfrequented parts of the country, as are far distant from the cities and towns ; and even there, no matter how remotely located in the solitudes of the frontier, there should never be any manner of contact or association between the whites and the blacks.

Unlike all people who are good for anything, the negroes are everywhere the recipients of charity ; but nowhere the granters of favors. Everywhere are they the coveters and the beggars of the property of others ; but nowhere are they the profferers of anything in the least worthy of acceptance. They ought to pay—and, but for their utter indifference to all good counsel, they would pay—some attention. to the terse and truthful words of Sir William Temple, who has said that,

"People who wholly trust to others' charity, and without industry of their own, will always be poor."

The negroes, like the poodles and the pointers, will always be the dependents and the parasites of white men, just so long as white men, unnaturally submitting to a wrongful relation, are disposed to tolerate the black men's infamously base and beggarly presence. Let the negroes be made to understand definitely, that, henceforth, they must desist from their daily importunacy in urging the acceptance of their dronish and dishonorable drafts upon the whites; and, in thus rightly and prudently dealing with the blacks, let the whites, as often as may be necessary, renew their recollection of the following rare words of "rare Ben Jonson:"

> "There is no bounty to be show'd to such
> As have no real goodness.   Bounty is
> A spice of virtue ; and what virtuous act
> Can take effect on them that have no power
> Of equal habitude to apprehend it?"

Truly and admirably, in the main, did the New York *Tribune*, not a great while since, say :

> "Nine-tenths of the Free Blacks have no idea of setting themselves to work except as the hirelings and servitors of white men ; no idea of building a church, or accomplishing any other serious enterprise, except through beggary of the Whites. As a class, the Blacks are indolent, improvident, servile and licentious ; and their inveterate habit of appealing to White benevolence or compassion whenever they realize a want or encounter a difficulty, is eminently baneful and enervating. If they could never more obtain a dollar until they shall have earned it, many of them would suffer, and some perhaps starve ; but on the whole, they would do better and improve faster than may now be reasonably expected."

Very significantly, and quite suggestively also, did Theodore Parker, in the course of a sermon which he preached in Boston, on the 31st of January, 1847, say :

> "Not a fiftieth part of the people of New York are negroes ; yet more than a sixth part of all the criminals in her State Prisons are men of color."

Something similar to what was then said of New York, might also, with equal truth, have been said of almost every other State of the Union—especially of those States wherein justice was impartially administered ; and, indeed, the same might be appropriately repeated now, of each and every State respectively, not only in reference to criminals, but also in reference to paupers and beggars— and the more particularly and preponderatingly so, after a reduction from the count, of the many Catholic criminals and paupers and beggars from Europe.

Certain it is that we owe it to ourselves—and we ought

to be able—to get rid of the negroes soon; but if they are to be retained much longer in the United States, (which may God, in his great mercy, forbid!) we may as well build immediately, for their relief and correction, in alternate adaptation, a row of hospitals and prisons, all the way from the Atlantic to the Pacific; and, upon the same plan, a range or series of almshouses and penitentiaries the entire distance from Lake Superior to the Gulf of Mexico!

All the devil-begotten imps of darkness, whether black or brown, whether negroes or Indians, whether Mongols or mulattoes, should at once be dismissed, and that forever, from the care, from the sight, and even from the thoughts, of the Heaven-born whites. Wherever seen, or wherever existing, the black and bi-colored races are the very personifications of bastardy and beggary. In America, these races are the most unwieldy occasioners of dishonor and weakness; they are the ill-favored and unwelcome instruments of disservice; they are the ghastly types of effeteness and retrogression.

At the earliest practicable moment, these inutile and baneful elements of our population must be either deported or fossilized. Of the two processes of displacement here suggested—deportation or fossilization—which shall we adopt? Whilst always cherishing a large and well-matured disposition to yield to the fairly-expressed preference of a majority of his countrymen, the voice of the writer hereof, as against the negroes, and as against all the other non-white races of mankind, is for quick and complete fossilization—precisely such a vindicable and effective system of fossilization as is now rapidly removing from the fair face of the earth all the aboriginal tribes of the New World. What says the reader? Rightly interpreted, in reference hereto, what is the will of Providence? what are the purposes and the decrees of the Almighty?

Let white men, all over the world, open their eyes, and serenely stretch out their vision upon the broad earth, and calmly survey the wide ocean, and contemplatively look upward in the direction of the high heavens; and let them rejoice with hearts overflowing with love and gratitude to God; for he hath ordered many good things to happen, and great things to come to pass. Soon are to transpire the unspeakably grand and glorious events which have been so long kept in reserve for us. The mighty and irresistible sword of the Lord hath been unsheathed against Ethiopia; and all the negroes, and all the other blacks and browns, whether in Ethiopia or out of Ethiopia, are to be laid low in the dust, and there fossilized! In the fifty-ninth part of a second after the final disappearance from the earth of the last member, respectively, of the black and the bi-colored races; in one instant, in the twinkling of an eye, after the whole world shall have been peopled exclusively by the whites, will the millenium dawn—but not till then!

CHAPTER V.

If the black man is feeble, and not important to the existing races, not on a parity with the best race, the black man must * * * be exterminated.—RALPH WALDO EMERSON.

It is a question of races, involving consequences which go to the destruction of one or the other. This was seen fifty years ago ; and the wisdom of Virginia balked at it then. It seems to be above human reason now. But there is a wisdom above human ; and to that we must look. In the meantime, do not extend the evil.—BENTON.

No fact in the long history of the world is so startling as the wide and repeated exterminations of its inhabitants.—DARWIN.

IN the event that a somewhat unusually capricious and tyrannical king should, as an act of brutality over certain of his subjects, introduce into their parlors teeming sows, and those sows should creep under the sofas and under the great arm-chairs, or topple them over pellmell, and among them give birth to litters of pigs, does it follow, therefore, that all the parlors of those of his subjects should be thenceforth and forever relinquished as drawing-rooms, and used only as pig-pens? Would it not, rather, be the duty of those sorely insulted and outraged subjects, to combine at once and overthrow the power of their king, and, at the same time, to oust all the sows and all the pigs from their parlors—and then to build for themselves new houses, and to furnish for themselves new parlors, which, under the more just and reasonable forms of republican government, should be perpetually guaranteed and protected, alike from the pestiferous authority of kings, and from the insufferable filth of sows and pigs?

For, all vitalized creatures, according to their nature, their dispositions, and their merits, suitable apartments or places should be prepared ; as, for instance, the parlor and the drawing-room for white people ; the kitchen and the coal-bin for negroes ; the swine-sty and the hog-pen for pigs.

When, under the auspices of monarchical institutions ; when, to pander to the cupidity of crowned heads ; when, to supply the vicious necessities of courtiers and sycophants, a pack of shirtless and shiftless negroes were brought from the coast of Africa and planted in America—a pack of black and beggarly barbarians, so bestial and so base as to prefer life to liberty—they, like all other foreign felons and outlaws, should at once have been returned to the places whence they came ; or to say the least, they should have been compelled to depart, with the greatest possible dispatch, from the land which they had so foully desecrated by their odious and infamous presence.

In the political organizations of mankind, it ought to be an axiom of peculiar and universal acceptation, that he who values life above liberty is unworthy to have his existence prolonged beyond the hour when to-morrow's sun shall set. This right and truthful proposition, practically established, would leave the whole earth absolutely negroless ere the lapse of two supper-times—a contemplated consummation which, even in the mere outlines of thought, is so prophetic of good, and, withal, so exquisitely exhilarating as to be most devoutly wished.

Still, there is no intention to assert that we ourselves should, by positive violence or by concert of action, exterminate the negroes ; it is only contended that we should pursue toward them the same enlightened and Heaven-approved policy which we have pursued toward the autochthones of our own continent; that is to say, that the negroes, like the Indians, being among the most mean and accursed representatives of those time-worn and effete races which are evidently foredoomed to destruction, we should effectually and forever separate them from ourselves—remove them at once to some far-distant territory or country—and there "let them alone severely," leaving them to the unerring care of God and Nature. This done, and the desired result would soon follow.

Upon the soil now embraced within the territory of the United States of America, Columbus and his immediate successors in discovery, found, it is said, no less than sixteen millions of Indians, all "native here, and to the manner born." This number, suffering a constant decrease during the last ten or eleven generations, has fortunately dwindled down to two hundred and sixty-eight thousand—being about equal in numerical strength, but far inferior in all other respects, to the present population of the city of Baltimore!

It was by no merit nor suggestion of his own, but rather by the demerits of both himself and his master, that the negro was brought to America. Not by any spirit of commendable enterprise was he induced to immigrate hither. He came under compulsion; and under compulsion he must (in the event of the failure of gentler admonitions on our part) be prevailed upon to emigrate back to Africa, to Mexico, to Central America, to South America, or to the islands of the ocean.

His coming to the New World was neither voluntary nor honorable. It was not for the purpose of bettering his condition in life. He sought not an asylum from the oppressions of rank and arbitrary power. In unresistingly allowing himself to be forced from his family and from his country, without even the promise or the prospect of ever being permitted to return, and in passively submitting to be taken in chains he knew not whither, he pusillanimously yielded to the most abject and digraceful vassalage.

For his passage across the Atlantic, he paid no money, no corn, no wine, no oil, nor any other thing whatever. He brought with himself no household property, no article of virtu, (nor principle of virtue,) no silver, no gold, nor precious stone.

He was hatless, and coatless, and trouserless, and shoeless, and shirtless—in brief, he was utterly resourceless, naked and filthy. He came as the basest of criminals— he came as a slave; for submission to slavery is a crime even more heinous than the crime of murder; more odious than the guilt of incest; more abominable than the sin of devil-worship.

With himself he brought no knowledge of agriculture, commerce, nor manufactures; no ability for the salutary management of civil affairs; no tact for the successful manœuvring of armies; no aptitude for the right direction of navies; no acquaintanceship with science, literature, nor art; no skill in the analysis of theories; no sentiment stimulative of noble actions; no soul for the encouragement of morality. Bringing with himself nothing but his own black and bastard body, benuded and begrimed, he came like a brute; he was a brute then; he had always been a brute; he is a brute now; and there is no more reason for believing that he will ever cease to be a brute, than there is for supposing that the hound will ever cease to be a dog—only that the black biped, the baser of the two, will be the sooner exterminated.

Yet this is the fatuous and filthy fellow whom, by certain degraded and very contemptible white persons, we are advised to recognize as an equal and as a brother! This is the incorrigible and groveling ignoramus upon whom it is proposed to confer at once the privilege of voting—the right of universal suffrage! This is the loathsome and most execrable wretch (rank-smelling and hideous arch-criminal that he is) who has been mentioned as one fit to have a voice in the enactment of laws for the government of the American people!

Shall we confer the elective franchise on this base-born and ill-bred blackamoor—this heathenish and skunk-scented idiot? No! Why not? Because he does not know, and cannot know, how to vote intelligently. It would therefore, to say the least, be an act of gross folly on our part, to extend to the negro the privilege of doing what the omnipotent God of Nature has obviously, and for all time, denied him the power to do.

Those of our half-witted and demagogical legislators who waste time in attempting to prove the equality of the negro, and in the drafting of absurd laws for his recognition in good faith as a citizen of the United States, might, with equal propriety, busy themselves in the ridiculous irrationality of framing codes for allowing the gorilla and the chimpanzee to attend common schools, and for the baboon and the orang-outang to testify in courts of equity! Let the blundering and baneful two-thirds majority of the Black Congress both blush and beware!

No man should ever be recognized as a citizen of the United States, nor be allowed to participate in any of the rights or privileges of citizenship, who did not come hither honorably and of his own accord—who did not immigrate to these shores, he or his ancestors, free, free from the gyves and chains of slavery. It was not of his own choosing, it was not at his own option, it was only in a state of the most abject and criminal servitude—a sort of compound felony between himself and his master—that the negro came from Africa. Therefore, for these and other sufficient reasons, the negro should have no

10

voice, no part nor lot, in any of the public affairs or private concerns of America.

(Here, if it be not asking too much, the writer would respectfully solicit his readers to cast their vision back a little way, and to reperuse and carefully ponder over the last preceding paragraph.)

Upon no principle of justice to ourselves, upon no basis of fair-dealing toward the white races in other parts of the world, upon no rule of action harmonizing with our duty to Heaven, can the negro in the United States ever be permitted to vote, to sit as a juryman, to hold any office whatever, nor even to remain permanently in the country.

Neither in courts nor out of courts should his oaths, nor any of his other statements in matters of importance, be accepted as worthy of the slightest credence— his regard for the truth being the same as the regard evinced therefor by his parental kinsman below, that other very mischievous nigger, the big nigger, with the ebony diadem, the uncouth and falsehood-telling progenitor of all the other niggers, the fire-inhabiting and forked-tailed Father of Lies.

Under no circumstances whatever should any one of the apish and impish children of the negro ever be allowed to enter any institution of learning devoted to the education of the whites.

If the negro marries an outcast white woman—of course no white woman who is not an outcast of the worst possible sort would ever think of marrying him—both he and she ought to be hung three minutes after the conclusion of the ceremony, or as soon thereafter as the necessary preparations could be made.

Over all the territory between the Atlantic and the Pacific oceans, and between the Great Lakes and the Gulf of Mexico, he should, after the 4th of July, 1876,

be excluded from every in-door and out-door employment. And, even between the present time and the date
here mentioned, he should be expelled from every city,
town, village, and hamlet, which contains a population of
more than sixty-seven whites. This, indeed, should be
done immediately—this year, or next year if possible, or
the year following at furthest.

He should never, under any circumstances whatever,
be permitted to reside in greater proximity to white people than the distance which separates Cuba from the
United States ; if the distance could be lengthened to
the extent of one thousand miles, so much the better ;
if, in point of duration, rather than in point of space,
the distance could be lengthened from now to the end of
time, (supposing such an end possible,) better still.

On the premises of no respectable white person ; in
the mansion of no honorable private citizen ; in no law-
fully-convened public assembly ; in no rationally moral
or religious society ; in no decently kept hotel ; in no
restaurant worthy of the patronage of white people ; in
no reputably-established store nor shop—in no place
whatever, where any occupant or visitor is of Caucasian
blood—should the loathsome presence of any negro or
negress ever be tolerated.

And as, in life and in health, the whites and the blacks
should always be separated—the further apart the
better—so also should they continue to be separated,
both in sickness and in death. No negro should, under
any circumstances, ever be admitted into any hospital or
asylum of the whites ; nor should the bastard and beastlike body of the black ever be buried in the cemetery of
the white.

If the very rude labor of the negro, which is the only
sort of labor that he is capable of performing, is fit for
anything (except for the cleaning of such nameless little

houses as are usually located in the more remote and secluded parts of farmers' gardens) it is fit for the fenced fields, for the cotton-fields, for the corn-fields, for the wheat-fields, and for the fields of other agricultural products ; but for the multifarious and more delicate indoor duties of the cities and towns, his labor is absolutely worthless, and not unfrequently so damaging and destructive as, in truth, to be ruinously worse than only passively worthless.

Away, then, in the first place, away with the negro from all incorporated communities ; in the second place, away with him from the rural districts ; in the third place, away with him from the entire territory of the United States ; in the fourth place, away with him from America at large; in the fifth place, away with him from the islands of the ocean; in the sixth place, away with him from Africa; and in the seventh and last place, away with him from all the exterior parts of the earth !

Precisely as it is here proposed to deal with the negroes, so also, in every respect, should we deal with the mulattoes, the Indians, the Chinese (in California and elsewhere) and all the other swarthy drones and dregs of mankind.

Under the euphemism of "Removal," the American government has already expelled, and rightly expelled, from time to time, more than one hundred thousand Indians from the States of the Atlantic slope, to the wild lands west of the Mississippi,—these expulsions by the government having been independently of the less systematic but (in the aggregate) much larger expulsions by unorganized communities of the white people themselves. It should also be recollected, that all the Indians thus expelled or "removed," were people of indigenous origin, autochthones, by whom the whole of America had, from time immemorial, prior to the days of Columbus, been held in fee-simple.

Now if we may rightfully expel the aboriginal owners of America from the old homes and possessions which they have enjoyed from a period of time so distant in the far past that it is absolutely untraceable, what may we not do with the alien and accursed negroes, who, base-minded and barbarous, and bound hand and foot with the fetters of slavery, were brought hither from the coast of Africa?

A very miserable fellow, indeed, is the Indian ; but yet he is a nobleman in comparison with the negro ; for while the latter has always most cringingly and criminally manifested a predisposition to be a slave, whereby many of the weaker sort of white men have been betrayed into the monstrous and disgusting sin of trafficking in human flesh, the former, justly regarding liberty as a boon far more precious and far more sacred than life, has, with becoming nerve and dignity, in every part of our country, disdainfully and defiantly refused to wear the yoke of bondage.

How we have despoiled the Indians of their landed property, and appropriated that property to our own uses ; how we have exterminated unnumbered thousands of red men, and driven others from the east to the west ; and how pursuing a somewhat similar policy toword a still more unworthy and dispicable people, it behooves us, as duteous instruments in the hands of Providence, to effectually separate from ourselves forever, the negroes and all the other dark-colored and death-doomed races, will, to a greater or less extent, be explained or suggested by perusing the following excerpts.

In his Annual Message to the Senate and House of Representatives, December 8, 1863, President Lincoln, speaking with words of the same noble import as those which had repeatedly animated the powers of utterance of many of his illustrious predecessors in the Chief Magistracy, says :

"The measures provided at your last session for the removal of certain Indian tribes have been carried into effect. Sundry treaties have been negotiated which will, in due time, be submitted for the constitutional action of the Senate. They contain stipulations for extinguishing the possessory rights of the Indians to large and valuable tracts of land."

The following extract from the "United States Statutes at Large," Volume XII., page 819, tells its own interesting story of progress in the right direction :

"An Act for the Removal of the Sisseton, Wahpaton, Medawakanton, and Wahpakoota Bands of Sioux or Dakota Indians, and for the Disposition of their lands in Minnesota and Dakota.—Passed by Congress, March 3, and Approved by the President, March 12, 1863."

"Be it enacted by the Senate and House of Representatives of the United States of America in Congress assembled, That the President is authorized and hereby directed to assign to and set apart for the Sisseton, Wahpaton, Medawakanton, and Wahpakoota bands of Sioux Indians a tract of unoccupied land outside of the limits of any State, sufficient in extent to enable him to assign to each member of said bands (who are willing to adopt the pursuit of agriculture) eighty acres of good agricultural lands, the same to be well adapted to agricultural purposes."

Almost all of our sessions of Congress are very fruitful of "treaties" with the Indians ; and, as a rule, all these compacts have the same bearing, and with the exception of the dates, the designations of tribes, territories, boundaries, and a few other particulars, most of them have pretty much the same phraseology. Here is a specimen, extracted from the "United States Statutes at Large," Volume XII., page 927 :

"Treaty between the United States, and the Dwamish, Suquamish, and other allied and subordinate Tribes of Indians in Washington Territory. Concluded at Point Elliott, Washington Territory, January 22, 1855, Ratified by the Senate, March 8, 1859. Proclaimed by the President of the United States, April 11, 1859.

    *   *   *   *   *   *   *   *

"The said tribes and bands of Indians hereby cede, relinquish, and convey to the United States all their right, title and interest in and to the lands and country occupied by them, bounded and described as follows. * * * There is, however, reserved for the present use and occupation of the said tribes and bands the following tracts of land. * * * All which tracts shall be set apart, and so far as necessary surveyed and marked out for their exclusive use ; nor shall any white man be permitted to reside upon the same without permission of the said tribes or bands, and of the superintendent or agent. * * * The President may hereafter, when in his opinion the interests of the Territory shall require and the welfare of the said Indians be promoted, remove them from either or all of the special reservations hereinbefore made to the said general reservation, or such other suitable place within said Territory as he may deem fit, on remunerating them for their improvements and the expenses of such removal, or may consolidate them with other friendly tribes or bands ; and he may further, at his discretion, cause the whole or any portion of the lands hereby reserved, or of such other land as may be selected in view thereof, to be surveyed into lots, and assign the same to such individuals or families as are willing to avail themselves of the privilege, and will locate on the same as a permanent home on the same terms and subject to the same regulations as are provided in the sixth article of the treaty with the Omahas, so far as the same may be applicable."

In another of these Indian "treaties" (Winnebago tribe—"United States Statutes at Large," Volume XII., page 1101) ratified by the Senate on the 16th day of March, 1861, and proclaimed by President Lincoln March 23, 1861, it is provided, as is similarly provided in the last foregoing extract, that,

"No white person, except such as shall be in the employment of the United States, shall be allowed to reside or go upon any portion of said reservation, without the written permission of the Superintendent of Indian Affairs, or of the agent for the tribe."

Now, if there is any portion of the Indian-occupied territory of the United States from which white men may properly be excluded, the Indians themselves may be, and ought to be, entirely and forever excluded from

all possible portions of the same ; and if any island belonging to our country, whether it be a sea-island, a
river-island, or a lake-island, may be reserved for the
particular residence or habitation of negroes, the whites
may have, and ought to have—and eventually must have,
and will have—all the islands and all the main-land, not
only of America, but of the whole world, for the exclusive occupancy and accommodation of themselves.

Significantly, in this connection, may we sing the little
ditty,

> "There's a snug little homestead well known in the West,
>   But the owner has passed like the snow ;
> John Redskin, the hunter, and all have confest
>   It was time he had gone long ago."

Much as I am opposed to military candidates for the
Presidency, yet the expression of such correct and manly sentiments as the following can never fail to command
my particulr respect and admiration for the man who,
irrespective of occupation or profession, gives them utterance ; and more especially would this be the case if
the words communicating the just and commendable
idea of fossilization here used, were so changed or am-
plified as to apply to the negroes no less than to the
Indians.   It was on the 1st of February, 1867, that Gen.
Grant, in the course of a letter on the subject of Indian
Affairs, addressed to the Hon. Edwin M. Stanton, Secretary of War, wrote thus :

"If our present practice of dealing with the aborigines of this
country is continued, I do not see that any course is left open to us
but to withdraw our troops to the settlements, and call upon Congress to provide means and troops to carry on formidable hostilities
against the Indians, until all the Indians or all the whites on the
great plains, and between the settlements on the Missouri and the
Pacific slope, are exterminated."

Daniel Wilson, Professor of History and English Literature in the University College, Toronto, Canada, in his " Prehistoric Man," Volume II., page 332, says :

" We see the American Indian in the fifteenth and subsequent centuries brought into contact and collision with the most civilized nations of the world, in periods of their matured energy. It was the meeting of two extremes ; of the most highly favored among the nations triumphing in their onward progress not less by constitutional superiority than by acquired civilization ; and of the savage, or the semi-civilized barbarian, in the stages of national infancy and childhood. Their fate was inevitable. It does not diminish our difficulty in dealing with the complex problem, to know that such had been the fate of many races and even of great nations before them. But if we are troubled with the perplexities of this dark riddle, whereby the colonists of the New World only advance by the retrogression of its aborigines, and in their western progress ever tread on the graves of nations, the consideration of some of the phenomena attendant on this same process of displacement and extinction, accompanying the human race from the very dawn of its history, may help to lessen the mystery."

Again in his " Prehistoric Man," Volume II., page 328, Prof. Wilson says :

" The native races of the islands of the American archipelago have been exterminated ; and of many of them scarcely a relic of their language, or a memorial of their arts, their social habits, or religious rites, survives. So, in like manner, throughout the older American States, in Canada, and over the vast area which spreads westward from the Atlantic seaboard, to the Rocky Mountains, whole tribes and nations have disappeared, without even a memorial-mound or pictured grave-post to tell where the last of the race is returning to the earth from whence he sprung."

Prescott, in his " History of the Reign of Philip II., Volume III., page 2, speaks of

—" The Indian race, that ill-fated race, which seems to have shrunk from the touch of civilization, and to have passed away before it like the leaves of the forest before the breath of winter."

10*

Waitz, in his "Anthropology of Primitive Races," Volume I., page 147, says:

"The belief that the Whites brought with them a virus, which they let loose upon the natives, prevailed all through New England, caused probably by the circumstance that shortly after the stranding of a French ship near Cape Cod, there broke out among the Indians, in 1616, a destructive pestilence, which so depopulated the coast for a distance of several hundred English miles, that the survivors were unable to bury the dead."

Sir Woodbine Parish, in his "Buenos Ayres and the Provinces of the Rio de la Plata," page 130, speaking of the Indians of the Pampas says:

"Whole tribes have been swept away by the small-pox—entire nations, I believe, whose languages have been lost. The plague is not a more frightful scourge than this disorder when it attacks the miserable inhabitants of the Pampas. They themselves believe it to be incurable—a feeling which adds to its lamentable consequences; for no sooner does it appear than their tents are raised, and the whole tribe takes to flight, abandoning the unfortunate sufferers to the certainty of perishing of hunger and thirst, if the virulence of the disorder itself does not first carry them off."

In his "History of the Conquest of Peru," Volume I., page 219, Prescott says:

"The Inca Capac himself, calling his great officers around him, as he found he was drawing near his end, announced the subversion of his empire by the race of white and bearded strangers, as the consummation predicted by the oracles after the reign of the twelfth Inca, and he enjoined it on his vassals not to resist the decrees of Heaven, but to yield obedience to its messengers."

Richard Lee, in the course of an address which he delivered before the London Anthropological Society, on the 1st of December, 1863, says:

"It has been estimated that the Hawaiians have been reduced as much as eighty-five per cent. during the last hundred years. The natives of Tasmania are almost, if not quite, extinct. The Maories are passing away at the rate of about twenty-five per cent. every fourteen years, and in Australia, as in America, whole tribes have disappeared before the advance of the white man."

On the 19th of January, 1864, Mr. Richard Lee delivered another address before the London Anthropological Society, in which he says:

"In 1815 the aborigines of Van Dieman's Land were estimated at 5,000, and this was probably a lower calculation than might have been justified. Five years later so great was the slaughter practised by the early settlers, that this number had been reduced to 340, of whom 160 were females. * * * In 1855, the numbers were further reduced, and the once numerous tribes of Van Dieman's Land had only sixteen representatives.

The New York Weekly *Evening Post* of the 16th of August, 1865, says:

"We learn from Hobart Town that the last man of the Tasmanian aboriginal population has shipped as a seaman on board a whaling barque, and was about to brave the perils of the deep in the whale fishery."

Charles Hamilton Smith, in his "Natural History of the Human Species," page 150, says:

"From the occasional destruction of whole races, which is sometimes caused, even in modern ages, by the sword, by contagious diseases, or by new modes of life, and the introduction of vices before unknown, it is evident that numerous populations of the human family have disappeared, without leaving a record of their ancient existence."

Mr. J. J. Freeman, Home Secretary of the London Missionary Society, in his "Tour through South Africa," page 68, foolishly lamenting the Heaven-decreed decimation of the blacks of Cape Colony, says:

"It is imposssible to conceal one's fears for the ultimate existence of most of the colored races in South Africa; I mean those in the first instance, within the colony, and those in the neighborhood of places where the emigrant Boers have lately settled. The lands of the native tribes become gradually encroached on; jealousies and animosities, wars and retaliations, arise; the native tribes are driven back, lose their property, their lands, their courage; they fall back on other tribes where they encounter more or less resistance, become weaker and weaker, and the white man advances, and absorbs the whole."

Still whimpering, instead of rejoicing, as he ought to rejoice, over a just and merry matter, this same Aminadab Sleek—otherwise called J. J. Freeman, Home Secretary of the London Missionary Society—in his "Tour Through South Africa," page 261, says:

"At present, it appears to me that the prospects of the colored races of South Africa, taken on the broadest scale, are such as Christian philanthropy may weep over. I see no prospect of their preservation for any very lengthened period. The struggle may last for a considerable time. Missionary effort may not only save many of the souls of men, but help to defer the evil day of annihilation as to many of the aboriginal tribes; but annihilation is steadily advancing; and nothing can arrest it without an entire change in the system of Government, wherever white British subjects come in contact with the native tribes."

The late lamented John Hanning Speke, in the introduction to his very interesting "Journal of the Discovery of the Source of the Nile," page 24, says:

"How the negro has lived so many ages without advancing, seems marvelous, when all the countries surrounding Africa are so forward in comparison; and judging from the progressive state of the world, one is led to suppose that the African must soon either step out from his darkness, or be superseded by a being superior to himself. Could a government be formed for them like ours in India, they would be saved; but without it, I fear there is very little chance; for at present the African neither can help himself nor will he be helped by others, because his country is in such a constant state of turmoil he has too much anxiety on hand looking out for his food to think of anything else. As his fathers ever did, so does he. He works his wife, sells his children, enslaves all he can lay hands upon, and, unless when fighting for the property of others, contents himself with drinking, singing, and dancing like a baboon, to drive dull care away."

Barrow, in his "Travels into the Interior of Southern Africa," Volume I., page 93, says :

"The name of Hottentot will soon be forgotten or remembered only as that of a deceased person of little note. Their numbers of late years have been rapidly on the decline. It has generally been observed that wherever Europeans have colonized, the less civilized have always dwindled away, and at length totally disappeared."

The New York Daily *Tribune*, of the 17th of September, 1860, says :

"The colored population of our State consists of some fifty thousand persons—at most a sixteenth part of our population. They are a less considerable fraction of the aggregate than they were fifty years ago."

Weston, in his "Progress of Slavery in the United States," page 158, uses this appropriate and pertinent language :

The population in America of European extraction has grown so large, and the accessions to it by immigration are so vast, that we can begin to see that the mission of the negro here is nearly completed, and that the limits of his possible expansion may be computed. In fifty years, the white races now in the United States, and their descendants, will number more than one hundred millions. While it is impossible to predict exactly the march of this great multitude, or to define precisely the regions it will occupy, it is easy to see that the negro in North America must be pressed into narrow bounds. And it is in North America only that he is formidable, because it is here only that his numbers are increasing ; the African race in South America and in the West Indies being either stationary or declining, except so far as it is kept up by the slave trade, which is reduced now to a single island, restrained even there within close limits, and menaced constantly by that complete extinction which it cannot long escape.

George M. Weston, a thorough anti-slavery man, now (or but recently) residing in the city of Washington, is originally from the State of Maine. He is one of the comparatively few able writers of the last decade who, while hating slavery and slaveholders with a sort of holy hatred, had, at the same time, the good sense to hold the negroes (as they everywhere deserve to be held) in equal contempt and detestation. His excellent work, from which the foregoing extract is taken, was first published in 1857. At that time, fifteen of the States of the United States were still Slave States ; and it was only in these fifteen negro-cursed and slavery-cursed States—States in which, to the grievous detriment and exclusion of many of the non-slaveholding whites, the system of slavery was upheld and fostered by legislative enactments—that there was any considerable increase of the black race. Now that the lazy and loathsome negroes are put, or are about to be put, exclusively upon their own resources, where they ought to have been put long ago, there can be no doubt that, erelong, they will all have so far disappeared from the face of the earth, that it shall be possible to find them only in the form of fossils.

Webster, "the great Expounder of the Constitution," the Demosthenes of Massachusetts, in the fifth volume of his works, page 364, says:

"In my observations upon slavery as it existed in this country, and as it now exists, I have expressed no opinion of the mode of its extinguishment or melioration. I will say, however, though I have nothing to propose, because I do not deem myself so competent as other gentlemen to take any lead on this subject, that if any gentleman from the South shall propose a scheme, to be carried on by this Government upon a large scale, for the transportation of the colored people to any colony or any place in the world, I should be quite disposed to incur almost any degree of expense to accomplish that object."

Clay, eloquent and magnanimous on all occasions—the Cicero of Kentucky—while a member of the House of Representatives, in 1827, spoke as follows:

"Of the utility of a total separation of the two incongruous portions of our population, (supposing it to be practicable,) none have ever doubted. The mode of accomplishing that desirable object has alone divided public opinion. Colonization in Hayti for a time had its partisans. Without throwing any impediments in the way of executing that scheme, the American Colonization Society has steadily adhered to its own. The Haytien project has passed away. Colonization beyond the Stony Mountains has sometimes been proposed; but it would be attended with an expense and difficulties far surpassing the African project, whilst it would not unite the same animating motives."

Jefferson, with whose views, upon whatever subject, the people of our country can never become too familiar—the man who, more than any other, has imparted high tone and true virtue to the American character, in the first volume of his works, page 48 says

"The bill on the subject of slaves, was a mere digest of the existing laws respecting them, without any intimation of a plan for a future and general emancipation. It was thought better that this should be kept back, and attempted only by way of amendment, whenever the bill should be brought up. The principles of the amendment, however, were agreed on, that is to say, the freedom of all born after a certain day, and deportation at a proper age. But it was found that the public mind would not yet bear the proposition, nor will it bear it even at this day. Yet the day is not distant when it must bear and adopt it, or worse will follow. Nothing is more certainly written in the book of fate than that these people are to be free; nor is it less certain that the two races, equally free, cannot live under the same government. Nature, habit, opinion, have drawn indelible lines of distinction between them. It is still in our power to direct the process of emancipation and deportation, peaceably, and in such slow degree, as that the evil will wear off insensibly, and their place be, *pari passu*, filled up by free white laborers. If, on the contrary, it is left to force itself on, human nature must shudder at the prospect held up. We should in vain look for an example in the Spanish deportation or deletion of the Moors. This precedent would fall far short of our case."

Again, in the fourth volume of his works, page 420, Jefferson says:

"The West Indies offer a more probable and practicable retreat for the negroes. Inhabited already by a people of their own race and color ; climates congenial with their natural constitution ; insulated from the other descriptions of men ; nature seems to have formed these islands to become the receptacle of the blacks transplanted into this hemisphere. Whether we could obtain from the European sovereigns of those islands leave to send thither the persons under consideration, I cannot say ; but I think it more probable than the former propositions, because of their being already inhabited more or less by the same race. * * * Africa would offer a last and undoubted resort, if all others more desirable should fail us."

History has furnished numerous instances, in various parts of the world, and at various intervals of time, of the enforced expatriation of whole tribes and peoples; and, if we may exercise full faith in the Bible, the voice of Jehovah never thundered with more unmistakable emphasis than when it was heard addressing the children of Israel, peremptorily commanding them to "drive out," on the one hand, and to "utterly destroy," on the other, all the inhabitants of Canaan.

About two thousand three hundred and seventy-seven years ago, the Tarquins were expelled from Rome.

In the year 1290, the Jews were expelled from England.

On the 30th of March, 1492, the very year of the discovery of America by Columbus, Ferdinand V. issued an edict, under which all the Jews—the number estimated to have been not less than eight hundred thousand—were expelled from Spain.

Boyer, the mulatto "president" of Hayti, on the 16th of June, 1831, ordered all the French white inhabitants of the island to leave there before the 15th of the following month—a twenty-eight days' notification. And so, the negroes having notified the whites to leave Hayti within a period of less than one calendar month, how many years (or months or days) ought the whites to give notification to the negroes, and 'to all other similar trash, that all persons who are not of pure Caucasian blood must depart, not temporarily, not merely for a season, but for all time, from the fair shores and superficies of America? To this important inquiry let us yield a manly consideration, and arrive, if possible, at a just and timely decision.

Dessalines, the black and barbarous "emperor" of Hayti, on the 29th of March, 1804, made proclamation for the massacre of all the white inhabitants of the island; whereupon many thousands were butchered.

Now if the negroes, being very greatly in the majority, may make public proclamation for cutting the throats of all their fair-complexioned neighbors, and if, besides, in consequence of overwhelming numbers, they carry into effect such proclamation—is it not, to say the least, a lamentable fact that the whites are not everywhere sufficiently strong to prevent such unpolished and sanguinary diversions on the part of the blacks? Unknown and unascertainable as may now be the name of the man or the woman who was the least and the vilest of the whites who thus perished by the murderous violence of the blacks, that man or that woman, although but a single individual, was of infinitely greater worth to the world than all the negroes and mulattoes who have ever lived.

It is the whites alone whose minds and souls are immortally bejeweled with the inextinguishable scintillations of divinity.

The bite and the injected venom of snakes occasionally benumb the vitals of men; but, for every person thus laid low in the dust, for every human heel thus injured, the heads of at least a thousand serpents are fatally bruised. So it has ever been; and so, in the good providence of God, will it ever be. The bad and the insignificant, the black and the base, will continue to decrease, until they shall all have disappeared forever; but the good and the great, the white and the worthy, will steadily gain, both in numbers and in strength, until the whole earth, and all the other worlds of the universe, shall present, among other scenes of exquisite grandeur and delight, one uninterrupted series of living and loving creatures, all exulting in a perpetual superabundance of enrapturing health, harmony and happiness.

Of the less favored races of mankind, some, of feeble and fameless destinies, have long since ceased to retain a foothold upon the earth; many, little better than those which first became extinct, have been completely hid among the fossilizations of later periods; and numerous others, similarly frail and futile, are now rapidly passing away.

Where, pray tell us, where are the Rephaim? the Caphtorim? the Gibborim? the Naphilim? the Emim? the Avim? the Anakim? the Zuzim? and the Zamzum-mim?

Where, pray tell us, where are the Jebusites, the Perizzites? the Girgashites? the Zemarites? the Tim-nites? the Amorites? the Arkites? the Arvadites? the Amalekites? the Hivites? the Hittites? and the Hama-thites?

Where, pray tell us, where are the Philistines? What has been the fate of the aboriginal races of Egypt and Assyria? Has there been seen, for many centuries past, any living representative of the autochthones of either Greece or Rome? Where may we look for the offspring of the Caucones? Is any German, or Frenchman, or Englishman, of to-day, an offshoot from the primitive in-habitants of any part of Germany, France, or Great Britain?

Where, pray tell us, where are the Narragansetts? the Nanticokes? the Alleghans? the Mandans? the Minri?

the Unamis? the Eries? the Illinois? the Antiwenda-
ronks? the Susquehannocks? and the Shawnees? Where,
pray tell us, where are the Mohawk braves and the
braves of the Algonquins? All these (but *not* alas!) all
these are dead. Soon also will be dead, dead and forever done for—if, indeed, not already done for—the
Penobscots, the Passamaquoddys the Oneidas, and the
Onondagas; the Wimponoags, the Winnebagoes, the
Kickapoos, and the Pequods; the Tuscaroras, the Pota-
watomies, the Mohegans, and the Micmacs; the Wyan-
dots, the Ojibways, the Choctaws, and the Cherokees.
Happily, also, will we soon be rid of all the other red-
skinned and yellow-skinned savages of America—the Indians and the Chinese. A day or a date, not far in the
future, must likewise be fixed for the irretraceable departure hence of all the negroes and mulattoes.

Where pray tell us, where are the descendants of the
people whom Columbus discovered in Hispaniola? How
long will yet last the lease of life of the few remnants of
the Caribs? the Quiches? the Camacans? the Zutugils?
the Kackiquels? the Warrows? the Chacos? and the
Araucanians? How (if at all) how is it to-day with the
Othomi? the Totonacs? the Miztecas? the Zapatecs?
the Aztecs? the Olmecs? and the Toltecs?

Safely may it be premised that nothing can be clearer
to the apprehension of the observant and well-informed
student of the operations of nature, than that all the
aboriginal tribes of both North and South America are
now in course of rapid extinction. Truly, too, "this is
the Lord's doing; it is marvelous in our eyes."

The dark-colored autochthones, also, of all the islands
of the Pacific, and of numerous other islands and places
throughout the wide world, are fast approaching the
close of their worthless existence. The Deity has devoted
them all to destruction; many are already dead; the sur-

vivors are drooping and dying. Erelong none of them—not one of them—will be left alive. "By the blast of God they perish, and by the breath of his nostrils are they consumed."

'Tis well; soon, very soon, indeed, will all the black and bi-colored barbarians be silenced forever. "Yet a little sleep, a little slumber, a little folding of the hands to sleep;" and then shall all the swarthy races find rest, as, in reality, they all richly deserve to find rest, in the deep sleep of death eternal!

During the six months which immediately succeeded the failure of the Slaveholders' Rebellion, it is said that not less than forty thousand negroes died in the Southern States from the prostrating diseases and penury entailed upon them in consequence of their sheer inability to act the part of either intelligent or useful beings. Indeed, and better still, in the course of a speech which he recently delivered in New Haven, Connecticut, Senator Doolittle, of Wisconsin, (who, as a White Republican, a patriot, a statesman, is doing much, and doing well) stated that it was the general opinion, among the more enlightened and accurate observers of our country, that at least *one million* of negroes, have perished in the South since the dawn of the present decade! Verily, "the Lord gave, and the Lord hath taken away; blessed be the name of the Lord"—and more especially so in all cases of this kind—for taking away!

Japan, and China, and India, and Egypt, and Algiers, and Soodan, and Madagascar; in a word, all Asia and Africa, and the islands adjacent, like the mighty Americas, like Polynesia and Oceanica, have, as it were, but recently been discovered by those Heaven-guided branches of the Caucasian race through whose irresistible energy and perseverance the whole world (when it shall be occupied by the whites alone) is yet to be brought under an unprecedentedly high and happy state of civilization.

In accordance with the pure and perfect fiat of Jehovah, all the black and bi-colored barbarians—and all who are either black or bi-colored are barbarians—must, at the exact time appointed for each race respectively, be utterly exterminated.

How nearly one of these death-doomed races has now arrived at its inglorious end, how fast the sands of its few remaining hour-glasses are running out, may be correctly inferred from the fact that the fossilizing substances of the earth have already, in an especial manner, been newly compounded and prepared for the reception of every negro, and for every blood-relative of the negro, in the world!

CHAPTER VI.

A SCORE OF BIBLE LESSONS IN THE ARTS OF ANNIHILATING
EFFETE RACES.

Ask of me,
And I shall give thee the heathen for thine inheritance,
And the uttermost parts of the earth for thy possession.
Thou shalt break them with a rod of iron ;
Thou shalt dash them in pieces like a potter's vessel.

PSALM II., 8–9.

I will deliver the inhabitants of the land into your hand, and thou shalt drive
them out before thee. Thou shalt make no covenant with them.

EXODUS XXIII., 31–32.

Thou art an holy people unto the Lord thy God, and the Lord hath chosen thee
to be a peculiar people unto himself, above all the nations that are upon the earth.

DEUTERONOMY XIV., 2.

IF it be true, as is most firmly and conscientiously believed by the writer hereof, that the white races of mankind should no longer degrade themselves by any manner of association with either the black or the bi-colored races, the question arises, What are the means necessary to be taken, and when should they be taken, to render the contemplated separation final and complete ?

An old proverb will have it, that, "Where there's a will, there's a way." Let us first *will* that the thing which ought to be done, shall be done, and the *way* to do it will, no doubt, soon manifest itself. Besides, the writer flatters himself, that, if, in this most momentous of all mere worldly matters, he alone shall be successful in creating the requisite *will*, it may not be expecting too much of others, that they will at least assist to suggest the *way*. Labor, everywhere, especially if the labor be highly honorable and important, should be equitably apportioned, and if one man were to perform both of the herculean tasks here referred to, he might, in a measure, perhaps, be forestalling one or more of his fellow-men in certain of their rightful prerogatives.

People professing great sanctity of character tell us that the Bible affords to man the only safe rule of faith and practice. Let us, therefore, carefully peruse that ancient tome, and, if possible, learn therefrom the particular policy which we ought to pursue toward the Ethiopians, against whom, according to Zephaniah, the sword of the Lord seems now to be so universally and so fatally drawn.

In the event that we, mere mortals that we are, should be found dealing with the reprobate and accursed blacks in just such manner as Almighty God himself is represented as having dealt with certain impious and hostile races of swarthy men, what possible exception could be taken to our conduct? Should we not, in some things at least, reverently and earnestly strive to imitate Him who alone, in the true sense of words, is Good and Great —to think (however imperfectly on our part) to think as he thought, to speak as he spoke, and to do as he did? Yet, even in the case supposed, if any objection, reasonable or unreasonable, should be urged, there would certainly be the less occasion for cavil just in the proportion that the means adopted for the removal of the blacks should recede in harshness from the summary proceedings which are said to have been employed by the Deity for the removal of the ancient but corresponding and equally-doomed enemies of human progress.

Without here recommending, or meaning to recommend, the effective plan of separation and extermination which is reported to have been sanctioned by Heaven, thousands of years ago, as against certain unfavored and effete races, let us now proceed to consider some of the more remarkable peculiarities and provisions of the plan itself.

The following biblical extracts which, for the sake of familiarity and simplicity, are here denominated *Lessons*, will fully explain the Hebrew account of God's method of ridding the world of those glaringly abortive and worthless races who, like the negroes, the Indians, and all the bi-colored fag-ends of mankind, have ceased to have a useful mission outside the superficies of this terrestrial ball.

HERE BEGINNETH THE FIRST LESSON.

(Numbers xxxiii., 50–56.)

"The Lord spake unto Moses, in the plains of Moab, by Jordan, near Jericho, saying, Speak unto the children of Israel, and say unto them, when ye are passed over Jordan into the land of Canaan, then ye shall drive out all the inhabitants of the land from before you, and destroy all their pictures, and destroy all their molten images, and quite pluck down all their high places ; and ye shall dispossess the inhabitants of the land, and dwell therein ; for I have given you the land to possess it. And ye shall divide the land by lot for an inheritance among your families ; and to the more ye shall give the more inheritance, and to the fewer ye shall give the less inheritance ; every man's inheritance shall be in the place where his lot falleth ; according to the tribes of your fathers ye shall inherit. But if ye will not drive out the inhabitants of the land from before you, then it shall come to pass, that those which ye let remain of them, shall be pricks in your eyes, and thorns in your sides, and shall vex you in the land wherein ye dwell. Moreover it shall come to pass, that I shall do unto you, as I thought to do unto them."

HERE BEGINNETH THE SECOND LESSON.

(Deuteronomy vii., 1–6.)

"When the Lord thy God shall bring thee into the land whither thou goest to possess it, and hath cast out many nations before thee, the Hittites and the Girgashites, and the Amorites, and the Canaanites, and the Perizzites, and the Hivites, and the Jebusites, seven nations greater and mightier than thou ; and when the Lord thy God shall deliver them before thee, thou shalt smite them, and utterly destroy them; thou shalt make no covenant with them, nor show mercy unto them; neither shalt thou make marriages with them; thy daughter thou shalt not give unto his son, nor his daughter shalt thou take unto thy son. For they will turn away thy son from following me, that they may serve other gods; so will the anger of the Lord be kindled against you, and destroy thee suddenly. But thus shall ye deal with them; ye shall destroy their altars, and break down their images, and cut down their groves, and burn their graven images with fire. For thou art an holy people unto the Lord thy God; the Lord thy God hath chosen thee to be a special people unto himself, above all people that are upon the face of the earth."

HERE BEGINNETH THE THIRD LESSON.

(Leviticus xxvi., 8–13.)

"Ye shall chase your enemies, and they shall fall before you by the sword. Five of you shall chase an hundred, and an hundred of you shall put ten thousand to flight; and your enemies shall fall before you by the sword. For I will have respect unto you, and make you fruitful, and multiply you, and establish my covenant with you. And ye shall eat old store, and bring forth the old because of the new. And I will set my tabernacle among you; and my soul shall not abhor you. And I will walk among you, and will be your God, and ye shall be my people."

HERE BEGINNETH THE FOURTH LESSON.

(Exodus xxiii., 1–3.)

"And the Lord said unto Moses, Depart, and go up hence, thou and the people which thou hast brought up out of the land of Egypt, unto the land which I sware unto Abraham, to Isaac, and to Jacob, saying, Unto thy seed will I give it; and I will send an angel before thee; and I will drive out the Canaanite, the Amorite, and the Hittite, and the Perizzite, the Hivite, and the Jebusite."

HERE BEGINNETH THE FIFTH LESSON.

(Exodus xxxiv., 11–14.)

"Observe thou that which I command thee this day; behold, I drive out before thee the Amorite, and the Canaanite, and the Hittite, and the Perizzite, and the Hivite, and the Jebusite. Take heed to thyself, lest thou make a covenant with the inhabitants of the land whither thou goest, lest it be for a snare in the midst of thee; but ye

11

shall destroy their altars. break their images, and cut down their groves."

HERE BEGINNETH THE SIXTH LESSON.

(Deuteronomy xx., 16–18.)

"Of the cities of these people, which the Lord thy God doth give thee for an inheritance, thou shalt save alive nothing that breatheth ; but thou shalt utterly destroy them ; namely, the Hittites, and the Amorites, and the Canaanites, and the Perizzites, the Hivites, and the Jebusites."

HERE BEGINNETH THE SEVENTH LESSON.

(Deuteronomy xxiii., 3–7.)

"An Ammonite or Moabite shall not enter into the congregation of the Lord ; even to their tenth generation shall they not enter into the congregation of the Lord for ever ; because they met you not with bread and with water in the way, when ye came forth out of Egypt ; and because they hired against thee Balaam the son of Beor of Pethor of Mesopotamia, to curse thee. Neverthless the Lord thy God would not hearken unto Balaam ; but the Lord thy God turned the curse into a blessing unto thee, because the Lord thy God loved thee. Thou shalt not seek their peace nor their prosperity all thy days forever.

HERE BEGINNETH THE EIGHTH LESSON.

(I. Samuel xv., 1–3.)

"Samuel also said unto Saul, The Lord sent me to anoint thee to be king over his people, over Israel ; now therefore hearken thou unto the voice of the words of the Lord. Thus saith the Lord of hosts, I remember that which Amelek did to Israel, how he laid wait for him in the way, when he came up from Egypt. Now go and smite Amelek, and utterly destroy all that they have, and spare them not ; but slay both man and woman, infant and suckling, ox and sheep, camel and ass."

HERE BEGINNETH THE NINTH LESSON.

(Exodus xv., 3–5.)

"The Lord is a man of war ; the Lord is his name.
Pharaoh's chariots and his host hath he cast into the sea ;
His chosen captains also are drowned in the Red Sea.
The depths have covered them ;
They sank unto the bottom as a stone."

HERE BEGINNETH THE TENTH LESSON.

(Exodus ii., 12.)

"And Moses* looked this way, and that way, and when he saw that there was no man, he slew the Egyptian, and hid him in the sand."

HERE BEGINNETH THE ELEVENTH LESSON.

(I. Samuel xxi., 11.)

"Saul hath slain his thousands,
And David his ten thousands."

HERE BEGINNETH THE TWELFTH LESSON.

(Numbers xxi., 31–35.)

"Israel dwelt in the land of the Amorites. And Moses sent to spy out Jaazer, and they took the villages thereof, and drove out the Amorites that were there. And they turned and went up by the way of Bashan; and Og the king of Bashan went out against them, he, and all his people, to the battle of Edrei. And the Lord said unto Moses, Fear him not; for I have delivered him into thy hand, and all his people, and his land; and thou shalt do to him as thou didst unto Sihon, king of the Amorites, which dwelt at Heshbon. So they smote him, and his sons, and all his people, until there was none left him alive; and they possessed his land."

HERE BEGINNETH THE THIRTEENTH LESSON.

(Numbers xxxi., 1–19, 32–35.)

"The Lord spake unto Moses, saying, Avenge the children of Israel of the Midianites. And Moses spake unto the people, saying, Arm some of yourselves unto the war, and let them go against the Midianites. Of every tribe a thousand throughout all the tribes of Israel, shall ye send to the war. So there were delivered out of the thousands of Israel, a thousand of every tribe, twelve thousand armed for war. And Moses sent them to the war, a thousand of every tribe, them and Phinehas the son of Eleazar the priest, to the war, with the holy instruments, and the trumpets to blow in his hand. And they warred against the Midianites, as the Lord commanded Moses; and they slew all the males. And they slew the kings of

---

* The chosen and ever-beloved servant of the Lord.

Midian, beside the rest of them that were slain ; namely, Evi, and
Rekem, and Zur, and Hur, and Reba, five kings of Midian ; Balaam
also the son of Beor they slew with the sword. And the children
of Israel took all the women of Midian captives, and their little
ones, and took the spoil of all their cattle, and all their flocks and
all their goods. And they burnt all their cities wherein they dwelt,
and all their goodly castles with fire. And they took all the spoil,
and all the prey, both of men and of beasts. And they brought the
captives, and the prey, and 'the spoil, unto Moses, and Eleazer the
priest, and unto the congregation of the children of Israel, unto the
camp at the plains of Moab, which are by Jordan near Jericho.

"And Moses, and Eleazar the priest, and all the princes of the congregation, went forth to meet them without the camp. And Moses
was wroth with the officers of the host, with the captains over thousands, and captains over hundreds, which came from the battle.
And Moses said unto them, Have ye saved all the women alive? Behold, these caused the children of Israel, through the counsel of
Balaam, to commit trespass against the Lord in the matter of Peor,
and there was a plague among the congregation of the Lord. Now
therefore kill every male among the little ones and kill every woman
that hath known man by lying with him. But all the women children
that have not known a man by lying with him, keep alive for yourselves. * * * And the booty, being the rest of the prey which
the men of war had caught, was six hundred thousand and seventy
thousand and five thousand sheep, and threescore and twelve thousand beeves, and threescore and one thousand asses, and thirty and
two thousand persons in all, of women that had not known man by
lying with him."

HERE BEGINNETH THE FOURTEENTH LESSON.

(Obadiah, xv., 16.)

"The day of the Lord is near upon all the heathen ;
    Yea, they shall drink, and they shall swallow down,
    And they shall be as though they had not been."

HERE BEGINNETH THE FIFTEENTH LESSON.

(L. Chronicles, xx., 1-3.)

" After the year was expired, at the time that kings go out to battle,
Joab led forth the power of the army, and wasted the country of the
children of Ammon, and came and besieged Rabbah. But David
tarried at Jerusalem. And Joab smote Rabbah, and destroyed it.

And David took the crown of their king from off his head, and found it to weigh a talent of gold, and there were precious stones in it ; and it was set upon David's head ; and he brought also exceeding much spoil out of the city.   And he brought out the people that were in it, and cut them with saws, and with harrows of iron, and with axes. Even so dealt David with all the cities of the children of Ammon."

HERE BEGINNETH THE SIXTEENTH LESSON.

(I. Chronicles, xix., 18.)

When David had put the battle in array against the Syrians, they fought with him.   But the Syrians fled before Israel ; and David slew of the Syrians seven thousand men which fought in chariots, and forty thousand footmen, and killed Shophach the captain of the host."

HERE BEGINNETH THE SEVENTEENTH LESSON.

(II. Kings, xix., 35, 36.)

"And it came to pass that night, that the angel of the Lord went out, and smote in the camp of the Assyrians an hundred fourscore and five thousand ; and when they arose early in the morning, behold, they were all dead corpses.   So Sennacherib, king of Assyria, departed, and went and returned, and dwelt at Nineveh."

HERE BEGINNETH THE EIGHTEENTH LESSON.

(Joshua viii., 24-29.)

"It came to pass, when Israel had made an end of slaying all the inhabitants of Ai in the field, in the wilderness wherein they chased them, and when they were all fallen on the edge of the sword, until they were consumed, that all the Israelites returned unto Ai, and smote it with the edge of the sword.   And so it was, that all that fell that day, both of men and women, were twelve thousand, even all the men of Ai.   For Joshua drew not his hand back, wherewith he stretched out the spear, until he had utterly destroyed all the inhabitants of Ai.   Only the cattle and the spoil of that city Israel took for a prey unto themselves, according unto the word of the Lord which he commanded Joshua.   And Joshua burnt Ai, and made it an heap for ever, even a desolation unto this day.   And the king of Ai he hanged on a tree until eventide."

HERE BEGINNETH THE NINETEENTH LESSON.

(Joshua, x., 6-11.)

"The men of Gibeon sent unto Joshua to the camp to Gilgal, saying, Slack not thy hand from thy servants ; come up to us quickly, and save us, and help us ; for all the kings of the Amorites that dwell in the mountains are gathered together against us. So Joshua ascended from Gilgal, he, and all the people of war with him, and all the mighty men of valor. And the Lord said unto Joshua, Fear them not ; for I have delivered them into thine hand ; there shall not a man of them stand before thee. Joshua therefore came unto them suddenly, and went up from Gilgal all night. And the Lord discomfited them before Israel, and slew them with a great slaughter at Gibeon, and chased them along the way that goeth up to Beth-horon, and smote them to Azekah, and unto Makkedah. And it came to pass, as they fled from before Israel, and were in the going down to Beth-horon, that the Lord cast down great stones from heaven upon them unto Azekah, and they died ; they were more which died with hailstones than they whom the children of Israel slew with the sword."

HERE BEGINNETH THE TWENTIETH LESSON.

(Joshua, chapters x. and xi.)

"Then spake Joshua to the Lord in the day when the Lord delivered up the Amorites before the children of Israel, and he said in the sight of Israel, Sun, stand thou still upon Gibeon ; and thou, Moon, in the valley of Ajalon ! And the sun stood still, and the moon stayed, until the people had avenged themselves upon their enemies. So the sun stood still in the midst of heaven, and hasted not to go down about a whole day. And there was no day like that before it or after it, that the Lord harkened unto the voice of a man ; for the Lord fought for Israel. And Joshua returned, and all Israel with him, unto the camp to Gilgal."

"But these five kings fled, and hid themselves in a cave at Makkedah. And it was told Joshua saying, The five kings are found hid in a cave at Makkedah. And Joshua said, Roll great stones upon the mouth of the cave, and set men by it for to keep them ; and stay ye not, but pursue after your enemies, and smite the hindmost of them; suffer them not to enter into their cities; for the Lord your God hath delivered them into your hand. And it came to pass, when Joshua and the children of Israel had made an end of slaying them with a very great slaughter, till they were consumed, that the rest which remained of them entered into fenced cities. And all the people returned to the camp to Joshua at Makkedah in peace ; none moved his tongue against any of the children of Israel.

"Then said Joshua, Open the mouth of the cave, and bring out those five kings unto me out of the cave. And they did so, and brought forth those five kings unto him out of the cave, the king of Jerusalem, the king of Hebron, the king of Jarmuth, the king of Lachish, and the king of Eglon. And it came to pass, when they brought out those kings unto Joshua, that Joshua called for all the men of Israel, and said unto the captains of the men of war which went with him, Come near and put your feet upon the necks of these kings. And they came near, and put their feet upon the necks of them. And Joshua said unto them, Fear not, nor be dismayed, be strong and of good courage ; for thus shall the Lord do to all your enemies against whom ye fight. And afterward Joshua smote them, and slew them, and hanged them on five trees ; and they were hanging upon the trees until the evening. And it came to pass at the time of the going down of the sun, that Joshua commanded, and they took them down off the trees, and cast them into the cave wherein they had been hid, and laid great stones in the cave's mouth, which remain until this very day."

"And that day Joshua took Makkedah, and smote it with the edge of the sword, and the king thereof he utterly destroyed, them, and all the souls that were therein ; he let none remain ; and he did to the king of Makkedah as he did unto the king of Jericho.

"Then Joshua passed from Makkedah, and all Israel with him, unto Libnah, and fought against Libnah, and the Lord delivered it also, and the king thereof, into the hand of Israel ; and he smote it with the edge of the sword, and all the souls that were therein ; he let none remain in it; but did unto the king thereof as he did unto the king of Jericho.

"And Joshua passed from Libnah, and all Israel with him, unto Lachish, and encamped against it, and fought against it ; and the Lord delivered Lachish into the hand of Israel, which took it on the second day, and smote it with the edge of the sword, and all the souls that were therein, according to all that he had done to Libnah.

"Then Horam king of Gezer came up to help Lachish ; and Joshua smote him and his people, until he had left him none remaining.

"And from Lachish, Joshua passed unto Eglon, and all Israel with him ; and they encamped against it, and fought against it ; and they took it on that day, and smote it with the edge of the sword ; and all the souls that were therein he utterly destroyed that day, according to all that he had done to Lachish.

"And Joshua went up from Eglon, and all Israel with him, unto Hebron ; and they fought against it ; and they took it, and smote it with the edge of the sword, and the king thereof, and all the cities thereof, and all the souls that were therein ; he left none remaining, according to all that he had done to Eglon ; but destroyed it utterly. and all the souls that were therein.

"And Joshua returned, and all Israel with him, to Debir ; and fought against it ; and he took it, and the king thereof, and all the cities thereof ; and they smote them with the edge of the sword, and utterly destroyed all the souls that were therein ; he left none remaining ; as he had done to Hebron, so he did to Debir, and to the king thereof ; and as he had done also to Libnah, and to her king.

"So Joshua smote all the country of the hills, and of the south, and of the vale, and of the springs, and all their kings ; he left none remaining, but utterly destroyed all that breathed, as the Lord God of Israel commanded.   And Joshua smote them from Hadesh-barnea even unto Gaza, and all the country of Goshen, even unto Gibeon. And all these kings and their land did Joshua take at one time, because the Lord God of Israel fought for Israel.   And Joshua returned and all Israel with him, unto the camp at Gilgal.

"And it came to pass, when Jabin, king of Hazor, had heard these things, that he sent to Jobab king of Madon, and to the king of Shimron, and to the king of Achshaph, and to the kings that were on the north of the mountains, and of the plains south of Chinneroh, and in the valley, and in the borders of Dor on the west, and to the Canaanite on the east and on the west, and to the Amorite, and the Hittite, and the Perizzite, and the Jebusite in the mountains, and to the Hivite under Hermon in the land of Mispeh.   And they went out, they and all their hosts with them, much people, even as the sand that is upon the sea shore in multitude, with horses and chariots very many.   And when all these kings were met together, they came and pitched together at the waters of Merom, to fight against Israel.

"And the Lord said unto Joshua, Be not afraid because of them ; for to-morrow about this time will I deliver them up all slain before Israel ; thou shalt hough their horses, and burn their chariots with fire.   So Joshua came, and all the people of war with him, against them by the waters of Merom suddenly ; and they fell upon them. And the Lord delivered them into the hand of Israel, who smote them, and chased them unto great Zidon, and unto Misrephothmaim and unto the valley of Mizpeh eastward ; and they smote them, until they left none remaining. And Joshua did unto them, as the Lord bade him ; he houghed their horses, and burnt their chariots with fire.

"And Joshua at that time turned back, and took Hazor, and smote the king thereof with the sword ; for Hazor beforetime was the head of all those kingdoms. And they smote all the souls that were therein with the edge of the sword, utterly destroying them ; there was not any left to breathe ; and he burnt Hazor with fire. And all the cities of those kings, and all the kings of them, did Joshua take, and smote them with the edge of the sword; and he utterly destroyed them, as Moses the servant of the Lord commanded. But as for the cities that stood still in their strength, Israel burned none of them, save Hazor only ; that did Joshua burn. And all the spoil of these cities, and the cattle, the children of Israel took for a prey unto themselves ; but every man they smote with the edge of the sword, until they had destroyed them, neither left they any to breathe. As the Lord commanded Moses his servant, so did Moses command Joshua, and so did Joshua ; he left nothing undone of all that the Lord commanded Moses.

"So Joshua took all that land, the hills, and all the south country, and all the land of Goshen, and the valley, and the plain, and the mountain of Israel, and the valley of the same; even from the mount Halak, that goeth up to Seir, even unto Baal-gad in the valley of Lebanon under mount Hermon ; and all their kings he took, and smote them, and slew them."

So striking, and so strange, are some of the passages in the foregoing extracts, that, to the end, that they may be more thoroughly comprehended, the following separate reproduction of a few of them is most respectfully submitted.

"Ye shall dispossess the inhabitants of the land, and dwell therein."

"Thou shalt make no covenant with the inhabitants of the land whither thou goest."

"Spare them not; but slay both man and woman, infant and suckling, ox and sheep, camel and ass."

"Thou shalt hough their horses, and burn their chariots with fire."

"If ye will not drive out the inhabitants of the land from before

11*

you, then it shall come to pass, that those which ye let remain of
them, shall be pricks in your eyes, and thorns in your sides, and shall
vex you in the land wherein ye dwell. Moreover it shall come to
pass, that I shall do unto you, as I thought to do unto them."

"David brought out the people that were in Rabbah, and cut them
with saws, and with harrows of iron, and with axes. Even so dealt
David with all the cities of the children of Ammon."

"They smote them until they left none remaining. They smote
all the souls that were in Hazor, with the edge of the sword, utterly
destroying them; there was not any left to breathe."

"For it was of the Lord to harden their hearts, that they should
come against Israel in battle, that he might destroy them utterly,
and that they might have no favor, but that he might destroy them,
as the Lord commanded Moses. And at that time came Joshua, and
cut off the Anakim from the mountains, from Hebron, from Debir,
from Anab, and from all the mountains of Judah, and from all the
mountains of Israel. Joshua destroyed them utterly with their
cities."

"So Joshua smote all the country of the hills, and of the south,
and of the vale, and of the springs, and all their kings; he left none
remaining, but utterly destroyed all that breathed, as the Lord God
of Israel commanded.

Now while, as already indicated, it is no part of our
purpose to deal with the negroes in such summary and
sanguinary manner as the Lord God of Israel is here represented as having dealt with the Canaanites, and with
other people of ancient Palestine, yet it is religiously believed that we ought so to deal with them as that the
will of Heaven, in reference to them, may meet no opposition. Notwithstanding the fact that we are mere mortals, and although the provocation is so great that it
sometimes seems to be almost irresistible, yet it would certainly not be proper for us to incur the labor and the
responsibility of a quick and indiscriminate extermination of the blacks, whether by force of arms or otherwise, when the great and good God himself stands ready
and anxious, and is actually pleading with us for the privilege to exterminate them by means of the more gentle
and beneficent agencies of nature.

Only let us at once decide upon a well-defined land-mark (or ocean-mark) of division between ourselves and the blacks, and then, with an equitable and final provision in their behalf, placing every one of them on the other side of the line of separation, leave them there, to be the recipients of such future care and protection as Providence may be pleased to extend to them. The salutary upshot of this arrangement would be (and must be) that some branch or wing of the white race would, in due time, act upon the felicitous suggestion of Jehovah, who, to the end that he may bless, is eager to be *asked*, saying "Ask of me, and I shall give thee the heathen for thine inheritance, and the uttermost parts of the earth for thy possession." Yes; in order that, as another vast conti-nent for the happy homes of white men only—the only men who know how to make happy homes—we may ere long obtain the whole of Africa itself, God has graciously and condescendingly asked us to ask him for it; and if we rightly ask it of him, he will assuredly give it to us, and that, too, to the total exclusion and extinction of the negroes, just as he has given (or is giving) us the whole of America, to the total exclusion and extinction of the Indians.

No permanent lodgment, no enduring part nor lot, must the black and baneful negroes be permitted to ac-quire in our country. Already have they outlived the period of their usefulness—if, indeed, they were ever use-ful at all; and the solidifying and concealing subsoil is now urgently claiming, as overdue to itself, those osseous parts of their frames which, for so long a time, have been fated and fitted for fossilization.

CHAPTER VII.

THE UNITED STATES OF AMERICA ; A WHITE MAN POWER.

The United States are young, fresh, and vigorous, abounding in wealth, exulting in strength, and eager for action. They come of a race, the Anglo-Saxon, seemingly endowed with a deathless spring and vitality—a race which crushed old Rome, when Rome oppressed the world—which reared the stupendous structure of British enterprise—which impelled the armies of the Reformation—which planted in the New World the hardiest of its colonists—and which now, commanding the citadel as well as the outposts of civilization, wields the destinies of all the tribes.—PARKE GODWIN.

Most distinctly do I deny that this country is great only because it is "spacious in the possession of dirt," because, like Russia, it is vast, or even because, like France, it is rich and warlike. Its real greatness I believe, with a belief having the clearness of conviction and the earnestness of faith, has its sole origin in the qualities of the Race by which the land was settled and reclaimed, and by which its government and its society were framed.—RICHARD GRANT WHITE.

> Freedom's soil hath only place
> For a free and fearless race.—WHITTIER.

LITTLE have I to say by way of introduction to the several subjects discussed within the compass of this chapter, which is, in the main, made up of extracts from such of my fugitive compositions as had, when first written, and still have, for their object the furtherance of the principles and purposes foreshadowed in the preceding pages. Each particular paper, whether good, bad, or indifferent, will tell its own story. Regardless of dates, the harmony of the views advanced will, I opine, scarcely be questioned.

Toward the close of a letter which I confidentially wrote to my friend W., under date of June 5, 1861, only a few weeks subsequent to the outbreak of the great rebellion, I said :

A trio of unmitigated and demoralizing nuisances, constituting, in the aggregate, a most foul and formidable obstacle in our way to a high and mighty civilization in America, are Negroes, Slavery, and Slaveholders. These three preëminently vexatious and revolting nuisances, everywhere exciting the detestation and abhorrence of noble minds, must be summarily abated and suppressed. Henceforth, therefore, until we shall have effectually reduced from power and from prominence, upon this continent at least, these three surpassingly base things of the earth, let us be busy with the war cry,

> Death to Slavery!
> Down with the Slaveholders!
> Away with the Negroes!

Two of the very important considerations here wished for—the first and second—having, by the great favor of Heaven, been recently consummated, I would keep the third still emblazoned upon the banners of just and necessary reform; and thereto I would also add a few other rightful and momentous demands, thus:

Away with the Negroes!
Away with the Mulattoes!
Away with the Chinese!
Detrition and Detrusion of the Indians!
Down with the Black Congress!
Down with the Pig-headed President!
Down with the Treacherous and Venom-fanged Copperheads!
Down with the Rancorous and Still-threatening Secessionists!
Down with all the Employers, Landlords, and Coadjutors of Swarth-colored Bipeds!
No Manner of Permanent Association nor Relation with Dark-skinned Caitiffs!

Up with the White Republicans!

Up with the Loyal Democrats!

Up with a New National Legislature!

Up with a New Chief Magistrate!

Up with all the Champions of a Pure and Perfect Caucasian Manhood!

Ultimate Fossilization of all the Nigrified and Dingy-hued Offshoots of the Genus Homo!

Universal, Supreme and Exclusive Dominion of the White Races!

And thenceforward,

Union, Peace, Prosperity and Good Fellowship, Everywhere and Forever!

———

To the American shipmasters, whose vessels were at anchor in the harbor of Buenos Ayres, on the 15th of November, 1862, I wrote thus:

For the first time since my assumption of the duties of this Consulate, during which period more than six months have elapsed, an extraordinary occasion, as I conceive, renders it particularly appropriate that I should hoist high, and display in its fullest and freest folds, the the flag of our country. To-day, as some of you will have perceived, the good old banner, of which every loyal son and lover of the new world has so much cause to be proud, is so hoisted, and so displayed. This I have done in celebration of advices received here yesterday, detailing the just, wise, and manly action, recently taken by our government on the subject of Slavery, which, *with the negro as a basis*, is at the bottom of all our present political trouble.

In a proclamation issued by President Lincoln, under date of September 22, 1862, it is auspiciously declared, in effect, that the slaves of all the states and territories of the United States found in armed rebellion against the Federal Government on the first day of January, 1863, shall be acknowledged, deemed, and treated, as absolutely and irrevocably free; and that the existence of Slavery in all such States and territories shall thenceforth cease forever.

By those of us who, peering into the future, have in view the highest and best interests of America, this timely declaration of the President of the United States may be regarded as second only in importance to the Declaration of Independence, in Philadelphia, on the 4th of July, 1776, which, but a few years afterward, was so gloriously followed by the permanent establishment of American nationality.

I beg leave to request, therefore, that you will, this day, in the hoisting of your respective flags, join me in doing honor to the patriotic, prudent and progressive policy foreshadowed in the President's proclamation.

I also seize this opportunity to inform you, that I have clipped from an English newspaper, and am now having framed in gold, a copy of an address lately delivered by Abraham Lincoln, favoring, as I understand it, the deportation of all the negroes from the United States, and which address, in my opinion, is so full of good sound sense, and so worthy of being earnestly, fully, and speedily acted upon in its leading recommendations, that I take great pleasure in thus commending it to your attention; and shall be but too happy to submit it for your perusal, whenever, from a desire to become familiar with its contents, you may be pleased to call at my office.

To my friend C., under date of September 20, 1864, I I wrote thus:

Often, of late, have I asked myself the question, What is C. thinking about just now? What is his opinion of the drift and ultimate end of the atrocious war which the slaveholders of the United States are now waging against the most sacred rights and liberties of mankind? Does his far-sighted vision enable him to see in the future of America the colossal and regenerated Republic which many great and good poets and political philosophers and prophets have promised to us in the days to come?

Can it be possible that, in an adverse and inexplicable providence, Faction, Sedition, Discord, Anarchy and Strife, the dire offspring of Slavery and Rebellion, are to be permitted to run riot in our land, and to desolate it from one end to the other? Or shall we not, rather, in the strength and wisdom of Anglo-American freemen, and with the approbation and blessing of Heaven, rally once more, and, crushing beneath our feet the traitorous wretches who have attempted to subvert the sublime principles and system of self-government which we have inherited from the immortal authors of the Declaration of Independence and of the Constitution of 'the United States, reëstablish ourselves in the matchless might and and majesty of a truly grand and glorious continental republic?

And meanwhile, what about those worse than worthless base-born blackamoors, those sable satellites of the slaveholders, the negroes and the mulattoes, the quadroons and the octoroons, those millions of despicable sloths and pests, who, as the fawning slaves of traitors, naturally and unintermittingly, from infancy to old age, teaching baseness by example, have been the primary cause of the most bloody and calamitous contest that ever marked the annals of time? Ought we not, as an act of justice and prudence toward all concerned, to separate them, every one of them, from our country forever? to colonize them in Africa? or to ship them, with our best wishes, and with suitable outfits in the way of provisions and implements of husbandry, to one or more of the West India Islands, to Mexico, to Central America, or to South America? It may, perhaps, be somewhat premature to discuss this matter earnestly just now; but, as for me, I cannot help but believe, as I have unflaggingly believed for the twelve or fifteen years last past, that to this wise and happy conclusion we are destined to come at last.

———

To my clerical and esteemed friend G., who wrote me a note by a big black negro, (an Erebus-doomed native of the Argentine Republic, who, like his illustrious African ancestors, had never, by voluntary emigration, gone beyond the shadow of his own pumpkin vines,) requesting me, in my official capacity, to give American protection to the said negro, I wrote thus, under the date of July 31, 1862:

Of the opinion that the United States of America are already burdened with about four millions too many eleemosynaries of the color, character and condition, of the bearer to me of your favor of to-day, I beg leave to decline adding, or in any manner whatsoever aiding in adding, even one more to the number. I trust, therefore, that you will pardon me for not issuing a paper of protection to the individual in question, seeing that he is not now, never has been, and I trust never will be, a citizen of the United States.

———

To my friend W., under date of September 4, 1863, I wrote thus:

Permit me to join you in exultation over our recent brilliant triumphs at Vicksburg and at Port Hudson, and to express the hope that I may, erelong, have the pleasure of rejoicing with you over the grand and final victories of the war, and over the reëstablishment of the Union in all its integrity—without slavery, without slaves, without slaveholders, and, ultimately, without negroes, without mulattoes, without Indians, without Chinese; in short, without anybody belonging to the inferior races of mankind, whether of the color of ebony, of the shade of ginger-bread, or of whatever other possible hue or tint differing from the transcendently superior white.

———

To my friend B., under date of October 12, 1863, I wrote thus:

We know the views which were entertained and promulgated by the immortal Jefferson,—views such as should be entertained and promulgated by every man in America,—in reference to negroes and negro slavery. The miserable rebels of the South, and other pro-slavery wretches, will yet learn how, by the white lover of liberty, they and their slaves can be held in equal detestation; how the man of a good head and a noble heart may treat both the negroes and their masters with the profound contempt and abhorrence which they so justly merit, and yet be a thoroughly consistent friend to Freedom, an absolutely uncompromising foe to slavery. * * * That the questions affecting the negro— what shall we do with him? where shall we put him? when? and how?—are soon to become the paramount questions in our country, compared with which all other political questions will, for the time, be but minor considerations and side issues, I have no more doubt than I have of my own existence; and that Sambo and Cuffy, Dinah and Chloe, will, in the interests of mankind at large, certainly in the interests of the better portion of mankind, ultimately cease to retain a foothold in the United States of America I pray daily and devoutly, and have full faith.

To my friend S., under the date of October 17, 1865, I wrote thus:

On the question of Negro Suffrage, which is now agitating the minds of many of our people, it may be that but little importance should be attached to the opinions of one so humble as myself. Yet as a faithful friend of the country, and as one who knows something of the lamentable unworthiness of the negro, I beg leave to tender you my sincere thanks for the very dignified and patriotic position which, if I have rightly comprehended one of your recent speeches, you have assumed in the discussion of the subject. * * * It is, I think, barely possible, not probable, that the American people may allow themselves to be so far misled as to do this foolish thing; but if they do, they will erelong repent it in sackcloth and ashes, and will undo it, just as they repented and undid the monstrous folly of which they were guilty in 1862-'63, when they elected, as Governors, Congressmen, and others, bad men, whose gross disloyalty and stratagems, even in such great States as New York, Pennsylvania, and Ohio, seriously threatened the circumvention of the National Administration—a circumvention which, at that momentous period, would have proved, by the delinquent North itself, the downfall of our preëminently grand and glorious republic.

Pray, do not apprehend, however, that I am disposed

to weary you with a long letter. My only object in thus addressing you is to tell you how sincere is my hope that but few of the leading statesmen of our nation are afflicted with that new and disgusting malady which, for some time past, has been manifesting itself among us, and which, in the irregular medical nomenclature of the day, is not inaptly designated Negro-on-the-Brain—a sort of delirious accompaniment to the Black Vomit!

———

To my friend S., under date of December 29, 1864, I wrote thus :

The Government of the United States, as at present organized, is, I believe, doing for America, and for the world at large, the noblest work that has ever been done by any Congress or community of men, since the discovery of the New World, by Columbus and his comrades, in 1492. Sincerely believing this, it was with real ecstasies of joy that I received, yesterday, intelligence of the unequivocal manner in which the good and true voters of our republic have, in their recent ballotings, indorsed the open policy, the pure and patent purposes of President Lincoln's administration.

By the late enlightened suffrages of our countrymen, every citizen of the United States, whether at home or abroad, whose head and heart have been trained to harmonize with the well-being of mankind, has broader and better ground to stand upon, and also an additional cause to feel justly proud of his nationality.

Thus have the enemies of republican institutions, the enemies of Freedom and the friends of Slavery, been completely and constitutionally discomfited at the polls ; may God (and Grant) grant that they may soon be irretrievably defeated, and forever foiled, on the field of battle!

To my friend C., (an old schoolmate,) under date of October 12, 1865, I wrote thus :

Now that the war is over, and that it has had a most rightful and auspicious termination, how do you feel, and what do you think?   How solidly glorious, how exquisitely comforting, has been the close of the contest!

Lee hath been unhorsed in the "last ditch;" and Beauregard hath been thrown far from the back, and far above the ears, of an he ass!   Longstreet is no lion's whelp; neither is B. Bragg a bull of Bashan!   John C., the son of Breckinridge, strolleth, in fatigue and melancholy, along all the highways and byways of the earth, but findeth neither rest nor pleasure therein; for his feet always alighteth on slippery ground; and, moreover, he sigheth, both day and night, and longeth exceedingly, and even crieth aloud, for the halcyon days of yore.   Yet hath his keen desire no promise of gratification in the time present, nor prospect of fulfillment in the time to to come.   George N., the son of Sanders, also panteth much for the pleasant places of the past; and Henry A., the son of Wise, (as wise as a stump-tailed steer!) smacketh his lips in vain for the fat things of old.   Oh Henry A., Henry A., Henry A.,

> "Be not *wise* in thine own eyes :
>   Fear the Lord and depart from evil :
>   It shall be health to thy navel,
>   And marrow to thy bones !"

More seriously, evermore let us offer up our deep-felt gratitude to God!   Let us give many thanks to the Most High; let our voices be tuned with ecstasies of joy; and may our hearts, like the harts upon the mountains, leap forward with gayety, and bound upward with delight!   Let us sing unto the Lord a new song, and unto the Lord of Hosts an hymn of exaltation.   Let us magnify his name above all names, and his ways above the ways of all the world. Not unto us, O Lord, not unto us, but unto thee belongeth the victory! Thy right arm hath not been shortened; thy left hand hath not suffered restraint. Mighty art thou in battle, and greatly to be feared. Terrible art thou to the doers of evil, and a swift witness against the workers of iniquity. Yet mercy and gentleness hath their dwelling-place in thine exalted habitation; and all goodness floweth forth from thee. Incline our hearts, O Lord, incline our hearts to honor thee with love and praise; for thou art the sum and the substance of all worthiness; and of thy most excellent majesty, there is no diminution. Even the hill-country and the plains shall praise thee; and the high hills and the mountains shall bow their heads in reverential acknowledgment of the sublimity of thy exceeding greatness. In all, and above all, art thou established forever! The fame of thy unapproachable power and perfection shall be extolled beyond the ends of the earth; and, with the music of thy transcendent glory, heaven itself shall resound forever and forever!

But enough of this rhapsody. The war is over. Peace has returned. Good times are coming. Let us be happy. Glory hallelujah!

And what about our old schoolmates and other friends in Carolina? Pray give me a sort of biographico-historical sketch of each and every one of them, during the last four or five years—so far, at least, as it may be in your power to do so conveniently—and also inform me what you think of the present and prospective state of affairs down in Dixie. Is there not in reserve for our entire commonwealth (soon, perhaps, to expand into continental dimensions) a superlatively grand and glorious future? I ween so; may God grant it so. Under no less a planet than the mighty Jupiter, did the American Republic spring forth into existence, full-grown and graceful, like the blue-eyed Minerva from the immortal brain of Jove.

Intelligence of the assassination of President Lincoln was received in the River Plate on Saturday, May 28, 1865. On the following Monday, many American citizens, resident in Buenos Ayres, met and appointed a committee to draft and report suitable resolutions. The committee, (of seven,) of whom I was one, offered four sets of resolutions ; but, after some little discussion, two of the sets entirely, and one for the most part, were withdrawn ; and the set handed in by myself was taken as the basis of the series which was afterward unanimously adopted in full meeting of all those who had taken part in the preliminary proceedings. An exact copy of the paper which, during the deliberations of the committee, was submitted by myself, is here transcribed :

Buenos Ayres, May 31, 1865.

Gentlemen :

In discharge of the duty which you imposed upon us day before yesterday, when it pleased you to constitute us a committee with specific functions, we beg leave to submit, for your approval, the following resolutions :

Resolved, 1.—That as loyal and ever-faithful citizens of the United States of America, now resident in Buenos Ayres, we have been sorely shocked, and, at the same time, filled with indignation of the deepest import, on the receipt here, on Saturday last, the 28th instant, of intelligence of the dastardly and fiendish assassination of the late eminently distinguished President of our country, Abraham Lincoln, in whom we have always recognized unswerving honesty and patriotism, and to whom we now assign in our memories a place among the very ablest and best statesmen of America;—a place no less exalted than that occupied by such representative benefactors as Washington, Adams, Franklin, Madison, Jefferson, and Jackson ; and that, among these, we know of but one name that will shine with more dazzling lustre on the impartial page of history.

Resolved, 2.—That to the grief-stricken family of the illustrious magistrate, who has thus fallen a victim to unexampled violence and atrocity—a magistrate for whom there had long since been awakened within us a feeling of affection as well as respect—we tender our most unfeigned and profound condolence.

Resolved, 3.—That, in celebration of the obsequies of our greatly esteemed and beloved President, Abraham Lincoln, whom we would solemnly proclaim and consecrate to posterity as the second Father of his Country, the Rev. William Goodfellow, an American clergyman in this city, be invited to deliver, at an early day, an appropriate discourse on the many distinguished virtues and abilities of the departed patriot.

Resolved, 4.—That as a measure emblematic of our sincere distress and bitterness of heart at this most lamentable occurrence, we will wear black crape around the left arm during the full period of thirty days.

Resolved, 5.—That, with similar experiences of pain and sorrow on our part, we have also heard of the attempted assassination, simultaneously with the assassination of President Lincoln, of another very able and worthy American statesman, William Henry Seward, Secretary of State; to whom, in the serious personal injury which he has suffered at the hands of a most vile and infamous wretch, we extend our warmest sympathies, and offer, at the same time, our best hopes and wishes for his speedy recovery.

Resolved, 6.—That we devoutly trust and pray, that the Cain-marked murderer, and his accomplices, if any, in these atrocious crimes, may be quickly apprehended.

Resolved, 7.—That we gratefully accept as a compliment to our country and to ourselves, the voluntary and considerate action of the authorities here, on Saturday last, the 28th instant, in causing all the national and provincial flags to be hoisted at half-mast, as a token of grief at the untimely loss of the honored and lamented subject of these resolutions ; and that, with our whole hearts, we thank Almighty God, that, amid the unparalleled trials and provocations of the most gigantic rebellion ever organized among the rash and misguided sons of men, our chief leaders and defenders have uniformly acted with so much moderation and justice, as to secure the enthusiastic sympathies and support of such enlightened and progressive statesmen as those whom we have the honor to know in the persons of President Mitre and his Cabinet, now at the head of the Argentine Republic.

Resolved, 8.—That, in a corresponding vein of thankfulness and gratitude, we make our acknowledgments to the Press of Buenos Ayres for appearing in mourning, on Sunday last, and for their numerous and well merited eulogiums upon our martyred President; also to the whole body of the Argentine Congress for their sympathetic resolutions of yesterday, among which was one to signify their sad and painful recognition of this solemn occasion, by wearing the badge of mourning during the space of three days ; and also to Gov. Saavedra and the Legislature of the Province of Buenos Ayres, for their complimentary resolution of last evening, declaring that the next new town or city which shall be organized within the Province, shall be designated Lincoln.

Resolved, 9.—That, to our fellow-citizens in the United States, we renew our pledge of continued and unfaltering fidelity to the Union, and to the Federal Government, as constitutionally organized in Washington; and entertain now, as heretofore, a deeply-cherished confidence in the ability and determination of the American people to carry out, in its fullest and most meritorious extent, without any manner of deviation, either to the right hand or to the left, the glorious and well-defined policy of President Lincoln's Administration.

———

Agreeably to due public notice, almost every respectable American citizen resident in Buenos Ayres (between fifty and sixty in number) assembled at the United States Legation, on the 20th of June, 1865; and there and then, in the course of other proceedings, adopted, verbatim, an address of sincere respect and confidence, which, in most cheerful compliance with a request which had been made of me some days before, I had drafted for presentation to our new Chief Magistrate, Andrew Johnson.* Verbatim, did I say? The only alteration pro-

———

* It will be remembered with what fullness of satisfaction and confidence committees of distinguished gentlemen from most of the great States and cities of the Union repaired to Washington, soon after Mr. Johnson became President, to offer him pledges of their sincere respect and support. The following address is in consonance with the spontaneous and generous sentiments which then actuated the masses of the American people. I deeply regret that the President has so .

posed, and which proposition was put to a vote and carried, was that the date should be changed from the 15th of June to the 4th of July, and that the address itself, with the date so changed, should not be forwarded hence until after that time.

Here follows a perfect copy of the address as it passed from me to the committee who reported it for adoption —and of which committee I had the honor to be named chairman :

BUENOS AYRES, June 15, 1865.

To ANDREW JOHNSON,
      President of the United States,

SIR :

Although residing far south in the southern hemisphere, nearer to Cape Horn than to the Equator, yet we are Americans ; we are your countrymen ; we are your friends ; and as such we beg leave to address you a few words of earnest faith and encouragement.

Mingled with the profound grief which has constantly harassed us since we first heard (a fortnight past) of the assassination of President Lincoln, there is brightening in our hearts an ever-present gleam of joy, and grati-

----

unnecessarily forfeited, in so great a measure, the esteem and affection of his countrymen. His pig-headedness (and this is the harshest term that I feel justified in employing against him) and his ill-timed and imprudent speeches in the West, have rendered him too unpopular to be any longer thought of in connection with the next Presidency. He is still, however, a better man, an abler man, than any one of his malicious accusers ; and his veto messages alone embody more enlightened and profound statesmanship than has ever yet found lodgment in the beggarly brains of the whole of the two-thirds majority of the Black Congress.

tude to God, that the mighty interests of America, the momentous concerns of the United States, the many considerations connected with the old homes and places forever endeared to us by the sweet memories of youth and manhood, have, as we confidently believe, been lodged in peculiarly safe and suitable hands.

Like you, we are animated by an unyielding solicitude for the perpetual unity, peace and prosperity of our whole country.

Like you, we believe that our Government has, in the main, been established upon the eternal principles of Right, Truth and Justice; and that, as a nation, we are now, and shall continue to be, so long as we adhere to these principles, under the friendly and all-powerful protection of Heaven.

Like you, we have unbounded faith in the past, present and future success of man's experiment as a self-ruler in the New World; and with you we concur in the opinion, that, ultimately the people of other countries, the inhabitants of other continents, will find the fullest and the best development of their affairs generally, their truest rank, and their highest earthly happiness, under improved forms of republican government.

Well assured are we that it will be quite safe and proper for us to leave all weighty and pressing considerations of American statesmanship, whether with regard to our domestic or our foreign relations, to yourself and to the other great and good men associated with you in managing the affairs of our Government. Calmly judging from what we know of the many approved services which you have already rendered to the public, both in and out of Congress, we entertain the most steadfast confidence in you as an eminently able and worthy representative of the free people of America; and we pray God, that he may still strengthen you, and, in strengthening you, strengthen us and every inhabitant of our land, in all that is good, noble and true.

Not in the desolating exploits of war and slavery, but rather in the renovating arts of peace and freedom, would we, as Americans, become renowned. Holding the sword in reserve, as we have been wont to do in years gone by, let us now go forward with the harmless weapons of progress and civilization, achieving successes which, by virtue of their intrinsic value and magnitude, shall enrobe our Republic with innocently earned and imperishable fame to the end of time. And, of many of the successes which shall be thus achieved, may we have it in our power to say to our children, and they to their children and to their children's children :—These are the grand results of measures inaugurated during the presidential administration of Andrew Johnson, the immediate successor of Abraham Lincoln, the reëstablishers and the promoters of a wise and magnanimous system of American legislation.

We remain, sir, with great esteem,
Your friends and fellow-citizens.

———

On the 4th of July, 1865, the leading American merchants and other citizens of the United States, resident in Buenos Ayres, (about five dozen in number,) gave a grand dinner, at which I had the honor and the pleasure to "assist." What a happy fellow I should be, were it possible and convenient for me to render such "assistance" every day of my life! What turkeys, and ducks, and chickens, and wild birds from the Pampas, all in excellent condition, and prepared under the most palatable fascinations of French cookery! What rich oyster-pies, lobster-salads, and vegetables, and side-dishes of good things innumerable! What delicate tarts and puddings, and custards, and cakes, and comfits of names and shapes unique! What delicious fruits, of smell and taste ambrosial! What fine wines, of aroma and flavor nectar-like! What a pleasing variety of abundant and wholesome cheer for the inner man! But why should the reader, or why should I, be tantalized by reference to these dainties, none of which, at this time, are within reach of either him or myself? Innocent hilarity prevailed from one end of the table to the other; and many well-worded toasts and speeches were pronounced. The paper copied below holds me responsible for some of the least meritorious expressions which were heard on that occasion. The toast to which I responded (and which had been handed to me two or three days previously, with the request that I would say something in reply) was in these words:

"Our erring Southern brethren, who have fought bravely, worthy of a better cause ; may their returning sense of justice bring with it a willing obedience to the Constitution of the United States."

Disconnected from all such little superfluities as "applause," "cheers," "bravos," and other complimentary demonstrations of approval on the part of the audience, the following is a correct copy of the remarks made by me, when, rising from my seat, I said:

Mr. Chairman and Gentlemen:
It has often been asserted—with truth, I think—that there are men who, if they assume an erect posture in the presence of a public assembly, have no command of themselves to say three words. Do you suppose that you have never seen a man of that sort? Then you deceive yourselves, for he now stands before you. Nevertheless, if it be in harmony with the general plan of the proceed-

ings of the evening, permit me to make a brief statement, and upon that a single inquiry. My friend, the author of the "Impending Crisis of the South," who is here with us, but who accepts as generally correct, and particularly so with reference to himself, the adage that *authors never make speeches*, has placed in my hands, on a paper now in my pocket, an expression of opinion in regard to the last toast; an opinion, however, exclusively his own, and not, in any manner, reflecting or expressing the opinion of others, except so far, if at all, as they may be pleased to indorse what he has written; and I would thank you to inform me whether it would be proper on my part to occupy eight or ten minutes of your time, by reading the paper in question.

"Certainly," "certainly," "most certainly," having resounded from every part of the hall, I took the paper from my pocket, and read as follows :

The sentiment of the toast just given is highly honorable both to the head and the heart of the gentleman* who proposed it. While, as I understand it, that sentiment very fully and properly acknowledges the strength and integrity of the Union, it, at the same time, whispers to our misled and overpowered countrymen of the South, assurances of manly kindness and conciliation. This is as it ought to be; and so, I am sure, it will be.

Considering the glorious victories which have everywhere crowned our arms, the complete suppression of the rebellion, and the perfect vindication of the great principles upon which our Government was founded, fitly may we continue the practice of moderation; well may we af-

---

* Mr. Wm. T. Livingston, formerly of New York.

ford to be generous to a fallen foe; safely and appropriately may we temper mercy with justice.

Only a few days since, an English gentleman, more liberal and kindly-natured than some of the other subjects of her Britannic Majesty, remarked in my presence—and I was pleased to hear the words fall from his lips—that, in his opinion, the unlooked-for leniency with which the United States had treated General Lee and his deluded comrades, would secure a speedy and happy re-adjustment of American affairs, both at home and abroad. This opinion of the Englishman was rightly conceived, and opportunely expressed; but, at the same time, let it be remembered that an honorable and lasting peace, with its long train of gladdening concomitants, may be secured, and in all probability will be secured, by the operation of other measures and other causes in proper conjunction with the one assigned.

Meanwhile let us not be cheated of any of the festival privileges and rejoicings, and free interchange of opinions, so eminently due to us on this occasion.

How often have the friends of our Government, especially those resident in foreign countries, been shocked and insulted by the misrepresentations of disunionists, chiefly disloyal Americans and other advocates of Slavery, who, in the face of facts, have falsely asserted that the South was a unit for secession! The number of times this wicked thing has been done, can only be known by criteria. In Buenos Ayres it has been done frequently. Our enemies made persistent efforts to weaken our cause by creating wrong impressions abroad. They always said that the war was popular at the South, and that it had been deliberately inaugurated by the masses of the Southern people. We know perfectly well, and always knew, that the war was not popular at the South, but that it was the unmixed measure of a small and most mischievous

minority of the people—a mere handful of factious demagogues, who had no higher object in view than the extension and perpetuation of negro slavery. Of the truth of
this we have conclusive proof in the great number of
Southern men who, under the most oppressive and cruel
proscription, and often at the sacrifice of life itself, have
firmly adhered to the flag of their fathers.

Bear with me two minutes, while I recount the honored
names of a few devoted sons of the South—men of South-
erd birth—who have fought and bled, and some of whom
have nobly died for their country, during the four years
last past. I will here mention the names only of such as
have been general officers in the army.

Virginia has given us twelve generals, whose surnames
are as follows :

THOMAS,	PRENTISS,	DENVER,
TERRELL,	NEWTON,	AMMEN,
COOKE,	DAVIDSON,	HAYS,
RENO,	STEVENSON,	GRAHAM.

Maryland, " My Maryland," has given us ten generals,
namely :

ORD,	EMORY,	SYKES,
COOPER,	FRENCH,	JUDAH,
BENTON,	KENLEY,	LANMAN,
	VANDEVER.	

Delaware has given us three generals, namely :

LOCKWOOD,	TORBET,	THOMAS.

Kentucky—the birthplace of President Lincoln, the
martyred and immortal patriot—stands in great measure
redeemed in the number and efficiency of the soldiers
whom she has sent into the field for the defence of the

Union. She has given us twenty-eight generals, whose names are :

CANBY,	POPE,	ROUSSEAU,
ANDERSON,	BOYLE,	BURBRIDGE,
REYNOLDS,	CRITTENDEN,	FRY,
NELSON,	McCLERNAND,	SHACKELFORD,
HOBSON,	McMILLAN,	JOHNSON,
HARROW,	CLAY,	JACKSON,
OGLESBY,	CLAY-SMITH,	WOOD,
BLAIR,	MORRIS,	WARD, and
GORMAN,	PALMER,	two BUFORDS.

Tennessee has given us five generals, namely :

CARTER,	HARNEY,	CAMPBELL.
ABERCROMBIE,	SPEARS.	

The District of Columbia has given us five generals, namely :

HUNTER,	ORME,	PLEASANTON.
BRANNAN,	GETTY,	

Alabama has given us three generals, namely :

Two BIRNEYS, and one CRITTENDEN.

North Carolina has given us two generals :

MEREDITH and JOHNSON.

South Carolina has also given us two generals :

HURLBUT and FREMONT.

Missouri has given us RENÉ; Louisiana, WEST; and Georgia, MEIGS.

Here we have a list of seventy-three Southern generals of land forces, many of whom have already, with their valor and blood, intermingled with the valor and blood of their compatriots from other sections of the country, added strength and indissolubility to the Union.

If we turn to the Navy we shall find from the South, four names at least, which will be famous in history so long as floating batteries or men-of-war shall be found upon the water. You know to whom I allude: Farragut, of Tennessee; Porter, of Louisiana; Goldsborough, of the District of Columbia; and Winslow, of North Carolina,—that brave and dauntless Old Coon, who sank the pirate Alabama.

Of men of Northern birth, the meanest and most infamous of all who have served as generals in the rebel army, I am happy to be able to name but nine; but am truly sorry, at the same time, that even one man, whether from the North or from the South, should ever have been found disgracing himself and his country by service so ignoble and atrocious. The names of the nine Northern renegades to whom I refer, are: Whiting, Ruggles, and Blanchard, of Massachusetts; Cooper, of New York; Pemberton and Duncan, of Pennsylvania; Leadbeater, of Connecticut; French, of New Jersey; and Ripley of Ohio.

And of these contemptible fellows, and their chief accomplices in the crime of treason, what shall be said? As for me, I hesitate not to say that, in my humble opinion, their memory ought either to be consigned to oblivion, or forever held in utter abhorrence.

Not the least among the seventy-odd names of distinguished army and navy commanders from the South who have heroically proved their devotion to the Union in the late terrible conflict—names which, in great measure, constitute the modern roll of Southern honor—is that of Andrew Johnson, formerly of North Carolina, now President of the United States, who is, perhaps, in many particulars, more like Andrew Jackson than any other man in America. They were both born in North Carolina, of which State President Polk was also a native. Both—all three in fact—emigrated to Tennessee, and, while residing there, were elected to the Presidency. The full name of each is composed of thirteen letters, the number being suggestive of the original thirteen States which, more than three-quarters of a century since, achieved their independence of Great Britain. Each has, (and very properly, as showing that their parents were persons of sense,) but one prenomen; and that is Andrew. The cognomen of each is a word of two syllables, and the terminating syllable of each is *son*. The prefix of the one surname is Jack, while that of the other is John. Now Jack and John, as is well known, signify one and the same thing. It follows, therefore, that, in Andrew Johnson, we have a man who is neither more nor less than Andrew Jackson—the same tough "Old Hickory," the able and incorruptible statesman, for whom it is said, the patriotic Dutchmen of Pennsylvania have been steadily voting, at every Presidential election, during the last forty years!

But the parallel does not end here. Both received appointment as generals of militia. Before becoming President, each served his adopted State, first as a Representative in Congress, and afterward as a Senator of the United States. Both were called to the Presidency in times of great national peril; both were Southern men, and it became the duty of both to deal stringently, and both did deal stringently, with the disaffection and treason of their slaveholding neighbors. One annulled nullification; and the other suppressed a gigantic rebellion.

As a new illustration of the fact that it is impossible to please everybody, (indeed, I fear there are in the world some persons who cannot, or will not, be pleased at all,) I may here mention that, prior to the dinner above referred to, several over-captious individuals raised very serious and pressing objections against the toast to which the foregoing response was made, on the ground that the sentiments which it conveyed detracted from the glory of the Union triumph! One of the Massachusetts invincibles seems to have carried his opposition so far, that, even at the table, he positively but silently refused to recognize the fitness of the toast, and (for once) did not drink, gruffly alleging, with an air of fastidiousness and self-importance, that *he* would never soil *his* lips with any liquid tinctured with such humiliating and unnecessary acknowledgments! He was a stiff-necked and stubborn man ; and, fond as he was of a glass, his refusal to drink, so far from adding anything to his Americanism, only betrayed, on his own part, such bitter and unreasonable prejudices, such implacableness of sectional rancor, as never finds nourishment in the breasts of the braver and the better classes of mankind.

This unkindly carper, before indulging so freely in caustic criticism against the discomfited traitors of the South, should have recalled to his mind the woeful defection and treachery which prevailed throughout all the loyal States themselves, during the first and second years of the war. He should have remembered how the people of even such powerful States as New York, Pennsylvania, and Ohio, by their votes, in 1862–63, virtually indorsed and approved the slaveholders' thrice-wicked rebellion. He should also have bethought himself of the fact, that it was a black-hearted editor of Wisconsin, who, in his own newspaper, first suggested an unspeakably atrocious crime to the fiend-like tragedian of Maryland, who became the accursed instrument of its perpetration:

Listen, says the New York Weekly *Tribune*, under date of April 29, 1865 :

" We recalled to mind recently a paragraph which appeared some months since in *The La Crosse* (Wisconsin) *Democrat*, instigating the assassination of Mr. Lincoln.   We have since received from a gentleman of this city the number of the paper containing it—that of August 29, 1864.   It is the closing paragraph of a fierce political leader, and is as follows :

" 'The man who votes for Lincoln now is a traitor.   Lincoln is a traitor and murderer.   He who pretending to war for, wars against the Constitution of our country, is a traitor ; and Lincoln is one of those men.   He who calls and allures men to certain butchery, is a murderer ; and Lincoln has done all this.   *Had any former Democratic President warred upon the Constitution, or trifled with the destinies of the Nation, as Lincoln has, he would have been hurled to perdition long since.   And if he is elected to misgovern for another four years, we trust some bold hand will pierce his heart with dagger point for the public good.' "*

Aye, not only during the war, but also before the war, and since the war, no small number of the most mean and malignant enemies of our Government have been Northern men, whose superior opportunities for knowing better, leave them, as it seems to me, even less excusable than the great majority of Southerners, who, until the glorious triumph of the armies of Liberty, had long been debarred from all sources of correct information.   Long and tenaciously did the Slaveholders cling to their filthy and disgusting idols of ebony ; yet, for these black and fanatical practices of paganism on their part, they were not wholly responsible. · Not from South Carolina, not from Georgia, not from Louisiana, not from Texas, have I met secessionists or rebels who were more recreant or rascally than many of the traitorous wretches whom I have seen, and others of whom I have heard, from Maine, from Massachusetts, from New York, and from Pennsylvania.

In the North, scarcely less than in the South, defection

and treason have been encountered and overcome ; but now that the war has had an eminently just and glorious termination, let us, in settling accounts with our white fellow citizens—and no others than the whites would we acknowledge as fellow citizens—be generous to all, unkind to none. When we were fighting the rebels, who, without good or sufficient reason, had raised their hostile hands against us, it was but right and dutiful on our part to press them hard ; but since they have been thoroughly whipped, and are now humbly petitioning for such terms as may be properly accorded to vanquished transgressors, let us deal gently with them. Flesh are they of our flesh, blood of our blood, and bone of our bone — countrymen and brothers all! Toward them, therefore, as toward all others, let our motto ever be : All Lion in War ; all Lamb in Peace.

Not so great is the sin of the Slaveholders as but that it may soon be expiated ; and then, having undergone purification from their very long and very vile association with the negro, they may assimilate with the other whites, and without any manner of distinction or discrimination, be incorporated with the great American body politic. Otherwise must it be with the negro himself. With him we must come to no terms ; with him we must have neither part nor lot. No, no ; of the matchless crime of his blackness and slavery and stupidity and self-imposed despicableness, there can be no forgiveness this side the grave ; I beg the reader's pardon ; I meant to have said this side the gully, this side the gutter, this side the Gulf of Mexico, or this side the Gulf of Guinea! As thoroughly and as speedily as possible must the negro be fossilized ; and then, by the better students of natural history, shall his bleaching bones be held equally sacred with the wire-strung skeletons of his first-cousin congeners, the gorilla and the baboon!

Objection was also made to my classifying as of the South such men as Fremont, Birney, and Blair, who, although born and reared south of Mason and Dixon's line, have nevertheless achieved or acquired much of their liberal and loyal manhood within the Free States; yet no one, I suppose, would be so rash as to contend that there is the least probability that they would ever have become Union soldiers, or soldiers of any sort, had they never been born! It is true that several of those whose names I have mentioned, have been greatly invigorated and benefited by inhaling, for a long while, the pure air of Liberty; and it is lamentable, indeed, that, during any part of their lives, it was ever binding upon them to breathe even one particle of the foul atmosphere of Slavery.   Yet, as in the case of General Thomas, Admiral Farragut, Attorney-General Bates and many others, we have abundant and most gratifying evidence, that the true and better type of mankind, as found developed in the white races, may, year after year, be exposed to daily contact with the contaminating influences of negroes, negro slaves and negro owners, and still be sufficiently strong and buoyant to save itself from shipwreck.

Besides the seventy odd Southern patriots whose names appear in the foregoing lists, there are many others, some of whom, by virtue of their whole-souled devotion and services to the Union cause, are worthy to be ranked among the very bravest and the best of those who have risked everything for the freedom and integrity of their common country.   To these from the South, as well as those from the North, who, with hands joined in sublime brotherhood, have forever crushed beneath their feet the fell spirit of Slavery, history will not fail to do ample justice.

Liberally large, however, as was the number of Southern officers and men, as compared with the general suppositions of those who pay little or no regard to statistics ; yet when we calmly consider all the adverse circumstances which affected the Union men of the South, we can readily understand how, after all, so few of them were found fighting on the right side. How terrible, indeed, throughout all the South, was the Reign of Terror! How many died of lawless and fiendish violence on the part of mobs, and how many by the sanguinary hands of desperate individuals, who, with impunity, were allowed to slay and slaughter at their own frenzied caprice, no tongue nor pen may ever tell.

At the mere remembrance of some of the appalling accounts of bloodthirstiness and torture and death which have been narrated to me personally, and of others which I have read in the newspapers (and in the substantial truth of which I have too much reason to believe) my heart sorely sickens, and shrinks from the recital of details. Yet precisely such barbarous conduct as, both during the war and before the war, characterized the men of the South, would, in the main, have also characterized the men of the North, had they, too, been brutalized by life-long association with negroes and negro slaves.

Living in communities composed exclusively of themselves, and not corrupted by personal intercourse with any inferior race, it is white men only who refine themselves from the dross, and who lift themselves above the savagery, of sheer revenge and cruelty. A state of refinement and amiability such as is here referred to, a state of refinement and amiability both of the head and the heart, the like of which has not hitherto been known among men, may be expected to make its simultaneous and permanent appearance in all parts of America, so soon as our country shall have been thoroughly cleansed of the vulgar and disgusting negroes and their next of kin, who must themselves be required to be the unreturnable bearers hence of their own worse than worthles bodies and nauseous odors.

Only let all the killow-colored refuse of humanity be whiffed beyond the confines of the life which, by their countless shortcomings and crimes, they have forfeited, substituting in their places white people; and then, from one end of our land to the other, from furthest side to furthest side, and from nadir to zenith, will be found prevailing, in exquisite and inexhaustible fullness, health, harmony and happiness.   Then will America be seen "ruling its destinies, preëminent alike in wealth and population, manners and religion, law, literature and arts."   Then, indeed, from the far east to the remote west, and from the outskirts of the north to the distant south,

> "Corn shall make the young man cheerful,
>   And new wine the maids."

Depart, therefore, ye wicked and abandoned blacks, into the regions of darkness and deep despair and oblivion prepared for you, and for all akin to you, from the foundation of the world; and let the radiant and gem-like gates of glory, affixed to pillars of gold, be opened wide for the reception of the righteous and Heaven-blessed whites, who, while ineffably happy amidst diamond-fenced fields of superb fruits and flowers, shall, with constantly-increasing joy, bask forever in floods of richly-perfumed and silvery-sparkling light!

CHAPTER VIII

THIRTEEN KINDRED PAGES FROM THE IMPENDING CRISIS.

I am not, and never have been, in favor of making voters or jurors of negroes ; nor of qualifying them to hold office, nor to intermarry with whites ; and I will say further, in addition to this, that there is a physical difference between the black and white races, which I believe will forever forbid the two races living together on terms of social and political equality.—LINCOLN.

I believe this Government was made by white men, for the benefit of white men and their posterity forever ; and I am in favor of confining citizenship to white men—men of European birth and descent, instead of conferring it upon negroes, Indians, and other inferior races.—DOUGLAS.

The proverbs of Theognis, like those of Solomon, are observations on human nature, ordinary life, and civil society, with moral reflections on the facts. I quote him as a witness of the fact, that there is as much difference in the races of men as in the breeds of sheep, and as a sharp reprover and censurer of the sordid, mercenary practice of disgracing birth by preferring gold to it. Surely no authority can be more expressly in point to prove the existence of inequalities, not of rights, but of moral, intellectual, and physical inequalities in families, descents and generations.—JOHN ADAMS.

Does there exist any good reason why the man who has fearlessly taken by the horns a brave bull, should timorously hesitate to seize by the ears a cowardly calf? Should the huntsman who has successfully bearded a lion in his den, shrink or recoil from combat with an opossum? If the traveler, who is in only moderate health, be able to contend single-handed with a wolf in the way, shall he not, when in the very vigor of manhood, be confident of his ability to worry a weasel?

There is, it is believed, a peculiar fitness in the fact that this exposure of the utter unworthiness and worthlessness of the negroes, should be made by one who had previously made a thorough exposition of the political follies and corruptions of the negro-owners themselves. The little David hereof, having, therefore, first attacked and overcome the strongest and the subtlest of mankind, now advances to wage vigorous and effective warfare against the weakest and the meanest—and woe to the black, woe to the brown, who allows himself to be confronted anywhere on the soil of America!

Evidences shall no longer be wanting that good men, the very best men in all the world—the real salt of the earth—may be hearty haters of slavery, and, at the same time, unconditional detesters of darkies. To hate slavery, or to abominate the slaveholder (so long as he willfully advocates and defends slavery) is a virtue. To love the slave, or to honor his master (so long as the condition of mastership is purposely and wantonly maintained) is a vice. To live in juxtaposition with the negro, or to tolerate his presence even in the vicinity of white men, is, to say the least, a most shameful and disgraceful proceeding—a proceeding which, if persisted in, will, sooner or later, bring down upon all those who are guilty of it, the overwhelming vengeance of Heaven.

By cringing and fawning like a cudgel-deserving dog, by passively yielding and submitting like a dumb brute, by mimicking and begging like a poll-parrot, the negro has but too generally succeeded in foisting himself, as a parasitical slave or servant, upon white men ; and has thus, upon all occasions, afforded incontestable proofs of the fact that he is, and ever has been, equally with his master, a sheer accomplice in the crime of slavery.

Richard Grant White, of the city of New York, in the course of a letter which he wrote to the London *Spectator*, only a few short months after the close of the slaveholders' rebellion, said with radiant truth and propriety :

"We have noticed, with some surprise, what we regard as a strange confusion of thought in England, in regard to the feeling here about slavery and about the negro. It seems to be taken for granted by most European, and even most British writers upon the subject, that opposition to slavery and a liking of the negro, or at least a special good-will to him, must go together, and *vice versa ;* and that consequently a war which was accepted rather than that the point of the exclusion of slavery from free territory should be yielded, and which was prosecuted in a great measure for the extinction of slavery where it had been already established, must have as its result the elevation of the negro to the political and social level of the dominant race, or else that its professed anti-slavery motive was a mere pretence. No supposition could be more erroneous. I tell you frankly that the mass of the people here were glad to fight against slavery, but had no intention of fighting for the negro. They felt that slavery was a great crime, a sin against human nature. They wished to purge the Republic of that wickedness, but they had no particular sympathy with, though most of them much compassion for, the race against whom the wrong was committed. You in Europe seemed to be thinking about the individual negroes ; we, in the mass, thought little or nothing of the individual negroes, but much of the barbarous institution of slavery."

Again, in another part of the same letter, Mr. Richard Grant White, with characteristic felicity and force of expression on his own part, related the following brief but highly significant anecdotes :

"In the last year of the war, a clergyman who had been a professor in the college where I studied, and who is one of those gentle, firm, wise men, with large souls, and wide sympathies, who can control men, and particularly young men, by mere personal influence, so that when the under-graduates were unruly or had a grievance, they would give up at once to Dr. ——— for pure love, when his colleagues could do nothing, and all the terrors of college discipline were laughed to scorn—this man went to the South on a tour of observation, and was placed in authority, as far as slavery was concerned, over a considerable reclaimed district by one of our most eminent generals. For years before the war, he had been one of our strongest anti-slavery men, and had by his writings done as much as any one person in the country, who was not a professed journalist or politician, to bring about the state of public feeling that provoked secession. I met him on his return home, and had not talked with him three minutes before he said to me, 'I come back hating slavery more than ever, but loathing the negro with an unutterable loathing. What a curse to have that people on our hands!' And not long ago, one of the editors of one of the leading anti-slavery papers in the country, and one which advocates giving suffrage to the freed slaves, said to me, 'These negroes are doubtless here by a dispensation of Providence, but,' with an earnestness which a whimsical smile could not conceal, 'O that the Lord had been pleased to dispense his negroes somewhere else!'"

Nearly ten years prior to the expression of these just and salutary views by Mr. Richard Grant White—and they are but the mere reflex or reproduction of the views of Washington, Adams, Jefferson, and other preëminently great men of America—the author of "The Impending Crisis of the South," with the modicum of ability which he possessed, portrayed the same views upon almost every page of his work. On the 145th page of the book just mentioned; the author—who is also the author of the book now in hand—said:

"All mankind may, or may not, be descended from Adam and Eve. In our own humble way of thinking, we are frank to confess we do not believe in the unity of the races. This is a matter, however, which has little or nothing to do with the great question at issue. Aside from any theory concerning the original parentage of the different races of men, facts, material and immaterial, palpable and impalpable--facts of the eyes and facts of the conscience—crowd around us on every hand, heaping proof upon proof, that slavery is a shame, a crime, and a curse—a great moral, social, civil and political evil—a stumbling-block to the nation, an impediment to progress, a damper on all the nobler instincts, principles, aspirations and enterprises of man, and a dire enemy to every true interest."

Again, on the 118th page of his work, the author of "The Impending Crisis of the South," said,

"In the Southern States, as in all other slaveholding countries, there are three odious classes of mankind: the slaves themselves, who are cowards; the slaveholders, who are tyrants; and the non-slaveholding slave-hirers, who are lick-spittles. Whether any one of these three classes is really entitled to the gentle regards of any respectable man or woman in all the world, is, indeed, a matter of grave doubt. The slaves, because of their mean and dastardly submission, are abominable; the slaveholders, because of their unjust and cruel exercise of power, are detestable; and the non-slaveholding slave-hirers, because of their unmanly endurance of usurpation and wrong on the part of the domineering moguls of unrighteousness, are contemptible;—and to a right-thinking public we submit the question, whether, with one grand concerted kick from all the decent peoples now living, every member of these three odious classes of mankind should not, as the just penalty of his flagrant demerits, be at once hurled headlong from the fair face of the earth into an abyss of oblivion."

Again, on the 118th page of his work, the author of "The Impending Crisis of the South," said:

"Every Southerner, who has any practical knowledge of affairs, must know, and does know, that every New Year's day, like almost every other day, is desecrated in the South, by publicly hiring out slaves to large numbers of non-slaveholders. The slave-owners, who are the exclusive manufacturers of public sentiment, have popularized the dictum that white servants are unfashionable; and there are, we are sorry to say, nearly one hundred and sixty thousand non-slaveholding sycophants, who have subscribed to this false philosophy, and who are giving constant encouragement to the infamous practices of slaveholding and slave-breeding, by hiring at least one slave every year."

Again, on the 349th page of his work, the author of "The Impending Crisis of the South," said:

"The table which we have here compiled from the Compendium of the Seventh Census (page 116) shows, in a most lucid and startling manner, how negroes, slavery and slaveholders are driving the native Non-slaveholding Whites away from their homes, and keeping at a distance other decent people."

Again, on the 432d page of his work, the author of "The Inpending Crisis of the South," said :

"The lazy and meanly-cunning proslavery officials of the South perpetuate the ignorance and degradation of their constituents, by withholding from them—especially from their miserably-duped, non-slaveholding constituents—the means of information to which they are justly entitled, and which they would receive, if represented by men whose sense of duty and honor was not irremediably debased by social contact with slaves and slavery. We are aware that this is very plain language ; but it is truthful also ; and slaves and slaveholders are welcome to make the most of it."

Again, on the 121st page of his work, the author of "The Impending Crisis of the South," said :

"To the Non-slaveholding Whites of the South, as a deeply-wronged and vitally distinct political party, we must now look for that change of law, for that reorganization of society, which, at an early day, we hope, is to result in the substitution of Liberty for Slavery; and it now becomes their solemn duty to mark out an independent course for themselves, and to utterly contemn and ignore the many base instruments of power, animate and inanimate, which have been so freely and so effectually used for their disfranchisement. Steering entirely clear of the oligarchy, now is the time for the Non-slaveholding Whites to assert their rights and liberties. Never before was there such an appropriate period to strike for Freedom in the South."

Again, on the 131st page of his work, the author of "The Impending Crisis of the South," said :

"Immediate and independent political action on the part of the Non-slaveholding Whites of the South, is, with them, a matter both of positive duty and of the utmost importance."

Again, on the 150th page of his work, the author of "The Impending Crisis of the South," said :

"Non-slaveholders of the South! up to the present period, neither as a body nor as individuals have you ever enjoyed an independent existence; but, if true to yourselves and the memory of your fathers, you, in co-equality with the non-slaveholders of the North, will soon become the honored rulers and proprietors of the most powerful, prosperous, virtuous, free and peaceful nation, on which the sun has ever shone."

Again, on the 185th page of his work, the author of "The Impending Crisis of the South," said:

"With reference to the two pictures here presented, we trust that the slaveholders will look, first on that, and then on this; from one or the other, or from both, they may glean a ray or two of wisdom, which, if duly applied, will be of incalculable advantage to them and to their posterity. We trust, also, that the Non-slaveholding Whites will view, with discriminating minds, the different lights and shades of these two pictures; for they are the parties most deeply interested; and it is to them we look for the glorious revolution that is to result in the permanent establishment of Freedom over the last lingering ruins of slavery."

Again, on the 344th page of his work, the author of "The Impending Crisis of the South," said:

"In what degree of latitude—pray tell us—in what degree of latitude do the rays of the sun become too calorific for white men? Certainly in no part of the United States; for in the extreme South we find a very large number of Non-slaveholding Whites over the age of fifteen, who derive their entire support from manual labor in the open fields. The sun (that brilliant bugbear of pro-slavery politicians) shone on more than one million of free white laborers—mostly agriculturists—in the Slave States, in 1850, exclusive of those engaged in commerce, trade, manufactures, the mechanic arts, and mining. Yet, notwithstanding all these instances of exposure to his wrath, we have had no intelligence whatever of a single case of *coup de soleil*. Alabama is not too hot; sixty-seven thousand white sons of toil till her soil. Mississippi is not too hot; fifty-thousand free white laborers are hopeful devotees of her out-door pursuits.   Texas is not too hot ; forty-seven thousand free white persons, males, over the age of fifteen, daily perform their rural vocations amidst her unsheltered air. * * * The truth is, instead of its being too hot in the South for white men, it is too cold for negroes ; and we long to see the day arrive when the latter shall have entirely receded from their uncongenial homes in America, and given full and undivided place to the former."

Again, on the 345th page of his work, the author of "The Impending Crisis of the South," said :

"Too hot in the South for white *men !* It is not too hot for white *women.*   Time and again, in different counties in North Carolina, have we seen the poor white wife of the poor white husband, following him in the harvest-field from morning till night, binding into sheaves the grain as it fell from his cradle. In the immediate neighborhood from which we hail, there are no less than thirty young women, non-slaveholding whites, between the ages of fifteen and twenty-five—some of whom are so well known to us that we could call them by their names —who labor in the fields every summer ; often hiring them-selves out during harvest-time, the very hottest season of the year, to bind wheat and oats—each of them keeping up with the reaper ; and this for the paltry consideration of twenty-five cents per day!"

"That any respectable man—any man with a heart or a soul in his composition—can look upon these poor toiling white women without feeling indignant at that accursed system of slavery which has entailed on them the miseries of poverty, ignorance, and degradation, we shall not do to ourself the vio-lence to believe. If they and their husbands and their sons and daughters, and brothers and sisters, are not righted in some of the more important particulars in which they have been wronged, the fault shall lie at other doors than our own. In their behalf, chiefly, have we written and compiled this work ; and until our object shall have been accomplished, or until life shall have been extinguished, there shall be no abatement in our efforts to aid them in regaining the natural and inalienable prerogatives out of which they have been so craftily swindled. We want to see no more ploughing, nor hoeing, nor raking, nor grain-binding, by white women in the Southern States; employment in cotton-mills and other factories would be far more profitable and congenial to them, and this they will have within a short period after slavery shall have been abolished."

Again, on the 375th page of his work, the author of "The Impending Crisis of the South," said:

How it is, in this enlightened age, that men of even ordinary intelligence can be so far led into error as to suppose that commerce, or any other noble enterprise, can be established and successfully prosecuted under the black and baneful sway of Slavery, is, to us, one of the most inexplicable of mysteries. Southern Conventions, composed of the self-titled lordlings of Slavery—Generals, Colonels, Majors, Captains and, Squires—may act out their annual programmes of farcical nonsense from now until doomsday; but they will never add one iota to the material, moral or mental interests of the South; nor will it ever be possible for them to do so, until their Ebony idol shall have been utterly demolished."

Again, on the 383d page of his work, the author of "The Impending Crisis of the South," said:

"So long as slaveholders are clothed with the mantle of office, so long will they continue to make laws expressly calculated to bring the non-slaveholding whites under a system of vassalage little less onerous and debasing than that to which the negroes themselves are accustomed. What wonder is it that there is no native literature in the South? The South can never have a literature of her own until after slavery shall have been abolished. Slaveholders are either too lazy or too ignorant to write it; and the non-slaveholders—even the few whose minds are cultivated at all—are not permitted even to make the attempt. Down with the oligarchy! Ineligibility of slaveholders—never another vote to the trafficker in human flesh."

Again, on the 146th page of his work, the author of "The Impending Crisis of the South," said :

"Not alone for ourself, as an individual, but for others also—particularly for six millions of Southern Non-slaveholding Whites, whom a most iniquitous pro-slavery statism has debarred from almost all the mental and material comforts of life—do we speak."

Again, on the 403d page of his work, the author of "The Impending Crisis of the South," said :

"Had we the power to sketch a true picture of life among the Non-slaveholding Whites of the South, every intelligent man who has a spark of philanthropy in his breast, and who should happen to gaze upon the picture, would burn with unquenchable indignation at that system of negro slavery, which entails unutterable stupidity, shiftlessness and degradation on the superior race."

Again, on the 41st page of his work, the author of "The Impending Crisis of the South," said :

"Our disappointment gives way to a feeling of intense mortification, and our soul involuntarily, but justly, we believe, cries out for retribution against the treacherous slaveholding legislators, who have so unpatriotically and so basely neglected the interests of their poor white constituents, and bargained away the rights of posterity. Notwithstanding the fact that the Non-slaveholding Whites of the South are in the majority, as six to one, they have never yet had any uncontrolled part nor lot in framing the laws under which they live. There is, indeed, in the South, no legislation except for the benefit of slaves and slaveholders. Under a cunningly devised mockery of freedom, the only political privilege extended to the great mass of the whites, is a shallow and circumscribed participation in the movements that usher slaveholders into office."

Again, on the 225th page of his work, the author of "The Impending Crisis of the South," said :

"Virginia, in particular, is a spoilt child, having been the pet of the General Government for the last seventy years; and, like many other spoilt children, she has become froward, peevish, perverse, sulky and irreverent—not caring to know her duties, and failing to perform even those which she does know. Her superiors perceive that the abolition of slavery would be a blessing to her. She is, however, either too ignorant to understand the truth, or else, as is the more probable, her false pride and obstinacy restrain her from acknowledging it. What is to be done? Shall ignorance, or prejudice, or obduracy, or willful meanness, triumph over knowledge, and liberality, and guilelessness, and laudable enterprise? No, never! Assured that Virginia and all the other Slaveholding States are doing wrong every day, it is our duty to make them do right, if we have the power; and we believe we have the power now resident within their (our) own borders. What are the opinions, generally, of the Non-slaveholding Whites? Let *them* speak."

Again, on the 89th and 90th pages of his work, the author of "The Impending Crisis of the South," said :

"We have been credibly informed by a gentleman from Powhattan County, in Virginia, that in the year 1836–'37, or about that time, the Hon. Abbott Lawrence, of Boston, backed by his brother Amos, and by other millionaires of New England, went down to Richmond with the sole view of reconnoitering the manufacturing facilities of that place—fully determined, if pleased with the water-power, to erect a large number of cotton mills and machine-shops. He had been in the capital of Virginia only a day or two before he discovered, much to his gratification. that nature had shaped everything to his liking. * * * To the enterprising and moneyed descendant of the Pilgrim Fathers it was a matter of no little astonishment, that the immense water-power of Richmond had been so long neglected. He, therefore, expressed his surprise to a number of Virginians, and was at a loss to know why they had not, long prior to the period of his visit among them, availed themselves of the powerful element that is eternally gushing

and foaming over the falls of James River. Innocent man !
He was utterly unconscious of the fact that he was "interfer-
ing with the beloved institutions of the South," and little
was he prepared to withstand the terrible denunciations that
were immediately showered upon him, through the columns
of the Richmond newspapers. Few words will suffice to tell
the sequel. Those negro-driving sheets, whose hireling policy
for the last five and twenty years has been to support the
worthless black slave and his tyrannical master, at the expense
of the free white laborer, wrote down the enterprise ; and the
noble son of New England, abused, insulted, and disgusted,
quietly returned to Massachusetts, and there employed his
capital in building up the cities of Lowell and Lawrence,
either of which, in the aggregate of those elements of material
and social prosperity that make up the greatness of States, is
already far in advance of the most important of all the seedy
and squalid slave-towns in the Old Dominion."

Again, on the 84th page of his work, the author of
"The Impending Crisis of the South," said :

"Once more to the Old Dominion. At the doors of Virginia we lay the bulk of the evils of slavery. The first African
sold in America was sold on the James River, in that State, on
the 20th of August, 1620 ; and although the institution was
fastened upon her and the other colonies by the mother country, she was the first to perceive its blighting and degrading
influences ; her wise men were the first to denounce it ; and,
after the British power was overthrown at Yorktown, she
should have been the first to abolish it. Sixty years ago she
was the Empire State ; now, with half a dozen other slaveholding States thrown into the scale with her, she is far inferior to
New York, which, at the time Cornwallis surrendered his
sword to Washington, was less than half her equal. Had she
obeyed the counsels of the good, the great and the wise men
of our nation—especially of her own incomparable sons, the
extendible element of slavery would have been promptly arrested, and the virgin soil of nine Southern States, Kentucky,
Tennessee, Louisiana, Mississippi, Alabama, Missouri, Arkan-
sas, Florida, and Texas, would have been saved from its horrid

pollutions. Confined to the original States in which it existed, the system would have been disposed of by legislative enactments ; and long before the present day, by a gradual process that could have shocked no interest and alarmed no prejudice, we should have rid ourselves not only of African slavery, which is an abomination and a curse, but also of the negroes themselves, who, in our judgment, whether viewed in relation to their actual characteristics and condition, or through the strong antipathies of the whites, are, to say the least, an undesirable population."

Again, on the 175th page of his work, the author of "The Impending Crisis of the South," said,

"The first Slave State that makes herself respectable by casting out slavery, and by rendering enterprise and industry honorable, will immediately receive a large accession of most worthy citizens from other States in the Union, and thus lay a broad foundation for permanent political power and prosperity. Intelligent white farmers from the Middle and New England States will flock to our more congenial clime, eager to give thirty dollars per acre for the very lands that are now a drug in the market, because nobody wants them at the rate of five dollars per acre ; an immediate and powerful impetus will be given to commerce, manufactures, and all the industrial arts ; science and literature will be revived, and every part of the State will reverberate with the triumphs of manual and intellectual labor."

Again, on the 123d page of his work, the author of the "The Impending Crisis of the South," with all the clearness and emphasis which he could impart to words, claimed that there should be

"THOROUGH ORGANIZATION AND INDEPENDENT POLITICAL ACTION ON THE PART OF THE NON-SLAVEHOLDING WHITES OF THE SOUTH."

And, further, on the same page, the same author stoutly insisted, and still insists, that there should be given

"THE GREATEST POSSIBLE ENCOURAGEMENT TO FREE WHITE LABOR."

Again, on the 143d page of his work, the author of "The Impending Crisis of the South," expressed a most earnest wish for the means "to send every negro in this country to the coast of Africa, whither, if we had the power, we would ship them all within the next six months." Other portions of the work here so liberally quoted from, were and are equally attestive of the author's perfect knowledge of the fact, that there should be immediately drawn between the Whites and the Blacks, a line of absolute and eternal separation.

Indeed, as already intimated, almost every page of the work here mentioned breathes a sincere and universal love for the Whites, and, at the same time, enunciates, in the loudest possible strains, a just and wholesome contempt for the Blacks. Yet, strange to say, there are many persons (not one of whom, however, has ever read the book) who absurdly persist in believing, or pretend to believe, that "The Impending Crisis of the South," was written specifically in the interest of the negroes! Such shallow-brained and babbling blockheads ought to have their necks wrung, with precisely the same energy and effect as, when there exists an unusually brisk and continuous demand for chicken-broth, the poulterers wring the necks of their pullets! Every man who is not an idiot, and who has read the book, knows perfectly well that it was written directly and pointedly in the interest of the Non-slaveholding Whites of the South ;—and it is very confidently believed that the non-slaveholding whites are the only species of white people who *now* inhabit, or ever will again inhabit, the Southern States! And as for those woolly-headed and rank-smelling individuals who are not white, they must all soon find accommodations elsewhere

—or be quickly fossilized in bulk beneath the subsoil of America!

High time is it that fools North and fools South should no longer deceive themselves, nor be deceived, with the preposterous notion that abolitionists, or anti-slavery men, must, as a matter of course, be hobnobbers with negroes. The better class of abolitionists, the genteel emancipationists, the anti-slavery men who are possessed of good common sense, the White Republicans—all white men, indeed, who are able to comprehend, with even moderate exactitude, the sublime works and laws of Nature—are always, and will ever be, particularly studious to shun and decline every possible sort of relationship with negroes.

Not to live together in close fellowship, as if they were of the same nature, not as the equals of each other, did God create the Horse and the Ass, the Sheep and the Goat; the Eagle and the Buzzard, the Swan and the Gull; the Whale and the Porpoise, the Shad and the Minnow; the Eel and the Snake, the Turtle and the Toad; the Cricket and the Cockroach, the Bee and the Bug; nor were White Men and Negroes placed upon the earth to be members of the same household, nor of the same community, nor even of the same continent.

It is to the gross ignorance and disregard of such very important truths as are here suggested, that we owe the malign existence of the Black Congress, which during many months past has been disgracing America with its multiplicity of crude and blighting enactments. The blatant and shameless charlatans of this Congress, who, by their constant efforts to do for the base blacks far more than they have yet manifested any disposition to do for the worthy whites, must all, at the expiration, respectively, of their present term of office, be taught certain lessons in political wisdom which it will be possible for

13*

them to learn only amidst the imperturbations and restraints of private life.

Let there be a full and settled determination on the part of the American people, on the part of the people of each State, respectively, that, with a few honorable exceptions, no member of the Senate, no member of the House of Representatives, who voted for the Negro Bureau Bill, or for any one of the thousand-and-one other black abominations of the Black Congress, shall ever again be elevated to any office of honor or trust under the government of the United States. On the contrary, let those guileful and nefarious framers of black statutes be made to feel that treason in themselves, just the same as treason in others, is a thing to be specifically detested and punished; and further, that so much greater is the enormity of their own treason than the treason of the traitor Jeff. Davis, that, whereas his perfidious purposes were practiced only against the Caucasian-blooded inhabitants of a single commonwealth (and a few negroes, whether few or many, not worth the mention) their wicked designs have been leveled against the general and peculiar welfare of the whites of the whole world!

In order, also, that the pure purposes of God and good men may no longer be thwarted upon the earth, (now that slavery and the champions of slavery have received their quietus,) let the Black Congress be assisted or urged to fritter itself away as quickly as possible; then, without delay, let a White Congress, and thenceforth and forever, none but White Congresses, be elected to enact laws for the salutary guidance of the Great Republic; let the negroes, and all the other swarthy races of mankind, be at once and completely fossilized; and 'let all the whites, who are blessed with sane minds and right reason, raise together their voices upon the key of a universal pæan; for all the lands and waters and pleasant places beneath the sun shall soon be theirs, to use and to occupy at discretion ; and then, for the first time in the long history of the world, will be more than realized the most popular and peerless promises of the painters, the poets and the prophets. All will be well; unexampled peace, plenty and prosperity shall everywhere be the established order of things ; and, in a single word, the long-talked-of and superlatively good time will have come at last !

CHAPTER IX.

WHITE CELEBRITIES AND BLACK NOBODIES.

In the just balance of nature, individuals, and nations, and races, will obtain just so much as they deserve, and no more. And as effect finds its cause, so surely does quality of character amongst a people produce its befitting results.—Samuel Smiles.

A person may cause evil to others not only by his actions but by his inaction ; and in either case he is justly accountable to them for the injury.—John Stuart Mill.

In the broad field and long duration of negro life, not a single civilization, spontaneous or borrowed, has ever existed to adorn its gloomy past.—Josiah Clark Nott.

Many very foolish and fanatical friends of the negro, claim that he possesses inborn qualities of manhood, physical, mental, and moral, which may, they say, be so developed, under a system of long and careful tutoring or training, that (except in color, which is certainly an amazingly big and black exception!) he will, as a rule, be found to be the equal of the White Man. Against the surpassing and dangerous absurdity of this claim on the part of the Black Republicans of the Black Congress and other negrophilists, I here raise my voice, in tones never, never to be lowered ; no, not even when the claim itself shall have been disallowed and abandoned forever, over the tumulus of the last of the Ethiops.

Weak in mind, frail in morals, torpid and apathetic in physique, the negro, wherever he goes, or wherever he is seen, carries upon himself, in inseparable connection with abjectness and disgrace, such glaring marks of inferiority as are no less indelible and conspicuous than the base

blackness of his skin.   Upon this point, all the records
of the past, all the evidences of the present, all the prog-
nostications of the future, are plain and positive.   In the
long catalogue of the great names of the world—names
which, whether they have caused nations to tremble with
fear and suspense, to quiver with awe and admiration, to
laugh with satisfaction and delight, or to weep with inno-
nocent sadness and love—there does not appear the cognomen of a single negro!   To overlook the ponderous
significance of this fact, to gainsay it, to wink it or to
blink it, let no unworthy attempt be made.

In nothing that ennobles mankind has any negro ever
distinguished himself.   For none of the higher walks of
life has he ever displayed an aptitude.   To deeds of true
valor and patriotism, he has always proved recreant.
Over none of the wide domains of Agriculture, Commerce, nor Manufactures, has any one of his race ever
won honorable mention.   Within the classic precincts of
Art, Literature and Science, he is, and forever will be,
utterly unknown.

If plainer proofs than those which are now possessed
by the reader, be required of the correctness of these assumptions on the part of the writer, it is but necessary,
in order to adduce them, to survey the several departments of human progress and renown.   Let this survey
be made thoroughly and in good faith ; and, in the labor
of it, let him who here sits and writes assist him who
there runs and reads.

Wherever or whenever we may begin our inquiries in
this regard, we shall find that the answers will be much
the same.

Not to delay our purposed investigations, therefore, let
us see, by way of commencement, who, at any time, have
attained remarkable eminence as Presidents, Emperors,
Kings, Princes and Potentates; who, as Conquerors, and

as the Founders and Enlargers of Nationalities ; who, in the Art of Good Government. You, sensible reader, or you, mawkish and deluded friend of the African, point out, if you can, the name of even one negro in the following Roll of Representative Men, which roll, if you are well informed, you cannot fail to perceive, designates the very greatest of the

GREAT RULERS OF THE WORLD.

David, Solomon, Jehoshaphat, and Hezekiah.
Cyrus, Darius, Xerxes, and Artaxerxes.
Antiochus, Mithridates, Saladin, and Othman.
Pericles, Pisistratus, Cleomenes, and Cleombrotus.
Alexander, Demetrius, Antigonus, and Pyrrhus.
Ptolemy, Lysimachus, Cassander, and Seleucus.
Constantine, Theodosius, Justinian, and Tiberius.
Romulus, Numa, Tullus, and Tarquin.
Cæsar, Augustus, Vespasian, and Titus.
Trajan, Adrian, Severus, and Aurelian.
Charlemagne, Otho, Conrad, and Frederick.
Rodolph, Albert, Sigismund, and Waldemar.
Gustavus, Peter, Nicholas, and Leopold.
Ferdinand, Alphonso, Ramirez, and Sancho.
Charles, Philip, Sebastian, and Pedro.
Clovis, Dagobert, Clotaire, and Pepin.
Louis, Francis, Bonaparte, and Napoleon.
Alfred, William, Richard and Edward.
Henry, James, George and Cromwell.
Washington, Adams, Jefferson, and Madison.
Monroe, Jackson, Polk,* and Lincoln.

---

* Although Polk was not so great a man as he might have been, yet his administration was eminently brilliant and successful.

Among the records of the White Race only, may we look for the names of justly celebrated Councilors, Diplomatists, and Ambassadors—such for instance as those who are here enumerated under the dignified heading of

STATESMEN AND ORATORS.

Demosthenes, Isocrates, Hermogenes, and Carneades.
Hyperides, Hierocles, Andocides, and Demades.
Cicero, Antonius, Crassus, and Gracchus.
Hortensius, Clodius, Mæcenas, and Metellus.
Fontanelli, Alberoni, Cavour, and Antonelli.
Ximenez, Olivarez, Perez, and Godoy.
Pombal, Villars, Turgot, and Sully.
Richelieu, Brissot, Mirabeau, and Montalembert.
Mazarin, Talleyrand, Guizot, and Thouvenel.
Oxensteirn, Sture, Reventlow, and Piper.
Nesselrode, Gortschakoff, Hardenberg, and Metternich.
Stedingk, De Witt, Gortz, and Heydt.
Bismarck, Schleinitz, Schurz, and Kossuth.
Mensdorff, Wollersdorff, Komes, and Werther.
Walsingham, Shaftesbury, Pym, and Pitt.
Raleigh, Throckmorton, Peel, and Brougham.
Hampden, Bolingbroke, North, and Erskine.
Walpole, Granville, Aberdeen, and Ashburton.
Melbourne, Canning, Russell, and Palmerston.
Bright, Cobden, Derby, and Gladstone.
Burke, Curran, Grattan, and O'Connell.
Otis, Ames, Henry, and Hamilton.
Gallatin, Pinckney, Quincy, and Forsyth.
Clay, Webster, Hayne, and Calhoun.
Everett, Legaré, Randolph, and Douglas.
Gaston, Macon, Crawford, and Clayton.
Livingston Clinton, Dallas, and Cass.
Rush, Rantoul, Phillips, and Winthrop.
Preston, Corwin, Marcy, and Marshall.

Benton, Crittenden, Prentiss, and Poinsett.
Seward, Sumner, Dayton, and Dickinson.
Fessenden, Stanton, Harlan, and Grimes,
Hale, Blair, Guthrie, and Colfax.
Wade, Sherman, Bingham, and Raymond.
Trumbull, Fenton, Banks, and Washburne.

———

Except among White Men, we have never found, and never will find, Renowned Patriots, Great Generals, Successful Commanders of Land Forces—such for instance, as those who are here denominated

MILITARY HEROES.

Joshua, Gideon, Jair, and Jephtha.
Miltiades, Aristides, Thrasybulus, and Agesilaus.
Leonidas, Cimon, Phocion, and Timoleon.
Epaminondas, Theramenes, Pelopidas, and Philopœmen.
Scipio, Coriolanus, Fabius, and Hannibal.*
Pompey, Regulus, Manlius, and Marcellus.
Marius, Sylla, Sertorius, and Stilicho.
Belisarius, Garibaldi, Gonsalvo, and Cordova.
Ruy Dias, Espartero, Cortez, and Pizarro.
Bolivar, Belgrano, San Martin, and Santander.
Almagro, Alvear, Mitre, and Urquiza.
Bayard, Godfrey, Turenne, and Montcalm.
Luxembourg, Rochambeau, Murat, and Moreau.
Lafayette, Pichegru, Soult, and Pelissier.
Eugene, Condè, Ney, and Hoche.
Tell, Winckelried, Ziska, and Suwarrow.
Sobieska, Poniatowski, Kosciusko, and Pulaski.

---

* Hannibal was a Carthaginian, of Caucasian ancestry.

Blucher, Schwartzenberg, Egmont, and Maurice.
Wrangel, Hofer, Steuben, and De Kalb.
Falkenstein, Manteuffel, Bittenfeld, and Benedek.
Marlborough, Clive, Fairfax, and Ponsonby.
Wellington, Abercromby, Havelock, and Cornwallis.
Wallace, Bruce, Glendower, and Llewellen.
Greene, Warren, Stark, and Putnam.
Marion, Sumpter, Lee, and Jasper.
Scott, Taylor, Worth, and Kearney.
Grant, Canby, Sheridan, and Sedgwick.
Sherman, Schofield, Birney, and Wadsworth,
Thomas, Hooker, Howard, and Hancock.
Meade, Fremont, Terry, and Mansfield.

———

No race of mankind except the White Race has ever given us (and no other race ever can give us) Valiant Admirals and Victors on the Water—such, for instance, as those who are here denominated

NAVAL HEROES.

Themistocles, Alcibiades, Lysander, and Pisander.
Callicratidas, Conon, Nearchus, and Lucullus.
Doria, Ricalde, Pisani, and Langara.
D'Estrées, D'Estaing, Du Casse, and De Grasse.
Villeneuve, Conflans, Suffrein, and Linois.
Tromelin, Brueys, Bruix, and Boissot.
Rupert, Van Tromp, De Ruyter, and De Winter.
Zoutmann, Bille, Kornileff, and Cornelison.
Dahlgren, Apraxin, Jeckethoff, and Tegethoff.
Drake, Anson, Leake, and Duckworth.
Blake, Duncan, Rooke, and Rodney.
Nelson, Cathcart, Hawke, and Hawkins.
Elphinstone, Collingwood, Benbow and Popham.

Howe, Hotham, Gambier, and Stopford.
Hull, Barry, Jones, and Lawrence.
Biddle, Dale, Reid, and Preble.
Decatur, Truxton, Rodgers, and Perry.
Bainbridge, Blakely, Ingraham and Stockton.
McDonough, Stringham, Stewart, and Mackeever.
Wilkes, Davis, Foote, and Drayton.
Farragut, Dupont, Worden, and Chauncey.
Porter, Rowan, Totten, and Stribling.
Goldsborough, Bell, Wise, and Cushing.

———

Nowhere except in the Genius-glowing Chronicles of
the Caucasian Races, may we look for truly Metrical
and Refined Expression—nowhere else can anything be
found at all comparable to the following list of White and
Heaven-inspired

POETS.

David, Solomon, Hosea, and Micah.
Isaiah, Jeremiah, Ezekiel, and Zephaniah.
Joel, Amos, Nahum, and Habakuk.
Homer, Hesiod, Orpheus, and Archilochus.
Linus, Oppian, Tyrtæus, and Timotheus.
Anacreon, Simonides, Theocritus, and Mimnermus.
Pindar, Hipponax, Nicander, and Terpander.
Virgil, Lucilius, Varius, and Varro.
Horace, Lucan, Hostius, and Tibullus.
Ovid, Catullus, Hyginus, and Propertius.
Dante, Petrarch, Tasso, and Alfieri.
Ariosto, Monti, Camoëns, and Miranda.
Calderon, Quevedo, Melendez, and Zorrilla.
Molière, Racine, Boileau, and Beranger.
Fréneau, Malherbe, Delille; and Ronsard.
Goethe, Klopstock, Heine, and Arndt.

Schiller, Ramler, Kleist, and Kinkel.
Dershavin, Kozloff, Pram, and Tegner.
Shakspeare, Chaucer, Spenser, and Jonson.
Milton, Young, Pope, and Dryden.
Byron, Moore, Keats, and Crabbe.
Shenstone, Cowper, Gray, and Thomson.
Wordsworth, Southey, Shelley, and Tennyson.
Burns, Ramsay, Beattie, and Campbell.
Bryant, Barlow, Drake, and Lowell.
Longfellow, Halleck, Stoddard, and Stedman.
Poe, Saxe, Percival, and Pierpont.
Holmes, Tuckerman, Hayne, and Burleigh.
Whittier, Whitman, Taylor, and Wallace.

———

Not among the Inane Annals of the Negroes—if, indeed
they have any annals at all—but among the Well-filled
Tomes and Manuscripts of White Men, and among these
only, may we expect to find emblazoned, as below, the
Patronymics of Phenomena-explaining and Profound

PHILOSOPHERS.

Job, Elihu, Bildad, and Zophar.
Confucius, Zoroaster, Demonax, and Cratippus.
Pythagoras, Xenophanes, Arcesilaus, and Parmenides.
Socrates, Empedocles, Thales, and Leucippus.
Plato, Anaxagoras, Protagoras, and Pherecydes.
Aristotle, Aristippus, Prodicus, and Democritus.
Heraclitus, Heraclides, Philolaus, and Lucretius.
Hermodorus, Hippasus, Thermistius, and Theophrastus
Xenocratus, Plotinus, Epicurus, and Diogenes.
Hippo, Pyrrho, Panetius, and Longinus.
Antisthenes, Anaximander, Zeno, and Cleantes.
Ammonius, Epictetus, Lælius, and Seneca.
Huarte, Campanella, Gassendi, and Spinoza.

Descartes, Helvetius, Simon, and Lammenais.
Voltaire, Rousseau, Comte, and Ampère.
Leibnitz, Schelling, Hegel, and Krüg.
Kant, Fichte, Wolf, and Rauch.
Bunsen, Fischer, Koppon, and Bilfinger.
Bacon, Locke, Hobbes, and Hume.
Newton, Hamilton, Berkeley, and Brewster.
Buckle, Spenser, Whewell, and Ferguson.
Franklin, Rumford, Marsh, and Loomis.
Jefferson, Henry, Hare, and Haven.
Bache, Draper, Redfield, and Maury.

———

White Men, such men for instance, as those whose names
are catalogued below, have always been, and will always
continue to be, the only Interesting and Instructive Nar-
rators of Past Events ; the only Diligent and Faithful
Chroniclers of Important Facts ; the only Erudite and
Truth-telling

HISTORIANS.

Samuel, Nathan, Ezra, and Nehemiah.
Sanchoniathon, Manetho, Appian, and Josephus.
Herodotus, Diodorus, Arrian, and Dionysius.
Thucydides, Theopompus, Hellanicus, and Xanthus.
Xenophon, Polybius, Herodian, and Zozimus.
Sallust, Livy, Nepos, and Vopiscus.
Tacitus, Suetonius, Nardi, and Botta.
Muratori, Davilla, Bentivoglio, and Jormini.
Guicciardini, Villani, Machiavelli, and Sismondi.
Herrera, Morales, Toreno, and Ocampo.
Solis, Oviedo, Muñoz, and Ayala.
Albuquerque, Andrade, Brito, and Souza.
Froissart, Ancillon, Thou, and Raynal.
Rollin, Guizot, Thiers, and Thierry.

Sturleson, Eichhorn, Lappenberg, and Becker.
Vossius, Hooft, Wagenaar, and Raumer.
Niebuhr, Schlosser, Voight, and Wachter.
Heeren, Rotteck, Dohm, and Dahlmann.
Holberg, Karamsin, Fryxell, and Ushakoff.
Gibbon, Raleigh, Hume, and Hallam.
Robertson, Alison, Tytler, and Grote.
Macaulay, Thirlwall, Finlay, and Froude.
Mitford, Belsham, Hinton, and Howell.
Roscoe, Coxe, Gillies, and Goldsmith.
Bancroft, Hildreth, Elliott, and Gayarré.
Prescott, Ramsay, Dew, and Howison.
Motley, Palfrey, Lossing, and Abbott.

———

Has there ever been born, in Africa, or out of Africa,
any negro whose powers of computation exceeded his
ability to enumerate the fingers on his left hand? Where
or when was there ever a negro who knew anything of
Arithmetic? of Mensuration? of Algebra? of Logarithms?
of Fluxions? of Geometry? of Trigonometry, of the Dif-
ferential Calculus or the Calculus of Variations? Nowhere—at no time. To the mentally dwarfed and dull-
brained negro, all of these methods of reckoning are so
unfathomably abstruse that about them he knows, and
ever has known, and ever will know, absolutely nothing.
It is only White Men, like those whose names are mentioned below, who possess the acute faculty to become
All-measuring and All-numbering

MATHEMATICIANS.

Euclid, Diophantus, Calippus, and Nicomedes.
Archimedes, Hypsicles, Apollonius, and Pytheas.
Heliodorus, Meton, Theon, and Vitellio.
Bernouilli, Ferrari, Valerius, and Manfredi.

Torricelli, Viriani, Vieta, and Varignon.
Regnault, Fermat, Pascal, and Pitot.
Rohault, Reyneau, Ramus, and Roberval.
D'Alembert, Condorcet, Clairaut, and Ozanam.
Legendre, Bossut, Quensel, and Hummelins.
Euler, Tschirnhausen, Snell, and Kastner.
Mercator, Reinhold, Ursus, and Achenwall.
Huyghens, Stifel, Hudde, and Hermann.
Vandermonde, Poppe, Hansen, and Gauss.
Napier, Oughtred, Hooke, and Barrow.
Gregory, Recorde, Molyneux, and Colenso.
Urquhart, Colquhoun, Minto, and Simpson.
Galloway, Babbage, Saunderson, and Maclaurin.
Parkinson, Peacocke, Stone, and Todhunter.
Playfair, Hayes, Vince, and Moxon.
Rittenhouse, Colburn, Davies, and Perkins.
Bowditch, Greenleaf, Docharty, and Hedrick.

———

Who are our Lofty-minded Delineators and Describers of the Upper Worlds? our Peerers into Space? Our Peepers at the Planets? our Sketchers of the Constellations? our Communers with the Stars? our Interlocutors with the Comets? Who are they that mark the Course of the Sun, and trace the Moon in her Path?—who are they that define the Orbits of the Asteroids, and show the safe conduct of the Satellites around their Attractive Superiors? Not negroes, certainly; but White Men only; such men, for instance, as those who are here fairly and fitly denominated

ASTRONOMERS.

Thales, Eratosthenes, Harpalus, and Anaximander.
Hipparchus, Sosigenes, Ptolemy, and Gallus,
Galileo, Cassini, Arago, and Pingre.

Lacaille, Lagrange, Lalande, and Laplace.
Delambre, D'Alembert, Picard, and Chacornac.
Leverrier, Gasparis, Laurent, and Chauvenet.
Copernicus, Rheticus, Elvius, and Hevelius.
Kepler, Euler, Longomontanus, and Tycho Brahe.
Struve, Roemer, Tiarks, and Schumacher.
Littrow, Lindenau, Luther, and Goldschmidt.
Encke, Hencke, Bessel, and Benzenberg.
Olbers, Temple, Bode, and Mädler.
Newton, Maskelyne, Harriot, and Horrocks.
Herschel, Halley, Bradley, and Flamsteed.
Rosse, Hind, Airy, and Whewell.
Ferguson, Pogson, Gillies, and Hubbard.
Mitchel, Peirce, Bond, and Gould.

———

From what human sources have we, at any time, derived Positive and Well-defined Right Rules of Action?—from whom have we inherited Just and Proper Principles of Civil Conduct? Who have been our most learned Counselors? Barristers? Attorneys? Advocates? Solicitors? Pleaders? Jurists? Judges? Not negroes certainly; but White Men only, such eminent and remarkable men, for instance, as those who are here ycleped

LAWYERS AND LAW-GIVERS.

Moses, Minos, Theseus, and Zaleucus.
Lycurgus, Solon, Draco, and Pomponius.
Publicola, Gaius, Paulus, and Numa Pompilius.
Tribonian, Papinian, Ulpian, and Gentilis.
Theophilus, Dragonetti, Macedo, and Puchta.
Montesquieu, Pothier, Hautefeuille, and Dupin.
Vattel, Domat, Brisson, and Pucelle.
Pellisson, Thibaut, Martens, and Savigny.

Bouvier, DeHauterieve, Cussy, and Labarthe.
Grotius, Wicquefort, Noodt, and Bynkershoek.
Puffendorf, Wetstein, Wolf, and Klüber.
Heffter, Struve, Reuvens, and Spangenburg.
Leeuwen, Schräder, Beckh, and Achenwall.
Kluet, Leyser, Mahn, and Mittermeyer.
Frelinghuysen, Grimke, Anthon, and Van Buren.
Blackstone, Coke, Hale, and Selden.
Stowell, Thurlow, Romilly, and Chitty.
Bentham, Shaftesbury, Yorke, and Yelverton.
Nottingham, Cottingham, Eldon, and Clarendon.
Lyndhurst, Cresswell, Twiss, and Merivale.
Pinkney, Marshall, Wythe, and Wirt.
Jay, Story, Kent, and Curtis.
Livingston, Rawle, Spencer, and Parsons.
Rutledge, Iredell, Tucker, and Gaston.
Wheaton, Wharton, Burrill, and Lawrence.
Ellsworth, Chase, Bates, and Woodbury.
Emmet, Brady, McLean, and O'Conor.
Choate, Field, Cushing, and Cutting.
Wayne, Swayne, Grier, and Clifford.
Stanbery, Evarts, Speed, and Sharkey.
Pearson, Ruffin, Reade, and Rogers.
Blatchford, Duer, Noyes, and Ketchum.

———

To whom are we particularly indebted for an Elucidation of the Principles upon which we may attain a High Degree of Individual and National Prosperity? Who are they that, by the Irresistible Force and Merit of their Suggestions, have been, and still are, the Promoters of our Private and Public Wealth? Who are the Statesmen-like Utilitarians, by the virtue of whose Wise and Well-timed Counsels we have all, of the present day, been more or less Assisted to direct our Footsteps in the

Way of Mutually-thrifty and Harmonious Management?
Whom have we to thank for Teaching us, (what, alas!) so
few of us have learned, Frugality and Prudence in all our
Expenditures? The correct answer to these questions,
in every instance, without any manner of exception or
qualification, is—White Men, and White Men only; such
men, for instance, as those who are here registered as

POLITICAL ECONOMISTS,

Sismondi, Sarchiani, Rossi, and Machiavelli.
Ricardo, Pinto, Uztariz, and Botero.
Quesnay, Chevalier, Dussard, and De Lolme.
Say, Legoyt, Constant, and Coquelin.
Garnier, Baudrillart, Dunnoyer, and Reybaud.
Blanqui, Riviere, Monjean, and Bastiat.
Storch, Unger, Lotz, and Vollgraff.
Schön, List, Krause, and Hermann.
Schmalz, Stein, Rau, and Wolowski.
Smith, McCulloch, Spencer, and Devenant.
Malthus, Hume, Cobden, and Cobbett.
Stewart, Godwin, Senior, and Mill.
Carey, Perry, Raymond, and Vethake.
Colwell, Bowen, Coxe, and Colton.
Ruggles, Tucker, Baird, and Blodget.

———

Who have been our most Erudite Condensers of
Knowledge? our Aiders and Assisters to a General Acquaintance with all the Sciences? our Philologists? our
Dictionarians? our Glossarists? our Explainers of Obscure and Antiquated Words? our Definers of Abstruse
Terms? Not negroes, certainly; but White-Men only;
such men,.for instance, as those whose names are here
catalogued as

ENCYCLOPÆDISTS AND LEXICOGRAPHERS.

Longinus, Proclus, Tullius, and Gesenius.
Forcellini, Baretti, Montucci, and Ernesti.
Taboada, Seoane, Escriche, and Velasquez.
Diderot, D'Alembert, Calmet, and Coetlogon.
Hénault, Roquefort, Boiste, and Du Fresnoy.
Bescherelle, Stocqueler, Lemprière, and Bouvier.
Heinsius, Gabelentz, Schneider, and Lackmann.
Adelung, Grimm, Neumann, and Ramshorn.
Ersch, Gesner, Freund, and Doderlein.
Lieber, Duyckinck, Zunz, and Zumpt.
Haydn, Schwan, Wachter, and Diefenbach.
Traille, Knight, Smellie, and Barrow.
Rees, Maunder, Smith, and Harris.
Chambers, Aiken, Gwilt, and Gregory.
Ure, Brande, McCulloch, and Postlethwayt.
Dunglison, Tweedie, Gardner, and Copland.
Kitto, Buck, Eadie, and Packard.
Ainsworth, Crabb, Tooke, and French.
Richardson, Nicholson, Jameson, and Elphinston.
Johnson, Ash, Kenrick, and Craig.
Walker, Todd, Bailey, and Barclay.
Webster, Worcester, Porter, and Goodrich.
Bartlett, Marsh, March, and Munsell.
Ripley, Dana, Homans, and Burrill.
Allibone, Arvine, Thomas, and Baldwin.
Andrews, Anthon, Baird, and Blake.

By whom, besides God himself, have we, for our own
Good, been led to Believe in the Immortality of the Soul?
By what Races of Mankind have we been taught true
Ethics and Religion? Among all our Fellow-men, who,
on the one hand, have been the most Zealous Inculcators

of Virtue, and, on the other, the most Ardent Inveighers against Vice? The answer is obvious—the White Races, the Caucasians. To White Men, and to White Men only, are we humanly indebted for all our Comforting Anticipations of Eternal Felicity—to such men, for instance, as those whose names are here calendared as

MORALISTS, THEOLOGIANS, PREACHERS.

Seth, Enoch, Noah, and Melchisedek.
Abraham, Isaac, Jacob, and Joseph.
Aaron, Zadoc, Josiah, and Daniel.
Levi, Eli, Elijah, and Elisha.
Matthew Mark, Luke, and John.
Peter, Paul, James, and Jude.
Ignatius, Ammonius, Justin, and Polycarp.
Origen, Irenæus, Hippolytus, and Eusebius.
Clement, Porphyry, Athanasius, and Basil.
Cyril, Artemon, Gregory, and Chrysostom.
Tertullian, Cyprian, Minucius, and Augustine.
Jerome, Rufinus, Ambrose, and Aquinas.
Arius, Arminius, Socinus, and Servetus.
Hilary, Barnard, Valdo, and Sorbonne.
Calvin, Bossuet, Mabillon, and Fléchier.
Fénelon, Abauzit, Bosc, and Quesnel.
Massillon, Bourdaloue, Prideau, and Martineau.
Saurin, D'Aubigné, Vinet, and Zschokke.
Luther, Kempis, Huss, and Zwinglius.
Melanchthon, Jansen, Semler, and Zinzendorf.
Mosheim, Neander, Swedenborg, and Schwegler.
Strauss, Bunsen, Oberlin, and Olshausen.
Schmucker, Odenheimer, Anthon, and Muhlenberg.
Weiss, Hagenbach, Spegel, and Benzelius.
Wycliffe, Bede, Becket, and Tyndale.
Latimer, Ridley, Usher, and Stillingfleet.
Knox, Fox, Penn, and Berkeley.

Hooker, Herbert, Baxter, and Bunyan.
Tillotson, Taylor, Fuller, and Warburton.
Horsley, Hill, Hall, and Heber.
Watts, Wesley, Whitfield, and Whately.
Dodridge, Paley, Clarke, and Chalmers.
Belsham, Lardner, Whiston, and Hoadley.
Robinson, Emlyn, Biddle, and Wakefield.
Priestley, Lindsey, Manning, and Disney.
Spurgeon, Firmin, Price, and Norton.
Dwight, Edwards, Hobart, and Wainwright.
Seabury, Doane, Potter, and Hopkins,
Hawks, Mason, Stiles, and Tyng. .
Bethune, Wayland, Spring, and Thompson.
Chapin, Barnes, Bush, and Bushnell.
Beecher, Cheever, Sears and Sawyer.
Simpson, Stevens, Durbin, and Dempster.
Deems, Weems, Soule, and Patton.
Buckminster, Pierpont, Ware, and Parker.
Channing, Dewey, King, and Conway.
Frothingham, Mayo, Furness, and Farley.
Bellows, Garnett, Hale, and Bowen.
Alger, Osgood, Wasson and Bartol.

———

Is the negro capable, in any degree, of Abstract
Reasoning? Has he ever acquired the reputation of
being an Investigator of the Laws or Principles of Cause
and Effect? Does he establish Premises, and therefrom
arrive at Conclusions? Has he, at any Period of the
World's History, been known to originate even one Respectable Hypothesis? Upon what subject or subjects is
he gifted with Intellectual Vision? Does any one of the
Sciences, does any Branch of Knowledge, owe to him its
Reduction from Theory? Did he ever possess an Idea,
or suggest a Problem, worthy, for one moment, of the

Attention of the White Man? In short, does the negro ever

> ———"To speculations high or deep
> Turn his thoughts, and with capacious mind
> Consider all things visible?"

No, verily; the negro is a nappy-headed and narrow-minded numskull, and little does he care for aught, except a plentiful supply of things to eat and things to drink. It is White Men only—such men, for instance, as those whose names appear below, who are justly and properly recognizable as

METAPHYSICIANS.

Aristotle, Seneca, Lælius, and Roscellinus.
Anselm, Vico, Mamiana, and Gioberti.
Campanella, Rosmini, Patrizi, and Gerando.
Cabanis, Poiret, Lamennais, and Jouffroy.
Condillac, Leroux, Cousin, and Collard.
Damiron, Bonald, Fourrier, and Proudhon.
Bouterwek, Krause, Herbart, and Dampe.
Schopenhauer, Keym, Volk, and Baader.
Cudworth, Reid, Hartley, and Hazlitt.
Coleridge, Home, Mill, and Stewart.
Emerson, Edwards, Tappan, and Upham.

Who are the gifted Sons of Genius to whom we are indebted for the Human-nature-portraying and Delightsome Entertainments of the Stage? Who in the Past, and who in the Present, have Proved themselves Worthy to be accounted good Comedians and Tragedians? Where, if not upon the Boards of the White Man, may we expect to Witness the most Soul-stirring and Soul-softening Theatrical Representations? There is, however, one Species of the Histrionic Art in which the negro is unparagoned; and that is in Farce, he himself being, by nature, the most Ridiculous and Absurd Farce in all the World! It is only White Men, such men, for instance, as are here named, who may be justly regarded as Ingenious and Genuine

DRAMATISTS. ·

Æschylus, Aristophanes, Thespis, and Phrynicus.
Euripides, Xenocles, Sophocles, and Menander.
Anaxandrides, Andronicus, Ennius, and Laberius.
Plautus, Pacuvius, Nævius, and Terence.
Boccaccio, Alfieri, Riccoboni, and Goldoni.
Moratin, Garcia, Barca, and Lope de Vega.
Molière, Corneille, Regnard, and Beaumarchais.
Racine, Arnault, Dufresny, and Rotron.
Boucicault, Barras, Sardon, and Ponsard.
Quinault, Scribe, Delavigne and Delongchamps.
Kotzebue, Holberg, Lessing, and Grillparzer.
Goethe, Schiller, Iffland, and Freytag.
Hooft, Vondel, Grabbe, and Gützkow,
Sumorokoff, Volkoff, Beskow, and Kexel.
Shakspeare, Jonson, Beaumont, and Fletcher.
Massinger, Vanbrugh, Ford, and Otway.
Congrève, Marlowe, Rowe, and Farquhar.
Wycherley, Sheridan, Crowne, and Taylor.
Knowles, Bulwer, Colman, and Talfourd.
Sargent, Boker, Payne, and Conrad.
Ingersoll, Godfrey, Stone, and Mathews.

———

Have the Africans ever given us any Readable Works of the Imagination? What pleasing Fancies or Conceptions have ever Betickled the Barren Brains of the Blacks? Are the negroes Romancers? Satirists? Tel-

lers of Good Stories ?   No, no, not at all ; of genteel Tales
and Anecdotes, they know nothing.   Still, although the
negroes are no Fictionists, yet they are the most Intolerable Fibbers under the Sun—and the Truth is never in
them.   White Men only, such men for instance, as those
whose names are tabulated below, have it in their power
to attain honorable distinction as

FABULISTS AND NOVELISTS.

Æsop, Heliodorus, Longus, and Lokman.
Pilpay, Phædrus, Tatius, and Juvenal.
Petronius, Apuleius, Centio, and Bandello.
Cervantes, Yriarte, Aleman, and Montemayor.
Rabelais, Marivaux, Le Sage, and La Fontaine.
Balzac, Vigny, Musset, and About.*
Novalis, Tieck, Hippel, and Zschokke.
Wetzel, Schulz, Apel, and Spiess.
Freytag, Pfeffel, Kuhne, and Vandervelde.
Steffens, Thummel, Anderssen, and Kryloff.
Smollet, Marryat, Fielding, and De Foe.
Scott, Thackeray, Reynolds, and Ainsworth.
Dickens, Sterne, Bulwer, and Trollope.
Reade, Jerrold, Lever, and Lover.
Lockhart, Fraser, James, and Haliburton.
Cooper, Paulding, Kennedy, and Kimball.
Simms, Melville, Poe, and Curtis.
Hawthorne, Neal, Cooke, and Clements.
Prentice, Shillaber, Derby, and Thompson.
Mitchell, Newell, Brown, and Browne.
Peterson, Webber, Carruthers, and Mathews.
Arthur, Fay, Cobb, and Bennett.

---

* Also Alexander Dumas, who but for the three drops of debasing black blood in his veins, might, years ago, have risen
to be the first man in all France.

The Newspaper and the negro—what knows the latter of the former? Is the black man a Journalist? a Gazetteer? a Reviewer? a Critic? an Essayist? Is he a writer of Magazines? Pamphlets? Serials? Tracts? Has he any more knowledge of Periodical Literature than is possessed by the warty toad or the bellowing bull-frog? Yet, let us 'not blame the black man too severely for his ignorance ; for why should the pitch-colored plodder busy himself with pen or pencil, when, by less laborious pursuits, he can easily get what he wants—a plentiful supply of stewed pumpkin? It is White Men only, such men, for instance as those whose names here follow, who constitute the abuse-abating and world-renovating army of

EDITORS.

Marmontel, Querlon, Boissy, and Arnaud.
Bertin, Linguet, Rabbe, and Desfontaines.
Marrast, Renaudot, Proudhon, and Proudhomme.
Troplong, Pichot, Bastide, and Flocon.
Morande, Lallemant, Roche, and Planche.
Fonblanque, Langlois, Le Clerc, and Le Blanc.
Jourdan, Limayrac, Malespine, and Dechamps.
Lewald, Schletter, Prutz, and Werther.
Molbeck, Westergaard, Tenzel, and Seckendorf.
Wöhler, Dingler, Urner, and Reventlow.
Zenger, Zamke, Wocel, and Katkoff.
Heinzen, Schurz, Schulz, and Siebenpfeiffer.
Nordhoff, Koff, Kopp, and Kolliken.
Lexow, Ottendorfer, Rapp, and Gross.
Raster, Becker, Balzer, and Bloede.
L'Estrange, Walter, Stoddart, and Sterling.
Cave, Lucas, Barnes, and Hannay.
Ingram, Miall, Nares, and Beloe.
Howitt, Hatton, Bayne, and Mackenzie.
Reeve, Masson, Elwyn, and Chapman.

Creasy, Mackay, Russell, and Rivington.
Niles, Sands, Gallagher, and Brackenridge.
Gales, Seaton, Rives, and Ritchie.
Blair, De Bow, Bailey, and Goodloe.
Prentice, Kendall, Force, and Forney.
Weston, Bradford, Holland, and Osborn.
Shillaber, Lunt, Dennie, and Dutton.
Garrison, Goodell, Powell, and Pillsbury.
Weed, Beach, Morris, and Willis.
Webb, Houghton, Fuller, and Congdon.
Bryant, Legget, Bigelow, and Godwin.
Greeley, Dana, Gay, and Wilkinson.
Raymond, Ottarson, Smalley, and Curtis.
Bennett, Hudson, Hosmer, and Halpine.
Marble, Tilton, Bowles, and Horton.
Brooks, Bickham, Mifflin, and McMichael.
Sweetser, Godkin, Perkins, and Hassard.
Prime, Stone, Swinton, and Hurlbut.

———

Who have been our most efficient Promoters of a Vigorous and Solid Literature? What Classical Treasures have the Whites ever inherited from the blacks? Has any negro ever distinguished himself in Biography? in Belles-Lettres? or in even ordinary Scholarship? With what Branch of Knowledge is the African familiar? What Department of Learning has its attractions for him? Alas! it is but too painfully evident, that, in Matters of the Mind, the negro is a nonentity. White Men only, such men, for instance, as those whose names are catalogued below, have the capacity to attain Honorable Recognition and Fame in the Republic of Letters. Time and space admit of the mention here of only a few of the more Elegant and Polite Miscellaneous

14*

PROSE WRITERS.

Plutarch, Eunapius, Photius, and Philostratus.
Suetonius, Lucian, Nepos, and Prudentius.
Varro, Medici, Vives, and Vinci.
Castiglione, Poggio, Maracci, and Moreri.
Abelard, Montaigne, Rochefoucald, and Fontenelle.
Voltaire, Marmontel, Charron, and La Harpe.
Malebranche, Rousseau, Lamennais, and Volney.
Chateaubriand, Lefevre, Biot, Bayle, and Bruyère.
Lamartine, Raynal, Hugo, Thoreau, and Michelet.
Erasmus, Vossius, Sturmius, and Bollandus.
Scaliger, Reuchlin, Gruber, and Foppens.
Gesner, Menzel, Schlegel, and Lessing.
Richter, Hettner, Grimm, and Moritz.
Adelung, Wieland, Heyne, and Herder.
Humboldt, Varnhagen, Duyckinck, and Verplanck.
Alcuin, Occam, More, and Melville.
Ascham, Oldham, Sidney and Raleigh.
Walpole, Bolingbroke, Ogilby and Camden.
Boyle, Middleton, Pepys, and Evelyn.
Addison, Steele, Swift, and Johnson.
Goldsmith, Pinkerton, Taylor, and Tooke.
Roscoe, Fosbrooke, Mackenzie, and Mackintosh.
Boswell, Lewes, Lamb, and Lockhart.
Brydges, Kinglake, Landor, and Trollope.
Carlyle, Helps, Disraeli, and De Quincey.
Ruskin, Smiles, Kingsley, and Gilfillan.
Irving, Paulding, Ticknor and Goodrich.
Sparks, Colton, Headley, and Griswold.
Whipple, Godwin, Strother, and Parkman.

Of things in Nature, what knows the negro? Has he
ever acquired any information in regard to the Multifarious and Marvelous Inhabitants and productions of the

Earth? No. With the negro, naught is the difference
between the Nightingale and the Gnat, the Pine and the
Pigweed, the Ruby and the Ragstone. Before his unap-
preciative eyes, almost everything lies unnoticed and unknown; and for nothing, except for the commonest needs
of the body, is his curiosity or concern ever awakened.
It is White Men only, such men, for instance, as those
whose names are here tabulated, who, by the Adorable
Creator of all, are Endowed with those Varied and Sublime Faculties of the Mind, which are always observable
in the Works of Learned

NATURALISTS.

Aristotle, Martius, Fabricius, and Spallanzani.
Pliny, Hernandez, Oviedo, and Guéttard.
Cuvier, Blainville, Pluche, and Deluc.
Buffon, Duvancel, Becquerel, and Beauvois.
Lamarck, Leblond, Daubenton, and D'Orbigny.
Swammerdam, Kaempfer, Koch and Oken.
Leeuwenhoeck, Hubner, Muller, and Eichwald.
Ehrenberg, Sparrman, Eschscholtz, and Moleschott
Agassiz, Burmeister, Ruschenberger, and Backman.
Darwin, Trembly, Kirby, and Jameson.
Owen, Wilson, Pennant, and Swainson.
White, Waterton, Ellis, and Goldsmith.
Audubon, Baird, Cassin, and Glover.
Gould, Marsh, Harris, and Holbrook.

From whom have we inherited or acquired the knowledge we possess of the Physical and Intellectual Properties of Man? Not from the negro, certainly; for from
him, (despicable dunce and drone that he is,) we have
inherited or acquired nothing of value. It is White
Men only, men of the Caucasian race, such men, for instance, as those whose names appear below, who are

known to the world, or who can, by any human possibility, be known, as justly distinguished

ANTHROPOLOGISTS AND ETHNOLOGISTS.

Quatrefages, Balbi, Broc, and Broca.
Dumeril, Desmoulins, Hilaire, and Gratiolet.
Levaïllant, Desnoyers, Pauly, and Pouchet.
Lartet, Perthes, Bey, and Collard.
Guyot, Pictet, Zeune, and Bollaert.
Blumenbach, Tiedemann, Camper, and Bischoff.
Soemmerring, Agassiz, Retzius, and Lepsius.
Waitz, Vrolik, Pulszky, and Steenstrup.
Durckheim, Müller, Wagner, and Weber.
Prichard, Lawrence, Smith, and Martin.
Knox, Latham, Burke, and Blake.
Crawford, Collingwood, Hunt, and Huxley.
Carpenter, Reade, Owen, and Wilson.
Balfour, Vincent, Edwards, and Embleton.
Morton, Pickering, Leidy, and Meigs.
Nott, Gliddon, Fisher, and Hawks.
Schoolcraft, Catlin, Stephens, and Squier.
Wyman, Brace, Folsom, and Francis.
Morse, Bartlett, Gibbs, and Gallatin.

———

Would we learn something of the Peculiar Formation and Structure of the Solidified Portion of the Globe? its Earths? its Rocks? its Minerals? its Organic Remains? And if so, from whom may we hope to obtain the desired information? From the negro? As well might we expect to hear Grammar from a Goose, Rhetoric from a Raven, or Logic from a Locust. It is White Men only, such men, for instance, as those whose names we here find outcropping conspicuously above the general level, who are entitled to full respect and recognition as

GEOLOGISTS.

Gismondi, Generelli, Moro, and Vallisneri.
Haüy, Villiers, Dolomieu, and Beaumont.
Herrissant, Saussure, Beche, and Brogniart.
Werner, Gesner, Lehmann, and Holbach.
Overmann, Bischoff, Weiss, and Hjelm.
Hermelin, Keutmann, Buch, and Schott.
Adelberg, Trippel, Studer, and Credner.
Hutton, Smith, Conybeare, and Buckland.
Lyell, Prestwick, Miller, and Mantell.
Murchison, Phillips, Dawson, and Maclure.
Jukes, Forbes, Houghton, and Portlocke.
Hitchcock, Hall, Shumard, and Cleveland.
Redfield, Hooker, Bruce, and Gibbs.
Dana, Eaton, Trask, and Rogers.
Emmons, Egleston, Kerr, and Denton.

In reference to the Vegetable Kingdom, what Volume
of Verity has the negro ever vouchsafed us? Has he
ever written or said anything about Trees? Shrubs?
Plants? Flowers? Lichens? Mosses? Alas! to our own
limited knowledge of these things, as of others, the negro,
in conformity with his usual practice, has added nothing.
Yet is the swarthy vagrant a Vine-grower; for the Pumpkin, which needs only to be planted, and pleads not for
the Plough, is his most Precious Product. Obvious is it,
however, that White Men only, have it in their power to
enlarge the circle of our acquaintance with the Verdant
Riches of Nature; and these are the men, such men, for
instance, as those whose names appear below, who are
alone worthy to be regarded and quoted as well-informed.

BOTANISTS.

Dioscorides, Camerarius, Lobelius, and Cæsalpinus.
Linnæus, Vahl, Arrhenius, and Retzius.
Candolle, Rivinus, Gesner, and Gronovius.
Endlicher, Swartz, Wahlenberg, and Wildenow.
Hasselquist, Hedwig, Juugermann, and Gærtner.
Grisebach, Ambodik, Kalm, and Füchs.
Schweinitz, Schlechtendal, Schleiden, and Schelhammer.
Tournefort, Cornutus, Jacquin, and Vaillant.
Jussieu, Plumier, Ventenat, and Delalande.
Heritier, Willemet, Dalibard, and Dalechamps.
Adanson, Petiver, Roxburgh, and Balfour.
Sloane, Banks, Ray, and Rutherford.
Lindley, Sibthorp, Loudon, and Paxton.
Hooker, Colden, Logan, and Darby.
Gray, Torrey, Barton, and Bartram.

Does the negro possess any knowledge of the Elements
or Ingredients of Compounds? Where are his Analytical
Laboratories? What knows he of Decomposition? of
Cohesion? of Combustion? of Assimilation? But, wherein, wherein, indeed, consists the pertinence of such questions as these? Very well do we know that White Men
ever have been, and that none but White Men ever
will be, or can be, earnest Investigators and Ad-
vancers of any Branch or Department of Science; and
that it is alone such men as these, such, for instance, as
those whose names appear below, who, with the Crucible
in one hand, and the Retort in the other, become distinguished as Wonder-working and World-improving

CHEMISTS.

Geoffroy, Fourcroy, Rey, and Rouelle.
Lavoissier, Berthollet, Saussure, and Lussac.

Regnault, Chevreul, Venel, and Thenard.
Morveau, Darcet, Chaptal, and Raspail.
Bœrhaave, Bergmann, Brandt, aud Bunsen.
Liebig, Schonbein, Glauber, and Poggendorf.
Wöhler, Scheele, Berzelius, and Angstrom.
Henkel, Erdmann, Kunckell, and Klaproth.
Wenzel, Stahl, Spielmann, and Kirchhoff.
Ashmole, Cavendish, Tennant, and Beddoes.
Wollaston, Millar, Kemp, and Kirwan.
Priestley, Nicholson, Ure, and Brande.
Davy, Mayow, Hunter, and Thomson.
Faraday, Tyndall, Dalton, and Draper.
Chilton, Hayes, Hare, and Henry.
Doremus, Gibbs, Beck, and Booth.
Youmans, Morfit, Hunt, and Cooke.

———

What knows the negro of the wonderful structure of
his own body? What knowledge does he possess cf the
peculiar Organization of any Species of Beast, Bird, or
Fish? What knows he of the Mysteries of Birth? of
the Phenomena of Life? of the Enigmas of Death? Is
he an Experienced Physiologist? an Ingenious Wound-
dresser? an Expert Dissector? We know that White
Men only, such men, for instance, as those whose names
are here registered, have it in their power, by virtue of
Nature's auspicious endowments, to become Eminent

SURGEONS AND ANATOMISTS.

Damocles, Ætius, Aretæus, and Rufus.
Ammonius, Servetus, Fallopius, and Scarpa.
Mondini, Asselli, Malpighi, and Morgagni.
Molinelli, Bertrandi, Moscati, and Rambilla.
Dupuytren, Peyronie, Morel, and Venette.

Desault, Lecat, Monthyon, and Paré.
Velpeau, Sabaurin, Lisfranc, and Flourens.
Nelaton, Garard, Bichat, and Berard.
Sequard, Levacher, Larrey, and Ledran.
Beclard, Verdier, Roux, and Petit.
Vesalius, Albinus, Swammerdam, and Deventer.
Camper, Rusch, Wirsung, and Vesling.
Heister, Theden, Gräfe, and Callisen.
Haller, Rödener, Platner, and Purrmann.
Horwitz, Ruschenberger, Gross, and Leidy.
Abernethy, Hunter, Ring, and Smellie.
Cooper, Liston, Ware, and Vance.
Wiseman, Cheselden, Pott, and Ramsay.
Pattison, Sharp, Monro, and Mayo.
Brodie, Douglas, Bell, and Bostock.
Carpenter, Lawrence, Owen, and Arnott.
Elliston, Simpson, Kerr, and Guthrie.
Mott, Dorsey, Wistar, and Shippen.
Carnochan, Kissam, Dowler, and Trevett.
Wyman, Warren, Jackson, and Beaumont.
Parker, Norris, Pope, and Carrington. .
Dalton, Mussey, Hammond, and Brainard.
Pancoast, Moore, Pim, and Flewellen.

Is the negro a good Doctor? Where or when was he
ever known to be successful as a Practitioner of Medicine? Has any one capable of telling the truth ever borne
testimony in his behalf as a Healer of the Sick? as a Curer
of Disease? as a Restorer of Health? as an Adapter of
Sanitary Measures? White Men only, such men, for instance, as those whose names here follow, have been
known to the world, and such only can be known, as
Skillful

PHYSICIANS.

Hippocrates, Herophilus, Asclepiades, and Serapion.
Erasistratus, Democedes, Nichomachus, and Athena-
    dorus.
Themison, Acron, Celsus, and Paracelsus.
Galen, Agathinus, Actuarius, and Andromachus.
Galvani, Achillini, Valli, and Volpini.
Cabanis, Astruc, Pidoux, and Pardoux.
Tissot, Selle, Alard, and Lænnec.
Lestocq, Virey, Sauvages, and Senac.
Ricord, Legallois, Mazet, and Helmont.
Erastus, Stahl, Vater, and Senkenberg.
Mœhsen, Bœrhaave, Rhyne, and Swieten.
Hüfeland, Rückert, Jahr, and Kraft.
Scheffel, Kuhn, Lauremberg, and Ledermutter.
Hahnemann, Stapf, Hempel, and Hartmann.
Preissnitz, Schiefferdecker, Weiss, and Wesselhœft.
Trall, Wier, Shew, and Shepard.
Harvey, Radcliffe, Glisson, and Cullen.
Arbuthnot, Sydenham, Todd, and Thomson.
Baskerville, Jenner, Uwins, and Tyson.
Heberden, Gilbert, Forbes, and Fordyce.
Ramsbotham, Imray, Barclay, and Graham.
Copland, Tweedie, Ashton, and Ferguson.
Dunglison, Gardner, Meigs, and Parish.
Boylston, Bard, Bond, and Bartlett.
Rush, Hosack, Paine, and Physick.
Chapman, Dickson, Kittredge, and Bigelow.
Delafield, Bedford, Woodward, and Metcalfe.

To what race of mankind did he belong, who first put
Europe in possession of the knowledge of a New World?

Who were the first to explore and describe the Insular
Continents of the South Pacific, and the numerous Islands and Islets of the Oceans? Has any negro (otherwise than as a slave, or as a scullion,) ever doubled Cape
Horn, or rounded the Cape of Good Hope? In whom
alone have we found the daring which braved the Icebergs
and the other Polar Perils of both the Arctic and Antarctic
Seas? White Men only, such men, for instance, as those
whose names are here recorded, have acquired fame—and
none but White Men can become famous—as

NAVIGATORS, AND MARITIME DISCOVERERS.

Hanno, Zarco, Picaro, and Groalva.
Columbus, Vespucci, Quiros, and Cabot.
Magellan, Cortereal, Ulloa, and Balboa.
De Gama, Orellana, Dias, and Torres.
Cabral, Pinzon, Mendana, and De Sola.
Solis, D'Urville, Le Maire, and La Salle.
Cassard, Freycinet, Diereville, and Perouse.
Bougainville, Bellot, Dampier, and Cartier.
Leif, Thorfinz, Biarne, and Ekeberg.
Tasman, Kotzebue, Wrangell, and Shelvocke.
Frobisher, Willoughby, Hudson, and Gilbert.
Baffin, Cook, Davis, and Parry.
Franklin, Ross, McClure, and McClintock.
Duncan, Richardson, Phipps, and Scoresby.
Middleton, Back, Liddon, and Lyon.
Wallis, Macham, Biscoe, and Briscow.
Cavendish, Carteret, Bass and Byron.
Wilkes, Lynch, Delano, and Kendrick.
Kane, Hayes, Hall, and Hartstene.
Herndon, Dehaven, Page, and Bonsall.

———

Not much, if at all, is the negro Moved or Impelled by
the Spirit of Adventure. Going abroad, (except under

Compulsion, as, for instance, when, as an Imp of Slavery, he has been Kidnapped or Bought, and is to be Sold,) is a Matter entirely *Foreign* to his Taste. Certain it is also, that he is not an Enthusiastic Sight-seer, nor a Graphic Describer of things Seen. As an Observer of the World and its Ways, he is scarcely less Dull and Meaningless than the Ox or the Ass. Who, indeed, does not know that the negro is no Journeyer? no Voyager? no Tourist? no Excursionist?—and that, by his own volition or preference, he is never found as a Rover or a Rambler, as a Palmer or a Pilgrim, as a Passenger or a Pedestrian, save only in the zigzag and uneven Paths which, within the circuit of a few small Acres, lead from one Pumpkin-patch to another? It is White Men only, such men, in truth, as those whose names appear below, who have ever gained, or can gain, a World-wide Reputation as

TRAVELERS AND COSMOPOLITES.

Marco Polo, Rosselini, Tschudi, and Belzoni.
Champollion, Gerard, Denon, and Labarthe.
Bonpland, Duperry, Fontanier, and Jacquemont.
Beauchamps, Orbigny, Moussy, and Vambery.
Du Chaillu, Caille, Renan and Volney.
Burckhardt, Seetzen, Dieffenbach, and Lepsius.
Lichtenstein, Hornemann, Siebold, and Poppig.
Schomburgk, Vogel, Krapf, and Overweg.
Gerstaecker, Kuttner, Kampfer, and Gützlaff.
Ruppell, Leichhardt, Kohl, and Wagner.
Froebel, Mundt, Hettner, and Humboldt.
Barth, Petherick, Rich, and Scoresby.
Layard, Fitzroy, Nash, and Madden.
Bruce, Parkyns, Duncan, and Campbell.
Park, Bowdich, Barrow, and Baldwin.
Denham, Clapperton, Laing, and Lander.

Livingstone, Speke, Grant, and Harris.
Wilkinson, Cumming, Martin, and Ritchie.
Palgrave, Eyre, Burton, and Moffat.
Atkinson, Dodwell, Giffard, and Hobhouse.
Ledyard, Riley, Adams, and Curtis.   .
Schoolcraft, Catlin, Squier, and Stephens.
Carson, Fremont, Lewis, and Clark.
Taylor, Brace, Miles, and Melville.

———

To whom are we indebted for Full and Accurate Descriptions of the Earth ? its Oceans and its Seas? its Rivers and its Lakes? its Continents, and its Islands? its Mountains and its Table-lands? its Nationalities and its other Political Divisions? Has the negro ever given to mankind a Chart? a Map? an Atlas? . What knows he of Latitude? of Longitude? of the Zones? of the Poles? of the Equator? of the Tropic of Cancer? or of the Tropic of Capricorn? Knows he anything, or cares he anything, about Circles? Degrees? Belts? Girdles? Parallels? Meridians? White Men alone have imparted to us a knowledge of these things; and it is White Men only, such men for instance, as those whose names appear below, who, at any time, have merited the distinction to be recorded as Able and Trustworthy

GEOGRAPHERS.

Strabo, Pytheas, Scymnus, and Scylax.
Artemidorus, Ptolemy, Hipparchus, and Eratosthenes.
Pausanius, Agathamerus, Isidore, and Dionysius.
Balbi, Riccioli, Ferrari, and Castro.
Malte-Brun, Mercator, Poirson, and Delamarche.
D'Anville, Baudrand, De Lisle, and Du Halde.
Gosselin, Bescherelle, Martinière, and Rougemont.

Ritter, Merleker, Engel, and Kombst.
Petermann, Berghaus, Kloden, and Kramers.
Krebel, Hoffman, Stein, and Moller.
Hassel, Hübner, Volger, and Von Roon.
Hakluyt, Sanson, Echard, and Vincent.
Johnston, Murray, Blair, and Blackie.
Rennel, Bigland, McCulloch, and Dalrymple.
Morse, Hillard, Smith, and Goodrich.
Lafon, Thomas, Baldwin, and Fisher.
Mitchell, Monteith, Colton, and Disturnell.

———

Has any African ever distinguished himself even in any one of the Out-door Employments—in any one of the Pastoral Vocations—which, of all other callings, are the most Natural to Man? When or where was the negro ever known as a respectable Shepherd? Gardener? Farmer? Grape-grower? Orchardist? Florist? Significantly may we, in our thoughts of him as a Tiller (or rather as a Non-tiller) of the ground,

> "Ask if in husbandry he aught doth know,
> To plough, to plant, to reap, to sow."

Yet it must be confessed that there are certain Seeds to which, as a Cultivator of the Soil, he Bends all his Energies, and they are the Seeds of the Pumpkin. We know, however, that White Men only, such men for instance, as those whose Names are here Furrowed in Paper, have gained the Honor of Recognition as justly Celebrated

RURALISTS AND AGRICULTURISTS.

Adam, Abel, Lot, and Laban.
Cincinnatus, Cato, Varro, and Virgil.

Scipio, Pliny, Columella, and Dentatus.
Palladius, Re, Herrera, and Olavides.
Ussieux, Duhamel, Quintine, and Tessier.
Dombasle, Tillet, Serres, and Serain.
Fellemberg, Wedenkeller, Stisser, and Potocsky.
Stockhardt, Sprenger, Koller, and Kretchmann.
Schwertz, Reichardt, Switzer, and Hartlibb.
Fitzherbert, Googe, Tull, and Tusser.
Blythe, Paxton, Young, and Dickson.
Bakewell, Loudon, Sinclair, and Repton.
Elkington, Thornton, Warner, and Wetmore.
Wadsworth, Garnet, Rhodes, and Blakeslee.
Bordley, Dearborn, Putman, and Tomlinson.
Olmsted, Mercer, Carter, and Colman.
Downing, Eliott, Miner, and Allen.
Mapes, Saxton, Rankin, and Ruffin.
Hitchcock, Sprague, Flint, and Kenrick.
Ogden, Wright, Langworthy, and Longworth.
Newton, Hovey, Hyde, and Holt.
Evans, Norton, Buist, and Wilder.

———

In what part of the world have we ever seen the negro busying himself in the construction of Stone-Highways? Railroads? Breakwaters? Docks? Wharves? Bridges? At what time, in the history of the past, has he been found occupied in the erection of Breastworks? Ramparts? Redans? Redoubts? or other Fortifications? White Men only, such men, for instance, as those whose names are here registered, have been, and none others can be, deservedly celebrated as

CIVIL AND MILITARY ENGINEERS.

Vitruvius, Zago, Pacheco, and Sangallo.
Archimedes, Ghega, Peruzzi, and Pardi.

Vauban, Montalembert, Ribes, and Burat.
Lefebvre, Flachat, Vicat, and Rignet.
Gauthey, Duvivier, Liard, and Laurent.
Monge, Talabot, Sommelier, and Papin.
Lesseps, Pambour, Viele, and Beauregard.
Wadstrom, Polhem, Absterdam, and Decher.
Howitz, Coehorn, Plaat, and Vermuyden.
Kurth, Roeder, Weitzel, and Weissenborn.
Graeff, Peltz, Zeller, and Ziegler.
Brindley, Fairbairn, Bell, and Myddleton.
Smeaton, Mitchell, Dodd, and Chapman.
Brunel, Rennie, Pelham, and Upton.
Stephenson, Rudd, Fowler, and Longridge.
Telford, Saunders, Lloyd, and Kennard.
Gillespie, Ellicott, Long, and Fulton.
Jervis, Ellet, Mahan, and Bulkley.
Olmsted, Kellogg, Darby, and Danby.
Barnard, Whiting, Gillmore, and Goldsborough.
Holley, Delafield, Cox, and McClellan.
Wood, Isherwood, Sewell, and Garvin.
Loring, King, Hoyt, and Haines.
Haswell, Swift, Garnett, and McNeil.
Ellison, Parker, Baldwin, and Chesboro'.
Craven, Shock, Roberts, and Robinson.
Latrobe, Whistler, Young, and Swain.

From whose brain has been evolved the Plow? the Reaper? the Thresher? the Corn-Sheller? the Grist-Mill? the Cotton Gin? the Spinning-Jenny? the Loom? the Sewing-Machine? the Trowel? the Plumb-Line? the Saw? the Plane? the Compass? the Quadrant? the Steam Engine? the Printing Press? the Telegraph? and the Telescope? Of what race are the Men of Might who have Wrested from Nature such secrets as show that the

whole Universe, in its relation to the Heaven-favored
branch of the Human Family, is Filled and Overflowing with Auspicious Possibilities? Well do we know
that it is White Men only, such men, for instance, as
those whose names are here catalogued, who have become,
or who can become, distinguished as

INVENTORS AND DISCOVERERS OF THINGS USEFUL.

Anacharsis, Lysistratus, Talus, and Erichthonius.
Dædalus, Danaus, Proetus, and Memnon.
Ctesibius, Archytas, Archimedes, and Anaximander.
Aretino, Fontana, Finiquerra, and Campani.
Torricelli, Volta, Galileo, and Galvani.
Borelli, Sansevero, Gioia, and Verochio.
Salva, Garay, Tagliabue, and Dondi.
Jacquard, Didot, Gobelin, and Gascoigne.
Daguerre, Mathiot, Ampère, and Froment.
Fourneyron, Foucault, De Caus, and De Jonge.
Chappe, Pascal, Bonnet, and Montgolfier.
Guttenberg, Faust, Worde, and Koster.
Schoeffer, Reuss, Van Eyck, and Von Füchs.
Huyghens, Leibnitz, Imgen, and Jansen.
Fahrenheit, Reaumur, Drebbel, and Schrotter.
Schroeder, Fessel, Guericke, and Gœinsfleisch.
Oberkampf, Reiffelsen, Gauss, and Kœnig.
Ericsson, Tschirnhausen, Moncke and Malzel.
Steinheil, Schweigger, Schilling, and Bohnenberger.
Reuter, Sennefelder, Schonbein, and Sturtevant.
Bechar, Gerbert, Miekles, and Menzies.
Hales, Hooke, Bacon, and Barlowe.
Worcester, Watt, Savory, and Newcomen.
Napier, Newton, Davy, and Faraday.
Wollaston, Harvey, Jenner, and Brewster.
Wheatstone, Pasley, Bain, and Babbage.
Caxton, Tilloch, Ged, and Applegath.

Arkwright, Wedgwood, Greathead, and Mac Adam.
Crompton, Heathcote, Cort, and Caithness.
Hodgkinson, Hargrave, Avery, and Bolton.
Franklin, Morse, Hughes, and House.
Fulton, Fitch, Stevens, and Rumsey.
Whitney, Godfrey, Hussey, and McCormick.
Whittemore, Dyer, Perkins, and Gobright.
Bigelow, Spencer, Hill, and Dearborn.
Herring, Lille, Yale, and Pike.
Howe, Wheeler, Grover, and Sloat.
Hoe, Longstreet, Phelps, and Alden.

———

Is the negro an Artisan? a Handicraftsman? a Maker
of Machines? What knows he of any one of the Mechanical Powers? Has he ever heard of the Lever? the
Wheel? the Axle? the Pulley? the Wedge? the Screw?
the Balance? the Inclined Plane? Knows he aught of
the Cog? the Ratchet? the Ball? the Socket? the Joint?
the Crank? the Chain? the Belt? the Band? It is
White Men only, such men, for instance, as those whose
names are here recorded, who have been, or who can
be, justly distinguished as Dexterous and Ingenious

MECHANICS.

Hiram, Tubal-Cain, Metius, and Magnus.
Regiomontanus, Camus, Rheita, and Porro.
Torriano, Ramelli, Mical, and Arnaboldi.
Vaucanson, Morin, Bouche, and Bregnet.
Maillardet, Rochon, Dessoir, and Lenoir.
Cassegrain, Guinand, Poncelet, and Lecomte.
Bourgeois, Cauchoix, Decondres, and Simonet.
Janvier, Brizont, Bouguer, and Dandrieux.
Amontons, Jubier, Langlois, and Mareschal.

Duparcq, Foucher, Cochot, and Larochette.
Petitjean, Amouroux, Bataille, and Dubois.
Lippersheim, Roemer, De Wyck, and De Vick.
Reichenbach, Reidenbeck, Steinbach, and Birkbock.
Fraunhofer, Fitz, Plossl, and Boscovich.
Weinbier, Wissler, Elzevir, and Maxheimer.
Grubermann, Ehrhardt, Guggolz, and Zettler.
Kempellen, Hahn, Droz, and Pflug.
Bohnenberger, Herz, Klix, and Gougelmann.
Appold, Tiemann, Dietz, and Bramah.
Dollond, Nasmyth, Rankine, and Moseley.
Earnshaw, Lassell, Dale, and Moreland.
Ramsden, Goddard, Hutton, and Harrison.
Whittingham, Clark, Palmer, and Marley.
Plimpton, Merrill, Harrington, and Dusenbury.

If we want any good thing, or any necessary thing—
anything conducive to our comfort or convenience—can
we get it from the negro? We know his inveterate and
rascally proneness to fabricate falsehoods? Is he also a
fabricator of Cloths? Carpets? Curtains? Gauze? Finery? Is he an artificer in Brass? a worker in Wood?
Is he a maker of Hats? Caps? Boots? Shoes? Garments?
Implements? Tools? Utensils? Vehicles? Umbrellas?
Arms? Ammunition? Hardware? Glassware? Cutlery?
Crockery? Needles? Pins? Furniture? Musical Instruments? Time-Pieces? Jewelry? Ornaments? White
Men only, such men, for instance, as those whose names
are here appended, have become, and none but White
Men can become, Extensive and Far-famed

MANUFACTURERS.

Biolley, Mantagnac, Lannay, and Bandoux.
Hamot, Bacot, Girardet, and Molyneux.

Poussin, Chatellier, Vavassen, and Koechlin.
Delasalle, Berteche, Courtois, and Jacqz.
Bodimier, Mellier, Druelle, and Paillard.
Delamaire, Brossette, Honette, and Desmarais
Erard, Pleyel, Alexandre, and Dupland.
Wülfing, Wurzburg, Banendahl, and Steezmann.
Kohnstamm, Nellessen, Elstob, and Dexheimer.
Schroeder, Westermeyer, Scherr, and Horstmann.
Steinway, Knabe, Lindemann, and Grovesteen.
Broadwood, Collard, Hastelow, and Chappell.
Howgate, Wrigley, Lupton, and Elworthy.
Grafton, Bradshaw, Wilton, and Monteith.
Crossley, Templeton, Lewell, and Hubbard.
Shorrock, Broadbent, Glegg, and Radcliffe.
Hawksworthy, Brinton, Thurston, and Finlayson.
Hargreaves, Mappin, Jessop, and Gillot.
Chickering, Boardman, Dunham, and Bradbury.
Wethered, Brewer, Stetson, and Pomeroy.
Slater, Sprague, Seagreaves, and Simpson.
Hazard, Bancroft, Evans, and Eddy.
Harris, Harding, Gardner, and Goodrich.
Lyman, Lawrence, Hassam, and Hinckley.
Norris, Rodgers, Poole, and Mason.
Simmons, Collins, Lingerwood, and Bogardus.
Naylor, Mellish, Cornell, and Shortridge.
Merrick, Secor, Winans, and Little.

———

Can the African hew out of Stone, cast of Metal, or make of any other Solid Substance whatever, life-like representations of Men? Beasts? Birds? Where or when has the Ethiopian executed an admirable Statue of any Hero? Demi-God? or other Renowned Personage? Is the negro a clever Modeler in Plaster? a cunning Carver in Wood? an expert Chiseler in Marble? Has

he ever, of Granite, of Bronze, or of Oak, formed famous
Images of the Lion? the Horse? the Dog? White Men
only, such men, for instance, as those whose names are
here registered, have been known, and none but White
Men can be known, as Highly-gifted and Accomplished

SCULPTORS.

Bezaleel, Aholiab, Scopas, and Bupalus.
Phidias, Myron, Lysippus, and Agesander.
Praxiteles, Diodotus, Polycles, and Polycletus.
Learchus, Zenodorus, Calamis, and Alcamenes.
Agoracrites, Demetrius, Chares, and Agasias.
Lombardo, Clementi, Buono, and Torretto.
Bernini, Rusconi, Penna, and Bracci.
Canova, Ghiberti, Monti, and Tacca.
Roubilliac, Goujon, Pradier, and Pigalle.
Houdon, Danton, Sarazin, and Quesnoy.
Lamoureux, Falconet, Cartellier, Clesinger.
Thorwaldsen, Rysbrach, Nollekins, and Schlüter.
Schwanthaler, Sergel, Nahl, and Kiss.
Dannecker, Schadow, Geefs, and Pimenoff.
Steinhaüser, Slodtz, Rauch, and Rauchmüller.
Flaxman, Gibson, Cibber, and Wyatt.
Chantrey, Westmacott, Lough, and Bailey.
Greenough, Crawford, Browne, and Palmer.
Powers, Rogers, Mills, and Akers.
Ward, Brackett, Strong, and Bartlett.

Has the African ever artistically Pictured, upon Canvas,
anything animate or inanimate? No, no. The negro can
show no Masterpiece in Landscape, no Pattern in Por-
traiture. It is the White Man only, who, self-supplied with
Easel and Brush, mysteriously seizes the Fantasies and
the Flights of the Imagination, and then, with steadiness

of nerve, deliberately fashions them into substances of
wondrous Form and Beauty.   None but White Men, such
men, for instance, as those whose names are depicted below, have gained, and none but White Men can gain,
meritorious recognition and eminence as

PAINTERS.

Zeuxis, Euphranor, Aglaophon, and Apollodorus.
Apelles, Timomachus, Nicomachus, and Nicophanes.
Parrhasius, Pausias, Pamphilus, and Polygnotus.
Protogenes, Timanthes, Nicias, and Antiphilus.
Aristides, Pauson, Evenor, and Eupompus.
Titian, Guido, Michael Angelo, and Salvator Rosa.
Raphæl, Massaccio, Correggio, and Spinelli.
Cano, Albano, Canaletti, and Carracci.
Cimabue, Pisano, Mabuse, and Mengs.
Velasquez, Murillo, Cespedes, and Spagnoletto.
Poussin, Petitot, David, and Delacroix.
Delaroche, Vernet, Scheffer, and Durand.
Gignoux, Vaux, De Haas, and Le Clear.
Düer, Burgkmair, Van Eyck, and Vandyck.
Holbein, Snyders, Ostade, and Vandervelde.
Rubens, Rembrandt, Huysum, and Hübner.
Winterhalter, Kaulbach, Schnorr, and Nehlig.
Vanderlyn, Suydam, Brandt, and Brevoort.
Bierstadt, Wenzler, Leutze, and Kuntze.
Reynolds, Thornhill, Haydon, and Nasmyth.
Wilkie, Opie, Etty, and Romney.
Turner, Jarvis, Cope, and Northcote.
Gainsborough, Barry, Morland, and Martin.
West, Copley, Cole, and Sully.
Allston, Fraser, Harding, and Huntington.
Trumbull, Rothermel, Hayes, and Hoppin.
Inman, Whittredge, Howland, and Hubbard.

Rossiter, Johnson, Cranch, and Kensett.
Powell, Carpenter, Church, and Chapman.

Not in Negroland have we found, nor, while the blacks
remain in possession of the country, can we find, Galleries
of Paintings, Halls of Sculpture, nor Cabinets of Curiosi-
ties.   Nor may we ever look to that part of Africa inhabited chiefly by the negroes, for Parlors embellished
with Engravings, for Antechambers adorned with Mezzo-
tints, nor for Saloons beautified with Lithographs.   True
it is, indeed, pitifully true, that the Ethiopan is no Etcher
upon Copper, no Graver upon Steel, no Delineator upon
Limestone.   Never have we seen from his hand even one
well-executed Woodcut, nor a single page of a Volume of
Vignettes.   White Men only, such men, for instance, as
those whose names are crayoned below, have been, and
none but white men can be, worthily known and heralded
as

ENGRAVERS.

Marcantonio, Raimondi, Cunio, and Dolci.
Bartollozzi, Morghen, Besi, and Porporati.
Volpato, Foschi, Longhi, and Botticelli.
Papillon, Jazet, Cousins, and Lecomte.
Thomassin, Girardet, Chalon, and Massard.
Richomme, Martinet, Desnoyers, and Brideaux.
Luycken, Ramberg, Klein, and Sadeler.
Kobbell, Vischer, Bolswert, and Ruscheweyh.
Reindel, Leybold, Merz, and Mandell.
Overbeck, Amsler, Lips, and Kessler.
Cruikshank,   Felssing, Rahl, and Rahn.
Hogarth, Bewick, Strange, and Vertue.
Willmore, Atkinson, Graves, and Ryell.
Woollett, Heath, Linton, and Landseer.
Bromley, Wallis, Evans, and Howison.

Lossing, Darley, Sartain, and Phillibrown.
Ritchie, Smillie, Buttre, and Corbett.
Howland, Orr, Stafford, and Cameron.
Toppau, Carpenter, Perkins, and Spencer.
Rawdon, Danforth, Hatch, and Causland.
Ormsby, Edmonds, Holyer, and Halpin.
Fairman, Wright, Goodall, and Wellstood.

Is the African a Builder of Houses? Did he ever dwell within the walls of a respectable and comfortable Domicile, designed and erected by himself, or by any one or more of his own kith and kin? Has he ever had regular shelter elsewhere than in his own miserable Mud-Hut, or in his master's Kitchen? Where, if anywhere, are his imposing Edifices?—his Capitols? his State Houses? his City Halls? his Town Residences? his Country Seats? his Castles? his Palaces? his Mansions? his Court Houses? his Custom Houses? his Warehouses? his Exchanges? his Mints? his Banks? his Post Offices? his Mills? his Factories? his Hotels? his Clubs? his Theatres? his Lyceums? his Asylums? his Hospitals? Has he ever, for purposes of worship, upraised a Church? a Cathedral? a Temple? or a Tabernacle? Where, if anywhere are the Superstructures, founded by him for facilitating the acquisition of Knowledge, or for the imparting of Intelligence? White Men only, such men, for instance, as those whose names are tabulated below, have gained, and none but white men can gain, enviable prominence and distinction as

ARCHITECTS.

Sostratus, Apollodorus, Demetrius, and Demetrianus.
Xenocles, Callicratus, Mnesicles, and Metagenes.
Andronicus, Anthemius, Vitruvius, and Isodorus.
Brunelleschi, Sanmichelli, Bramante, and Sansovino.

Palladio, Ligorio, Scammozzi, and Visconti.
Pannini, Peruzzi, Sangallo, and Fontana.
Perrault, Bullant, Verniquet, and La Barre.
Soufflot, Huyot, Lescot, and De Lorme.
Lenoir, Jardin, Pugin, and Duthoit.
Dottzinger, Steinbach, Heitz, and Eidlitz.
Weinbrenner, Fischer, Tessin, and Zwiner.
Klenze, Schinkel, Gildemeister, and Vanbrugh.
Wren, Jones, Wyatt, and Chambers.
Donaldson, Fergusson, Taylor, and Smirke.
Hawksmoor, Savage, Rennie, and Reveley.
Nash, Wykeham, Barry, and Gibbs.
Haviland, Soane, Milne, and Wilkins.
Paxton, Gwilt, Towke, and Cockerell.
Upjohn, Hanford, Earle, and Duckworth.
Meigs, Walter, Penchard, and Ranlett.
Holley, Winham, Cleaveland, and Hatfield.
Gilman, Hunt, Cabot, and Clarke.
Atwood, Renwick, Jaffray, and Gambrill.

May we, may any one, in any part of the world, see or know the negro as a Naval Constructor? Is he a Shipwright? a Builder of Ocean-Steamers? a Layer of the Keels of River-craft? Where, if anywhere, may we find his formidable Men-of-War? his Iron-Clads? his Frigates? his Corvettes? —his Monitors? his Dunderbergs? his Dictators? his Kearsarges? his Tonawandas? his Monadnocks? his Miantonomahs? his Quinsigamonds? Where, if anywhere, are his Freight-carrying Merchantmen?—his Great Easterns? his Great Westerns? his Great Republics? his White Swallows? his White Clouds? his Mountain Waves? his Heralds of the Morning? his Seaman's Brides? his Empresses of the Seas? his Queens of Clippers? White Men only, such men for instance, as those whose names are here registered, have become, and none but White Men can become, from actual Skill and Merit on their own part, Distinguished

SHIPBUILDERS.

Noah, Arman, Oswald, and Hoste.
Descharges, Puget, Lome, and Lemont.
Armand, Trufant, Duthie, and Brunel.
Dubord, Soule, Currier, and, Minot.
Von Somm, Wettenberg, Rickmers, and Marbs.
Kirchhoff, Domke, Leibke, and Nuske.
Hansen, Carlsund, Moller, and Lindberg.
Throengaard, Toll, Lange, and Schillig.
Klawitter, Stridolff, Groot, and Mitzlaff.
Rosevelt, Westervelt, Brandt, and Bogert.
Eckford, Slade, Deane, and Tippet.
Symonds, Manby, Fairbairn, and Batcley.
Fearnall, Walker, Scott, and Hall.
Ditchburn, Fletcher, White, and Thompson.
Taylerson, Napier, Laud, and Russell.
Gower, Fincham, Dimon, and Moorson.
Hepworth, Wigram, Denny, and Lanson.
Webb, Collyer, Patterson, and Perrine.
Steers, Sneden, Joyce, and Erksine.
Hammel, Stack, Vaughan, and Lyne.
McKay, McGilvery, Quiggin, and Connell.
Cooper, Slicer, Robb, and Gardner.
Ashcraft, Fardy, Booze, and Abrams.
Raynes, Crobsy, Pearce, and Pettigrew.
Hotchkiss, Halleck, Greenman, and Gildersleeve.
Curtis, Tilden, Manson, and Magoun.
Jackman, Hayden, Briggs, and Lapham.
Stetson, Townsend, Milledge, and Rideout.
Tewksberry, Gibbs, Noyes, and Dunning.
Metcalf, Norris, Patten, and Pickett.
Southard, Ferrin, Meeker, and Dinsmore.

Stover, Lamport, Perkins, and Packard.
Doxford, Larrabee, Burgess, and Titcomb.

———

Have we ever known the negroes, or is it possible for us ever to know them, as honorable and extensive Exchangers of Commodities? Are they Buyers by Bulk? Are they Sellers by Wholesale? Are they Exporters by the Cargo? Are they Importers by the Shipload? What are the names of their Firms? the titles of their Partnerships? May we not, within the space of three short lines, sum up the whole history of their Mercantile Transactions, thus:—SAMBO, CUFFEY & Co.; Hucksters in Hot Corn: WOOLYHEAD, FLATFOOT & Co.; Melon-Mongers: BLACKAMOOR, BLOBBERLIP, & Co.; Peddlers in Pumpkins? Who, indeed, are

> "They that go down to the sea in ships,
> That do business in great waters ;
> That see the works of the Lord,
> And his wonders in the deep?"

Not negroes, certainly, but White Men; for White Men only, such men, for instance, as are here ledgered, have acquired, and none but White Men have the capacity to acquire, fame and fortune as

MERCHANTS.

Brossard, Dorbec, Stoude, and Lalonde.
Seillière, Desmotreux, Broche, and Latour.
Manigault, Leroux, Milleschamps, and Marjollin.
Tocquart, Thébaut, Lorillard, and Lachaise.
Labouchère, Jumel, Gracie, and Perit.
Lanier, Quintard, Polhemus, and Guion.
Schieffelin, Upstein, Steiglitz, and Leupp.
Havemeyer, Kohne, Rosevelt, and Vanderbilt.

Opdyke, Nölte, Bruck, and Fugger.
Harbeck, Shultz, Voorhees, and Haughwout.
Zimmermann, Peltzer, Mallmann, and Freyer.
Ropes, Hale, Perry, and Folmar.
Lumb, Armstrong, Drabble, and Drysdale.
Gresham, Marsden, Wigram, and Cuthbert.
Maitland, Baines, Shipley, and Tapscott.
Stewart, Lennox, Abbott, and Silsbee.
Whittridge, Yardley, Beatty, and Morris.
Halliwell, Cope, Warner, and Willing.
Endicott, Pitman, Sutton, and Dunbar
Bussy, Lowell, Amory, and Upton.
Edgerton, Hoyt, Lord, and Taylor.
Grinnell, Minturn, Spofford, and Tileston.
Howland, Aspinwall, Coghill, and Coleman.
Alsop, Hurlbut, Lathrop, and Ludington.
Stone, Starr, Broome, and Butler.
Phelps, Dodge, Savory, and Wetmore.
Chittenden, Hewitt, Morgan, and Marshall.
Claflin, Mellen, Skiddy, and Kingsland.
Goodhue, Lambert, Hone, and Hicks.
Brooks, Sturgis, Hunt, and Fish.
Gray, Perkins, Lawrence, and Appleton.
Bowen, McNamee, Haight, and Bulkley.
Halsey, Haines, Low, and Corning.

———

In what part of the world, if in any part, may the
negro be found as a masterly Money-Maker? Was he
ever, is he now, can he possibly be, the Possessor and
discreet Manager of great Treasures of Silver and Gold?
Where, if anywhere, is he an Accumulator of Property?
an Amasser of Wealth? a Gatherer of Riches? Where,
if anywhere, does he live in Affluence? in Opulence? in

Easy Circumstances? What are the sources and the extent of his Revenue? the bases and the amount of his Income? Is he a Millionaire? Questions similar to these may be fitly propounded in reference to the Caucasian, but not in reference to the African, who is an almost total stranger to all monetary terms and realities of greater value than the half-dime. White Men only, such men, for instance, as those whose names are catalogued below have attained, and none but White Men can attain, honorable and substantial distinction as

CAPITALISTS, FINANCIERS, AND BANKERS.

Crœsus, Isidorus, Claudius, and Lucullus.
Galba, Palma, Paparo, and Candamo.
Medici, Miro, Llavallol, and Anchorena.
Thellusson, Touro, Ouvrard, and Beauvois.
Fould, Guyot, Colbert, and Calonne.
Laborde, Vaudeville, Mirey, and Lafitte.
Durasse, Bezard, Offroy, and Fouchet.
Hottinguer, Jaricot, Fernex, and Baudard.
Lorillard, Groelet, Pereire, and Greffulhe.
Girard, Vacassy, Vassar, and Vermilye.
Astor, Belmont, Schuchardt, and Gebhard.
Rothschild, Erlanger, Sintz, and Seibert.
Stettheimer, Bischoffsheim, Oppenheim, and Gobel.
Zellwegger, Schuttler, Eichthal, and Van Vleck.
Osterwald, Groesbeck, Cammann, and Vonhoffman.
Seligmann, Salomon, Goldschmid, and Speyer,
Rhinelander, Roosevelt, Fischer, and Havemeyer.
Cavendish, Forbes, Glynn, and Neild.
Paterson, Patterson, Wood, and Child.
Lloyd, Satterthwaite, Hankey, and Rodgers.
Hope, Morrison, Ellison, and Robinson.
Baring, Colston, Spenser, and Thornton.
Jennings, Elwes, Day, and Arkwright.

Coutts, Pultney, Barclay, and Heywood.
Ridgeway, Thorndike, Biddle, and Morris.
Peabody, Thayer, Cooper, and Macdonough.
Corcoran, Riggs, Lawrence, and Baldwin.
Duncan, Sherman, Clewes, and Livermore.
Satterlee, Belknap, Stout, and Kissam.
Howes, Macy, Fiske, and Hatch.
Winslow, Lanier, King, and Kellogg.
Cooke, McCulloch, Hogg, and Whitney
Halsted, Dodge, Bogart, and Babcock.
Bingham, Lockwood, Carter, and Clymer.
Hemmenway, Gray, Jayne, and Parrott.
Stewart, Stuart, Steward, and Stevens.
Heywood, Ketchum, Hayden, and Hoyt.
Taylor, Lord, Brown and Greene.
Spofford, Jerome, Denny, and Detmold.
Dows, Morgan, Webb, and Watson.
Patton, Lennox, Young, and Clark.
Drew, Corning, Minturn, and Mitchell.
Phelps, Law, Coghill, and Crawford.

Does there flow, did there ever flow, from the breast
of the negro, even so much as a tea-spoonful of the
Milk of Human Kindness? In what community is any
one of his race recognized as a Benefactor? Where,
and in what manner, have we seen displayed the evidences of his Public Spirit? Is he a Promoter of Virtue and Knowledge? a Rewarder of Merit? a Comforter
and Protector of Widows and Orphans? a Sympathizer
with the Unfortunate? a Reliever of Distress? an
Assuager of the Tears of the Afflicted? Where are
the grateful witnesses to his Works of Charity? the
heart-softened Recipients of his Bounty? Is he a

Man of Mercy? a Good Samaritan? a Healer of the
Woes of his Fellows? an Exemplar of Disinterested
and Ennobling Actions? But, even if the negro were, as
a rarity in the history of the world, disposed to ameliorate the condition of mankind, or to do a needed and
special favor, would he not—poorest of the poor, as he
is—still and forever labor under the chronic inability to
carry out his good intent? White Men only, such men,
for instance, as those whose names are here recorded,
have been, and none but White Men can be, True and
Efficient

PHILANTHROPISTS.

Aristides, Odescalchi, Pinelli, and Pestalozzi.
Mæcenas, Nicoli, Rolli, and Las Casas.
Turgot, Sicard, Appert, and Coram.
Esquirol, Courcelles, La Garaye, and De Lessert.
Faneuil, Touro, Demilt, and Benezet.
Girard, Vassar, Bowdoin, and Boudinot.
Guggenbuhl, Metz, Falk, and Van Dun.
Schimmelmann, Berchtoed, Hein, and Hulse.
Rickoff, Hencel, Bergh, and Adler.
Rutgers, Astor, Schmid, and Schoffler.
Howard, Newdigate, Bass, and Tiptoft.
Gurney, Buxton, Firmin, and Lettsom.
Ashmole, Brampton, Guy, and Granville.
Hawes, Vernon, Chantrey, and Sheepshanks.
Penn, Hodgkin, Fitch, and Bates.
Wadham, Boyle, White, and Wildey.
Bodley, Radcliffe, Williams, and Marvell.
Smithson, Colston, Hunt, and Harley.
Wilberforce, Sharp, Swift, and Clarkson.
Watkinson, Duncan, Cotton, and Coit.
Yale, Tufts, Dudley, and Lawrence.
Jay, Jefferson, Chambers, and Perkins.

Peabody, Farmer, Stearns, and McKim.
Garrison, Phillips, Smith, and Tappan.
Birney, Buffum, Howe, and Hopper.
Cooper, Grinnell, Packer, and Packard.
Cornell, Appleton, Reed, and Bolton.

Has the Diffusion of written or printed Knowledge, as
a vocation collateral with Authorship, ever been a Spe-
ciality with the African? Was he ever actuated by the
noble ambition to become an Agent for the Wide-Spreading of Intelligence? an Instrument for the Enlighten-
ment of Mankind? Has he ever been the Enunciator of
Important Facts? the Announcer of Good News? the
Proclaimer of Glad Tidings? the Promulgator of Newly-
Discovered and Sublime Truths? No, no. White Men
only, such men, for instance, as those whose names are
here scheduled, have acquired, and none but White Men
can acquire, honorable and extensive reputation as

PUBLISHERS AND BOOKSELLERS.

Manutius, Cotta, Nicolai, and Andrade.
Hachette, Gosselin, Baudry, and Mandar.
Didot, Delalaine, Gravier, and Renard.
Baillière, Hervier, Didier, and Dufart.
Pierer, Elzevir, Schuberth, and Brockhaus.
Tauchnitz, Hoffmeister, Palm, and Blum.
Bohn, Witzendorf, Zumsteeg, and Damköhler.
Trübner, Westermann, Voorhies, and Van Nostrand.
Zell, Leypoldt, Radde, and Duyckinck.
Chambers, Bagster, Moxon, and Tonson.
Routledge, Oliphant, Longman, and Chapman.
Bentley, Whitaker, Low, and Hurst.
Grigg, Elliot, Carey, and Baird.
Lippincottt, Cowperthwait, Childs, and Peterson.

Lindsay, Blakiston, Lea and Blanchard.
Harding, Butler, Baldwin, and Bancroft.
Crocker, Brewster, Phillips, and Sampson.
Gould, Lincoln, Crosby, and Nichols.
Ticknor, Fields, Little, and Brown.
Hickling, Swan, Jewett, and Sanborn.
Merriam, Brewer, Case, and Taggard.
Harper, Scribner, Barnes, and Lockwood.
Appleton, Sheldon, Leavitt, and Allen.
Carleton, Putnam, Mason, and Widdleton.
Ivison, Phinney, Fowler, and Wells.
Hurd, Houghton, Derby, and Miller.

———

To what extent, or in what degree, is the negro a Man of Melody? Knows he aught of the Laws of Harmony? of the Principles of Cadence? of the Rules of Rhythm? Have his acoustic organs ever been enraptured by the Music of the Spheres? Was he ever, even for a moment, the Pupil of any one of the Tuneful Nine? Is he a Pianist? an Organist? a Player upon the Harp? Has he ever composed an Opera? an Oratorio? an Overture? Has he ever charmed the Heart with his Fantasias? with his Recitatives? Has he ever delighted the Soul with his Symphonies? with his Madrigals? Where may be heard his Choruses? his Trios? his Duets? his Divertisements? Is he the author, or is he the setter to music, of Psalms and Hymns and Spiritual Songs? Has he ever planned or prepared a Chaunt in honor of Jehovah? an anthem in praise of the Almighty? a Doxology in Thanksgiving to God? an Hosanna to the Lord? Has he ever arranged even a single Note in Exaltation of the Most High? Does he possess one grain of knowledge about the Breve? the Semibreve? the Minim? the Crochet? the Quaver? the Semiquaver? the Demisemiquaver?

White Men only, such men, for instance, as those whose names are sounded below, have become, and none but White Men can become justly Distinguished

MUSICIANS AND COMPOSERS.

Jubal, Asaph, Herman, and Jeduthon.
Amphion, Arion, Alcman, and Orpheus.
Verdi, Donizetti, Scarlatti, and Zingarelli.
Bellini, Piccini, Clementi, and Martini.
Rossini, Cherubini, Perti, and Pitoni.
Jomelli, Agostini, Sarti, and Rastrelli.
Durante, Ximines, Perez, and Yriarte.
Rameau, Herold, Miquel, and Monsigny.
Halevy, Mehul, Berlioz, and Auber.
Handel, Haydn, Himmel, and Hummel.
Mozart, Schubert, Bach, and Albrechtsberger.
Beethoven, Kalkbrenner, Ries, and Mitzler.
Gluck, Chotek, Dussek, and Döhler.
Mendelssohn, Weysc, Krug, and Kucken.
Meyerbeer, Bendix, Meyer, and Beyer.
Weber, Wiegel, Lobe, and Lortzing.
Thalberg, Flotow, Wagner, and Schneider.
Liszt, Radziwill, Pychowsky, and Chopin.
Gottschalk, Strakosh, Bergmann, and Anschutz.
Purcell, Morley, Arne, and Atwood.
Lawes, Hayes, Kemp, and Carey.
Callcott, Crotch, Nares, and Tomkins.
Tallis, Dibdin, Croft, and Ravenscroft.
Onslow, Weldon, Greene, and Pierson.
Balfe, Wallace, Burney, and Bennett.
Fry, Willis, Mason, and Bristow.
Dwight, Root, Foster, and Fridell.
Woodbury, Kingsley, Sanderson, and Patterson.

Nor is it alone in Instrumental Music, nor in the more Solemn or Sacred Offices of the Voice, that the negro has shown himself an indifferent Producer of Strains— an Effector of sorry Sounds.   No Bard is he, nor Troubadour, nor Minnesinger.   Nothing knows he of the Carol, of the Ballad, of the Lay, nor even of the Lullaby.   Yet, have we not heard of him as a Minstrel?   Yes ; but he is a Minstrel only in Name ; not in Reality.   It is his White Superiors only, who (under the counterfeit of the blackness of lampblack) have created a somewhat Popular Interest in a Species of Entertainment miscalled Ethiopian Minstrelsy.   In order to reach the low level of the negro's Musical Tastes and Abilities (if, alas! we must go *down* instead of *up*) it is necessary for us to descend from Psalmody to Love Songs, from Operas to Ditties, and from Organs and Pianos to Reed-whistles and Jews-harps.   White Persons only, such persons, for instance, as those whose names are here noised abroad, have been known, and none but White Persons can be known, as justly Celebrated

MALE SINGERS.

Farinelli, Naldi, Redi, and Benelli.
Stradella, Rubini, Mongini, and Graziani.
Tamburini, Everardi, Brizzi, and Brignoli.
Mario, Ronconi, Garcia, and Pandolfini.
Nourrit, Duprez, Millex, and Santley.
Mantius, Wurda, Krebs, and Reichel.
Formes, Raff, Blum, and Pischeck.
Incledon, Braham, Reeves, and Linley.

———

Nor yet may we forbear Disclosure of the African's Poverty of Sweet Accents—the Ethiopian's Undisciplined

and Discordant Inflexions of Voice.   Alike ignorant is he
of both the Symbols and the Tones of Music.   Scarcely
has he heard, nothing has he learned, of the Diatonic and
Chromatic Scales.   What knows he of the Tenor? of the
Treble? of the Bass? of the Barytone? of the Alto? of
the Falsetto? of the Soprano?   Of these, indeed, as of
the Gamut, the negro knows little more than knows the
goose.   And, as of the black man, so of the black woman.
Not creditably known is she, nor can she be creditably
known, as a Chantress, as a Songstress, as a' Cantatrice,
as a Prima Donna.   White Persons only, such persons,
for instance, as those whose names are trilled in this
connection, have become, and none but White Persons
can become, Meritorious and Favorite

FEMALE VOCALISTS.

Grisi, Alboni, Patti, and Persiani.
Lotti, Crurelli, Berini, and Bondini.
La Grua, Mara, Pasta, and Gordosa.
Piccolomini, Lessi, Zucchi, and Galetti.
Volpini, Catalani, Morensi, and Biscaccianti.
Malibran, Castellan, Ugalde, and Novello.
Viardot, Artot, Devrient, and Damoreau.
Lind, Laborde, Schechner, and Schebest.
Sontag, Colson, Weinlich, and Van Zandt.
Rudersdorf, Murska, Lutzer, and Tietjens.
Schroeder, Kreutisch, Bettelheim, and Heinefetter.
Hayes, Bishop, Pyne, and Thillon.
Paton, Austin, Shaw, and Sherreff.
Galton, Stanesby, Robinson, and Phillips.
Kellogg, Whiting, Hauck, and Hinckley.

———

As a Stage-Player, is it possible for the negro to perform well in any character higher than the Harlequin or

the Buffoon—to the perfect acting of either of which, however, he would only need to be natural? Would not the very donning of Sock or Buskin on his part, partake correspondingly of the Absurdity of Boots or Breeches on a Monkey? Yet, in addition to his fitness to appear in either or both of the characters just named, he might, perchance, gain applause as a Personator of one of his most Distinguished Relatives in America—the "What Is It?" at Barnum's. Still, White Men only, such men, for instance, as those whose names are here announced, have been, and none but White Men can be, justly Celebrated

ACTORS.

Susarion, Bathyllus, Pylades, and Roscius.
Talma, Poisson, Larrivée, and Larnette.
Desforges, Rouvière, Suette, and Devrient.
Iffland, Schroeder, Wolf, and Dohring.
Bingley, Dewitzer, Haase, and Seydelmann.
Fechter, Beil, Beck, and Boekh.
Hendrichs, Esslair, Baïson, and Baumeister.
Cibber, Alleyn, Tarleton, and Macklin.
Garrick, Ross, Cooke, and Mountfort.
Kemble, O'Keefe, Quin, and Quick.
Henderson, Palmer, Terry, and Mossop.
Siddons, Dogget, Liston, and Elliston.
Macready, Emery, Yates, and Wigan.
Kean, Bernard, Miller, and Fawcett.
Buckstone, Collier, Reeve, and Robson.
Wallack, Burton, Sothern, and Wheatley.
Forrest, Murdoch, Booth, and Baker.
Hackett, Holston, Stone, and Clarke.

All the way have we come, (or we are now coming,) from the Philosopher to the Fiddler, having seen men earnestly engaged in almost every important Calling or Vocation, and yet, in nothing have we found the African equaling the Caucasian. Such, with reference to the negro, is the state of things now; it has always been so; and, as it was in the past, and as it is in the present, so will it ever continue to be in the future. Inferiority and Despicableness are the very Groundwork of the negro's Nature ; and, for these Fate-fixed Misfortunes, he can find no permanent Remedy nor Relief, save only in the utter Extinction of his Race. White Men only, such men, for instance, as those whose names are thrummed below, have been known, and none but White Men can be known, as Genius-favored and First-rate

VIOLINISTS.

Paganini, Viotti, Campagnoli, and Raimondi.
Corelli, Gemimiami, Sivori, and Tartini.
Nardini, Bazzini, Rolla, and Pinto.
Giardini, Lolli, Polledro, and Pixis.
Jullien, Sainton, Mayas, and Molique.
Allard, Boucher, Beriot, and Baillot.
Vieuxtemps, Leonard, Rode, and Remeny.
Kreutzer, Romberg, Proch, and Bohm.
Sphor, Griebel, Mayseder, and Reichardt.
Hauser, Hansel, Schon, and Stamitz.
Mollenhauer, Bull, Konski, and Lipinski.
Hohnstock, Blumenthal, Ernst, and Speyer.
Eichler, Foder, Maurer, and Steinberg.
Eckart, Gerke, Stor, aad Gassner.
Shuttleworth, Mangold, Fisher, and Corbett.

In the list of the Names of Female Vocalists, we have already had before us some evidences of the brilliant and fascinating Merits of the White Man's Sister. Can anything be fitly said or shown in behalf of the Black Man's Daughter? Is Dinah Beautiful? is she Good? is she True? We know that she is not Fair. Alas! how unfortunate for all the black and bi-colored Races of Mankind, who have it not in their power to boast of the companionship of a Fair Sex! Is Dinah Graceful? is she Attractive? is she Lovely? It is but too obvious that she is no Pattern of Feminine Elegance or Refinement; no Prototype of Lady-like Accomplishments. Is Dinah known in the World of Fashion? in the Rounds of Etiquette? in the Circles of Good Society? Certain it is that she has never been celebrated for her Modesty; for her Maidenhood; for her Matronship. Have the poets ever measured her as a Blue-eyed Belle? a Bonny Lass? a Blushing Bride? Her Auburn Hair, her Flaxen Curls, her Golden Tresses—where are they? Alas, for dusky Dinah! the bewitching Locks and Ringlets, the heart-moving Eye-brows and Eye-lashes, which, with White Damsels, are universal Appurtenances of Beauty, are, with her, quite as scarce as hens' teeth! Has any one ever seen her Rosy Cheeks, her Daisy Dimples, her Cherry Lips? No love-sick serenader has ever sung the praises of her Snowy Neck, her Alabaster Shoulders, her Lily Hands. Who, if any one, since the birth of time, has beheld her Well-proportioned Waist? her Delicately-shaped Ankles? her Prettily-rounded Insteps? It is said that her armpits, (to say nothing of other malodorous parts of her person—her feet, for instance,) are more rank than the billy-goat! Would it be possible to introduce her into a Parlor, or to present her in a Drawing-Room, without the danger of stinking every one else out of it?

In all seriousness, the Negress, like the Negro, is a notorious nuisance; and it is now getting to be high time

that both she and he should be so effectually and finally
abated, as that the earth may never again be darkened
by the presence of either the one or the other. White
persons only, such persons, for instance, as those whose
names are lisped below, have been known, and none
but White Persons can be known, as truly Estimable and

DISTINGUISHED WOMEN.

Sarah, Rebekah, Miriam, and Deborah.
Rachel, Abigail, Huldah, and Hannah.
Naomi, Ruth, Esther, and Judith.
Mary, Martha, Salome, and Priscilla.
Helen, Hypatia, Sappho, and Penelope.
Artemisia, Berenice, Zenobia, and Cleopatra.
Cornelia, Lucretia, Julia, and Virginia.
Octavia, Paulina, Ildico, and Isabella.
Boadicea, Elizabeth, Anne, and Victoria.
Catharine, Maria Theresa, and Maria Louise.
Maddalena Fernandez, and Marianne Martinez.
Constanza Monti, and Louiza Conti.
Eleonora Fonseca, and Adelaide Ristori.
Cecilia Arrom, and Grace Aguilar.
Joan of Arc, and Jeannie Hachette.
Philippone Roland, and Annie Dacier.
Hortense Beauharnais, and Sophie Grouchy.
Pauline Guizot, and Marie Dudevant.
Frances D'Arblay, and Lætitia Barbault.
Chantal Sévigné, and Henriette Castleneau.
Joanna Baillie, and Charlotte Brontë.
Rosa Bonheur, and Octavia LeVert.
Harriet Martineau, and Lydia Sigourney.
Louise de Staël, and Julianna Krüdener.
Margaret Klopstock, and Amelia Von Schoppe.
Ida Pheiffer, and Ida Hahn-Hahn.
Frederika Bremer, and Jenny Lind.

Electrina Freiberg, and Anette Hülshoff.
Louisa Muhlbach, and Margaret Van Eyck.
Jane Swisshelm, and Caroline Chisholm.
Angelina Grimke, and Lee Hentz.
Hannah More, and Mary Mitford.
Stuart Wortley, and Wortley Montague.
Jane Taylor, and Jane Grey.
Cowden Clarke, and Barrett Browning.
Felicia Hemans, and Letitia Landon.
Maria Edgeworth, and Eliza Cook.
Amelia Opie, and Mary Howitt.
Florence Nightingale, and Grace Darling.
Burdett Coutts, and Elizabeth Fry.
Eleanor Franklin, and Priscella Wakefield.
Agnes Strickland, and Anne Kemble.
Martha Washington, and Abigail Adams.
Dolly Payne, and Margaret Mercer.
Catharine Sedgwick, and Maria McIntosh.
Josepha Hale, and Margaret Fuller.
Annie Lynch, and Mercy Warren.
Emma Southworth, and Emma Willard.
Alice and Phœbe Carey, and Julia Howe.
Catharine Beecher, and Beecher Stowe.
Mattie Griffith, and Amelia Welby.
Lydia Child, and Eliza Follen.
Maria Chapman, and Elizabeth Stanton.
Eliza Leslie, and Lucretia Mott.
Cora Ritchie, and Elizabeth Ellet.
Charlotte Cushman, and Ann Stephens.
Hannah Gould, and Frances Osgood.
Caroline Kirkland, and Caroline Gilman.
Estelle Lewis, and Alice Neal.
Eliza Farnham, and Mary Dennison.
Anna Dickinson, and Clara Barton.
Dorothea Dix, and Annie Andrews.

Jessie Fremont, and Susan Warner.
Abigail Dodge, and Harriet Prescott.
Virginia Terhune, and Sarah Lippincott.
Augusta Evans, and Caroline Chesebro.

———

Parallels between the enterprising and progressive spirit of the Whites, and the stupidity and uselessness of the Blacks, might be drawn almost *ad infinitum.* In whatever sphere of human action we may, anywhere or at any time, be pleased to move, there will we invariably find the Africans, if we find them at all, at the very feet of their Caucasian superiors—or, if not at the feet, loitering so far in the rear as never to be able to overtake even the hindermost of the Whites who have surpassed them. A thousand and one employments are insufficient to satisfy the bold and restless activity of the Anglo-Saxon. It would appear that the African experiences an excess of contentment in having ignored every other pursuit than that of raising pumpkins!

We know how greatly white men have distinguished themselves in all the high callings of life; and that, in many of these callings, no negro's head nor hand, even as the least possible agent, has ever been seen. Not among Presidents, Emperors, nor Kings; not among Statesmen, Orators, nor Heroes; not among Poets, Historians, nor Jurists; not among Naturalists, Moralists, nor Metaphysicians; not among the devotees of Literature, of the Arts, nor of Science; not among Farmers, Inventors, nor Engineers; not among Merchants, Manufacturers, nor Mechanics; not among Bankers, Millionaires, nor Philanthropists—not among any of these, nor among others of corresponding merits and renown, have we found, nor can we find, the Ethiopian a shining light. We might extend our investigations to many other depart-

16

ments of human concern and progress; but the results, in
every case, so honorable to the Whites, and so disgraceful
to the Blacks, would be the same. Fully assured of this,
and deeply impressed with the significance and force of
the assurance, it is difficult to withstand the temptation
to offer, in support of the fact, new proofs in close connection with those already adduced. Let us, therefore,
by cursory examination, or by brief inquiry, ascertain, if
we can, whether the negroes have ever been, or whether
it is possible for them ever to be, able and distinguished.

INSURERS, UNDERWRITERS;

Such Insurers, such Underwriters, for instance, as
those whose names are here appended :

Depeyster, Dantignac, Geroux, and Paulmier.
Luqueer, Didier, Despard, and Delamater.
Ostrander, Bierwirth, Habicht, and Van Norden.
Uhlhorn, Rokenbaugh, Bancker, and Bleecker.
Angerstein, Hilger, Kahl, and Teneyck.
Wesendonck, Bouck, Keeler, and Michelbacker.
Pell, Griffith, Knevitt, and McDonald.
Hoxie, Clarkson, Corning, and Comstock.
Lathrop, Lambert, Hone, and Neilson.
Martin, Willmarth, Oakley, and Hibbard.
Winston, Briston, Lyman, and Underhill.
Satterlee, Satterthwaite, Cocks, and Condict.
Valter, Bigelow, Jones, and Seaver.
Reese, Huntington, Walker, and Waddington.
Ward, Savage, Platt, and Pratt.
Hope, Cobb, Howell, and Halsted.
Lathers, Winans, Stokes, and Collins.
Harriott, Benson, Thorne, and Churchill.
Pinkney, Graham, Hodges, and Stansbury.
Brokaw, Barker, Laing, and Skidmore.

Have the negroes ever been, or can they ever be, enterprising and successful

EXPRESSMEN?

Such Expressmen, for instance, as those whose names are here given:

Adams, Berford, Williams, and Wescott.
Butterfield, Freeman, Lansing, and Pullen.
Wells, Fargo, Kinsley, and Clarke.
Carrington, Studley, Farnsworth, and Fitzgerald.
Harnden, Dodd, Reeves, and Lockwood.

———

Have the negroes ever been, is it possible for them ever to be, popular and prosperous

AUCTIONEERS?

Such Auctioneers, for instance, as those whose names are cried below:

Tattersall, Wrigglesworth, Chadwick, and Galsworthy.
Humphreys, Robins, Hammond, and Hawkins.
Croxford, Underhay, Tindale, and Southgate.
Billinghurst, Gowland, Hatch, and Hichborn.
Henshaw, Leonard, Phinney, and Mortimer.
Nicolay, Schenck, Herts, and Muller.
Draper, Haggerty, Bangs, and Merwin.
Wilmerdings, Mount, Bogart, and Haydock.
Leeds, Ludlow, Miner, and Fairchild.
Bleecker, Mathewson, Gaffney, and Townsend.

———

Never having been, is it possible for the negro ever to be, honorable or distinguished

BROKERS?

Such Brokers, for instance, as those whose names are here mentioned:

Fordyce, Overend, Barker, and Little.
Parmelee, Wenman, Stokes, and Thomson.
Beebe, Montgomery, Hawley, and Smalley.
Saltonstall, Bulkley, Strong, and Norton.
Bayliss, Conant, Dow, and Drake.
Rathbone, Earle, Woodbridge, and Dunderdale.
Caswell, Haskell, Waddell, and Maxwell.
Harding, Merritt, Bedell, and Southwick.
Hazen, Hallet, Boyd, and Brower.
Rawlings, Sandersen, Stebbins, and Studdiford.

———

Have the negroes ever been, is it in their nature ever to be, Zealous and Self-denying

MISSIONARIES?

Such Missionaries, for instance, as those whose names are here recorded; earnest, well-meaning men, who, regardless alike of the inevitable hardships and perils of " Greenland's icy mountains," of " India's coral strand," of "Africa's sunny fountains," and of other inhospitable and benighted regions, have gone forth, without the expectation of any manner of earthly reward, and with the willingness to sacrifice their own lives, if necessary, in promoting the temporal and eternal welfare of strangers:

Xavier, Ignatius, Regna, and Las Casas.
Valverde, Fernandez, Olmedo, and Pasco.
Gerbillon, Biart, Carheil, and Le Clerc.
Huc, Labot, Lafore, and Le Jeune.
Despard, Bounard, Ralle, and Fouquet.

Dobritzhoffer, Gutzlaff, Ausgar, and Zerbe.
Willibrod, Winifred, Visdelow, and Rebmann.
Schoffler, Schneider, Kircher, and Kanouse.
Van Lennep, Van Doren, Van Dusen, and Van Meter.
Cary, Gardner, Forde, and Sterling.
Livingstone, Brownlee, Moffat, and Maidment.
Eliot, Tenant, Bliss, and Brainerd.
Judson, Morrison, Rankin, and Hitchcock.
Scudder, Ward, Shuck, and Wiley.
Apthorp, Lyman, Bradley, and Bardwell.
Kidder, Fletcher, Carrow, and Goodfellow.

———

To the Whites, to the Men of Might and Merit, thousands of ways are ever open, or opening, for the realization of honorable and substantial distinction. If they find it too difficult to achieve success in the regular roads or rounds of life, their versatility of talent, their energy and their perseverance, will, in due time, secure to them prosperity in new and unbeaten paths. No amount of opposition, no number of disappointments, no combination of reverses, can turn them aside from the straight forwardness of their course, nor swerve them a hair's breadth from faithful adherence to the respective duties which devolve upon them in their multifarious pursuits. With manly nerve and fixedness of purpose, forward they go, eventually overcoming all obstacles, and in a manner, as it would seem, in certain cases, winning or wringing friendship and favors from even Fate itself! If not prominent in one of the fifty-odd normal vocations which we have already examined, we shall assuredly find them conspicuous and thrifty in some other career.

It may be a matter of little moment to the reader to know how much time I have spent in preparing the more elaborate of the foregoing Lists of Celebrities ; but if he will himself similarly arrange, in regular order, the names of two or three score of the respective leaders of a few of the other departments of human enterprise and progress, he will have acquired a somewhat adequate knowledge of the labor;—a labor so tedious and perplexing that he will, I dare say, heartily tire of it before he finishes a single page. Let his subjects, for instance, be Teachers, Instructors ; Linguists ; Hunters ; Fishers ; Preparers and Venders of Good Medicines ; Wine-Makers, Brewers, and Distillers ;—or whatever other subjects he may prefer ; and, in writing down the names, let him pay due attention to Universality, Nationality, Chronology, and Euphony, not unfrequently, however, prudently yielding one consideration to another, and having almost incessantly to contend with numerous claims and counter-claims for precedence of mention, and he will very soon learn, at the cost of much wear and worriment of mind, that his undertaking is no easy task.

As already explained, it was for the purpose of exhibiting the varied and sublime greatness of the Caucasians in contrast with the pitiable and predestined nothingness of the negroes, that I undertook the compilation of the brilliant array of names embraced within the limits of this chapter. Hundreds of times, in the course of my labors, have I had occasion to regret profoundly, that, so far as I know, there has never been published a biographical dictionary based upon any plan similar to the one here adopted. Had I been able to find such a work, well-arranged and complete, it would, indeed, have saved me a great deal of strenuous thought and research.

Fully persuaded am I that when a majority of the more worthy and discriminating people of the United States shall have minutely examined the many important branches of speculative and productive industry which have, from time immemorial, engaged men's minds and hands, and when they find that no negro has ever been, and further, that no negro ever can be, a chief actor in any respectable calling, they will at once come to the just conclusion, that, even in the estimation of the great and good God himself, no less than in the estimation of the right-thinking portion of mankind, the Africans, like all the other swarthy races now inhabiting the earth, are fit, and fit only, for unexceptive and immediate fossilization. Like the Mastodon, the Mylodon, the Megatherium, and other extinct animals, the Ethiopians belong to a preterlapsed age; and any attempt to prolong the tenure of their incommodious and pernicious existence among us is, as I firmly believe, not only an atrocious crime against the great body of the Whites, but also a proceeding of most indecent and impious opposition to the will of Heaven.

Yet to men of good sense there still remains this supreme consolation, that from the pure and necessary fiats of the Almighty there is, and can be, no appeal; and that among those fiats is one which declares, in tones as if issuing from Sinai itself, that the insignificant ends for which the black and bi-colored races of mankind were created, have been fulfilled; and that these effete races must, therefore, now disappear from the face of the whole earth, leaving it free and clean, henceforth and forever, for the exclusive occupancy and control of their Caucasian betters.

Fools and knaves of the worst possible type are those short-witted and hypocritical blatherskites of the Black Congress, and their silly satellites, who, alternately howling and whining in the interest of the accursed negroes, are incessantly crying out "no aversion to color," "no prejudice against color," "no disability on account of color"—as if, forsooth, color was the only matter or thing of difference and dispute! With this absurd outcry against the natural and rightful disposition of the white man to abominate the most abominable of all bad colors, the Black Republicans hope to divert public attention from a majority of the real issues, and thereby to gain time for the further prosecution of their infamous designs. Fortunately, however, there is not the least danger that the American people will, for any considerable length of time, permit themselves to be hoodwinked in that way.

Rejecting all mere partisan statements, and relying alone on their own good sense and sight, the intelligent white citizens of the United States will soon subject the negro to a most rigid and thorough scrutiny; and then, seeing him exactly as he is, and convinced that he is an exceedingly heterogeneous and unworthy element in our Republic, they will at once assign to him his proper place —a place within the limits of some foreign land—and thither it will be prudent for him to repair without delay.

As has already been shown in many of the preceding pages, quite obvious and abundant are evidences of the fact that the negro is a widely-different and very inferior sort of man. A close and critical examination of him will reveal not only his loathsome color,—his base and black complexion—but there will also be repulsively apparent his woolly hair; his receding forehead; his dense skull; his depressed nose; his mucous-dripping nostrils; his protruding tongue; his slobbering mouth; his thick lips; his retreating chin; his swayed back; his ungainly belly; his colossal buttocks; his calfless legs; his projecting heels; his flat feet; his slow gait; his imbecile mind; his idle disposition; his drowsy propensities; his vile stench; his filthy habits;—and numerous other characteristics equally mean and contemptible.

Yet, of all these last-mentioned defects and disadvantages—natural defects and disadvantages which almost invariably show themselves in the negro—the two-thirds majority of the Black Congress, and other Black Republicans, would have us lose sight entirely. The atrocious game which these demagogical and unprincipled white men are now trying to play is, in some of its features, not unlike that of the incendiary, who, immediately after committing arson in one part of the city, runs swiftly in an opposite direction, bawling out, at the very top of his voice, Fire! Fire! Fire! Tallying with this ruse of the incendiary to conceal and to mystify an evil purpose and a guilty action, is the strategical alarm-cry of the Black Republicans, who, in order to shield themselves for a while longer, from the overwhelming responsibilities of having become the apologists and the excusers of the bastard and devil-begotten blacks, are now, in the bass tones of a big bull-frog, vociferously bellowing out, Color! Color! Color!

High time is it that the deceitfulness and trickery of this color cry of the two-thirds majority of the Black Congress, and of other Black Republicans, should be unmeasuredly exposed, denounced, reprobated. No longer must the clamorous and canting clowns of the Black Congress, nor their coarse-mouthed coadjutors, be permitted to cover or screen their deep-dyed complicity with the crimes of an accursed race, by the jargon-like or frog-like cry of Color! Color! Color! Their persistent attempts to blind the eyes of the public to the true state of things, by the loud and constant babbling of their silly protests touching Color, constitute a species of evasion and subterfuge which, considering the fatal consequences that might result from such miserable shifts and sophistries, should at once brand every one of them with life-long infamy. Bad as is the color of the negro, (and how

16*

very bad it is we have already seen in two of the preceding chapters, entitled respectively, "Black; a Thing of Ugliness, Disease, and Death," "White; a Thing of Life, Health, and Beauty,") yet that is only one of more than a hundred of other notoriously vile and detestable qualities of his nature.

Holding in view the highest and best interests of this continent at large, we White Republicans, in affiliation with the Loyal Democrats, mean to look at these things fairly and squarely, and to take action accordingly. We mean to take the Government of the United States of America entirely out of the hands of the Black Congress, and to elect a new Congress—a White Congress—of far more capacity, respectability, and honor. It is our determination that even the separate States themselves, the counties and the cities, aye, and the small towns, too, shall, erelong and forever, cease to be controlled by Black Republicans. With as little delay as possible, we mean to overhaul all the unconstitutional legislation of the Black Congress, (chiefly its legislation since February, 1866,) and either repeal it altogether, or so modify it as to make it conform to the everlasting principles of Nature, Truth, and Justice. We mean to open the way for the early ingress into the Southern States of hundred of thousands of white immigrants from New England, from the Middle States, from Europe, (especially from Germany,) and from other parts of the enlightened world—the more the better—and we are resolved that the negroes and the hybrids, the blacks and the browns, of all races, nations, tongues, and tribes, (all of them, without any manner of exception,) shall soon find an eternal exit from every part and parcel of our common country.

In order to accomplish, within a reasonable length of time, these prudent and beneficent purposes, it is our intention, after we shall have taken the reins of government into our own hands, to offer to the negroes, and to other persons of impure and pestilential presence, during a limited period of years, liberal premiums or inducements to take themselves, at once and forever, out of our way; that is to say, to emigrate to Africa, or to some other foreign and far-distant land, never, under any circumstances whatever, to return to America. If necessary, we mean to place the sum of fifty or sixty dollars, more or less, at the disposition of every negro in this country, who may wish to avail of it in that way; and also, in certain cases, an ample supply of agricultural implements. But, what if the negroes, manifesting and proving anew their inherent destiny to be, everywhere and at all times, so long as they survive, a common nuisance, should refuse the offer, and decline to go? In that case we intend to provide the requisite means, and to fix a time within which such means shall be used or employed, for securing their absence by main force. But even prior to the fixing of the time here referred to, and in the hope of being able to avoid the necessity of having to fix it at all—so far as we ourselves are concerned—we mean to bring to bear upon the negroes certain very suggestive and salutary lessons.

Not only do we mean to hire, and have about us, white persons only, but, with due regard to public decency and general morality, we mean that all our white neighbors and countrymen shall do so likewise. We mean that, after the lapse of a certain time hereafter to be determined and promulgated, every negro, (or other non-white,) still remaining in the country, shall pay into the national treasury a special fine, or an extra tax, of not less than one hundred dollars per annum; and that every white person who employs a negro, or who even tolerates a negro on or about his premises, whether as servant, tenant, or in whatever other capacity, shall pay into the national treasury, for each and every such negro, (or other non-white,) a special fine, or an extra tax, of not less than two hundred dollars per annum. From all hotels, restaurants, boarding-houses, and other similar establishments, whether public or private, in which negroes, (or other non-whites,) are employed, it shall also be a particular duty with us to withhold our patronage and support.

Meanwhile, even before the arrival of the time when it shall have become feasible and convenient for us to oust or deport the negroes from all sections of our country, we mean to dislodge them entirely from our cities and towns. Whether by persuasion or by force, they must all soon go into the agricultural districts; and upon the same just principles that we remove the Indians westwardly, along the paths and the by-ways of extinction, so also will we remove the negroes southwardly, along the stratums and the streams of fossilizing properties.

CHAPTER X.

SPANISH AND PORTUGUESE AMERICA.

However our present interests may restrain us within our own limits, it is impossible not to look forward to distant times, when our rapid multiplication will expand itself beyond those limits, and cover the whole northern, if not the southern continent, with a people speaking the same language, governed in similar forms and by similar laws ; nor can we contemplate with satisfaction either blot or mixture on that surface.—JEFFERSON.

Whoever is afraid of submitting any question, civil or religious, to the test of free discussion, is more in love with his own opinion than with truth.—RICHARD WATSON.

Our planet, before the age of written history, had its races of savages, like the generations of sour paste, or the animalcules that wriggle and bite in a drop of putrid water. Who cares for these or for their wars? We do not wish a world of bugs nor of birds ; neither afterward of Scythians, Caribs, nor Feejees.—RALPH WALDO EMERSON.

THE Spanish and Portuguese discovery and settlement of South America were so nearly simultaneous with the Saxon and Anglo-Saxon discovery and settlement of North America, that the difference in time is, in the general history of such grand achievements, a mere bagatelle. Yet it is a fact well established in the annals of the greater part of the four last centuries, that the daring countrymen and kinsmen of Columbus took precedence of all the Germanic races, both in the finding of new countries and in the planting of colonies in the western hemisphere.

The first important European conquests in America, such, for instance, as those of Mexico and Peru, were Spanish conquests, and the first cities and towns which were built in America, after European models, were built by the Spaniards. Even in our own country, the oldest town of which we can boast, Saint Augustine, in Florida, is of Spanish origin, it having been founded by a company of Castilians during the reign of Philip II., in 1565.

Seventy-eight years before the Dutch settled New York, the Spaniards had settled Buenos Ayres; that is to say, the city of New York was founded in 1612; the city of Buenos Ayres in 1534.

Not only Buenos Ayres, but also Lima, Rio de Janeiro, and other important seaports in South America, were settled before we had any permanent settlement in North America.

Yet how often, in speaking of the primitive manners of the people, the lack of progress, the backwardness of civilization in South America, as compared with the present advanced condition of mankind in North America, do we not hear the former excused on account of their alleged youth and inexperience! How preposterous! The elder, under a species of self-deception, claiming to be the younger! The shriveled matron, who became a mother many, many years ago, coquettishly setting up pretensions to beauty and attractions eclipsive of the charms of her own blooming and buxom daughter of sweet sixteen!

Of what is not true let us hear no more. The absurdity of these claims for the newness of the Spanish and Portuguese settlements in South America, in contrast with the Saxon and Anglo-Saxon settlements in North America, is only equaled by the absurdity of the claims which, within the sixty or seventy years last past, have been so frequently advanced for the juvenility of the negro race; as if, forsooth, the evidences were not both palpable and abundant, that the negro race is the oldest and the rudest and the rustiest and the rottenest —indeed, by far the most superannuated and worthless —in all the world.

It is not, therefore, because of priority of settlement

that North America has so greatly surpassed South America in agriculture, commerce and manufactures ; in science, literature and art ; no, certainly not because of priority of settlement, for, as we have already seen, South America was settled first. Nor is the reason to be found either in the climate or in the soil ; for these, upon a general average, are good alike.

Yet for the difference which obtains here, as indeed for every other difference in the universe, there is a good and sufficient reason ; and for the very important reason connected with this difference, it behooves us to look further. The real reason, then, if tell it we must, the real reason is a Reason of Race, or rather of races, for there are many races in South America ; and all except one— all except the white race—have long since ceased to be the creatures of a useful existence.

Connected with this Reason of Race, which is the primary and principal reason of the comparatively unprosperous condition of Spanish and Portuguese America, there is also a Reason of Religion, which, though but secondary and attendant, is nevertheless very powerful, not for good, but for evil ; and toward this latter reason we are now approaching.

Within the circle of human agencies, events occur thus and so, pro and con, not merely because men are men, but because they are men of a certain sort—because they are men who, in their physical, mental and moral constitutions, are, by nature, under the control of irresistibly powerful and specific differences. It is safe to say, therefore, that in all the particulars wherein mankind are affected, whether affected momentously or but slightly, whether affected gloriously or ingloriously, Race, whether characterized by positive or by negative peculiarities, whether acting or acted upon, has more or less to do in inducing the change of condition.

North America is strong and influential, great and good, because a large majority of its inhabitants are unmixedly white—Caucasians of pure descent. South America is comparatively feeble and insignificant, unprosperous and bad, because a very large majority of its inhabitants are black and bi-colored—negroes, Indians and hybrids.

With the exception of the Hottentots, the Bushmen, and a few of the other incomparably stolid peoples of Africa, almost all the races of mankind, regardless alike of color and habitat, are susceptible of certain impressions which, naturally indulged, lead to moral convictions. The convictions thus formed are, in most cases, so rigidly observed as to be adopted into systems of faith and practice which, considered collectively, are called Religion.

Of the different religions which, in this maner, have been organized and promulgated (each in its turn, solemnly recommended by its respective devotees as affording the only sure means of eternal salvation!) there are, at the present time, in all the world, not less than one thousand. This, however, is a very small number in comparison with those which have flourished, waned, decayed, died out, and disappeared forever.

Very unfortunately, indeed, most of the merit which manifested itself in the unwritten inception of many of these religions was lost in the process of reducing the religions themselves to such propositions, plain or abstruse, as was thought to be necessary to render them sufficiently intelligible, interesting and acceptable to others.

Even the most enlightened and progressive of the white races, governed respectively by such lofty, and profound powers of mind as the Almighty has been pleased to grant them, have chosen for themselves, to say the least, numerous widely-different and debatable modes of worship.

All the religions which are now obsolete were either false or ill-founded ; and some of them passed away only with the nations that foolishly adhered to them. And as, in this respect, it has been heretofore, so it may possibly be hereafter. This reflection may, with peculiar force and significance, come home to the Italians, the Spaniards, the Portuguese, and other peoples of the south of Europe, and their descendants, who, with a blind and bigoted zeal, are clinging to a religion which is every whit as spurious and nonsensical as Judaism or Mahometanism on the one hand, or as Buddhism or Brahminism on the other.

The very worst system of religion which has fallen to the lot of any of the white races, has been ardently embraced and tenaciously retained by the Spaniards. Yet irrational and ridiculous as is the religion of the Spaniards, it is far, very far, from being so irrational and ridiculous as the best of the religions of the black races.

The Fetichers, who are negroes, prostrate themselves in adoration before snakes and sticks and stocks and stones. The Brahmins, who are East Indians, with a species of impressively solemn and awful reverence, kneel down before white elephants and other light-colored beasts, in the bodies of which they most firmly but fatuitously believe that the spirits of their great-great-grandfathers have found blissful tenancy ! The preposterousness of this religion is, however, somewhat relieved in the fact that its foolish followers are, after all, sufficiently wise not to believe that the body of any *black* beast could ever afford, or would ever be desired to afford, lodgment to the soul of any person whomsoever! The Catholics, who are Italians, Spaniards, Portuguese, South Americans, and others, worship men and women and effigies and statues and pictures. People possessed of well-balanced minds, that is to say, people endowed with the prime gift of common sense, such people, for instance, as are to be found in Germany, Switzerland, Sweden, Denmark, Holland, Great Britain, North America, and elsewhere, offer up their devotions to the one only living and true God, and to no other spirit, nor creature, nor thing whatever.

What the Catholic religion is in South America—and it is much the same in every country where, under the forms of law, it is recognized as a co-ordinate power of the government, in other words, where, under legislative enactments, it is succored and maintained as the Religion of the State—has, from time to time, been graphically described by many South Americans themselves, and especially so by a Mr. Vicente Pazos, a native of Peru, who was educated for the priesthood, but who, more than half a century since, becoming thoroughly enlightened as to the superstitions and corruptions of Romanism, manfully renounced, and unmasked anew, the whole system.

It was while the Spanish American colonies were struggling to cast away from themselves the burdens of European domination, that Mr. Pazos, from whose book we shall now quote somewhat at length, wrote a very important series of "Letters on the United Provinces of South America, addressed to the Hon. Henry Clay, Speaker of the House of Representives of the United States of America," detailing, among other matters of special interest, the monstrous and glaring villainies of Catholicism, which were generally practiced at that time, and which, with equal bigotry and hypocrisy, and with no less of perniciousness and infamy, are as generally practiced now.

In the course of his eleventh Letter, commencing on the eighty-third page of the admirable volume of which the title is given in the last preceding paragraph, Mr. Pazos says:

"Among the evils suffered by the Indians, and which has been a source of much unhappiness to them, as well as to all South America, is the Roman Catholic religion, which was introduced among them by the Spaniards. This religion, in countries where it predominates or is connected with the government, is widely different from the same religion as it appears in the United States of America. Instead of being employed, as all religions ought to be, in directing the morals purifying the heart, and restraining the vices of the people, it is so prostituted in Spanish countries that it has become nothing but a mass of superstitious ceremonies, and the instrument of avarice and oppression.

"And in every country, where there is an exclusive religion which is connected with the government, no matter what it is, it will necessarily be intolerant, and become a most tremendous calamity to the people. And it may be questioned, whether in any community the purity of morals can be preserved, without difference of religious sentiment, and those useful checks and balances which the emulation of sectarians is calculated to produce, in adding animation and strength to public virtue. If the reformation of Luther, to which is attributable in a great degree the present progress of light and liberty in the world, is not a complete proof of this truth, the practical lesson afforded by the United States, leaves no doubt that religious liberty and the rivalship of different sects, is the best means of maintaining in their purity the morals of the people.

"Unhappily for South America, the most intolerant of all religions fell to her lot, which made penal every attempt to investigate its character; and, consequently, the hand of reform could never be applied. An exposition of this religion in South America would fill a volume. * * * The bishops, who are three in number, in Peru, including the Archbishop, and four in Rio de la Plata, are generally Europeans. They have annual incomes of from 40,000 to 60,000 dollars, varying according to the amount of tithes. These ecclesiastics, before obtaining their offices, are required to take an oath to preserve these dominions under the Castilian crown, and consequently their first care is to impress upon the minds of the people a blind obedience to the king, who is called the 'Lord's anointed,' and 'Vice-God in the World!' The Bishops, who are learned men, are generally employed in writing homilies for the church for the same object; and the late Archbishop of Charcas, San Alberto, a man of great disinterestedness and charity, and of extraordinary eloquence, employed the power of his pen in composing a Royal Catechism for the use of his diocese, in which he exerted himself to the extent of his abilities to inculcate the doctrine of passive obedience ; and certainly the Brahmins of India could not exceed him in their efforts to establish this slavish doctrine. This catechism has been republished in Rome, and has received the approbation of his Sanctity the Pope, who ordered it to be translated into Italian. This was one of the best of the Peruvian Bishops ; as for the others, they have generally been men of infamous characters.

"The instruction which is given to the Indians by the curates, is to teach them the prayers of the Roman Church, which are said before mass, and to attend mass on the Sabbath. On this day they preach to them one quarter of an hour some abstract doctrine, which the Indians cannot understand. They urge them, particularly when sick, to call in the confessor, and also to send their children to be baptized — the first, not to lose the profits of the burial, and the second, to ascertain the number of children that are born, of which an exact account is kept, in order to know the amount of the poll tax. The census is taken every five years, and, for the reason above mentioned, it may be regarded as accurate. This motive of avarice is the reason why the Indians are persuaded to marry young.

"The Sabbath is a great market day, when the people transact all their business with the Indians, who come from a great distance to attend mass. At the same time, justice is administered to them, and the poll tax collected. * * * The *obvenciones* are one of the modes of obtaining money, which is practiced under the Roman religion. They include benedictions, masses, festivities of Christ, of the Virgin, and the Saints, processions, marriages, funerals, and souls in purgatory. The curates and friars inculcate, with the most ardent zeal, the doing of good works here, in order to be happy hereafter. These good works consist in the festivities before mentioned, and in saying masses. Every mass costs two dollars ; if chanted, the price is double. At Buenos Ayres it is but one dollar. * * * Besides the festivities in honor of the saints in heaven, there are others for souls in purgatory. The second of November in every year is the day appointed by the Romish Church for that festivity. On that day hundreds of monks and priests inundate all the cities, villages, towns, and country chapels, in search of *responsos*, which are 'Pater nosters,' said to liberate souls from purgatory. This service, which occupies but a moment, costs sixpence ; and, although the price is so trifling, it is a source of large income to the priests, as the people universally order *responsos* for their deceased relatives and friends. It is indeed a cheap service to produce such wonderful benefits as liberating souls from the terrible torments of purgatory ! * * * The king of Spain has a part in the sale of bulls, with which he is plentifully supplied by his Holiness the 'Vicar of Christ.' These bulls are billets or drafts of pardon, not only for the sins of the living, but also of the dead. Such, for instance, is the *bula de difuntos*, or bull for the dead, which is paid for according to the rank and wealth of the deceased. The living have the *bulas de cruzada, de lacticinios, de carne*, and *de composicion*. The first, which had its origin in the crusades, is to gain the graces and indulgencies of the Church, the meaning of which I never understood; the second to eat cheese, eggs, and milk, in Lent, and the third, to retain everything obtained by theft or fraud. * * * The business of bulls, which is a branch of public revenue, has in latter times fallen into contempt in Buenos Ayres, and has been abolished; and the people of that city who, ten years ago, believed in their efficacy, now laugh at the imposture. * * * From their religious festivities I now pass to their funerals. The tax levied upon these solemnities is most painful to the Indians, and the most barbarous avarice is displayed in its exaction. The sum which the Indian is obliged to pay is in proportion to his wealth, varying from $5 to $100. His property is narrowly investigated, and the violence of oppression unites to aggravate the afflictions of a man who has lost a father, a brother, or a wife. I have seen the poor Indian weep till his heart was well nigh broken, at the levying of this unjust contribution. But the European curates, whose hearts are harder than the gold they covet, turn a deaf ear to the wailing of the widow, whose children are taken from her, to pay this tax. A religion so abused and transformed into a systematic mode of thieving and robbery, is a calamity more dreadful than a pestilence. * * * The days of public solemnity under the Roman Catholic religion, are those of Corpus Christi, the Holy Thursday, and of the titular saint of every city. For celebrating the day of the Corpus Christi, there are erected sumptuous altars and triumphal arches; and the streets through which the host passes are covered with fine carpets, and strewed with flowers. The altars are very high, and built in a conic form; the upper part is covered with splendid looking-glasses from Germany, artificial flowers made of paper and silk, and beautiful feathers. The lower part is surrounded with steps leading to the table of the sacrament; and which are filled with saints and angels dressed in the richest silks and laces, and profusely decorated with jewels; the whole disposed with great symmetry and taste, and by artists who are educated to the business. Everything rich and rare is employed to beautify these altars and triumphal arches, which display the most gorgeous spectacle to the eye, and at the same time exhibit the immense riches of the country. On the

eve of this festivity, the altars and triumphal arches are hung with
blazing chandeliers of great beauty and value, and the streets are
crowded with people to gaze upon them. * * * Before the procession
the titular saints of every church are carried, which are from twelve
to twenty-five in number in every city.   These saints are all of the
ordinary size of the human figure, except St. Christopher, who, as
the legends tell us, was a giant, and who is generally made about
twelve feet high.   They are all richly dressed and covered with gold
and silver ; they are placed on pedestals of massy silver, each weighing 1,600 ounces at least ; and which is borne on the shoulders of from
40 to 60 Indians.   In the midst of the saints are carried the Virgins
of Carmen, Mercedes and Rosario, which attract much public devotion. * * * It will not be foreign to my purpose to show how this
wealth is accumulated.   The foundation of the monastic institutions
of this country, is the work of piety , as it is called, of rich men, who
bequeath their property to this object for the good of their souls.
This property is made productive, being vested in houses and lands,
yielding a rent which amounts to 5 per cent.   Another principal
source of wealth to these institutions, are the bestowing of alms and
the indulgencies of the Pope.

"The nuns are entirely dead to the world ; and no person can see
them after their initiation, which generally takes place at the age of
eleven.   All their worldly consolation is to augment their riches,
which are enjoyed in common, and employed only to improve and
extend their establishments.   Every nun, upon entering a convent, is
required to bring with her, as her dower, $4,000 (in gold or silver)
which is put into the common fund ; and, besides, they are obliged
to provide a contingent fund to defray their extraordinary expenses.
These dowers, by being rendered productive, have necessarily greatly
augmented their property.   This wealth is employed in various ways,
in rebuilding churches, forming gold and silver utensils for the uses
of religion, and making altars which are of pure silver.   The body of
the patron saint or virgin is ornamented with diamonds and pearls,
collected from all parts of the world, and so profusely, that the body
is literally covered all over with them ; and on the head is a crown of
gold, studded with brilliants and pearls of the highest value.   There
are also two or three sets of this jewelry for the saint, for changes on
particular occasions.   These jewels, when once consecrated to these
holy purposes, can never be converted to any other use ; and for this
reason their accumulation is so great, that it is sufficient to maintain
armies, or to defray the expenditures of a nation.   Such, however,
has been the superstition on the side of both the patriots and the roy-

alists, during the present revolution, that no part of the property of the churches has been touched.

"On a visit which I made to the nunnery of Concebidás, in La Paz I was shown two boxes of four feet and a half long, and two feet broad, filled with doubloons. Indeed the cash and bullion which are buried in these nunneries, is incalculable. * * * As property is not a necessary qualification for the profession of a monk or friar, it is generally embraced by the lower classes of society. In their monastic institutions, everything is provided for their support, and, being the masters of money, they become infamous in their conduct. In their contests for the high places in the Church, they conduct in the most scandalous manner, sometimes resorting to the sword to settle their disputes; and it not unfrequently happens that the soldiery are ordered out to quell their bloody affrays.

"The immense wealth acquired in the modes I have mentioned, is squandered by the monks in the most disgraceful manner, in every kind of debauchery and gross sensuality. Yet, notwithstanding this profusion of the monks, the churches are full of riches."

Again, in his Letters on South America, page 101, Pazos says :

"The curates have large incomes, and consequently live in the most splendid manner ; and it is easy to conceive that young men of fortune, of the first rank and consideration in the community, will readily fall into all manner of immoderate pleasures and dissipation, more especially as they are condemned to perpetual celibacy. This barbarous law, which, warring against the law of nature, plunges all who are subject to its operation into the most shameful disorders, is a fruitful source of vice and immorality among the people. This law of celibacy, which was dictated by the wickedness and corrupt ambition of the Roman court, is the cause of many calamities to Catholic countries ; yet so blind are the people of South America in their prejudices, that, although they well know its injurious operation, they cherish it, with its host of abominations. South America will forever remain ignorant and enslaved, so long as the freedom of religious opinion is restrained, and the institutions of the friars, and the law of clerical celibacy supported. At Buenos Ayres, the abolition of this law has been attempted ; and it was demonstrated that the Pope was only bishop of Rome, and could not interfere with the internal economy of the church, which possessed the right of electing its own pastors. But the clergy of Buenos Ayres, who are well aware of these truths, and who in their hearts laugh at the canon laws, have not yet had sufficient resolution to effect a reformation."

Again, in his Letters on South America, (almost in the very beginning of his book) page 15, Pazos truthfully declares, that,

"A system of religion which obliges its professors to act as self-accusers, and to regard the doctrines and counsels of their priests as oracles of Heaven, is, without doubt, the most potent engine of despotism which has ever been devised."

If the writer of the line which is, at this very moment, engaging the reader's attention, has seemed to warm up somewhat upon the subject of Romanism, it is because he has long been deeply impressed with the conviction that the Catholic religion, in every place where it exists, operates as a powerful barrier to the progress of general knowledge and good morals, and that it is particularly inimical to both civil liberty and republican government. As long ago as 1857, the writer here referred to, in his "Impending Crisis of the South," page 135, wrote thus :

" Although the Whig, Democratic, and Know-nothing newspapers, in all the States, free and slaves; denounced Colonel Fremont as an intolerant Catholic, yet it is now generally conceded that he was nowhere supported by the peculiar friends of Pope Pius IX. The votes polled at the Five Points precinct, (in the city of New York,) which precinct is almost exclusively inhabited by low Irish Catholics, show how powerfully the Jesuitical influence was brought to bear against him. At that delectable locality, as we have already shown, the timid Sage of Wheatland received *five hundred and seventy-four* votes—whereas the dauntless Finder of Empire received only *sixteen !* True to their instincts for Freedom, the Germans, generally, voted the right ticket, and they will do it again, and continue to do it. With the intelligent Protestant element of the Fatherland on our side, we can well afford to

dispense with the ignorant Catholic element of the Emerald
Isle.   In the influences which they exert on society, there is
so little difference between Slavery, Popery, and Negro-driving Democracy, that we are not at all surprised to see them
going hand in hand in their diabolical work of inhumanity
and desolation.

George Bancroft, in his excellent address on the Life,
and Services of Abraham Lincoln, delivered before both
houses of Congress, in the city of Washington, February
22, 1866, thus quietly, but opportunely and effectively,
castigated the anti-republican spirit of Popery.

"It was the condition of affairs in Mexico that involved the Pope
of Rome in our difficulties so far that he alone among temporal sovereigns recognized the chief of the Confederate States as a President,
and his supporters as a people ; and in letters to two great prelates
of the Catholic Church in the United States gave counsels for peace
at a time when peace meant the victory of secession. Yet events
move as they are ordered. The 'blessing' of the Pope at Rome on
the head of the Duke Maximilian could not revive in the nineteenth
century the ecclesiastical policy of the sixteenth ; and the result is
only a new proof that there can be no prosperity in the State without
religious freedom."

Such was the singularly infamous action toward our
country on the part of that despicable Old Beast of Italy
—Pope Pius IX.   And was there, in the United States,
or out of the United States, a single Catholic who, by
virtue (or rather by the vices) of his religion, was not
bound to sympathize and co-operate with the disorganiz-
ing and anti-republican labors of that blind and beggarly
bigot ?

For the love and reverence which we bear to God, for
the health and safety of our own souls, and for the honor
and the interests of America, let us be careful to adopt
timely and efficient measures for the purpose of prevent-
ing, if possible, any further extension of the pestilential
powers of popery;—at least, let us make it our business

to see that this pernicious system of papal paganism shall gain no additional foothold in our own particular part of the New World.

Not only in our own Protestant country, but also in Catholic countries themselves, in such countries, for instance, as Italy, Spain, Portugal, Mexico, Central America, and South America, let us calmly contemplate the diabolical workings of Catholicism, and take warning accordingly.

What very melancholy spectacles do we not witness to-day, in poor pontiff-oppressed and pope-polluted Italy? in poor priest-ridden Spain? in poor monk-pestered Portugal? in poor friar-befouled Mexico? and, indeed, in all the Romanized and ecclesiastically-enfeebled States of Central and South America? May the omnipotent Author and Ruler of the Universe, in his infinite goodness and mercy, unceasingly shield our own country from all such monstrous hierarchical pretensions and corruptions as have, for many hundred years, restrained from rising into view the splendid but yet obscured fabric of Italian nationality; and may all such portentous anomalies, in mere sublunary geography, as States of the Church, soon be completely and finally obliterated from every map of the earth.

Otherwise it cannot be, in the good providence of God, than that a day is fast approaching for the final downfall of Catholicism. All the signs and events of the times warrant us in this happy inference. Even the king of Italy himself, the brave Victor Emmanuel, is, at this very moment, one of the staunchest champions of religious liberty. He it was—his potential voice still echoing and re-echoing throughout the land—he it was who, at the recent opening of the first Italian Parliament held in Florence, gave utterance to these noble words:

"By doing away with old traditions, we shall be enabled to separate the Church from the State, and confiscate all religious corporations. If a new and inevitable struggle arise, I trust all Italians will rally round me in defence of the rights of Italy; for we must initiate a national policy, and, with our strong arms, leave the great work fully accomplished for our descendants."

It has been by such manly expressions as these, that Victor Emmanuel has achieved the great merit of having provoked the formal anathemas of that frail and foolish old fellow in the Vatican, called Pius IX. (as pious as a pig!) who is, with the single exception of James Buchanan, of Pennsylvania, the veriest old granny that was ever seen in male attire. Rather, however, as both of the masculine-feminine fogies here mentioned have a mixed reputation of being miserable old bachelors one day, and hysterical and antiquated maids the next, it might, perhaps, be more appropriate to speak of them as a couple of androgynous spinsters! After Old Buck, the strangely-sexed tenant of Wheatland, and Pius Nine, the he-she occupant of the Vatican, the third rank or place in man womanhood belongs of right to their own particular friend and correspondent, Jefferson Davis, formerly of the House of Dixie, who has of late, it is said, manifested a very extraordinary and peculiar *penchant* for petticoats!

Rome, not Florence; the "City of Seven Hills," not Turin; the "Eternal City," not Milan; is where, and where alone, all the Italian parliaments ought to be held. Rome, and Rome alone—Rome, not with popes nor with cardinals; not with prelates nor with priests; not with monks nor with nuns; but Rome, inhabited only by people of sane minds; Rome, affording protection only to persons engaged in some respectable and useful vocation, should immediately become, and henceforth and forever remain, the capital of the whole of Italy, including Venice.*   And as Rome ought to be, so it must be;—onward,

---

* This was written in the early part of last year, while Venice was still under the domination of Austria.   Only a few short

then, heroic Italians, on to Rome! and if Gallic soldiers
or other soldiers be found as adversaries in your way,
let all such liberty-despising and despot-serving enemies
be quickly overcome and trampled in the dust!

Marcos Paz, Vice-President of the Argentine Republic,
in the course of his Message to the National Congress,
in Buenos Ayres, Sunday, May 6, 1866, (President Mitre
being absent, as Commander-in-Chief of the allied forces
then fighting against Paraguay) said, speaking of our
own country:

"President Johnson has received our Minister to the United States
with the most marked attention. The object of this mission to the
Great Republic is not merely to bind more firmly our friendly relations, but also to study the institutions and try if possible to discover the secret which, in so short a space of time, has secured for that
nation such unexampled prosperity."

No particular secret about it, Mr. Paz. An American,
who sat immediately in front of you, on the occasion of
the delivery of your message (by the clerk who read it)
could have told you, in words which would have occupied
but few phrases, the whole "secret"—which, however, as
already stated, is no secret at all—of the truly wonderful success and prosperity of the good people of the United States. Had you asked that American to name the
means which he would prescribe for arriving, in the Argentine Republic, at a high degree of national prosperity
and progress, he would have cheerfully complied with
your request. This, too, he would have done in plain
terms, and in a somewhat laconic style; as, for instance,

months since, Venice very properly returned to her dear old
mother; now, henceforth and forever, let her stay at home—
and be happy !

with a preliminary exhortation to study closely, and to
practice faithfully, the leading principles contained and
foreshadowed in the Constitution of the United States,
he would have said, as, indeed, he would solemnly say to
every Catholic country in the world,

1.

Lay no obstacles athwart the paths of Destiny; for if
you do, those obstacles will, sooner or later, be made to
rebound against you, and will do you irremediable harm.

2.

Stand aside a little while, and let Michæl and his
mighty host of associate military angels have a fair sweep
at all the negroes, Indians, and bi-colored hybrids; and
very soon afterward the last of these involuntary candidates for fossilization will cease to be a pest to the worthy
portion of mankind.

3.

Fill your country with white people, and with white
people only—the more of Germanic stock, whether Sax-
ons, Anglo-Saxons, or others akin to them, the better.

4.

With all its nonsensical and ridiculous ceremonials,
renounce Catholicism at once, and beat it back, heels
over head, in an easterly direction, until it shall find exclusive companionship with the superstitious and heathenish Hindoos, who gave it birth.

5.

Between yourselves and the State, do not, under any
circumstances whatever, permit any form or system of
religion to intervene.

6.

Let all ecclesiastical organizations live and flourish

solely by their own merits, or languish and die by their demerits.

7.

Turn half of your churches into school-houses, libraries, and lecture-rooms; and the other half into founderies and machine-shops.

8.

Use your monasteries for agricultural colleges, and for academies of civil engineering; and your nunneries as institutions for promoting a knowledge of the useful arts, and of the sciences generally; and also of the fine arts in the few cases wherein nature is pleased to develop in her children the essential requisites of great genius.

9.

After your bishops, curates and monks, shall have ended their serio-comic engagements as star-actors in idolatry, place in their hands implements of husbandry, such as hoes, spades, and mattocks; and with these, rather than with rosaries, pyxes, and crucifixes, or other engines of jugglery, let them learn to earn for themselves an honest and respectable livelihood.

10.

Kindly, but firmly and fully explain to your sweethearts, wives, and daughters—who, as the victims and instruments of an exceedingly crafty clergy, are about the only lay church-goers among you—that any system of religion which is not good for men, cannot, by any manner of means, or upon any basis whatever, be justified or vindicated as good for women.

11.

Show your sons, and the young men of the State generally, that they have adopted a most extravagant and ill-founded view of the importance of pomatums, kid gloves, and suits of black broadcloth.

12.

Recollect that the English language—the language of Bacon, Locke, and Newton ; the language of Shakspeare, Milton, and Byron ; the language of Raleigh, Sidney, and Bolingbroke; the language of Hampden, Pitt, and Peel ; the language of Burke, Canning, and Cobden ; the language of Erskine, Bright, and Russell ; the language of Brougham, Mill, and Gladstone; the language of Hume, Gibbon, and Macauley ; the language of Addison, Swift, and Scott ; the language of Bulwer, Thackeray, and Dickens ; the language of Franklin, Henry, and Ames ; the language of Washington, Adams, and Lincoln ; the language of Jefferson, Madison, and Monroe ; the language of Jackson, Seward, and Johnson ; the language of Hamilton, Jay, and Everett ; the language of Marshall, Story, and Kent ; the language of Pinkney, Wirt, and Benton ; the language of Livingston, Clinton, and Marcy; the language of Webster, Clay, and Crittenden ; the language of Wheaton, Choate, and Douglas ; the language of Morton, Carey, and Draper ; the language of Prescott, Bancroft, and Motley ; the language of Hildreth, Palfrey, and Abbott ; the language of Channing, Edwards, and Dwight ; the language of Irving, Cooper, and Hawthorne; the language of Emerson, Whittier and Poe ; the language of Bryant, Holmes, and Longfellow—is now, and promises to be permanently, the principal language of the world. Recollect also that this is the only important and universally spoken language that is comparatively free from the befoulments of Catholicism, and from the baneful sophistries of other ecclesiastical nonsense and corruption. With as little delay as possible, let this copious and noble language, alike in the nursery and in the school, alike in law and in religion, alike in the family and at the forum—everywhere and on all occasions—take the place of your own.

13.

Establish, if possible, free libraries in every city and town ; and, at the public expense, have them kept open every day (Sundays not excepted) from six o'clock in the morning until eleven at night. Sundays, as a matter of course, should not be excepted ; for many, who have little or no time to read on other days, would gladly avail themselves of the opportunity, while resting from six days' labor, to read on the seventh ; and it would be infinitely better for them to spend their time at the libraries, than to be in the situation of those who have to seek recreation at the groggeries and at the gambling-saloons, because there are, unfortunately, no inducements nor conveniences for them to frequent places of real interest and respectability. As another measure equally well calculated to promote the temperance and good health of the masses of the people, physically, mentally, and morally, construct, without delay, numerous first-class public pumps, at suitable distances, and with permanent and unexceptionable conveniences for drinking (water) in all your larger cities and towns.

14.

Divide and subdivide your large but unimproved landed estates ; and, by legislative enactments, prepare the way for as many as possible of the more industrious and deserving of your white tenants to become owners in fee simple of the little homes which they occupy.

15.

Do away with all systems of peonage and other forms of labor bordering upon servitude ; and encourage the springing up among yourselves of a virtuous and stalwart white yeomanry, with good facilities for acquiring at least a tolerable education, and with well-protected proprietary interests in the soil.

16.

Devote more attention and labor to agriculture, gardening, and pomology ; and let at least one male member of every one of your families be a good farmer.

17.

Foster industry in the mechanic arts.

18.

Encourage the erection, and, by your patronage, contribute to the support, of manufacturing establishments all over the country ; and, if possible, cease at once to be dependent on foreign nations for such things, of whatever kind or nature, as may be produced at home.

19.

Let your merchants and others engaged in commerce, acquire wealth by the sale and exchange of home products, rather than by the introduction of foreign fabrics.

20.

Discountenance the unnecessary and nauseating "de" and its synonymes, and the incommodious and vomit-provoking "y" and its equivalents, which your exceedingly shallow-brained snobocracy have adopted in writing their worthless patronymics. In this matter, modesty and simplicity are inestimable virtues. If any man be of real importance in the world, his merits will, in due time, be discovered and acknowledged ; and the more especially so, if he be blessed with an easily pronounced and rememberable name—a short, jolly name, which, in all its fullness and belongings, should never be composed of more than two words, of from one to three syllables each, and each syllable of as few letters as possible—such a name, for instance, as we find dazzling like a diamond in the far-famed and immortal John Smith!

21.

Lose no time in subjecting to a thorough revision the whole body of the shabbily-framed and slovenly-executed laws now in force among you; and for all such unfortunate persons as are under judicial arraignment or restraint, provide speedy and equitable trial by jury. Make good the title of those of your institutions called courts of justice, whether for the decision of civil or criminal causes; and at least render it possible that a man, urged by actual grievances, may, without ruining himself financially, be enabled to obtain legal redress— to recover and maintain his rights, and to vindicate his character. It is a gross shame, nay, it is a heinous crime, that, on the one hand, poor plaintiffs and defendants, accusers and deniers, whether right or wrong, whether innocent or guilty, are required to dance life-long attendance before your sham tribunals, without ever being the recipients of even so much as a respectful hearing; while, on the other hand, litigants in affluent circumstances are almost invariably fleeced of their entire possessions.

22.

Enact, at your earliest convenience, a stringent and efficient law for the prevention of cruelty to animals; and see to it, that no infringement of any one of its provisions be allowed with impunity. Horses should not be flailed out of their shape, as if they were sheaves of wheat, nor work-oxen goaded three inches deep at every thrust of the metal-pointed shaft, as if, forsooth, their skins and flesh were made of Goodyear's gutta percha! One of the sections of the law thus suggested, should provide for the burning, in a bonfire, on the first day of next January, all the blind bridles in your country; it should, moreover, under heavy penalties, prohibit harness-makers from ever manufacturing other like instruments of torture.

. 23.

As for the lotteries and other legalized games of chance, which are so common among you—so common, in fact, in all Catholic and other semi-civilized communities —abolish them without delay. Neither in principle nor in practice, are they in any manner right, expedient, or respectable.*

---

* Of the baleful influences and effects of lotteries, Say, in his "Political Economy," page 459, thus speaks :

"When a government derives a profit from the licensing of lotteries and gambling-houses, what does it else but offer a premium to vice most fatal to domestic happiness, and destructive of national prosperity. How disgraceful is it, to see a government thus acting as the pander of irregular desires, and imitating the fraudulent conduct it punishes in others, by holding out to want and avarice the bait of hollow and deceitful chance! Lotteries and games of hazard, besides occupying capital unprofitably, involve the waste of a vast deal of time, that might be turned to useful account; and this item of expenditure can never redound to the profit of the exchequer. They have the further mischievous effect of accustoming mankind to look to chance alone for what their own talents or enterprise might attain ; and to seek for personal gain, rather in the loss of others, than in the original sources of wealth. The reward of active energy appears paltry beside the bait of a capital prize. Moreover, lotteries are a sort of tax, that, however voluntarily incurred, falls almost wholly upon the necessitous ; for nothing but the pressure of want can drive mankind to adventure, with the chances manifestly against them. The sums thus embarked are, for the most part, the portion of misery ; or, what is worse, the fruit of actual crime."

24.

Know that all public beggary, and all barefaced mendicancy—all beggary and mendicancy, whether in the market-places, in the streets, or in the highways—and most of the private solicitations on the part of the alms-seeking fraternity of circumforaneous negroes and Catholics, are disgraceful in the extreme. Adopt measures at once for the prohibition of all these shameful proceedings, and while guaranteeing to all good people, throughout the whole length and breadth of your land, absolute exemption from the distressful besiegements and importunities of proletarian paupers, make ample provision for supporting comfortably, at the public expense, all worthy persons, who, whether from calamitous accidents, or from other adverse causes, are incapable of taking care of themselves—persons who, if truly worthy, are, in all cases, without exception, of pure white complexion.

25.

To-morrow is a term which, in many cases, conveys an inauspicious announcement of procrastination, and is more or less inimical to the progress of the nineteenth century—and also of the twentieth, the thirtieth, the fortieth, and other centuries, which will all come along in the regular order prescribed for them by the Author of cycles, epochs and periods. To-day is a vocable of better promise; and this latter, as indicating the time when you ought to begin to improve yourselves in every good word and work, is particularly recommended as a first-rate substitute for the former, which is now so proverbially, yet so fruitlessly popular among you. To-day, for instance—not to-morrow—but to-day, this very hour, this very minute, this very moment, is the time for you, and equally for all of you, to begin, (by planning at least,) to bring about the complete and irrecoverable downfall of the Ro-

man Catholic religion.   Do this, do it in good faith, do
it with prudent earnestness, and God will always keep
you profusely supplied and environed with His blessings,
both here and hereafter.

26.

Among none of you—among none of the Latin races
—does there exist, in its true sense, any knowledge of the
endearing word Home, nor of its more endearing realities.   In regard to this precious and paradisiacal monosyllable, which has come down to us as a godsend from
Heaven, bestir yourselves quickly, and be no longer ignorant.   This word, which, in its best and happiest signification, describes the family relation in its highest state
of mundane perfection, will find a place in all your larger
vocabularies, (and the memorable and attractive places
which it suggests, will become enchantingly conspicuous
over the whole area of your commonwealth,) just so
soon as the pernicious power of popery shall have been
irretrievably prostrated.

27.

Pass a law that every person who writes a book, magazine, pamphlet, newspaper article, or other essay or statement of whatever bearing, sort, or character, shall be
required to publish it, if published at all, under his own
proper name; and that all anonymous writings shall be
promptly and sweepingly condemned as being at once
disingenuous, mischievous, and immoral—and their pub-.
lication and circulation prohibited accordingly.

28.

Enact by statute the conditions which shall justly and
wisely qualify and accept, or disqualify and reject, every
candidate for the exercise of the elective franchise.   To

this end, let there be appointed for every County, or other corresponding division of territory in the State, or for every ward of the city, a commission of three highly respectable and responsible citizens, whose duty it shall be to examine within their respective districts, all white males over the age of twenty-one; and if found worthy and well-qualified, to enroll their names accordingly, and, immediately thereupon, to issue to them amply descriptive and identifying certificates—no certificate, however, to be recognizable or valid without the holder's autograph; and let every person, upon the production of such certificate, vote without further challenge of his right to do so. Among other conditions which the commission so appointed should invariably require of the candidate in question should be these:

1. That he be of Pure Caucasian Descent.

2. That he be Able to Read and Write.

3. That he be a Citizen of at least Five Years' Residence.

4. That he has Attentively and Studiously read the Constitution of his Country at least Three Times.

5. That he is a Regular Subscriber to, Payer for, and Reader of, at least one Secular, (not Sectarian,) Newspaper; and further, that he is the Sole and Absolute Owner of at least Two Hundred and Fifty Dollars' worth of Property.

6. That he Owes and Acknowledges Supreme Allegiance to the Country of which he claims to be a Citizen—the Monstrous Pretensions of those Shameless Hypocrites and Impostors, the Popes of Rome, to the Contrary Notwithstanding.

7. That, under Penalty of Complete Disfranchisement, and the Forfeiture of all Manner of Political Rights and Privileges, and a Fine of at least Ten Thousand Dollars, he will never Offer nor Accept anything whatever having either the Shape or the Significance of a Bribe.

It would also be just and prudent to enact that, under penalty of the forfeiture of one hundred dollars, every well qualified voter be required to exercise personally, or by proxy, the right of suffrage at every constitutional election held within the limits of his own particular precinct.

29.

Cultivate with assiduity the arts of peace, and learn to frown upon war, (between white men,) as a thing which belongs more properly to the earlier part of the period of the Dark Ages.

30.

In opposing, as, without delay, and with the most earnest and uncompromising action, it is your duty to oppose, the machinations of factious military and political demagogues, learn to place a just estimate upon the words of Glanville, who has well assured us, that " It is a greater credit to know the ways of captivating Nature, and making her subserve our purposes, than to have learned all the intrigues of policy." What the world wants now, what the world sighs for, are Pacific Railways and Atlantic Telegraphs, not Waterloos nor Hohenlindens; Suez Canals and Darien Dykes, not Royal Prerogatives nor Papal Privileges; Croton Aqueducts and Fairmount Water-Works, not Holy Alliances nor Pragmatic Sanctions; Niagara Bridges and Hoosac Tunnels, not Jesuitical Concordants nor Spanish Inquisitions.

31.

Settle all domestic disputes by an impartial appeal to the ballot; and adjust all foreign differences by diplomacy and arbitration.

Thus, in the case supposed, would have ended, for a time at least, the remarks of the American who attentively listened to the clerical reading of the message of Vice-President Paz—the ostensible (and doubtless real) author of the message himself being also present. But when once warmly interested in the subject, that America might have been willing to say something more—not exactly in regard to the country at large, but rather in special reference to the cities and towns; and had any desire been expressed to hear him in behalf of these, he would have indicated some of his views of village and metropolitan proprieties, by drafting and offering for proper signatures a petition to the local authorities of the principal borough and municipal corporations in the vicinity of the River Plate—a petition worded, for instance, somewhat as follows:

BUENOS AYRES, May 7, 1866.

To the Honorable, The President of the Municipality of Buenos Ayres,

DR. LORENZO TORRES:

DISTINGUISHED SIR: We, the undersigned, petitioners to your Honor, respectfully represent, that, whether as permanent or temporary residents of the city of Buenos Ayres, we are all influenced alike by considerations for the substantial good and glory of the metropolis. We are, therefore, in favor of the enactment of any and every municipal measure which may be calculated to build up and strengthen the sanitary, the mental, the moral, and the material importance of Buenos Ayres, or which may add lustre to its civilization and renown.

Entertaining these sentiments, your Honor may readily and rightly infer that we are earnestly opposed to all such practices and proceedings, and especially to the toleration of all such nuisances, as are unequivocally detrimental to the true interests of the city. As humble petitioners, we therefore entreat your Honor, to cause, in

the most effectual and final manner, the abatement of at
least two disgusting and disgraceful nuisances, which, in
the rankness of their growth and prevalence throughout
the city, have long since become to us almost intolerable.

The first nuisance to which we allude, and from which
we beg your Honor to give us speedy relief, is the foul
and shameless habit of the men, or of the beasts or things
in the shape of men, who daily and hourly, and indis-
criminately, use the walls of our houses for the deposit of
the effete and offensive liquids of their bodies; thus, with
impunity, polluting the very fronts of our dwellings, nas-
tying the sidewalks, and shocking the sensibilities of all
persons of gentle and polite breeding.

Our wives and daughters, whether at their doors or
windows, or within a carriage, are ever liable to be
abashed and mortified by this abominably obscene and
crying nuisance ; and when they go out to visit, to make
purchases, or to promenade, the sidewalks, so far from
being, as they ought to be, in clean condition to receive
them, are everywhere slippery and bestunk with streams
and puddles of filth (such as should never be seen outside of a privy or a livery-stable) through which, to the
sore discomfort and cost of both themselves and us, they
are literally obliged to wade, and to bedraggle their
dresses.

Under these peculiarly annoying and distressful circumstances, we respectfully ask that your Honor, in connection with the other esteemed and worthy gentlemen
associated with you in the government of the city, may
be pleased to pass an ordinance that, after the fourth day
of July, or from a date as soon thereafter as may be convenient and agreeable for you to decide upon, every person who may be discovered perpetrating, on the side-
walk, in the street, or against any private or public
building, anywhere within the limits of the city, the vile

indecency here complained of, shall be required to pay to the Municipality, for the support of a police force sufficient to enforce the law, and for other local purposes, a fine of not less than one hundred paper dollars, for each and every offence so committed. And that the guilty in this regard, even those, if any there be, who have no water-closets to repair to, may not be left with any excuse for gross vulgarity of conduct, we would respectfully recommend to your Honor, that all the Livery-stables throughout the city, of which stables there are many, might, with propriety and general satisfaction, be legalized as places of resort for those who may have occasion to enter them with the motive here implied.

The second insufferable nuisance from which, through your Honor, we seek deliverance, is the howling wilderness of dogs, by which we find ourselves encompassed on every side, whether in the city proper, or in the suburbs, where alike, as it seems to us, they are all absolutely useless; barking, and biting, and bruising about, and behaving with a license and lust of action more appropriate to the wild wolf-lands of the west, than to the enlightened and progressive city of Buenos Ayres. Only a short while since, the writer of this petition, stopping for a few moments, without changing his position, in one of the principal streets of Buenos Ayres, counted twenty-eight dogs, among which, it is needless to say, there were prominently visible " mongrel, puppy, whelp, and hound, and cur of low degree," all within the narrow limits of his momentary observation ; and he has seen as many as thirteen miserable creatures of this kind at, and all apparently belonging to, a single farm-house in one of the southern extremities of this city.

We trust that your Honor may be induced to put an early stop to this snarling and snapping nuisance, by imposing an annual tax of three hundred dollars, more or less, on every dog allowed to run at large, within the municipal bounds, strictly requiring, at the same time, that the mouth of every animal thus taxed and permitted to live, shall be kept well muzzled.

We have noticed with regret, and we dare say your Honor must have noticed with indignation, that the present law, requiring the muzzling of dogs, is contemptuously evaded by certain sorry-witted gentry, who merely tie a real muzzle, or a myth of a muzzle, about the dog's neck, and, having done so, claim (preposterously enough, to be sure,) that the dog is then legally muzzled! A fine of five hundred dollars, more or less, for each and every offence of this sort, would probably cure these dissembling dog-fanciers of their contempt for the law, and thus, for the future, would they be taught more proper respect for your Honor's just and necessary ordinances.

In conclusion, we may be permitted to suggest to your Honor, that the issue from you, at an early day, of an ordinance embodying, with suitable provisions and penalties, and with ample powers of enforcement, the Dog Law and the Law of Decency here proposed, would, as we believe, be an act of public prudence on your part, which, in the salutary example that would be given to the younger and less important cities and towns throughout all the countries bordering on the River Plate and its tributaries, would justly entitle Señor Torres, as President of the Municipality of Buenos Ayres, to take rank with Alsina as Governor of the Province, and with Mitre as President of the Republic, in marking, in Argentine annals, a brilliant epoch of wise and wholesome legislation.

———

Thus far would the American, in conference with the worthy and patriotic Mr. Paz, have been willing to advance an outline of some of the views entertained by an invited visitor—a stranger in a strange land—in regard to both national and municipal matters. Nor would that American, on the particular occasion referred to, have been averse to hazarding an opinion of his own in opposition to the numerous and desolationg wars which, owing, in great measure, to the lamentable defects and rottenness of Catholic ethics, have almost incessantly marked the course of events over the whole of Spanish and Portuguese America. On this subject, had his opinion been asked, he would have replied in the words of a communication which he addressed to a friend, on the 17th of April, 1865, immediately after the outbreak of the fierce and bloody contest which (at the very time of the writing hereof) is still going on between Brazil, the Argentine Republic, and Uruguay, in alliance on the one side, and Paraguay on the other — a communication which was couched in these words :

A new revolution—no new thing, however, in this part of the southern hemisphere—has just broken out between the Argentine Republic, in alliance with Brazil and Uruguay on the one side, and the petty power of Paraguay on the other.

This triple alliance against Paraguay, which, as it would appear, she herself has wantonly provoked, can hardly fail to result in her speedy downfall ; and there are few, perhaps, beyond the limits of that Japanese-like State, whose eyes would moisten with sorrow at such result.

It would seem, indeed, as if an avenging angel were hovering over the people of all Spanish and Portuguese America, inciting them, ever and anon, in one place or another, to acts of intestine strife and mutual destruction. Otherwise it is very difficult for a person of mere ordinary calibre, like myself, to account for the constantly recurring revolutions so characteristic of all the countries situated between New Mexico and Patagonia.

To all appearances in Buenos Ayres, never did the sun rise more peacefully on a nation, than it rose yesterday on the Argentine Republic. To-day it rose here, amid the rolling and the rattling of gun-carriages, and the quick tramp and the bustle of regiments and battalions.

How sudden the transition from tranquillity to commotion! From peace to war within twenty-four short hours! Men, acting under hastily issued but regularly executed commissions from the national authorities, preparing to rush at each other with all the unreasoning ferocity of tigers! No proposition, no suggestion, not even a whisper, for arbitration! No appeal on either side, to the calmer and better judgment of any person or persons whomsoever? Not one moment allowed for the subsidence of the first fierce and frantic passions! No listening for, no desire to hear, the still small voice of generous and lofty admonition.

Even here in Buenos Ayres, the very capital of the Argentine Republic, where the people, as a community, are, perhaps, more enlightened, more amiable, more enterprising, and more generally imbued with just and noble sentiments, than in any other part of South America, with the possible exception of Chili, it was, to use a figurative expression, painfully apparent, throughout the whole of last evening, and during much of the night, that they, equally with their antagonists, had fallen under the fascinating influences of a most subtle and illusory spirit, who, with gleeful grimace, and with laughter in the sleeve, was alluring them both to deeds of common death.

Instead of receiving with quiet yet brave and profound regret, intelligence from Paraguay of the actual rupture by the Government of that country of all friendly relations with this, the entire populace here seemed to hail the news with as unmistakable demonstrations of joy, as if a divine messenger, with love and healing in his wings, had descended from the heavens! Bonfires, rockets, crackers, and all the improviso paraphernalia of great and glorious occasions, were conspicuous in every street of the city; so that if, twelve or fifteen hours since, there had arrived here, for the first time, any man belonging to a race not marked for absorption on the one hand, nor for extinction on the other, he might have supposed that the country, so far from being engaged in the solemn service of inaugurating fresh and fatal hostilities against their neighbors and kindred, had just begun to emerge, after the fashion of Troy of old, from the desolations of a ten years' war.

Were I something of a philosopher, and the possessor of a pipe, (but am neither the one nor the other) I should at once betake myself to a quiet corner, especially if the day were rainy, and there, in the happy mood of a meditative cat, seek, in the somewhat mazy but very certain problem of cause and effect, for a full explanation of the heterogeneous and ever-conflicting elements of these abortive and misborn republics.

I can readily conceive it possible, that, in the course of a stoic philosopher's cogitations on this subject, he might be led to the conclusion, that the principal secret of the cause which thus unceasingly besets and bedevils the people of all the countries of Central and South America, is to be found in the very unfortunate and disgraceful commixture of the first European settlers with certain grossly inferior races of mankind, who are totally undisciplined and undisciplinable, unschooled and unschoolable, unfitted and unfittable for civilization. It may be, moreover, that a philosophical mind, in the process of analyzing different theories, might be led to the further conclusion, that the only true remedy for the evils here alluded to, must be looked for in the eventual dominance, throughout all these countries, of a population composed chiefly—all the better if composed entirely—of Germanic, of Anglo-Saxon, and of Anglo-American origin. This condition of things, or a condition of things not very unlike it, God will assuredly bring about in his own good time.

———

Here, politely taking leave of Senor Paz, and hoping that his reveries and cogitations may lead him to continue the performance of as truly honorable and noble deeds in the future as have marked his career in the past—especially his career as a civilian—let us pause for a few moments, and then proceed to the consideration of such un-canvassed questions of interest and importance as are still awaiting our attention.

Throughout the length and breadth of all Spanish and Portuguese America, we behold the glaring and revolting evils of a commixture of the superior and inferior races, and also of the various inferior races among themselves. As has already been intimated, it is to the manifest fault-iness of Catholic education and training, that most of these evils owe their origin.

Look at the Empire of Brazil, which, like that upstart of a monarchy, Mexico, should be overthrown as quickly as possible, and converted into a Republic inhabited exclusively by white Protestants; look at the Argentine Republic; look at Paraguay; look at Chili; look at Peru; look at Bolivia; look at Ecuador; look at Venezuela; look at New Granada; in brief, look at all the States of South America; look at all the States of Central America; look at Mexico—and there is presented to your view one vast and unbroken conglomeration of mean-blooded and base-born hybridity, a most miserable and monstrous conflux of bastardy, whose dissolute and adulterous parents (one possessed of hideousness of colors, the other possessed of hideousness of characteristics, and both equally reprobate) are Savagery and Catholicism!

It was a clear perception of this deplorable condition of things that induced General Scott to decline the rulership of Mexico, which was voluntarily tendered to him by a number of wealthy and influential Mexicans immediately after his brilliant conquest of the old home of Montezuma,— a truly memorable declination of power, which, when viewed in connection with the continuous revolutions to which that war-worn and woe-begone country has so long been subject, one scarcely knows whether to applaud or to regret.

Sooner or later, Mexico, and all other parts of the vast continent of which it is a section, must be Americanized —Republicanized, Caucasianized, Protestantized; and if General Scott could have materially contributed to the advancement of these just and noble ends, it is not too much to believe that his refusal of the sway now so perniciously exercised by a hypocritical and half-witted hireling of the house of Hapsburg, has, for a time (but only for a time) retarded the development of the grand and glorious events which, as the essential stepping-stones to the climax of true greatness, are yet in reserve for the whole of Spanish and Portuguese America.

The manner in which General Scott rejected the overtures of power made to him by influential and distinguished Mexicans, has, as follows, been interestingly criticised and quoted by Dr. Francis Lieber, in his "Civil Liberty and Self-Government," page 330—a work which (if the fact may be here stated by way of digression) the writer of this line recollects having heard the late lamented William Curtis Noyes enthusiastically praise as by far the best book that he had ever seen on the subject of which it treats :

"General Scott, in his account of the offer which was made to him in Mexico, to take the reins of that country into his own hands, and rule it with his army, twice mentions the love of his country's institutions, which induced him to decline a ruler's chaplet. He himself has given an account of this affair in some remarks he made at a public dinner at Sandusky, in the year 1852. The generals of most countries would probably charge the victorious general with folly, for declining so tempting an offer. We delight in the dutiful and plain citizen who did not hesitate; and as the occurrence possesses historical importance, the entire statement of the general is here given. I have it in my power to say, from the best information, that the following account is 'substantially correct,' and as authentic as reports of speeches can well be made.

"'My friend,' said General Scott, 'has adverted to the proposition seen floating about in the newspapers. I have nowhere seen it *correctly* stated that an offer was made to me to remain in that country and govern it. The impression which generally prevails, that the proposition emanated from Congress, is an erroneous one. The overture was made to me privately, by men in and out of office, of great influence—five of whom, of enormous wealth, offered to place the bonus of one million of dollars to my credit in any bank I might name, either in New York or London. On taking possession of the city of Mexico, our system of government and police was established, which, as the inhabitants themselves confessed, gave security—for the first time perfect and absolute security—to person and property. About two-fifths of all the branches of government, including nearly a majority of the members of Congress and the Executive, were quite desirous of having that country annexed to ours. They knew that upon the ratification of the treaty of peace, nineteen out of twenty of the persons belonging to the army would stand disbanded, and would be absolutely free from all obligations to remain in the army another moment. It was entirely true of all the new regiments called regulars, of all the volunteers, and of eight out of ten of the rank and file of the old regiments. Thirty-three and a third per cent. were to be added to the pay of the American officers and men retained as the nucleus of the Mexican army. When the war was over, the government overwhelmed me with reinforcements, after there was no possibility of fighting another battle. When the war commenced, we had but one-fourth of the force which we needed. The Mexicans knew that the men in my army would be entitled to their discharge. They supposed, if they could obtain my services, I would retain these twelve or fifteen thousand men, and that I could easily obtain

18

one hundred thousand men from home. The hope was, that it would immediately cause annexation. They offered me one million of dollars as a bonus, with a salary of $250,000 per annum, and five responsible individuals to become security. They expected that annexation would be brought about in a few years, or if not, that I could organize the finances, and straighten the complex affairs of that government. It was understood that nearly a majority of Congress was in favor of annexation, and that it was only necessary to publish a pronunciamiento to secure the object. We possessed all the fortresses, all the arms of the country, their cannon foundries and powder manufactories, and had possession of their ports of entry, and might easily have held them in our possession if this arrangement had gone into effect. A published pronunciamiento would have brought Congress right over to us: and, with these fifteen thousand Americans holding the fortresses of, the country, all Mexico could not have disturbed us. We might have been there to this day, if it had been necessary. I loved my distant home. I was not in favor of the annexation of Mexico to my own country. *Mexico has about eight millions of inhabitants, and out of these eight millions there are not more than one million who are of pure European blood. The Indians and mixed races constitute about seven millions. They are exceedingly inferior to our own.* As a lover of my country, I was opposed to mixing up that race with our own. This was the first objection, on my part, to this proposition. May I plead some little love of home, which gave me the preference for the soil of my own country and its institutions? I came back to die under those institutions; and here I am."

Alluding to the proverbial instability of the governments of all the States of Spanish and Portuguese America, one of the writers for the New York *Times*, in a recently issued number of that newspaper, says :

"An eminent statistician records that our neighbors, the Mexicans, have had twenty-seven new constitutions or plans of government, varying between the extremes of conservatism and radicalism, within the period of forty years of anarchy which they have been pleased to term their independence. The North American memory becomes utterly bewildered and demoralized in trying to recall the long trains of presidents, dictators, and military chieftains that have passed and repassed upon the political stage. We even fail to remember the names, much less the history, of many of them."

In Bolivia, where, according to the latest advices from that wretched country, four fellows, respectively representing four separate and antagonistic factions, are all, each for himself, fighting for the rulership! the changes of government have been even more frequent than in Mexico, the former, within a period of exactly forty years, having undergone forty-four complete revolutions! —an average of more than one revolution for every year of its national existence! A similar mutation of public affairs has been constantly going on in all the nationalities of both South America and Central America, ever since they were first colonized by the Latin races. At the very moment of penning these lines, there is scarcely an independent State or territory between Lower California and Cape Horn that is not engaged in stubborn and deadly conflict, either with its immediate neighbor or neighbors, or with its mother country. Especially is this the case with the principal powers here alluded to— the Argentine Republic, Chili, Peru, Bolivia, Paraguay, Brazil, New Granada, and, as a matter of course, Mongrel and miserable Mexico.

Much of the disastrous puerility and fickleness of purpose which has all the while characterized the people of both Spanish and Portuguese America, has been inherited from the more southerly Catholic-cursed portions of Europe. On this subject, the New York *Evening Post*, of August 23, 1865, says :

"It is calculated that within thirty years, there have been in Spain about fifty different premiers and four hundred ministers, so frequent have been the changes in the Cabinet."

Whether we look at Italy, at Spain, at Portugal, or at any of the countries of Spanish or Portuguese America, conspicuous evidences of the mischief-breeding folly of tolerating any manner of statute connection between the State and the Church, and palpable proofs of the festering evils of priestly domination, are apparent on every hand. In the constitution or supreme law of all the nationalities thus mentioned or referred to, it is substantially declared—irrationally and despotically declared, declared in effect, if not in words—that,

"The Apostolic Roman Catholic religion shall be the religion of the State. The law shall protect and guarantee the exclusive recognition of this religion ; and shall prohibit the exercise of whatever other.

The constitution of the United States, based upon the principles of Reason and Liberty, declares that,

"Congress shall make no law respecting an establishment of religion, or prohibiting the free exercise thereof."

When the politically and religiously oppressed colonists of Spanish America overthrew Monarchy, and yet failed to overthrow Catholicism, they omitted, to say the least, one-half of a mighty and momentous duty. Indeed, it is but too obvious that, in this respect, those colonists came lamentably short, aye, culpably short, of the most solemn and important obligations which they owed to themselves.

At the very worst, however, hurtful and hateful as Monarchy undeniably is, it can hardly be said to be more than a mere despotism over the body. Catholicism, on the other hand, even at the best, is not only a despotism over the outer man ; it enslaves the mind ; it lessens the brain ; it shrivels the heart ; it dwarfs the soul.

If, then, the people of Spanish America would choose in reality what, thus far, they have chosen only in name —if they would sincerely adopt and put in practice the true principles of republican government—they must, as the first step necessary to be taken toward the accomplishment of that end, cause a thorough and final separation between themselves and that dismal chaos of irrationalities and superstitions, the Church of Rome.

To talk of Republicanism and Catholicism in the same State, each in good faith concerting and concurring with the other, is to talk the sheerest possible nonsense. The two are absolutely diverse in their natures, and can never, by any manner of procedure, whether of gentleness or of force, be made to harmonize, nor to work well together. Republicanism is something very good. Catholicism is something very bad. Prominent among the regular attendants of Republicanism, are Knowledge, Truth, Virtue, Peace, Power, Prosperity, and Progress. Prominent among the regular attendants of Catholicism, are Ignorance, Falsehood, Vice, War, Weakness, Adversity, and Retrogression.

A genuine republic, a republic entirely free from all heterogeneous and hostile elements, would be as barren of Catholics as Heaven is of Demons ; as unincumbered with Jesuits as the earth will be with negroes, Indians and bi-colored hybrids, when the superlatively superior whites shall be found to be the sole living representatives of the human race ;—God speed the day !

Of the many so-called republics of Spanish America, not one of them is republican in fact ; nor is it possible for any one of them ever to become so, so long as the stumbling-blocks and dead-weights of Catholicism are permitted to clog the wheels of progress. Monarchy, Dictatorship, Absolutism, and Catholicism, are all foul birds of a feather, which flock together ; and with none of these, at any time or place, or under any circumstances whatever, can Republicanism so far degrade itself as to form relations of lasting alliance.

When we see the very best men of Spanish and Portuguese America (as, indeed, we may see the very best men of every Catholic country in the world) overawed and paralyzed by the insidious arts of a most bigoted and fanatical priesthood, what degrees of jesuitical tomfoolery and fraud may we not be prepared to witness among the masses?

Between the northern confines of Mexico and the southern limits of Patagonia, there is a very small number of good men, white men, men of pure Castilian descent, such men, for instance as Mitre, Elizalde, Costa, Sarmiento, Paz, Gutierrez, Zuviria, Urquiza, and Ugarte, In everything, except in their blind and disgraceful submission to Catholicism, these gentlemen, and a few others like them, are eminently able and exemplary; but, then, they are as only a dozen stalwart and impatient lions among vast multitudes of slow-gaited pismires—and who, forsooth, has ever heard of a great or glorious nation of pismires?

The pismires here referred to, are two-legged pismires, frail-limbed, and weak-headed, and are more diversified in color than Joseph's coat—the very dull and deleterious colors peculiar to negroes, Indians, and non-white hybrids, being predominant. In the immediate fossilization of all these pismires, and in the complete extinguishment of the Roman Catholic religion, the most pressing and important interests of both Heaven and Earth would be promoted. Let these uppermost and transcendent interests be promoted accordingly!

From the anarchical and ruinous condition of things which, for so long a while, has prevailed all over Spanish and Portuguese America, have not we, of Germanic and Anglican America, certain special and important lessons to learn? What is the real character of those men who, having conspicuously portrayed before them the Principles of Good, on the one hand, and the Principles of Evil, on the other, at once precipitate themselves into a loud acclaim of the latter as more estimable and worthy than the former ? The most charitable view that we can take of such men, is that they are led into error through the impulses of very frail and faulty judgments ; and it is alone with this view of them, that there can be found any manner of excuse for their fatal proceedings. The only other view which, upon any basis of reason or probability, we may take of the action of such men, is that they are unconscionable hypocrites, and that they are influenced by motives of downright deception and dishonesty. With our feet well balanced upon these two stand-points of vision, and with even moderately good eye-sight, we shall be able to discern clearly, at a single glance, and at a distance so near as to excite disgust, the deplorable character of the two-thirds majority of the Black Congress.

If we would have North America reduced from its lofty position of Peace, Prosperity, and Progress, and lowered down to the deep depths of Disorder, Disrepute and Desolation, which have been reached in South America ; if we would have our Southern States debased into a Mexico, a Central America, a Jamaica, or a Hayti ; or if we would otherwise labor to degrade Heaven-descended white men from the high and sacred civilization which they have attained, and to place them, and to keep them forever, upon the low level of base-born and barbarous black men—then we should be very zealous and particular to continue in power the two-thirds majority of the Black Congress. On the other hand, however, if we would tenaciously and virtuously retain in our possession all the good which, under a beneficent Providence, we have thus far achieved ; if to that we would add something better ; if

we would steadily grow in grace, and in the knowledge
of God ; if we would, as far as possible, make ourselves
the efficient advocates and furtherers of every good word
and work ; if, with the instinct and foresight of true
statesmanship, we would, in no measure, oppress the
Southern States, but give them a fair chance to recover
from all the disasters which Negroes, Slavery, and Rebellion, have brought upon them,—aye, a just and fair
chance also to surpass, if they can, in Mental, Moral, and
Material progress, even the most advanced of the other
states themselves,—then, as the first step fit and necessary to be taken in order to accomplish these noble ends,
must we use at once, every constitutional means at our
command, to send, as soon as the statutes of elections
will allow, all of the more Radical members of the Black
Congress back to their own private homes, and there, to
say the least, until they shall have become perceptibly
better and wiser, hold them rigidly aloof from all public
pursuits.

Let us do these things without unnecessary delay. At
the very next regular elections, let us choose, in lieu of
the degenerate and degraded Black Congress, a White
Congress ; let us also elect a White Republican President ; and, with White Republicans filling all the minor
offices of the land, and with the negroes and all other
non-whites subjected to a just and effective process of
fozzilisation or removal, we shall soon be on the high-
road to a degree of excellence, greatness, and power,
hitherto altogether unknown and unexpected in the affairs of men.

CHAPTER XI.

THE FUTURE OF NATIONS.

In the most civilized countries, the tendency always is, to obey even unjust laws, but, while obeying them, to insist on their repeal. This is because we perceive that it is better to remove grievances than to resist them. While we submit to the particular hardship, we assail the system from which the hardship flows.—BUCKLE.

In all the large movements of human affairs, as in the operations of nature, the great law is gentleness—violence is the last resource of weakness—NICHOLAS BIDDLE.

I have said that I do not understand the Declaration of Independence to mean that all men are created equal in all respects. Certainly the negro is not our equal in color—perhaps not in many other respects. * * * I did not at any time say I was in favor of negro suffrage. Twice—once substantially, and once expressly—I declared against it. * * * I am not in favor of negro citizenship.—ABRAHAM LINCOLN.

EXPLANATION.

Soon after the news of the assassination of President Lincoln was received in the River Plate, a rumor reached Buenos Ayres, from Rosario, that Captain R., formerly of Kentucky, who had been known as one of Morgan's most daring and efficient raiders, but who had been captured and finally released, and, at his own request, permitted to leave the United States—and who is now residing near Rosario, in the Argentine Republic—had given a dinner in celebration of that surpassingly foul and flagitious crime.

The rumor had been in circulation but a little while, when Captain R. came down to Buenos Ayres, and, in company with Colonel M., formerly of Charleston, South Carolina, who had also been in the rebel service, called on me, at the Consulate, and assured me, in the most earnest and solemn manner, that there was not one word of truth in the report. Although Captain R.'s name and exploits had been frequently mentioned to me, yet I had never seen him until, accompanied by Colonel M., he called at the Consulate.

I quickly perceived that Captain R. was really and deeply grieved at the circulation of a false report, which was calculated to render him odious in the estimation of every loyal American who heard it, whether at home or abroad. He seemed to be particularly anxious that the rumor might be restricted to the limits which it had already reached, and that it should, if possible, be prevented from spreading to his friends in Kentucky. Yet he was aware that one or more of the departments of government at Washington would be likely to receive information of what was here current against him; and, in order to counteract the prejudices and wrong impressions which might result from such information, he asked me if I would assist him in making the facts of his case known to the Hon. Wm. H. Seward, Secretary of State. Fully persuaded of the Captain's innocence, I cheerfully signified my willingness to comply with his request; and advised him to return to Rosario, and there procure, and forward to me, the several exonerative affidavits which he said he could, if necessary, obtain from the very persons who were reported to have been invited by him to partake of the dinner in question.

Captain R. did as I suggested; and I lost no time in transmitting to our Government the solemn declarations of himself and friends, in disproof of a most heartless and atocious calumny—a calumny of which, it would seem, a fellow-Kentuckian, an unprincipled personal enemy, was the author.

In the course of his conversation with me, Captain R.

was very frank; and, in speaking of the political opinions
and actions of various members of his family in Kentucky, he said many things which I could not but regard
as far more complimentary to them than to himself. He
told me that he was the only member of his family who,
of his own accord, had gone into the rebel service;
and that, when he had made up his mind to go, and began to make the necessary preparations, his father took
him aside, and used every manner of argument and
entreaty to induce him to abandon his rebellious intentions. But he had deliberately volunteered to add himself to the rebel ranks; was hot-headed, hare-brained,
and headstrong; and, therefore, to all his father's friendly
counsel he turned a deaf ear; and would listen to no
voice that was not elevated to a high pitch of rancor and
wrath against the Union. His aged mother, (who, however, was the youngest of a large family of children,)
then came to him, and, weeping bitterly, addressed him
substantially in these words:

"My son, oh! my son, you are making this the unhap-
piest day of my life! Remember that you had three
uncles in the American army at the battle of King's
Mountain. There, eighty years ago, on the soil of South
Carolina, they fought to establish the independence of
our common country. There, in defending and immor-
talizing the flag of the Union, one of them was killed
outright, and another was dangerously wounded. Oh!
it is, indeed, the bitterest experience of my life, thus to
realize that I have borne a son who would raise his hand
to strike down the honor and the greatness of his country.
In no event may I reasonably expect to remain much
longer upon the earth. If you take part with the rebels
in their treasonable insurrection against the lawfully constituted authorities, I can hardly hope ever to see you
again. I, therefore, beseech you, with all the solemnity

of a mother's dying request, that you will at once desist from all your purposes of hostility to the Government of the. United States."

Captain R., regarding his mother's devotion to the Union as a mere womanish whim, heard her with comparative indifference, and continued to prepare himself for departure for the rebel camp. He had two sisters. They both came to him. The younger of them, with the most sisterly affection, threw her arms about his neck, and kissed him, and then, overcome by the anguish of her heart, she fell upon her knees at his feet, and, sobbing aloud, begged and adjured him not to disgrace his country, his family, and himself, by going voluntarily into the rebel service. The elder sister, of sterner mettle, stood before him, and said, in effect,

"Brother! you know how tenderly we have always loved you. Our poor old father and mother have both reasoned with you, pleaded with you, and, with all the sincerity and solicitude of parental concern, have warned you against the inevitable dangers and dishonor of taking sides with the enemies of your country. In harmony with what they have said, we are here to add the weight of our own solicitation and caution. We implore you not to offer yourself for so base a sacrifice. But, hear me further; sister and myself have come to say to you, and we say it with no less genuineness of the import of words, than with sorrow, that if you do go into the rebel service, we hope and pray never to see you return home alive!"

"Yes," substantially responded the younger sister, rising resolutely, and standing before him with firmness of purpose, "we have considered this matter well, and have come to say what sister has told you. We are mutually pledged to each other, to unite our prayers to Heaven, that if our brother ever raises even the little finger of his hand to impair, in any degree, the consecrated union of these States, we may never see him alive again!"

But, owing to the very bad influences in the South under which the young men there have been reared, that is to say, owing to their life-long association with negroes and negro slaves, whose only power over the white race seems to be to develop in it whatever is cruel, vicious, and detestable, Captain R.'s nature was so hardened and distorted, that no amount of persuasion on the part of his parents, no measure of entreaty on the part of his sisters, could turn him aside from his rebellious purpose. Nor was he to be deterred from it by the threatened invocations for the vengeance of Heaven. Off he went to the rebels in arms, and joined them; was engaged in many battles and skirmishes; "broke the crust," it is said, of most of the fights in which he participated; was finally captured, paroled, and, in accordance with his own request, permitted to leave the United States; and at the very moment at which I write, is, as I learned last evening, harvesting two hundred and fifty acres of as fine wheat as ever grew on the banks of the Parana.

Captain R. is a better man to-day than he was yesterday; and was better yesterday than he was before the war. It would be a pleasant little task for me to say something of this sort, if I felt certain that I could say it with truth, of the humble writer, and also of all the gentle readers of these lines!

Should we ever become involved in a war for the maintenance of what is popularly known in our country as the Monroe Doctrine—in other words, should it ever come to be necessary for us, in (fractional) support of that doctrine, to oppose and put down the monarchy of Maximilian in Mexico—as it certainly will, if that adventurer does not soon leave the country, or dash away his insulting and disgusting crown—I could hardly expect to find by my side, in any contest of that sort, a truer American, or a better soldier, than Captain R.

Under date of September 22, 1865, in the course of the second letter which he wrote to me in reference to the false rumor against him, Captain R. says :

"Only let me be judged with calm and dispassionate feelings. 'To err is human—to forgive divine,' is one of the many moral maxims taught me by my mother, who, I verily believe, is now in heaven ; and trust me, Mr. Helper, I would as soon have thought of giving a dinner in celebration of her death, as that of Mr. Lincoln's."

His good old mother, now no more, was certainly worthy to be ranked with the very best of the public-spirited matrons of Sparta and Rome ; and, as for his inflexibly loyal and Union-loving sisters, were I not a Carolinian, I might regret that I am not a Kentuckian ; for it could never be otherwise than a matter of just pride with me to be able to say that they and I were of the same State ; and yet we are of the same STATE, in a much larger and better sense than if we had all been born and reared in Carolina or in Kentucky, in Massachusetts or in New York, in Pennsylvania or in Ohio. We are all AMERICANS ; we are all of the same nation, of the same continental commonwealth ; and it is in this more expanded, enlightened and liberal sense, that I have the pleasure and the honor to greet them.

It is true that part of their bearing toward their erring brother may, in the estimation of some, appear to have been rather rigid and exacting ; but, considering it in the main, how patriotically, how laudably, does it contrast with the follies of thousands of foolish and fretful women in the South — fire-eating termagants, shrews, vixens, and viragoes — who, instead of employing their feminine graces in an attempt to allay the fury of fraternal strife, only added frenzy and fierceness to the terrible conflict! In the examples afforded by the latter class of females in the Southern States, we have additional evidences of the alarming and brutalizing debasement brought upon the Whites, by living in juxtaposition with the Blacks.

Nor was it only in serious matters that Captain R. was interestingly frank and communicative. He told me several little anecdotes, *à la Lincoln*, of the views, plans and purposes of the rebels in his part of Kentucky. The first thing which they meant to do, was to acquire and irrevocably establish their independence, under a separate and distinct nationality. That, as a preliminary and all-important proceeding, was a matter well understood and well arranged. There were also certain little indemnities and vengeances which were to receive attention in the treaty of peace between the United States of America and the Confederate States of Jefferson Davis. The United States of America aforesaid, would have to pay all the expenses of the war, whether incurred in the North, in the South, in the East, or in the West; and, in addition thereto, would be required to deposit in the Treasury of the Confederate States of Jefferson Davis aforesaid, one hundred millions of dollars in hard money current with the merchant, as security for good behavior in the future!

More than a score of ogre-like, anti-slavery heads, including the excessively ugly and stubborn one belonging to the writer hereof, were to be demanded for immolation, as a preliminary *sine qua non*, to the ratification of peace! It was well known (in Kentucky) that Abraham Lincoln, just prior to his nomination for the Presidency, had, for many months, been closeted in Washington city, with the nominal author of "The Impending Crisis of the South;" and that they two, facing each other at the same table, had then and there, contrary to the peace and dignity of Dixie, concocted, written, and compiled, that saucy volume! Although I had, on various occasions, frequently heard the authorship of "The Impending Crisis of the South" attributed to sundry able and distinguished gentlemen, such, for instance, as James Gordon Bennett, Horace Greeley, and John Sherman ; yet this was the first time that I had been honored by hearing it attributed, in any of its outlines or details, to a man so great and so good as Abraham Lincoln.

After Captain R. had explained and re-explained to me, both verbally and by writing, the several really interesting facts in his case, it occurred to me that something ought to be done to shield, in a general way, all those who might be similarly situated, from the gross and unfounded accusations of mere personal enemies, whose passions and prejudices, as between the persons hated and themselves, would seem, in certain instances, especially in negroized communities, to blind them to almost every principle of honor, truth, and justice. Indeed, I may not disguise the fact, that, so constantly and heavily did this matter weigh upon my mind, that during intervals of leisure from Consular labors, for several days in succession, I found myself involuntarily walking backward and forward, from one side of my office to the other, engaged with numerous imperfect thoughts, first upon one plan, and then upon another, for remedying at least one or two of the many evils into which tens of thousands of our good people have fallen, not only in the South and in the North, but also in the West and in the East.

The result of these humble but well-meant meditations on my part, is the following paper, addressed to the public of the Argentine Republic; and here it may not be amiss for me to state that when I began to write it, it was my intention to offer it for the acceptance and action of several prominent Southerners in and about Buenos

Ayres, some of whom, like Captain R., had already assured me that they had ceased to harbor any feelings of ill-will against the government, or against any part of the people, of the United States. As I proceeded, however, fearing that, even in the best republic of the River Plate, some question of international law might arise from my comparatively unqualified freedom of expression against monarchical and other anti-republican forms of government, or that I had said something that might cause complaint of a disposition, on the part of Americans resident in a foreign country, to be too unreserved in communicating to the world their political opinions; and also in some doubt, as to whether what I had said would meet the approval of those in whose behalf I had written, I gave up the idea of offering it for any action or recognition at that time; and, without exhibiting it, or even mentioning it, to any person whomsoever, (except in friendship and confidence, to our Ministers Resident, respectively, in the Argentine Republic and in Paraguay, the Hon. Robert C. Kirk and the Hon. Charles A. Washburn,) concluded to dispose of it in this manner. No one, I venture to say, will, at any time, be more surprised at what I have thus written, than Captain R. himself, should it ever come to his knowledge.

TO THE ARGENTINE PUBLIC.

We, the undersigned, hitherto known as having manifested more or less sympathy with those who, from four to five years since, defying the authority of the Government of the United States, attempted to secede from the American Union, and to construct of the States of the South a sovereign and independent nationality, deeming it but just, alike to the several communities of the Argentine Republic in which we respectively reside, and to ourselves individually and collectively, and also to our relatives and other friends at home, that our status as Americans may not be misunderstood, do hereby solemnly declare the feelings and purposes which actuate us under the present and prospective posture of public affairs.

First. We accept the result of the late civil war in the United States, as the final overthrow of Slavery, and the perfect and perpetual establishment of the constitutional supremacy of the Federal Government as contradistinguished from State Governments. We, therefore, both for the present and for all time to come, utterly repudiate and abandon the doctrine of State Sovereignty.

Second. In a country like ours, where the masses are not only noted and admired for their native intelligence and education, but who are also equally noted and admired for their possession of an unusually large share of personal independence, and for their exemption from undue selfish motives, we believe that the decision of all questions affecting their political welfare may, with certain wise limitations and restrictions touching the voters themselves, be safely submitted to their .suffrage ; and that the will of the majority, in all fairly conducted elections, should be quietly and unequivocally acquiesced in, without dissension and without murmur ; and, further, to speak with perfect candor, that armed opposition to the will of the majority, in such cases, is a flagrant crime against the most essential and sacred principles of republican government.

Third. Assured, as we háve been, that the government of the United States, in the hands of that part of our people who have been successful in sustaining it, will never seek to employ against us, nor against any member of our families, any feelings of mere rancor or revenge, but, on the contrary, in a spirit of manly freedom from passion, is disposed to extend all reasonable and proper encouragement for us to resume, under the late laws of Congress, and the proclamations of the President, our rank as citizens of the Great Republic, we, on our part, do freely and fully withdraw from the said Government, and from all our victorious countrymen, every general desire and purpose of resentment, and every secret sentiment of hostility.

Fourth. At the same time that we are far from the disposition to evade any just responsibility which we may have incurred, yet in behalf of our friends in the northern hemisphere, no less than in our own behalf, we indulge the hope that there may be no failure to discriminate equitably as to how much of the burden of the rebellion belongs to the generality of the people, and how much to the small number of wily leaders, whom the masses had been accustomed to follow. And, with reference to the handful of prominent leaders, mere noisy politicians, who have evinced so much fatal ignorance of the genius and tendency of American institutions, we trust that they may, for a term of years at least,—until, for instance, they shall have become well instructed in a better school of politics—be denied all positions of a public nature, whether of honor, trust, or profit.

Fifth. Disinclined as we are to differ pointedly from the views entertained by our most immediate friends at home, yet, as Americans, we cannot acknowledge ourselves as bound in political faith with those who have seemed to see, as a thing antagonistic to equitable government, an undue growth or extension of the territory of the United States. So far from this, indeed, it is our settled conviction that the vigorous and expansive principles of republican government, as expounded by Madison and others in the *Federalist*, and also by Monroe and his compatriots, may be prudently and auspiciously applied, under one President, to every fertile acre, to every genial acre, to every desirable acre, on the contintinent of North America.

Henceforth, therefore, if it shall be the pleasure of a majority of our countrymen, let us readopt, with greater earnestness and enthusiasm of action than we have ever displayed in the past, the policy of Cohesion, not the policy of Disintegration ; the policy of Union, not the policy of Disruption; the policy of Annexation, not the policy of Secession. Under the ægis of a government so great as ours would thus become,—so much greater than it now is, and yet, as it is, unquestionably the greatest in the world,—and with public virtue and intelligence keeping pace with our national enlargement, what paramount good for ourselves and for our children, in the way of exemption from oppressive taxation, and in the consciousness of having secured lasting peace and prosperity at home, and absolute safety and respect abroad, might we not accomplish?

After mature deliberation, far is it,—we speak frankly, —far is it from a feeling of regret that we have failed to become citizens of a confederacy of less territorial extent than the Republic under which we were born, of a confederacy established by madmen on the black basis of Slavery, rather than of the good old Republic established by our fathers on the white basis of Liberty.

Turning to the page of history, we perceive, in pressing proximity to the details of the wreck and ruin of sixty centuries, vast accumulations of proof of the inevitable weakness, instability, and general disadvantages of small governments. Larger and more enduring nationalities, now in course of consolidation in various parts of the world, are, we believe, the forerunners of better days —the foundations of greater degrees of tranquillity and healthful progress than the wisest statesmen ot any age or country have ever dared to plan, or even prophesy.

Pygmean commonwealths, unallied and without protection, have always, and everywhere, been the bane of mankind. Look we back along the stream of time, commencing our survey from the present hour, and extending our view down to the very first period of which there is vouchsafed to us any authentic record, and what do we behold? What, indeed, but the constant clashing and crumbling, the alternate conquest and reconquest of diminutive states? What, indeed, but the despoliation or the death of individuals, the pitiless expulsion of families, the scattering of tribes, the overthrow of principalities, and the subversion of kingdoms;—what, indeed, but the appalling devastations of war, the track of the destroyer, and the path of the plunderer, visible over every part and parcel of the petty power?

Quailing before the mighty sword of Adonizedek, no less than three score and ten kings are said to have been dethroned; and, dead or alive, thirty-one regal rulers succumbed to the unflinching prowess of Joshua. Failure of national consolidation, or lack of international league, even for the prudent purpose of, self-preservation, is plainly apparent in the case of these one hundred and one calf-witted kings, who were thus forced to surrender their sceptres to two ferocious and rapacious dogs of war; and, as we may safely infer, it was this fact, this universal weakness of littleness, this inevitable feebleness of division, which finally led to their complete discomfiture.

Of what astonishing glory and greatness did not the Jews in general give evidence, when once well organized under a single national ensign, and when governed by kings of unquestioned ability and worth, like David and

Solomon ?   Dissension and division damned them. There must needs be, as they most foolishly and fatally surmised, two kingdoms ; the kingdom of Judah, and the kingdom of Israel. The day of their separation was the day of the beginning of their decadence, the dark day of the commencement of their downfall ; and where are they at this time, and who are they, and what have they been for the last twenty-five hundred years? What, indeed, among nations, but a hissing and a byword, a puppet and a football ? Whilst we eschew the absurdities of the religion of the Jews, let us be careful not to become converts to their political errors.

Greece—how has it always been with Greece, poor, uncohesive, subdivided Greece? Oh! how gloomy, how grievous, indeed, has been the fate of Greece! Without some previous preparation on our part to withstand the shock of dismay, let us not at once unfold her annals of mutual and inhuman slaughter, her chronicles of intestine and relentless bloodshed, lest, becoming astounded, we ourselves fall aghast with horror and with faintness of heart, and expire suddenly. Against the untold and untellable havoc of the Peloponnessian war,—an internecine strife of twenty-seven years' duration, when day by day Greek met Greek in deadly fray,—let us shut our eyes, praying God that such dark days of desolation may never return again to plague his people anywhere. Of the war of the Seven Greek Captains, the Messenian wars, the Athenian wars, the Spartan wars, the Corinthian war, and the Macedonian war, all domestic; and of their foreign wars with the Trojans, the Persians, the Romans, the Huns, and the Turks, we have no heart to speak, save only with sighs and sadness.

Yet, in this late era of the world's progress, it is graciously permitted to mankind, doubtless for some wise purpose, possibly for some special good to ourselves, to read, in letters prominently imprinted with the unerring types of truth, the doleful secret of the ever-recurring misfortunes of Greece. As a whole, the country was little; rather less, indeed, than the State of Kentucky. Divided and subdivided into a score of independent sections, some of which were not larger than Wake County in North Carolina, her several parts became contentious; and, following fast in the first steps of strife, unallayable hostilities among themselves soon opened the door for the invasion of hosts of hungry wolves from foreign lands.

Too great frequency of elections, by which the public mind was not only kept in an almost constant state of ferment, but also often frensied by the harangues of rival candidates, and the ridiculously brief term of office in all posts of importance, (even the archonship, the chief magistracy, having been a function of annual rotation,) had also much to do, as indirect agencies, in the direful demolition of the Grecian democracies,—often miscalled republics. And, if we may fitly ask the question on this occasion, is not the matter of frequent elections an ominous principle in our own system of government? Such, certainly, is our conviction; and, in this regard, we feel assured that more than one salutary amendment might be made. For Presidents, and for other eminent public servants,—ah, servants, plain, sturdy, trusty, republican servants, not masters,—give us good men, capable, upright, incorruptible men, men like Washington, Adams, Jefferson, Madison, Monroe, Jackson and Lincoln; but do not impose upon us the unnecessary burdens and vexations, the perilous labors and excitements, of having to find, once in every period of four years, or oftener, inexperienced and doubtful successors.

When our country was of but comparatively small extent, with a population of only about three millions, the four years' term may possibly have been sufficient; but now that, with more than thirty millions of inhabitants, we are rapidly becoming a nation of continental magnitude, let us have terms of service more appropriately corresponding with the enlarged circumstances of the times. Give us Presidents for not less than seven years; Governors for six years; Judges, if good, for life; and others for four or for five years, or for periods indefinite, during blameless and efficient behavior. With greatness let greatness grow.*

Again to Greece. Lamentable, indeed, was the lack of alliance, the absence of mutual support, among her several parts. Cut up into twenty different democracies, all of which, if combined into an extended whole, would, in this progressive age of great things, be too small for one republic, her glory took wings of rapid flight, and flew away; and now we scarcely know her except as an historical wreck among the bright shining nations of antiquity. Much as we admire the political theories of Solon, Lycurgus, Pericles, Demosthenes, Phocion and other distinguished statesmen of Greece, yet we cannot repel from our vision the obvious insufficiency of their miniature governments.

Let us array before our eyes for a few moments the number and the names of the independent Grecian communities, which so fatally failed to understand the great political truth, so transcendently important to be

----

* The author is persuaded that his views upon this subject acquire at least some measure or degree of force and value, from the fact that they were thus expressed many months *after* he had voluntarily and deliberately *resigned* the only office which he has ever held; namely, that of United States Consul at Buenos Ayres. Of this fact, the two American Ministers mentioned on page 425, and the Hon. Secretary of State of the United States, are fully cognizant.

understood and practiced by all the component parts of a nation, that, "in unity there is strength."

If we have learned well our lessons in history, these are the names which indicate the number of the

ANCIENT DEMOCRACIES OF GREECE.

Attica.	Achaia.
Laconia.	Epirus.
Arcadia.	Thessaly.
Messenia.	East Locris.
Corinthia.	West Locris.
Ætolia.	Megaris.
Bœotia.	Phocis.
Eubœa.	Doris.
Acarnania.	Elis.
Sicyonia.	Argolis.

Futile was the Amphictyonic Council; and preposterous was the Achæan League. Nations, worthy of the title, are something more, in both extent and property, than mere pleasure-grounds or public parks; and no bond upon paper, no constitution upon parchment, no treaty upon vellum, can save from national disaster the people who fail to surround themselves with the solid and wide-spreading realities of national attributes.

As the world counts greatness, Alexander the Great, Themistocles, and Timoleon, were great men; so also were Miltiades, Leonidas, Epaminondas, and other herculean heroes of Hellas; but it was owing to the unsuppliable want of greater men than any of these—men whose far-reaching statesmanship would have consolidated twenty independent democracies into one powerful Republic—that ancient Greece, the Greece of glory, sinned, sorrowed, sickened, and died.

Italy, in early times, was also subdivided into numerous undersized nations and nationalities, always warring among themselves, and so vulnerable, by default of a prudent combination of forces, as to invite the invasion of the Carthaginians and other foreigners, who laid waste many of the fairest portions of the Italian peninsula. We have not forgotten the accounts of the three Punic wars, which had an aggregate duration of forty-three years, nor the domestic feuds between the Plebeians and the Patricians,—the respective partisans of Marius and Sylla, Cæsar and Pompey,—and their bloody predecessors and successors in sedition, who, in the long career of their excesses, prepared the way for the influx of so many ruthless and irresistible hordes of barbarians.

These, we believe, were the

INDEPENDENT COMMUNITIES OF ANCIENT ITALY.

Latium.	Samnium.
Etruria.	Sabini.
Umbria.	Lucania.
Picenum.	Bruttia.
Campania.	Apulia.
Liguria.	Calabria.

More recently, not at once, but at different epochs, we have seen Italy swept of all her old organizations of government, newly constituted into an equal or even greater number of minute kingdoms, dukedoms and democracies, each asserting independence of the other, but all of them devoid of that solemn dignity and power, that grandeur of simplicity and impartiality, that loftiness of aim and tendency, that matchlessness of enterprise and achievement, that excellence of general system and procedure, which are so peculiarly characteristic of great republican commonwealths.

Had it not been for the devastating wars which have so frequently fallen to the lot of Greece and Italy, and the other countries bordering on the Mediterranean, all of which have been so profusely favored by nature, what gardens of Eden, what paradisiacal places of residence, what Elysian fields of abode, what an aggregation of Utopias realized, would not those countries be to-day!

These, it appears, are the names of the territorial sub-divisions which indicate the principal

INDEPENDENT COMMUNITIES OF MEDIÆVAL AND MODERN ITALY.

Sicily.	Ravenna.
Sardinia.	Lucca.
Naples.	Parma.
Lombardy.	Pisa.
Tuscany.	Placentia.
Piedmont.	Rome.
Savoy.	Milan.
Sammarino.	Genoa.
Modena.	Venice.
Ferrara.	Florence.

Even the present hour of Italy is fraught with lessons of the deepest import to the discerning students of national and international history, who perceive that, for one country, two or more supreme governments, so far from contributing to the best interests of the people anywhere, are, immediately or remotely, inimical to the true welfare of all. Ah, even in this advanced day of the nineteenth century, do we not behold poor war-worn (and otherwise worn) Italy acting the insane farce of running hither and thither in search of a capital, as if, indeed, for Italy proper, there ever was, or is, or can be, any other capital than Rome?

Spain also ranks prominently in the catalogue of those countries which have boundaries indicated by nature, but which have ever staggered and tottered, and eventually toppled, under the giddy and gouty evils of independent subdivisions of territory.

These, if we err not, were the

ANCIENT KINGDOMS OF SPAIN.

Arragon.	Catalonia.
Valencia.	Asturias.
Andalusia.	Galicia.
Estremadura.	Murcia.
Old Castile.	Biscay.
New Castile.	Leon.
Navarre.	

How infinitely better for the Spaniards generally, had they been favored from the first with that unity of nationality which, in 1479, they so happily found under Ferdinand and Isabella!

France, as we see her at this time, is but an agglomeration of the remains of a dozen or more independent mediæval communities, whose fierce and sanguinary conflicts among themselves, have ever wanted a pen adequate to their description.

These, it would seem, were the principal

SOVEREIGN SUBDIVISIONS OF FRANCE DURING THE MIDDLE AGES.

Burgundy.	Lorraine.
Normandy.	Touraine.
Gascony.	Dauphiné.
Picardy.	Bretagne.
Orléans.	Ile de France.
Champagne.	Guienne.
Provence.	Anjou.
Languedoc.	

Of these fifteen insignificant nationalities, any number less than the whole might have striven, separately or together, till doomsday; yet, owing to the impossibility of enlisting sufficient forces in concert, they could never have come forward with such an acceptable offering to the world as the France or the Paris of to-day.

England, during most of the perturbed time which elapsed between the fifth and the ninth centuries, was subdivided into seven kingdoms, called collectively the Saxon Heptarchy; Ireland, in the twelfth century, into five kingdoms; Wales, in the ninth century, into three kingdoms; and Scotland, in the eighth century, into two kingdoms.

These, as we gather from the statements of various historians, were the

ANCIENT KINGDOMS OF ENGLAND, IRELAND, WALES, AND SCOTLAND.

ENGLAND.	IRELAND.	WALES.	SCOTLAND.
Kent.	Ulster.	North Wales.	The Kingdom
Essex.	Munster.	South Wales.	of the Picts,
Wessex.	Leinster.	Powys-Land.	the Lowlands;
Sussex.	Meath.		and the King-
Mercia.	Connaught.		dom of the
East Anglia.			the Scots, the
Northumberland.			Highlands.

Here we have the names of seventeen kingdoms, all of which, and more, under one strong central government, have been losers of State Sovereignty, but gainers of National Freedom—relinquishers of little and precarious Independence, but acquirers of large and lasting Liberty,

It was not under the Heptarchy that London grew up to be the largest city upon the face of the whole earth; nor was it until England became a unit in point of nationality, that the East India Company was Chartered; nor yet until all the independent subdivisions of Great Britain and Ireland were joined together in the peaceful bonds of a common and coöperative sisterhood, that dozens of wrangling Asiatic principalities, covering in the aggregate an area of twelve hundred thousand square miles, and occupied by at least one hundred and eighty millions of inhabitants, came to acknowledge, as they still acknowledge, their allegiance to the British crown.

Happily for the present dynasty of Great Britain, there seems to be no prospect of a renewal in England of the War of the Roses, nor of the Rebellion of the Pretenders, nor of any one of the other thirty-five civil discords which have there, within the last eight centuries, overturned society and deluged the country in blood. In this respect, at least, let us strive to be so much wiser than the English, that, whereas, since William the Conqueror took their island from them in 1066, they count their domestic wars by the dozen,—the total number amounting to thirty-seven,—we, having had but a single one, may never have another.

Yet it is by no means to the past only, that we are indebted, as a matter of warning to ourselves, for illustrations of the bad working of small independent communities.

Germany, in her present political organization, affords a multiplicity of proofs of the general correctness of our assumptions.*   With a territory not quite twice the size

* The two diplomatic gentlemen whose names are mentioned on the 425th page of this book,—the only persons to whom I read, or whom I permitted to read, any part of my manuscript, —will bear me witness that they read the greater part of this chapter, or heard it read, (in the city of Buenos Ayres,) early in November, 1865.—And here an old saying holds good, that

of Texas, she is, at the present time, subdivided into no less than thirty-six self-ruling, self-stultifying, self-subversive States, including the Empire of Austria and the Kingdom of Prussia. As if determined to develop, in contrast, or otherwise, the respective advantages and disadvantages of every known system of government, the designations of Statehood are, (considering the comparative smallness of the region affected,) here called into requisition, and are represented, in unprecedented variety. One Empire, five Kingdoms, eight Principalities, ten Duchies, six Grand Duchies, one Landgraviate, one Elecrate, and four Free Cities, complete the inventory of the real estate of this joint-stock company.

What paltry substitutes of shadow for substance, what pompous appropriations of the mere names of independent political communities, do we not discern, in the apple-orchard governments of Hesse-Cassel and Hesse Darmstadt! What poverty of domain, what ridiculous pretensions to nationalities, do we not perceive in the potato-patch principalities of Schwarzburg-Sondershausen and Schwarzburg-Rudolstadt! What impotent and preposterous imitations of sovereign commonwealths do we not behold in the horse-lot bodies politic of Lippe-Schaumburg and Lippe-Detmold! What unblushing

---

"the first shall be last, and the last shall be first;" for this last chapter was written first, and the first one herewith bound was written last. As is well known, the Needle-gun war in Europe did not break out until June, 1866,—seven months after what I have here said of Prussia and the other states of Germany was written. Without the alteration of a line, word or letter, I leave the text precisely as I wrote it. How well things have worked as I wished; how exactly great political changes have taken place in accordance with my advocacy; how wonderfully certain events have transpired as I virtually predicted, will be apparent to all candid and accurate observers.

burlesques upon the noble and ponderous distinctions of true Statehood do we not observe in the Sheep-pasture duchies of Saxe-Meiningen and Saxe-Coburg-Gotha! Big names, indeed, but little things! High-sounding terms, truly, but tiny territories! Frogs in abundance, but no oxen! No political common sense, alas! but an over-supply of Buncombe and Schleswig-Holstein!

A noble people are the Germans, brave, true and trusty; but they are still deplorably inexperienced in the art of good government. Are our worthy Teutonic friends really concerned to learn the limits of a nation whose ample and unbroken dimensions harmonize with the progressive grandeur of the nineteenth century? Then let them come, (on a visit, or to remain permanently;—they shall be most heartily welcome in either case,) to the United States of America, or go to Russia in Europe and Asia. Let them also confer with their enlightened and heroic republican neighbors, the invincible Switzers,—the countrymen of Tell and Winckelried,—who, from long experience, will teach them that mankind are endowed with certain talents, energies, dignities, and powers, which can be developed to perfection only in the absence of monarchical institutions. Yet one gigantic monarchy, objectionable as is the form of government, is better than a dozen dwarfish democracies; and even mild despotisms in bulk, with general good order and peace, are preferable to lawless liberty in detached fragments, with incessant anarchy and bloodshed.

When the Germans shall have consolidated their three dozen sovereign states under one grand central power, rightly administered, whether that power be known by the name of Republic, Empire, or Kingdom, it will be the first step in fulfillment of the promise of their universally-recognized, yet dormant greatness. Then, but not till then, will they occupy among the nations of the earth, that position of prominence and importance which belongs to them by virtue of their many inherent and eminent qualities of manhood. Then will it be, that, strengthened by the wise and patriotic administration of some modern Charlemagne, Otho, or Conrad, the citizens or subjects of the minor Germanic communities, residing in foreign countries, will have no disposition, no necessity, to apply to any representative of the government of the United States, nor to the representative of any other government except their own, for a redress of such grievancies as the exigencies of war, or other irregularities of the times, incident to their new places of abode, may entail upon them. Yet we know that less than two years have elapsed since very positive and importunate application of this sort was made to an officer of the government of the United States, now on duty in the Argentine Republic. And had we, who belonged to the strict State Rights school, succeeded in our hotspur attempt to establish State Sovereignty over South Carolina, and other States of the American Union, how long,—let us ask ourselves,—how long would it have been before we or our children, short of a navy of the requisite strength to command respect abroad, and lacking the support of a powerful home government, might have been found, weakened and distressed by some overwhelming outrage, seeking satisfaction by making similar overtures to a representative of Great Britain, or of France, or, with more propriety, and with better prospect of success, to a representative of our excellent old mother, the Model Republic?

It is not pleasant to have to suffer deprivation of personal liberty; nor is compulsory military service in foreign armies an agreeable pastime. The demand for indemnification for loss of property unlawfully seized and consumed, or carried away, is both natural and right;

and in those instances, where the ministers of justice are, unfortunately, rather nominal than real, there is no harm in having the power to inspire them with certain principles of international equity.

Long-settled are we in the belief, and with us deep-seated is the conviction, that this factious world of ours is cursed with many public quarrels, many national tumults, many bloody antagonisms, many mutually destructive conflicts, only because there are many jarring and ill-founded governments to foment them. Henceforth, instead of war, rapine, and ruin, let us promote peace, progress and prosperity. Let us reduce the number, but increase the size, and improve the form of the ruling powers of the earth. By doing this, many of the sanguinary dangers of public commotion, whether internal or external, may be greatly lessened, and the golden periods of tranquillity and thrift gloriously lengthened.

Only by decreasing the number of mischief-makers shall we ever be enabled to guard ourselves effectually from the entangling meshes of mischief itself. Only let us do away with the contentious causes of war, and the disastrous effects of it will soon disappear.

Another important reason why we are opposed to diminutive political powers is because the commonalty are, as a rule, even in times of peace, oppressively taxed to support them. National governments, if well organized, require vast and expensive systems of machinery, —systems of machinery so vast and expensive, indeed, and withal so intricate, and, in great part, of such rare material, that it is impossible for the comparatively few inhabitants of the smaller sovereign and independent States to furnish them, without having to endure, at the hands of the assessor, the most onerous and oft-repeated exactions.

For popinjays, and for others who wear such baubles as crowns and cockades, it is doubtless desirable to have the world cut up into numerous national territories, called empires, kingdoms, duchies, and other subdivisions, which we generally find corresponding in size with the insignificant littleness of their rulers; but for mankind at large, the true bone and sinew and salt of the earth, a very small number of great republics, like the United States of America, would, we believe, be infinitely better. And, ere the lapse of many years, may it not be so? It ought to be so; and with God's approval, it will, it must, it shall be so! Indeed, among all the ordinary affairs of mankind, there is certainly nothing more grossly unjust, nothing more unblushingly iniquitous, than to require that the recuperative energies and substance of the industrious masses, should be so frequently wrung from them for the mere purpose of pampering the pride and the pomp of petty princes.

Away, then, with the enforced necessity of enormous revenues to be squandered by the prodigal and insatiable vampires of monarchy! Away with the ostentation and extravagance of imperial retinues, equipages, and liveries! Away with the locust-like standing armies of crowned usurpers, who are ever and anon disturbing the peace of the world: and for whose costly maintenance the yeomanry are everywhere taxed and straitened to the very point of despair! Away with the glittering gewgaws and tinkling cymbals of royalty! Away with the ridiculously be-titled, be-gartered, and be-ribboned grandees of dwarfish and dwindling dynasties! Aye, away, away with all these; and instead of them, give us the solid advantages of the institutions of mighty Republics; of governments founded upon the principles of common sense, economy, justice, and patriotism; of free and enlightened commonwealths, where neither masters nor slaves are tolerated, and where no person, nor persons, of whatever name, claim, or condition, are invested with public authority, except such as are duly elected by the unbiased suffrages of their more intelligent fellow-citizens, and who, moreover, are, at any time, and at all times, removable or dismissable at the good pleasure of their constituents.

Thus, by this hasty retrospect of the history of dead nations; by this succinct review of the great bodies politic of our own time; by this concise inquiry as to the probable diminution of the number but increase of the size of sovereign and independent governments throughout the world, with reference to the future; and by other kindred considerations, have we already learned to regard with a large degree of contentment, amounting almost to perfect satisfaction, the new and truly momentous and irreversible triumph of the enlightened principles of the American system of self-government.

Even to the most superficial observer of human affairs, it is plain that Slavery and the Southern Confederacy are as physically dead as Julius Cæsar, and as morally dead as any other Cæsar, or successor of Cæsar. Therefore, under all the circumstances of the case, common sense, patriotism, and self-interest, alike suggest to us but one course; and that course, with frankness and firmness, we have resolved to pursue.

With our countrymen, in whatever part of the world we desire to renew relations of fellowship, friendship and loyalty; and to this end, we hereby mutually pledge ourselves to produce, at an early day, to the United States Consul within whose jurisdiction we severally reside, a copy of this declaration of sentiments, bearing the signature of our respective selves, and thereupon request his recognition and approval of the same (in so far as it may be proper for him to recognize and approve it,) by issuing to each of us a new certificate of our status as unqualified citizens of the United States of America.

Inquiry may here possibly be made whether we have not gone out of our way to say something more than was exactly pertinent to the primary object of this paper; and if so, we answer, that the free-spoken citizens of America, unlike the tongue-tied subjects of despotic governments, have no aptitude, no capacity, no intention, to accustom their lips to the use of padlocks. Not Servility and Slavery, (as have been foolishly and wickedly asserted,) but Freedom of Speech and Freedom of the Press, are, indeed, the principal corner-stones of our republican edifice.

If, perchance, it should be asked, by any one who is not an American, if this be not a somewhat extraordinary proceeding on our part, let us inquire, by way of reply whether the Americans have not always been a somewhat extraordinary people? Never yet have we known how to accept defeat at the hands of a foreign foe; and we confess to the fact that it is now one of our most earnest desires that this preëminent distinction of the American character may be rendered permanent and perpetual.

Providence, ever ready to contravene the projects of overweening ambition, seems to have ordained that we should not prove superior to our own countrymen; and we have no disposition whatever to attempt to thwart the decrees of destiny. No good, we are persuaded, nothing but evil, and that continually, evil on the right hand, and evil on the left, evil to ourselves and evil to others, could come from keeping alive in our breasts, disaffections and animosities, which are at once impotent and immoral.

Unfettered from passion and prejudice, and reëstablished under the wholesome influences of serenity and reason, we gladly hail this opportunity to resume our accus-

tomed championship of the free institutions of America;
and, responding to the gleeful strains of the friends of pop_
ular governments all over the world, our voices, intonated
with patriotic fantasies fresh from the head and the heart,
shall always be heard in unfaltering accents, keeping
time with those who exult with most warmth of affection
in the chorus of a nation redeemed. And as we ourselves
shall live, so also will we teach our children to live,—
with faith and works promotive of at least one Republic
of colossal power and magnitude, which, while generously
offering, or actually affording, a refuge for all the oppressed victims of the decaying systems of monarchy,
shall flourish, in undiminished invulnerability and vigor
so long as the earth itself shall endure.

ADDENDA.

Thus far had I written for the consideration and action of such Americans, resident in the Argentine Republic, as had been indentified with the Slaveholders' Rebellion; but for the reasons already assigned in the course
of my explanatory remarks at the beginning of this chapter, I did not tender the projected address, nor even
mention it, to any one of them.

It is believed that no person of even ordinary compre-
hension, after reading the foregoing paper, can fail to
perceive that, in connection with the preceding chapters,
it has, among other features of its special scope and design, the achievement of the three following propositions :

First. The reduction of the numerous little and insignificant States of the world into a small number of
large and powerful Nationalities.

Second. The extension of improved and refined forms
of Republican Government (such, for instance, as we

have in the United States of America) to each and every one of the newly enlarged and consolidated Commonwealths.

Third. The coöperative dominance of the White Races over every square foot, over every superficial inch, of land and sea ; and the non-hindrance of the apparent purposes and plans of Providence tó exterminate forever, from the fair face of the earth, all the Black and Bi-colored Riffraff.

Scattered over the six grand divisions of the earth, there are, at this time, (not to speak of the numerous clans and tribes of self-ruling barbarians,) about one hundred and ten sovereign and independent States; of which more than one one-third are in Europe. Might not these one hundred and ten nationalities, many of which are miniature and rickety monarchies, and few of which are of sufficient importance to send and support representatives abroad, be advantageously reduced to twenty or twenty-five great Republics? This inference appears to me to be most clearly warranted by considerations of universal good order.

In the Old World, within the last half century, how incessant and excited has been the clamor for a reconstruction of the States of Europe! The Congress at Vienna, which assembled in November, 1814, and adjourned in June, 1815,—having been in session nearly nine months,—pompously proclaimed the present limits of the countries of Europe ; but the men who composed that Congress were, unfortunately, a mere cabal of narrow-minded monarchists, whose puerile proceedings have never been, and can never be, accepted as satisfactory to any number of the more liberal and progressive people of the continent.

Nor is it only in Europe that a reconstruction of nationalities would seem to be necessary. Territorial reconstruction, in its application to peoples and governments, is needed all over the world ; and if I could raise my feeble voice so as to be heard in a matter so important as this, my plan of a general and systematic apportionment, should be marked by such divisions of the earth, into vast Republican Commonwealths, as would be delineated upon a map similar to the one foreshadowed in the following outlines·:

EUROPE.

1. To Russia (in lieu of Turkey, reserved for Austria) I would give both Sweden and Norway.

2. To Germany, including all the kingdoms and minor states and free cities of the Zollverein, I would give Switzerland, Holland, and Denmark.

3. To Austria, including Hungary, I would give all of European Turkey, and the whole of Greece.

4. To Italy, including Rome and Venice, I would give all the islands of the Mediterranean, on this condition, however, that that despicable hypocrite and impostor, the Pope, whether he be the present pope or a future pope,—if, indeed, the world is doomed to be afflicted and disgraced afresh with a future pope,—should first be hanged, banished for life, or condemned to ninety-nine years of hard labor in some isolated and dismal penitentiary.

5. To Spain, I would give Portugal.

6. To France, I would give both Belgium and Luxemburg.

7. To Great Britain and Ireland, in addition to their immense Asiatic and African possessions, I would

give all of the comparatively out-of-the-way islands of the world, (except those which constitute the West Indies, reserved for the United States of America; and those of Oceanica, reserved for Australia) which are not already under the protection and control of one or more of the nations of pure Caucasian blood. Nor would I favor, on the one hand, any secession from England, of either Scotland or Wales ; nor, on the other hand, any withdrawal from Protestant-blessed Great Britain, of Catholic-cursed Ireland; only so far as the Catholic curse of Ireland could be withdrawn, driven away, or obliterated.

Enough, and too much, have we already heard of the nonsense of a sovereign and independent Ireland; a sovereign and independent Poland; a sovereign and independent Hungary; a sovereign and independent Schleswig-Holstein; a sovereign and independent Southern Confederacy. God grant that the sore affliction, the galling humiliation, and the deep disgust, may not yet be in reserve for us, to hear of a sovereign and independent Vermont; a sovereign and independent Rhode Island; a sovereign and independent Delaware: a sovereign and independent Buncombe !

Europe, therefore, according to the arrangement thus proposed, instead of being subdivided, as she now is, into nearly fifty sovereign and independent nationalities, would be reduced to the more convenient and auspicious number of seven, as follows:

1. GERMANY, with Prussia as the central and better basis.	4. GREAT BRITAIN.
	5. FRANCE.
2. RUSSIA.	6. ITALY.
3. AUSTRIA.	7. SPAIN.

The democratic masses of Europe have not forgotten the republican spirit which, in 1848, awakened them to an unsatisfied and still accumulating foretaste of greatness and glory. From the buoyant Boyhood of Democracy, let them unfalteringly ascend to the mighty Manhood of Republicanism. This done, and the evil days of crowned princes and mitred potentates will soon have passed away, never, never to return.

NORTH AMERICA.

To THE UNITED STATES OF AMERICA, I would give the whole of North America, from Behring's Strait in the north to the Isthmus of Darien in the south, and from Cape Race in the east to Vancouver's Island in the west; also Cuba, Hayti, Jamaica, Porto Rico, and all of the other West India islands.*

SOUTH AMERICA.

SOUTH AMERICA, in my humble way of thinking, should be reduced to three nationalities, each of which should possess sea-shore on both the east and west coast of the continent.

---

* As already stated, on page 438, the greater part of this chapter was written by me, and was read by two of my esteemed friends (whose names are mentioned on the 425th page of this book) in Buenos Ayres, in the early part of November, 1865. Thanks to our Bismarckian Secretary of State, William Henry Seward—a greater Councilor and Diplomatist than Bismarck himself—we have recently acquired (from Russia) a very considerable and important part of the continental territory here claimed. With Seward, and with other eminently able White Republicans, as our Helmsmen of State, British America, Mexico, Central America, and the West Indies, will all soon find excellent and permanent shelter under the wide-spreading wings of our mighty Eagle !

1. To New Granada (or the United States of Colombia), should be given Venezuela, the three Guianas, and so much of Brazil and Ecuador as may be found north of the equator.

2. To Brazil, divested of both Slavery and Monarchy, I would give so much of Bolivia, Peru, and Ecuador as could be found north of the twentieth parallel of south latitude.

3. To the Argentine Republic, I would give the whole of Chili, Patagonia, Uruguay and Paraguay, and so much of Peru, Bolivia, and Brazil, as may be found south of the twentieth degree of south latitude.

Or, in default of the success of this arrangement, all the countries west of the Andes might, for the present, be put under one republican government, and the other part of the continent subdivided into two or three republics, (but into no empire nor kingdom) with latitudinal limits similar to those suggested in the foregoing proposition. In the course of time, when the Anglo-Saxon and other Caucasian races shall have taken the places,— as, at some future time, (the sooner the better) they certainly will take the places,—of all the feeble-minded and spindle-shanked hybrids who now occupy both slopes of the Andes, the whole continent might, perhaps, be fitly formed into one republic.

ASIA.

Let all Asia, and the Islands adjacent thereto, be so apportioned into half a dozen great powers, under the exclusive control of Caucasian-blooded people, as that the Russians in the north, the English in the south, and the French in the interior, may not only be permitted, but encouraged, and if necessary, assisted to maintain, strengthen and extend their foothold upon that vast section of the habitable globe.

AFRICA.

As it seems to me, Africa, like South America, should be subdivided, by parallel lines running from east to west, into three nearly equal parts ; the northern third of the continent to be colonized and governed by the French ; the middle or equatorial by the Germans, or by the people of the United States of America ; and the southern by the English ;—all to be held and fostered in the paramount interest of the White Races (between whom and the blacks there should ever be the most absolute and uninterrupted separation) until they, the Whites, shall have become numerous enough, and strong enough, not only to establish and maintain governments of their own, but also to put in unfailing practice, with reference to the worthless negroes, a fossilizing policy, similar to that which has been so naturally and so successfully pursued by the Anglo-Americans, with reference to the good-for-nothing Indians.

OCEANICA.

To AUSTRALIA (the whole island-continent organized under one republican government) I would assign New Zealand, New Guinea, Van Dieman's Land, and all the other Islands of Oceanica, including those of Polynesia.

Upon the comprehensive plan of adjustment here indicated, the whole world, as will now be seen, would be brought under only twenty-one sovereign and independent nationalities, thus :

North America 1
South America 3
Europe 7
Asia 6
Africa 3
Oceanlca 1

Total, 21

The governments of all of these countries, the governments of all countries (all communities of men everywhere) should be so organized as to be essentially and truly republican ; and, therefore, as a matter of course, tolerant of no favoritism to families, no absolutism in politics, no mere worldly and absurdly prescribed form of religion ; such religion, for instance, as we find established, under State recognition, by the Roman Catholics, the Mohammedans, the Brahmins, the Buddhists, and other booby-brained bigots.

In the furtherance of these highly important measures, a Congress of the most able and distinguished representatives of White People from every influential division of the earth, should, at an early day, be assembled in the city of Washington, in London, in Paris, or in Berlin ; and should there sit, in earnest and prudent deliberation until they had matured the outlines of a plan under which the great changes thus contemplated could be speedily and peacefully effected.

As soon as it could be seen that the world had been territorially reorganized upon a basis well answering to these suggestions, I would take still another step in fulfillment of the auspicious promises and predictions of man's destiny to attain, upon the earth, a far higher and better state of existence than he has ever yet known From the twenty-one world-embracing republics thus formed, I would convene, with perfect numerical equality of representation, alternately, at intervals of ten years, in first one and then another of the several cities indicated, or elsewhere, sixty-three of the most discreet and impartial statesmen who could be found,—such statesmen, for instance, as, from America, William H. Seward, Charles Francis Adams, and Reverdy Johnson,—every one of the sixty-three (three from each republic) to be elected by the whole body of the people of their respective commonwealths, for the term of seven years, at a salary of not more nor less than $17,000 each per annum, who, with their successors, should constitute a perpetual World Congress, invested with full powers to hear and definitely determine, without an appeal to arms in any case whatever, all serious controversies between the different governments; and also to lend whatever combination of forces might be necessary for the immediate suppression of all unjust and foolhardy rebellions, regardless alike of the place, the time, or the circumstance of their outbreak.

Other special and clearly defined labors which should devolve upon this International Congress, would consist in devising ways and means for the prevention of any more wars among the Caucasian families of mankind ; or, in other words, for the preservation of peace, and for earnest and coöperative action, among all the White Races, until, at least, all the effete peoples now inhabiting the earth, all negroes, all Indians, all mulattoes, all bi-colored hybrids, should be so far annihilated as that it might never be possible to find even a vestige of any one of them, save only in the fated form of fossils.

Here, for a few moments, let a part of the Ottoman Empire receive attention. One of the most stupendous acts of folly and wickedness which the world has witnessed in modern times, was the successful but infamous part played, to the great detriment of civilization and progress, in 1854-'5, by the combined forces of Great Britain, France, and Sardinia, in prolongation of the long-since forfeited life of that despicable and death-doomed "Sick Man of the East," whom the brave old Nicholas of Russia, acting under the noble impulses of an exalted desire for the regeneration of Europe, had prepared to bury irrecoverably in the deep bowels of the Bosphorus.

No one, except he who, through sheer perversity, closes his eyes to the unfailing signs and evidences of coming events, is so dim of sight as not to be able to perceive that the Asiatic interlopers, the Mohammedan fanatics, who now hold that unhappy and despoiled country called Turkey in Europe, must, in fleeing, for a time, from the vengeance that awaits them, soon retire to their own side of the Dardanelles, and even there, erelong, be hunted down, harassed, and finally supplanted. Not to the Mongol, but to the Caucasian ; not to the copper-colored, but to the fair-complexioned ; not to the black man, but to the white man, rightfully belongs the whole earth ; and to these, not to those, shall, in due time, be given, in all its entirety of atmosphere, land and liquid, " this spheroidal orb of our present habitation." God's heralds of destiny, heaven's messengers of justice, may, by divine sufferance, be somewhat slow in coming ; yet, with the most absolute and unerring certainty, will they come within the good time appointed ;—and then, ah, then, (glorious hour to anticipate!) a quick and eternal farewell to all that's black, whether simple, quaint, or compound!

As early as December 9, 1835, Mr. Henry Wheaton, our universally and justly distinguished author on International Law, writing from Berlin, at which capital he was most ably and honorably discharging the duties of an American diplomatist, said to Mr. Forsyth, who, at that time, was our Secretary for Foreign Affairs :

"If I am not wholly misinformed, the Emperor of Russia is not disposed much longer to postpone the execution of those designs upon Turkey, which he has inherited from the traditionary policy of his predecessors—a policy, in the actual nature of things, requiring the possession of Constantinople and the Dardanelles, in order to give complete development to the natural resources of Russia, and to enable her to advance in the career of civilization, in which she is now impeded for want of the complete command of this channel of communication with the Mediterranean and its rich coasts and islands."

Daniel Webster, from his high seat in the Senate, (see his works, Volume III. page 79), spoke thus:

"The Ottoman power over the Greeks, obtained originally by the sword, is constahtly preserved by the same means. Wherever it exists it is a mere military power. The religious and civil code of the state being both fixed in the Koran, and equally the object of an ignorant and furious faith, have been found equally incapable of change. 'The Turk, it has been said, has been *encamped* in Europe for four centuries.' He has hardly any more participation in European manners, knowledge, and arts, than when he crossed the Bosphorus. But this is not the worst. The power of the empire is fallen into anarchy, and as the principle which belongs to the head, belongs also to the parts, there are as many despots as there are pachas, beys, and viziers. Wars are almost perpetual between the Sultan and some rebellious governor of a province ; and in the conflict of these despotisms, the people are necessarily ground between the upper and the nether millstone."

With as little delay as possible, the truculent Turks, who, by their intrusive and blighting tread, are now desecrating the sacred soil of Europe, ought to be forced to transmigrate, heels over heads, or otherwise, in the direction of their inhospitable old haunts in the east, until every one of them shall have either found a final resting-place in the depths of the Hellespont, or been pushed so far beyond its banks as never to be able to return. And so thoroughly and speedily should this be done, that all the other countries of Europe, making common cause, should array themselves in irresistible columns, and accomplish their praiseworthy undertaking, in its fullest scope, within the brief period of a single campaign, which might, and should, be limited in its duration to ninety days.

Whether Turkey, wholly reclaimed from the deleterious grasp of the Moslem, should be absorbed by Russia, by Austria, or by one of the other great powers of Europe, would matter little. Brought under the sole occupancy and control of the pure white race, (the only race fit for continued habitation upon the earth,) there could be no doubt as to the dignity and splendor of its future career in the grand march of civilization. Still, had I the disposal of it, it should, as already indicated, be assigned to Austria;—and to Russia should pass the two (the twin) kingdoms of Sweden and Norway; not from any ill-will toward either of these States, nor toward any one of the other diminutive bodies politic designated for absorption, but from deeply ingrafted convictions that the true welfare of both the greater and the lesser powers would be equally promoted by an extensive and well-devised system of consolidation.

Events of the greatest possible importance in the political world will, it is confidently believed, soon begin to transpire among the rotten and tottering monarchies of Europe. Large and influential parties, deeply imbued with the sentiments and principles of free governments; justly alarmed at the unremitting encroachments upon their liberties; grossly wronged and insulted by the presence of a drone-like prince or potentate on almost every square league of territory, (when, as with negroes, Indians, and bi-colored hybrids, there should not be one in all the world,) and naturally anxious for a change for the better, are now rapidly developing themselves there; and that, too, with so much determination and unanimity of purpose, that their patriotic labors, in the end, are morally certain to be crowned with success. Germany, grand, glorious old Germany, the venerated Fatherland of the Anglo-Saxons and of the Anglo-Americans,—a country from which we always look for so much that is good, and for so little that is bad,—is the mighty centre around which all the republican parties of the Old World are now, with prudent forecast, rallying their friendly forces, their faith, their hopes, their expectations.

A few excellent suggestions, looking to the ends here held in view, are contained in the following extract from a letter recently written by Garibaldi to his friend Karl Blend, who resides in London, and who is there editing a newspaper which urgently and ably advocates the union of all the German States under one great central Republican Government.

"The world is in want of a leading nation; not for domineering over it, but for conducting it on the path of duty, which is nothing more than the fraternity of nations and the overthrow of the barriers which political egotism has raised. Yes, the world is in want of a leading people, which, similar to the knights-errant of old, would devote itself to redress the wrongs, to take the side of the weak, and to sacrifice for a while its own material welfare in order to attain to a far more valuable good, namely, the satisfaction of having mitigated the sufferings of fellow-men. A people that came courageously to the front with such a noble object would rally round itself all those who are oppressed, all those who would fain rise from the abyss of misfortune into which the perversity of governments has thrown them. This paramount post of honor, which the vicissitudes of modern times has left vacant, could be occupied by the German nation. The serious and philosophical character of your compatriots, would be a guarantee and a pledge of stability for us all. Shake, then, you with your robust Germanic arms, the rotten fabric of your thirty tyrants. Form, in the heart of Europe, which you inhabit, the imposing unity of your fifty millions; and we shall all throw ourselves with enthusiastic eagerness into your brotherly ranks."

Well said, heroic Garibaldi! Germany will not forget your noble words, nor will the republicans of other portions of Europe fail to hold them in deeply-cherished and significant' remembrance. Victor Hugo, of France; Joseph Mazzini, of Italy; and Emilio Castelar, of Spain, are still alive: and under these, and under their brave comrades and successors, shall many a tyrant, (however disagreeable to him may be the lesson,) learn to tremble, and to totter from his throne!

While the Slaveholders' Rebellion in the United States was in most wicked progress, Thomas Carlyle, a sort of self-constituted and loud-mouthed yelper for the time-bewasted institutions of the Old World, said, in effect, and with lachrymose demonstrations, that, if the democratic masses of America were successful in putting down Slavery and the Slaveholders, England and all the other countries of Europe would at once prepare for an easy transit from Monarchy to Democracy. For the term *Democracy*, in this particular instance, the stentorian Thomas, the vociferous Carlyle, the boisterous and bellowing beef-eater, might, with a display of far greater elegance of taste in the selection of words than his style usually evinces, have substituted its best synonyme, REPUBLICAN-ISM:—a synonyme to which, in the extensiveness and importance of its signification, even the precious old word Democracy is itself subordinate.

Unintermittingly, from the birth of history to the present moment, has the world been the victim of both anarchy and strife; but this has not been because of the lack of democracies, but rather because of the lack of Republics. Thus far, during man's sojourn upon the earth, there have already been, and ceased to be, many thousands of democracies; yet there has never been but one real Republic. Most fortunately, however, for both the present and the future of the human race, and not unfortunately for the past, *that* Republic still exists; and, by the grace of God, it will forever continue to exist, in a form similar or superior to that in which it is now found embodied in the UNITED STATES OF AMERICA. At various epochs, both ancient and modern, democracies in Europe and elsewhere have been almost as numerous and inutile as monks in Italy, or as nuns in Spain; but in no part of the world, except that between Canada and the Gulf of Mexico, has a Republic, in the true definition of the term, ever been known. It is said that Aristotle, who lived in the fourth century before Christ, wrote the history of eighteen hundred democracies which existed and flourished, but every one of which had completely expired, prior to his own time ; and these, by those who ought to know better, are often wrongly mentioned as having been so many Republics. Consoling would it be to be able to believe that no narrow-minded monarchist, while under the lingering influences of passions engendered by unreasonable jealousies, envyings, and prejudices, has done this with malice prepense. He who is to write the whole history of any one republic is yet unborn. The historian here dimly held in view in the far future will find all the items of his chronology between the year 1776 and the very distant time to come—if come it must—when the sun, and the moon, and the stars, and all the hosts of other shining orbs and glittering globes, shall have been forever eclipsed in total darkness, and, to the wreck and ruin of all nether space, hurled headlong from the heavens!

Democratic government, good as far as it goes, but too circumscribed in its functions for all the weighty and complicated requirements of a great nation, had its origin in Europe; republican government, an extensive and independent organization of infinitely superior scope and power, a political system of far more stately and wide-spreading growth, is indigenous to America. Comparing great things with small,—using a figure of speech the very antithesis of exaggerated hyperbole,—while a Democracy, on the one hand, is a rich and carefully cultivated one-acre lot, a Republic, on the other, is a surpassingly fertile and thoroughly-tilled thousand-acre field. Very different from either the Republic or the Democracy, is the Monarchy, which, wherever seen, is, indeed, but a sorry sight,—a mere blighted and barren eight-acre goose-pasture.

Humiliatingly limited, indeed, is an accurate knowledge of the differences which exist between the two forms of government now under consideration, the republican and the democratic; and hence the frequent and absurd confounding and classifying of the one as synonymous with the other. Let Americans, at least, be no longer guilty of this inexcusable weakness. No system of government that has ever been instituted by the wisdom of mankind, is so worthy to be perfectly known and appreciated as our own; for, as yet, it is unique in its excellence, and bids fair, by virtue of its having been established as the first of a series of indestructible forms for the proper management of public affairs, to become unapproachably preëminent in the length of its aggregate duration.

In order that the reader may be enabled to perceive with entire clearness of vision some of the special points of the superiority of a Republic as compared with a Democracy, I beg leave to offer for his perusal the following perspicuous definition of certain important differences and distinctions between them, which may be found detailed at length in the truly statesman-like writings of Madison. See the *Federalist*, No. XIV., page 61, from which what here follows is a priceless quotation:

"The error which limits republican government to a narrow district, has been unfolded and refuted in preceding papers. I remark here only, that it seems to owe its rise and prevalence chiefly to the confounding of a republic with a democracy; and applying to the former, reasonings drawn from the nature of the latter. The true distinction between these forms, was also adverted to on a former occasion. It is, that in a democracy, the people meet and exercise the government in person; in a republic they assemble and administer it by their representatives and agents. A democracy, consequently, must be confined to a small spot. A republic may be extended over a large region.

"To this accidental source of the error, may be added the artifice of some celebrated authors, whose writings have had a great share in forming the modern standard of political opinions. Being subjects, either of an absolute or a limited monarchy, they have endeavored to heighten the advantages or palliate the evils of those forms, by placing in comparison with them the vices and defects of the republican, and by citing, as specimens of the latter, the turbulent democracies of ancient Greece and modern Italy. Under the confusion of names, it has been an easy task to transfer to a republic, observations applicable to a democracy only; and among others, the observation that it can never be established but among a small number of people, living within a small compass of territory.

"Such a fallacy may have been the less perceived, as most of the popular governments of antiquity were of the democratic species; and even in modern Europe, to which we owe the great principle of representation, no example is seen of a government wholly popular, and founded, at the same time, wholly on that principle. If Europe has the merit of discovering this great mechanical power in government by the simple agency of which the will of the largest political body may be concentred, and its force directed to any object which the public good requires, America can claim the merit of making the discovery the basis of unmixed and extensive republics. It is only to be lamented, that any of her citizens should wish to deprive her of the additional merit of displaying its full efficacy in the establishment of the comprehensive system now under her consideration.

"As the natural limit of a democracy is that distance from the central point, which will just permit the most remote citizens to assemble as often as their public functions demand, and will include no greater number than can join in those functions; so the natural limit of a republic is that distance from the centre which will barely allow the representatives of the people to meet as often as may be necessary for the administration of public affairs. Can it be said that the limits of the United States exceed this distance? It will not be said, by those who recollect, that the Atlantic coast is the longest side of the Union; that during the term of thirteen years, the representatives of the states have been almost continually assembled; and that the members from the most distant states are not chargeable with greater intermissions of attendance than those from the states in the neighborhood of Congress."

Once have I solicited the reader to peruse this lucid exposition (from the *Federalist*) of some of the more notable differences which exist between a Republic and a Democracy. Twice, at least, will he peruse it, if he has not already done so, in the acquisition of certain jewels of political knowledge, of which, in this otherwise well-informed age, it would be a gross shame and disgrace to be entirely ignorant.

In 1787, during the period of his ambassadorship to France, and while the learned writers of the *Federalist,* and other literary patriots, were busily engaged in discussing the several proposed provisions of our imperishable Constitution, not then adopted, Mr. Jefferson, (see his works, Volume II., page 220,) in the course of one of his unofficial letters from Paris, said:

"Above all things, I am astonished at some people's considering a kingly government as a refuge. Advise such to read the fable of the frogs who solicited Jupiter for a king. If that does not put them to rights, send them to Europe to see something of the trappings of monarchy, and I will undertake that every man shall go back thoroughly cured. If all the evils which can arise among us from the republican form of government, from this day to the day of judgment, could be put into a scale against what this country suffers from its monarchical form in a week, or England in a month, the latter would preponderate. Consider the contents of the Red-book in England, or the Almanac royale of France, and say what a people gain by monarchy. No race of kings has ever presented above one man of common sense in twenty generations."

Again, under date of August 14, 1787, (see Jefferson's Works, Volume II., page 249,) writing unofficially from Paris, he said:

" With all the defects of our constitution, whether general or particular, the comparison of our government with those of Europe, is like a comparison of heaven and hell. England, like the earth, may be allowed to take the intermediate station. And yet I hear there are people among you who think the experience of our government has already proved that republican governments will not answer. Send those gentry here to count the blessings of monarchy."

To David Hume, the brilliant Scottish metaphysician and historian, who was certainly one of the very best thinkers and writers of his time, the world is indebted (see his Essays, Volume I. page 461–2) for the following well-merited tribute to the principles of republican government,—a tribute which accords so harmoniously with Mr. Madison's, on a preceding page, that, but for absolute knowledge to the contrary, the reader might be . strongly inclined to surmise that both papers had for their author the same great mind :

" Though it is more difficult to form a republican government in an extensive country than in a city, there is more facility, when once it is formed, of preserving it steady and uniform, without tumult and faction. In a large government, which is modeled with masterly skill, there is compass and room enough to refine the democracy, from the lower people who may be admitted into the first elections or first concoction of the commonwealth, to the higher magistrates, who direct all the movements. At the same time, the parts are so distant and remote, that it is very difficult, either by intrigue, prejudice, or passion, to hurry them into any measures against the public interest.

Even Machiavelli, who, with consummate ability, said so many bad things (especially in his Essay on the Prince) that most of his political ethics have, for more than three centuries, been utterly contemned and abominated, was, nevertheless, constrained to give expression to many good words, true and strong, among which some of the very best were these :

"Republics furnish the world with a greater number of brave and excellent characters than kingdoms ; the reason is that in republics virtue is honored and promoted ; in monarchies and kingdoms it incurs suspicion.

Yet Machiavelli knew nothing of Republics only so far as, with the eye of an astute political seer, he foresaw them in the future ; or rather, perhaps, in his case, I should say, only so far as republics were and are but diminutively and imperfectly represented by democracies ; which is as much as to say that, although the ship and the yacht are both vessels of universally recognized good qualities, yet the one is very much larger and better than the other. A Monarchy is a common flat-bottomed boat, a sort of ugly and ominous mud-scow, in which everyone who is so silly or unfortunate as to take passage, is not only certain to be most foully and frequently bedaubed, but will, besides, even in the best of weather, have distressingly slow and perilous progress.

Even toward democracies, however, which may be said to be the mere but yet sacred and delicate germs or buds of Republics, the servile advocates and supporters of Monarchies have ever cherished the most mean and inveterate hostility. A remarkable instance of this has been strikingly adduced by one of great Britain's ablest historians, (see Robertson's Charles V., Volume II., page 322,) who, notwithstanding the fact that he, too, has fallen into the common error of miscalling Republics those diminutive powers which are simply pure and unmixed Democracies, significantly says :

"The Republic of Venice, which at the beginning of the sixteenth century, had appeared so formidable, that almost all the potentates of Europe united in a confederacy for its destruction, declined gradually from its ancient power and splendor."

The charming historian Motley, in his glowing description of the rise and fall of the Dutch Democracy, which

came so near expanding into the magnificent proportions
and properties of a Republic, that he deemed it becoming
on his part to honor it under that appellation, has rendered conspicuous, for all time to come, another very grievous instance of monarchical hostility to free governments. Switzerland also, ever since her adoption of the
enlightened principles of civil and political liberty, has
constantly experienced the bitter jealousies and animosities of her monarchical neighbors. So also has it ever
been, thus far, with every country, whether in Europe or
out of Europe, where mankind have sought to regain the
natural and inalienable rights and privileges which, under the tyrannical institutions of monarchy, have been
filched from them.

Scarcely is there a civilized people on the face of the
globe who have not, on more than one occasion, preferred
their reasonable claims for recognition as the sole and
rightful rulers of themselves ; but so close and powerful,
hitherto, has been the alliance of absolutism against
them, that nowhere, save only in the United States of
America, have they ever been able to establish a Republic under which it was found practicable to secure to every one of its worthy and well-qualified citizens, perfect
constitutional equality. But, although there has ever
been, and ever will be, on the part of crowned heads, or
on the part of the sycophantic advocates of kingcraft, the
sternest opposition to all democratic ideas and movements, yet, in the progress of time, shall the people everywhere have the great good fortune to witness the downfall of all the regal and other despotic forms of government, and, with enraptured vision, to behold, upon the
ruins of these, the permanent upbuilding of a score, more
or less, of world-embracing and weal-working Republics.

Of kings themselves, and of how hereditary kingship

commonly affects the households of royalty, a few words may not be out of place in this connection. Says the learned and philosophic Jefferson, (see his works, Volume V., page 514,) in the course of a letter which, on the 5th of March, 1810, he wrote to Governor Langdon, of New Hampshire :

"When I observed that the King of England was a mere cypher, I did not mean to confine the observation to the mere individual now on that throne. The practice of Kings marrying only in the families of Kings, has been that of Europe for some centuries. Now, take any race of animals ; confine them in idleness and inaction, whether in a sty, a stable, or a state-room ; pamper them with high diet, gratify their several appetites ; immerse them in sensualities ; nourish their passions ; let everything bend before them ; and banish whatever might lead them to think ; and in a few generations they become all body and no mind ; and this, too, by a law of nature, by that very law by which we are in the constant practice of changing the characters and propensities of the animals we raise for our own purposes. Such is the regimen in raising Kings ; and in this way they have gone on for centuries. While in Europe, I often amused myself with contemplating the characters of the then reigning sovereigns of Europe. Louis the XVI. was a fool, of my own knowledge, and in despite of the answers made for him at his trial. The King of Spain was a fool ; and of Naples the same. They passed their lives in hunting ; and despatched two couriers a week, one thousand miles, to let each other know what game they had killed the preceding days. The King of Sardinia was a fool. All these were Bourbons. The Queen of Portugal, a Braganza, was an idiot by nature. And so was the King of Denmark. Their sons, as regents, exercised the powers of government. The King of Prussia, successor to the great Frederick, was a mere hog, in body as well as in mind. Gustavus of Sweden, and Joseph of Austria, were really crazy ; and George of England, you know, was in a straight waistcoat. There remained, then, none but old Catherine, who had been too lately picked up from the commonalty to have lost her common sense. In this state Bonaparte found Europe ; and it was this state of its rulers which lost it with scarce a struggle. These animals had become without mind and powerless ; and so will every hereditary monarch be, after a few generations. Alexander, the grandson of Catherine, is as yet an exception. He is able to hold his own. But he is only of the third gener-

ation. His race is not yet worn out. And so endeth the book of
Kings, from all of whom, for all time to come, may the good Lord
deliver us !"

Elsewhere, toward the close of one of the many excellent epistles with which he was accustomed to favor those
who had the honor and the intellectual profit of corresponding with him, this same Thomas Jefferson, who was
a notably stanch and genuine republican of the good old
times ; who was also a most wholesome hater of both
crowned heads and woolly-heads; and who was, moreover, an exquisite despiser of all manner of cant and hypocrisy and wrong hypothesis, said that, during the whole
period of his several years services and travels in the Old
World, he never saw a king nor emperor whose mental
calibre would have been a match for the mind of one
of even the second rate parsons of Virginia. It is a matter of regret with me, that I have lost the reference to
the letter thus alluded to, and have no time now to read
anew the nine ponderous and precious volumes of his
works, in order to recover it ; otherwise, I should here
reproduce, in his own fitly-chosen words, what he himself said concerning the numerous sorry kings and king-
lings—the " beastly divinities and droves of silly gods"
—whom he met, a thousand times, more or less, in the
leading courts of Europe.

Herbert Spencer, the greatest living philosopher of
England, in his admirable work on Education, (see page
67,) says :

"As in past ages the king was everything and the people nothing ;
so, in past histories the doings of the king fill the entire picture, to
which the national life forms but an obscure background. While
only now, when the welfare of nations rather than of rulers is becoming the dominant idea, are historians beginning to occupy themselves
with the phenomena of social progress."

It has ever seemed to me, that both masters and slaves, having assumed toward each other relations which are clearly incompatible with true manhood, ought to be equally and profoundly ashamed of themselves, and that no one of them, of either class, while persisting in the maintenance of his disreputable status, should ever be tolerated in good society ; and as with these, so with kings and subjects ;—I could never regard either the former or the latter, except with feelings of the deepest aversion, indignation and disgust. In fact, Master and King, on the one hand, and Slave and Subject, on the other, are synonymous terms ; and as the two words have one meaning in the former case, so have both the same signification in the latter. These several terms involve such crooked and arbitrary conditions between men as are no longer (if, indeed, they ever were) consistent with the common rights and interests of either individuals or nations. They are no longer consonant with substantial dignity ; they are no longer accordant with the spirit of ennobling progress.

In the future, therefore, let the democratic masses of republican America be less reserved in their championship of free institutions, whether in words or in deeds, than they have been wont to be in their serene and self-satisfied experiences of the past. Fortunately, there are, in certain parts of the world, some things so intrinsically good as to be worthy of universal praise and acceptance; and these, it cannot be questioned, ought to be earnestly recommended to all those who live in less favored lands. One of the things of this sort,—a thing meritorious of unlimited confidence and adoption,—is Republicanism, which, among all the systems of government hitherto devised for the well-being of mankind, is alone adequate to the full and perfect accomplishment of each and every high end proposed.

After very careful consideration of the subject, it has seemed to me that the people of the United States of America, whilst fast attaining to a degree of renown and genuine greatness unexampled beneath the sun, have, nevertheless, in one point at least, come short of their duty to mankind at large. Hitherto, as Americans, in my humble opinion, we have always been too diffident and too silent in our defence and advocacy of republican institutions, as compared with the monarchical institutions of the Old World. Unnecessarily long, as it seems to me, have we waited and labored to accumulate an overwhelming fund of fact and argument for our own vindication, and for the vindication of others who have followed, and who are yet to follow, our example in annulling the usurpations of kingcraft and tyranny. As the citizens generally of a gigantic and still growing commonwealth, which, by its regular and healthful accretions, would seem to be gathering to itself all the fair and fertile parts of a vast continent, let us now manfully put aside our reticence in this regard. Let us, with becoming modesty, but yet with firmness of purpose, and, above all, with convincing truthfulness of statement, proclaim to the world the full efficiency and the perfect adaptability of the principles of republican government for every emergency, and for all the conditions of enlightened humanity. In short, let us, with ardor and diligence, teach all the nations of the earth, (exhibiting to them, meanwhile, evidences of the incontrovertible correctness of our teachings,) that Republics, in their highest and best developments, are political sublimities; and that, except under the mighty ægis of these, mankind will always in vain aspire to a grand and glorious future beneath the heavens.

Time and space here exhort me to be brief, and to bring to a close this special labor. Have I fairly met and answered the expectations of my readers? Have I scrupulously preserved these pages from a plethory or redundance of levity and jest? May what I have here written, taken as a whole, be said to be a work of real and enduring usefulness? Have I, with earnestness and truth, spoken of things solid and substantial? Have I given prominence to subjects worthy to be further considered? Have I, with becoming dignity, dwelt upon matters of terrestrial moment to mankind?

Little, certainly, have I said of celestial creatures or concerns; for of these, little (if anything) did I know. Yet have I a strong and steadfast faith, that the three-score and ten years, more or less, allotted to man upon the earth, were not given in vain,—were not given except for his general good, and for his comparative exemption from the numerous troubles which, through the gross ignorance and folly of both himself and his fellows, now beset him.

I believe in man's capacity to discover and enjoy, upon any one of the six grand divisions of the earth, a far better condition of life than the world has ever yet known; and I believe, further, that, independently of his own volition, he is happily destined gradually to advance in the path of improvement, until he shall have permanently attained a degree or measure of perfection to which, as yet, he is an almost total stranger. Then, indeed will there be no more Wars, nor Rumors of Wars; no more Slavery, Slaves, nor Slaveholders; no more Monarchies, Kings, nor Subjects; no more Bigotry, Priestcraft, nor Catholicism; and, (the Lord be thrice specially praised for the prospect,) no more Negroes, Indians, nor bi-colored Hybrids!

Better now than later, let us learn, if possible, both

with accuracy and with reverence, what the one only
good and great God himself hath irreversibly decreed
concerning us, and concerning others. As Americans,
we must either soon recognize and accept the fact that,
with reference to the world at large, Providence has ordained the sole and universal ascendency of white men,
and, at the same time, made equitable provision for the
extinction of all the black and copper-colored races, or
else we ourselves, as delinquent offshoots of the Caucasian type, are absolutely certain to be expunged from the
earth, and will deserve to be so expunged, for our willful
blindness and disobedience. Of this startling fact, let all
the Black Republicans, and mere especially the driveling
and knavish negro-kissers, who compose the two-thirds
majority of the Black Congress, take due notice, and
govern themselves accordingly.

It is white men only who ever did, or do, or would, or
will, or could, or can achieve greatness; and it is these,
and these alone, to whom I have reference when I speak of
the actual or possible existence of an approximately perfect
manhood. Clearheaded poets and prose writers may very
properly evolve their inspirations in glowing promises and
predictions of better days to come; for come they will; but
then, before the all-cheering and all-pervading light of
such days shall have dawned upon us, we must spread the
Caucasians, the whites, our own kith and kin, in exclusive occupancy and control, over the whole earth;—having previously fossilized, or put in process of fossilization,
all the inferior species of the genus *homo*, whether of
color black or of color brown.

If the reader will revert to the title-page of the book
in hand, he will at once perceive the words, "A QUESTION
FOR A CONTINENT," which imply a conviction on the part
of the author, that there is, now under discussion in the
United States, a certain matter of such transcendent im

portance, that it should, until rightly and definitely disposed of, take precedence of every other public problem. I need scarcely add that the question to which I thus allude, is "THE NEGRO QUESTION." How I have treated this question, may be seen and read in the preceding pages. How it is to be eventually determined, I deferentially submit to God, and to the majority of Anglo Americans.

Nor, if I may be permitted to suggest the fact, have I strictly confined myself to the examination of a single question, nor to the interests of a single continent. On the contrary, I have, I think, in my humble way, discussed several questions, and turned, at times, my attention to all the continents. In doing this, if I have performed something more than I promised, it is better, perhaps,—if, as I believe, the things aimed at be good in themselves,—than if I had come short of the mere apparent purport of my self-imposed task.

Of the gentle and confiding souls who have come with me thus far, I must now take my leave. It is not for nothing, however, that we have been so long together. Upon every one who has read these lines, as well as upon him that wrote them, new obligations have been laid. From every relation and circumstance in life we are expected, by a superior intelligence, to acquire knowledge, both for our own special improvement, and for the betterment of the world at large. As it always behooves us to be studious not to disappoint the just expectations of our fellow-men, so also, in a much greater degree, doth it behoove us not to disappoint, not to baffle, not to contravene, the ever-rightful expectations of Heaven. By virtue of our joint investigations, researches, and inquiries, and in consequence of the corresponding convictions with which we have all become more or less impressed, my readers and myself have alike incurred at least one great moral and preponderating responsibility, which can be discharged only under the bonds of such vigorous and constant co-operation between us as shall, at the earliest practicable moment, place people of pure white complexion in exclusive and permanent possession of the whole earth.

From America quickly must the negro take his depar- ture; from every part of the world must the Indian and the bi-colored hybrid soon hie away. No new golden age, no general jubilee, no Eden-like millennium, no prolonged period of uninterrupted peace and joy, until in the total absence of all the swarthy and inferior races of men, the happy time thus contemplated shall be ushered in amidst the rapturous melody of a grand and universal chorus of the Whites!

THE END.

INDEX.